# Hanged Man's Gambit

# Books by Douglas J. Bornemann:

*The Demon of Histlewick Downs* (Book 1 of the Dreamweaver Chronicles). This stand-alone novel explores historic events that set the stage for the rest of the Heiromancer Trilogy.

**The Heiromancer Trilogy:**

    *Practical Phrendonics*

    *A House of Cards*

    *Hanged Man's Gambit*

*Shady Fortunes*

Website: dougbornemann.com
Facebook: https://www.facebook.com/djbornemann/
Twitter (X) @DougBornemann

# Hanged Man's Gambit

Book Four of
The Dreamweaver
Chronicles

and

Volume Three of
The Heiromancer
Trilogy

## Douglas J. Bornemann

Published by SORCELERITY

First Print Edition
ISBN 978-0-9906281-7-0

*To Tam...and the joy of thinking for thinking's sake*

# Table of Contents

# ÒRAMATIS PERSONAE

**Albert Graves**
> *Curator of Profanities in the Holy City; the Primal's confessor*

**Alexi Reysa**
> *Dona's classmate at Exidgeon University, member of Reston's secret society*

**Alistair Nevinander**
> *Aging patriarch of the Nevinander family*

**Alphonse**
> *Alexi's fencing buddy*

**Amanda Merinne**
> *Dona's mother and Rayen's sister and caretaker*

**Amehtan Shoruga**
> *Hathaway Professor at Exidgeon University; Shunese defector*

**Arerio**
> *Marguerite's manservant*

**Armand Goodkin**
> *Monsignor, brother to the Primal and Inquisitor General of the Church*

**Arne**
> *Woodcarver and purveyor of fine objects suitable for enchantment in Trifienne's market*

**Aunt Olivia**
>   *Nathalie Nevinander's sister*

**Clarke Reston**
>   *Professor of History at Exidgeon, leader of secret society studying Phrendonic Heresy*

**Constable Connelly**
>   *Constable of Trifienne; Miranda's father*

**Count Laslo**
>   *Blond-haired advisor of Crown Prince Nathan of Trifienne*

**Crown Prince Nathan**
>   *Sovereign of Trifienne, father of Princess Julienne*

**Crown Princess Irina**
>   *Wife of the Crown Prince*

**Damien Nevinander**
>   *Alistair and Nathalie's eldest son*

**Darron Goodkin**
>   *Primal and brother of Monsignor Armand Goodkin*

**Dominick Everson**
>   *Professor of Grammar at Exidgeon*

**Dona Merinne**
>   *Daughter of Henry and Amanda Merinne; student at Exidgeon University*

**Dreamweaver**
>   *Legendary niece of Phrendonian, reputed to have invented Daemonology*

**Eloise**
>   *Nathalie and Alistair Nevinander's maid*

**Francesca Harcourt**
>   *Mother of Jonas and Mathilda; they called her 'Nanna'*

**Father Cartier**
>   *Priest of St. Sophia's Church in Trifienne*

**Garvin**
>   *Caretaker at St. Sophia's Church—killed in magical attack on St. Sophia's vicarage*

**Giles Boothby Harcourt**
>   *Jonas and Mathilda's dead father, Francesca's husband*

**Gregory Delauren**
>   *Dona's friend and sometimes classmate; an up-and-coming tenor at the opera*

**Hasset Bey**
> *According to legend, was responsible for Dreamweaver's capture and execution*

**Helena Dunkirk**
> *Dona's friend and roommate at Exidgeon*

**Inquisitor Grummon**
> *In charge of the day-to-day operations of a battalion of Inquisitors*

**Jedidiah Nevinander**
> *One of the twin sons of Alistair and Nathalie*

**Jonas Mapleton Harcourt**
> *Traveling merchant dealing primarily in spirits*

**Josephus Vane**
> *Inquisitor with a reputation for ruthlessness and discretion*

**Madame Rhozhia**
> *Acclaimed Trifienne dress designer, competitor of Nils Calenti*

**Magister Treust**
> *A Magister at the Academy, former mentor to Michlos, creates Amulets*

**Marguerite Serrola**
> *Matriarch of the Serrola family, mother of Michlos and Crown Princess Irina*

**Mathilda (Tilly) Harcourt**
> *Sister to Jonas, owns and runs a brothel in Trifienne*

**Michlos Serrola**
> *Santine, aide to the Crown, and son of Marguerite and Spiros Serrola*

**Miranda Connelly**
> *Dona's friend and roommate at Exidgeon, Constable's Connelly's daughter*

**Mr. Lop Ears**
> *Dona's childhood stuffed toy, a copy of which Dona found in Exidgeon's Ossarium*

**Mrs. Laverne Temrich**
> *Hard-of-hearing member of the Venerable Assembly of Church Mothers*

**Nathalie Nevinander**
> *Alistair's wife, Verone's mother, member of the Venerable Assembly of Church Mothers*

**Nils Calenti**
> *Acclaimed Trifienne dress designer, competitor of Madame Rhozhia*

**Newcomb**
> *Princess Celeste's manservant and personal guard*

**Old Bart**
> *One of Princess Celeste's gaolers*

**Ordinal Bittern**
> *Close ally of Ordinal Laitrech*

**Ordinal Isrulian**
> *One of Darron's more recent and regrettable Ordinal appointments*

**Ordinal Laitrech**
> *Advisor of Primal Darron Goodkin; one of his more recently appointed Ordinals*

**Ordinal Barclay Lavicius**
> *Charming and rapacious Ordinal; A patron to the Accipitrines*

**Phrendonian**
> *Legendary codifier of Phrendonic Heresy*

**Princess Celeste**
> *Sovereign of the Island that is home to the Artists' Colony and the Academy*

**Princess Julienne**
> *Youngest daughter of the Crown Prince and Princess of Trifienne*

**Professor Amberton**
> *Scrawny Professor at Exidgeon, confidant to Professor Reston*

**Professor Fenton Tamry**
> *Professor at Exidgeon, confidant to Professor Reston*

**Randolph Brent**
> *Bursar at Exidgeon, descendant of a Chervillian who escaped the fall of Exidgeon through the Ossarium*

**Rayen the Magnificent**
> *Dona's uncle; subject to occasional seizures—he believes they reveal the future*

**Reginald Nevinander**
> *One of the twin sons of Alistair and Nathalie*

**Shelby**
> *One of Mathilda's "girls"*

**Spiros Serrola**
> *Marguerite Serrola's dead husband*

**Thaddeus Nevinander**
> *Alistair and Nathalie's youngest son, younger brother to Verone, artist at the Artists' Colony*

**The old priest**
> *Thurman's mysterious ally*

**The Widow Bainbridge**
> *Reston's mysterious visitor at the University*

**Thoren Theratigan**
> *Famous demon hunter*

**Thurman Goodkin**
> *Armand Goodkin's son and assistant*

**Venji**
> *Verone's horse*

**Verone Nevinander**
> *Daughter of Alistair and Nathalie Nevinander*

**Zachary Hepplewhite**
> *Professor of Rhetoric and Theology at Exidgeon, old friend of the Monsignor*

# TRIFIENNE

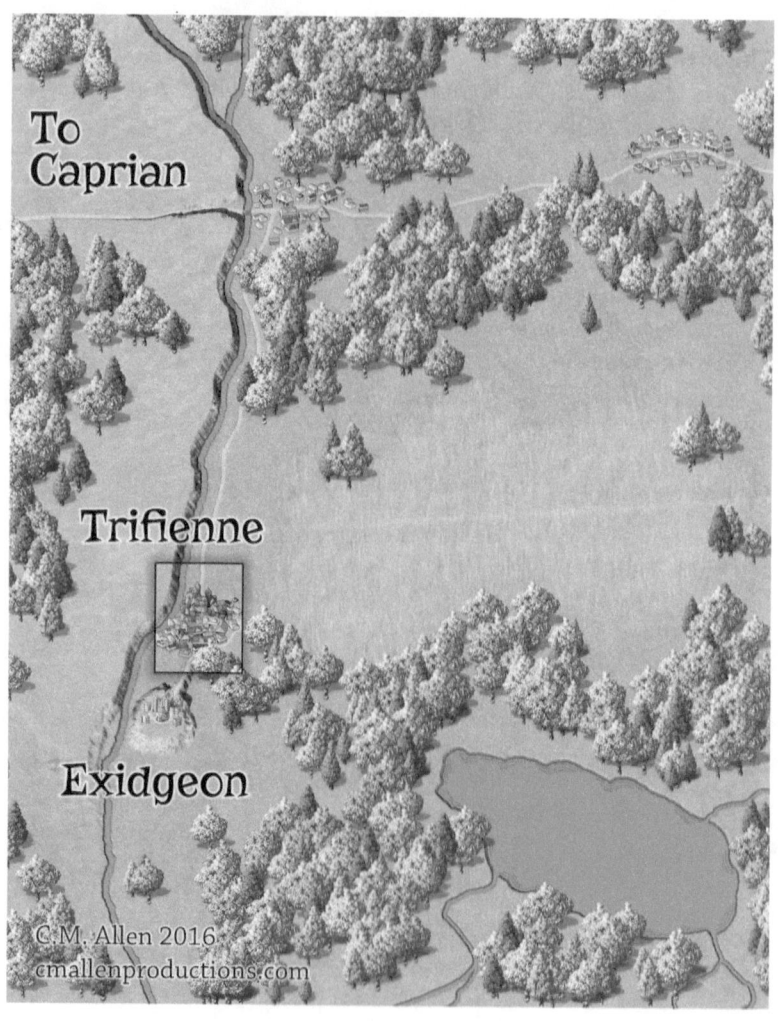

To Caprian

Trifienne

Exidgeon

Holy City

Trifienne

Nevinander

Royal Palace

Expatriate

Ranselard

Main Docks

Opera House

Serrola Estate

Market

The Sultan's Respite

# ORGANIZATIONAL CHART

*• = Primary Character*

## Holy City ▪

**Primal**
• Darron Goodkin

**Inquisitor General**
• Armand Goodkin

**Armand's Assistant**
• Thurman Goodkin

**Curator of Profanities**
Albert Graves

**Ordinals**
Laitrech
Isrulian
Lavicius
Bittern
Kuypers
Marius
Shelby
Stohl
Cronsett

**Accipitrine Order**
Prentiss

**Demon Hunter**
Thoren Theratigan

**Other**
• Old Priest

**Inquisitor**
Josephus Vane

## Exidgeon University ▪

**Chancellor**
Harald Wiggins

**Professors**
• Clarke Reston
• Dominick Everson
Zachary Hepplewhite
Amberton
Fenton Tamry
Bartholomew Driessen
Rutledge

**Bursar**
Randolph Brent

**Librarian**
Mathers

**Students**
• Dona Merinne
Helena Dunkirk
Miranda Connelly
• Alexi Reysa
Alphonse
Gregory Delauren
Arietta Charwick
Caroline Caldor
Adam Deargard
Charles Danforth
Terulla Kardell

**House Mother**
Miss Maxtine

## Trifienne

**Crown Prince**
Nathan

**Crown Princess**
Irina

**Law Enforcement**
Constable Connelly

**Advisors to the Crown**
• Michlos Serrola
Count Laslo

## Local Church ▪ Artists' Colony ▪ Academy

**Priest**
• Father Cartier

**Church Mothers**
• Verone Nevinander
Nathalie Nevinander
Laverne Temrich
Myra Curtsik
Mrs. Muscany
Mrs. Tibbleman
Caroline Caldor

**Princess**
• Celeste

**Manservant**
Newcomb

**Prison Guard**
Ol' Bart

**Provost**
Wellsbrough

**Magisters**
Treust
Celeric

**Former Students**
• Michlos Serrola
Josephus Vane

## Nevinanders

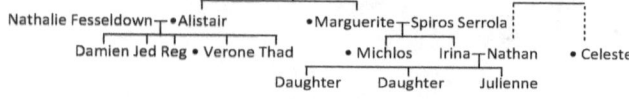

Nathalie Fesseldown ⊤ •Alistair          •Marguerite ⊤ Spiros Serrola
   Damien Jed Reg • Verone Thad        • Michlos    Irina ⊤ Nathan     • Celeste
              Daughter    Daughter    Julienne

## Harcourts

Boothby Harcourt ⊤ Francesca Ravennan ⊤ Barclay Lavicius
        • Jonas         • Mathilda        • Thurman

## Theratigans

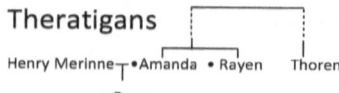

Henry Merinne ⊤ •Amanda    • Rayen    Thoren
        • Dona

## Goodkins

Roman Goodkin ⊤ Antoinette Barget
   • Darron (Primal) • Armand (Monsignor)
              • Thurman (adopted)

# SYNOPSIS

The *Hanged Man's Gambit* is the third installment of the *Heiromancer Trilogy*, following *Practical Phrendonics* and *A House of Cards*. *The Demon of Histlewick Downs* serves as a stand-alone prelude that sets the series' historical stage. The trilogy follows two principle events. The first is a sprawling scheme by Verone Nevinander to influence the inheritance of her wealthy father Alistair's estate. The second follows various factions in a plot to poison the Primal, the head of the Church.

These main events spawn various subplots that draw in an ensemble cast of characters that can be sorted into four main camps:

**The Nevinanders, Serrolas, and the Crown:** Verone's cousin, Irina, is married to the Crown of the city state of Trifienne. Verone's father, Alistair Nevinander, is brother to Irina's mother, Marguerite Serrola. Like the Nevinanders, Irina's brother Michlos and their mother Marguerite Serrola are both closeted Phrendonic Heretics. Though the Nevinanders and Serrolas are estranged, both families are on good terms with the Crown's distant relative, Celeste, Princess of the Artists' Colony, a small independent island in the center of Trifienne.

**The University Group:** Exidgeon University is situated in the rebuilt ruins of an ancient fortress just south of Trifienne, and it falls within the Crown's jurisdiction. Professor Clarke Reston leads a group of Exidgeon students and faculty who have secretly been delving into Phrendonic Heresy, a form of magic forbidden by the Church. One of

Reston's colleagues, Dominick Everson, has gone rogue. By throwing in his lot with Verone, Everson has embroiled Reston's group in her schemes. Reston's protégé, Alexi Reysa, is a student at Exigeon University. Alexi pulled another of Reston's students, Dona Merinne, into Reston's group when he allowed her access to Reston's copy of the heretical text *Practical Phrendonics*.

**The Church:** All agree that Darron Goodkin, the Church's ruling Primal, is not well, but not everyone believes the Primal's confidant, Ordinal Laitrech, when he claims the Primal is suffering from a terminal brain disease. Darron's implicit trust in Laitrech complicates the situation for those who doubt Laitrech's diagnosis. Laitrech is one of the Church's nine Ordinals, who rank just beneath the Primal. Although not an Ordinal, Armand Goodkin is the Primal's brother as well as the Inquisitor General. The Monsignor's son, Thurman, serves as his assistant. Thurman, and an old priest with whom he associates, are among those who doubt Ordinal Laitrech.

**The Harcourts:** Siblings Jonas and Tilly Harcourt were children when their family lost everything during the Caprian Inquisition forty years previously. Jonas sells spirits on a traveling cart, and Tilly is madam of a local brothel. Jonas has been recruited by the old priest to obtain a medallion to aid in their plans.

**The Backstory:** As part of her scheme, Verone tricks Everson into creating a large sphere of darkness—obvious Phrendonic magic—at Exidgeon University, though he escapes capture. The Church responds by sending the Inquisitor General, affable Monsignor Goodkin, accompanied by his son Thurman, to investigate. Through several chance meetings, Dona befriends the Monsignor. When the Primal calls the Monsignor back to the Holy City, the Monsignor leaves Thurman in charge of the Exidgeon Inquisition. Unlike his father, Thurman has a fire-and-brimstone approach to heresy that escalates the Inquisition, and he requests the Holy City send a of battalion of Inquisitors as backup.

Unbeknownst to the Monsignor, Thurman and the old priest hatch a plot to determine the Primal's true health status. Since that plan involves doctrinal gray areas, Thurman and the old priest operate in secret, even from the Monsignor. They enlist the aid of Jonas Harcourt, but when he fails to deliver what he promised, Thurman's inquisitors and mercenaries pursue him to his sister Tilly's brothel. Nanna, who is Tilly and Jonas's mother, sacrifices herself to enable her children to escape. By chance, Dona and Alexi were present at the time, and they all go briefly into hiding.

Dona's absence causes her mother Amanda to rush to the University to search for her. Amanda brings her brother Rayen along because he requires watching due to a condition that predisposes him to seizures. After one of his seizures, Rayen meets Verone at the infirmary, where she has gone to visit Everson after he's injured on one of her errands. Rayen declares he's seen Verone before in visions, and that they are destined to be together. Verone overlooks Rayen's bizarre behavior because she overhears Dona's mother say she is looking for Dona. Since Verone also seeks Dona to obtain Reston's book from her, Verone offers to aid in Amanda's search by enlisting her church group, nominally led by her friend Father Cartier. The Monsignor returns to Exidgeon ahead of the battalion to find that Ordinal Isrulian, (Laitrech's accomplice) arrived first. Thurman flees to the Holy City, and Cartier assumes nominal control of the Exidgeon Inquisition under Isrulian. Isrulian uses the battalion to capture the Monsigor, along with Dona and Alexi. The three, together with Randolph Brent, the University Bursar, collaborate to escape through long-forgotten tunnels beneath the old fortress. Once the Monsignor escapes, he convinces the Crown to exile Isrulian from Trifienne.

Back in the Holy City, Thurman and the old priest's investigation reveals the Primal is being poisoned. Since the Primal still trusts Laitrech, Thurman and the old priest are forced to abduct him using a plan that takes advantage of Phrendonic Heresy. They leave for Trifienne, hoping the Monsignor can talk sense into him.

Eager to distinguish himself in his new role, Cartier discovers evidence (planted by Verone) that suggests Marguerite may be behind the heretical incidents at the college. Since Marguerite is connected to both Verone and the Crown, Cartier secretly hires Inquisitor Josephus Vane (who's also a closet Phrendonic Heretic) to take Marguerite into Church custody. Marguerite escapes Vane's ambush and sends her son Michlos to neutralize him. Michlos catches up with Vane, but Vane defeats Michlos and leaves him for dead. Princess Celeste and her security force rescue Michlos and capture Vane.

When Verone learns of Vane's attack on Marguerite, she approaches Cartier pretending the charges are ridiculous but offering to help Cartier capture Marguerite to clear her name in return for Inquisitorial Indulgences—documents that would prevent the Church from prosecuting Verone or her parents for heresy. Documents in hand, Verone confronts her father and suggests she should inherit his estate, because otherwise the Church will shortly discover his Heresy and confiscate his properties. She tells him he must decide soon, since they're already closing in on his sister Marguerite. Alistair reluctantly agrees, but to goad Verone, he requires that she must be married to inherit and gives her only one week to do it. When Rayen hears, he proposes on the spot, and Verone accepts. The ceremony is planned for the courtyard of Princess Celeste's palace, Ranselard Keep.

Dona is invited to the Nevinander villa to assist with the wedding plans. She sneaks out of her room to her uncle's at night to make sure he understands what he's getting into. When she tries to return to her room, a man leaps from the shadows and holds a knife to her throat.

# HANGED MAN'S GAMBIT

# CHAPTER ONE

## ᏥᎦᏟ ᏟᎡᎥᏌᎬS ᎠᏁᎠ ᏟᎥSᎠᎬᏟᎬᎠᏁᎣᏒS

Ordinal Lavicius filled Prentiss's glass from a bottle that had been hand-blown employing techniques obsolete for more than a century. They sat at a table to one side of Lavicius's tastefully appointed office. His collection of ancient tomes and manuscripts filled several nearby floor-to-ceiling bookcases. The only thing arguably more impressive, in a room clearly devoted to impressiveness for its own sake, was the full-length portrait of Lavicius as a young man on the wall behind his desk.

"The carriage driver was clueless," he said. "We are unlikely to learn anything useful about the Primal's whereabouts from him."

Indeed, Lavicius felt everything about the Primal's flight was a puzzle. One minute the man was on his deathbed; by the next, he'd ordered his pet demon hunter imprisoned and fled town. Prentiss's Accipitrines intercepted the Primal's carriage on the road to Caprian, but the Primal was no longer aboard. His nephew, Thurman—the Primal's last scheduled meeting—had also vanished. And all this occurred shortly after the Primal claimed a demon impersonating Ordinal Laitrech had attempted to abduct him. Laitrech, the Primal's erstwhile favorite, was discovered unconscious in the Chapel Ordinalis missing both his Relic and his vestments. While still unclear as to all the forces in play, Lavicius recognized a power vacuum when he saw it, and he was not one to waste such an opportunity.

"And the demon hunter?" Prentiss asked.

Ah, what would he do without Prentiss's razor-sharp insights and grim efficiency? "I've invited him to join us. Since you've been unable to find Thurman, he's the only lead we have."

"We did locate a cottage Thurman frequented, but recently abandoned. It was rented by an old priest, but the landlord didn't know much else. We have it under surveillance in case either of them returns."

This was the first Lavicius had heard that Thurman was associating with an old priest. Though he didn't immediately see why that detail was relevant, he trusted Prentiss did. Prentiss had an uncanny knack for such things. "Did he have a name?"

"Father Anton. Ring any bells?"

Lavicius shook his head. "I'll check the rolls. We might at least be able to find where he was ordained and maybe get a family name. And what of our good friend Ordinal Laitrech? Any news?"

"He and Ordinal Bittern have set up shop in the Chapel. I'm sure you'll appreciate that makes the details of their activities difficult to obtain. There has been a steady procession of Ordinals in and out."

Of course they'd retreated to the Chapel. Despite his youth, Laitrech was shrewd enough to appreciate the protection against his rivals' prying ears the Chapel's arcane defenses could provide, even if someone—or something—had recently breached them.

Fortunately, Lavicius didn't rely solely on eavesdropping minions to supply his intelligence needs. "Perhaps it's time I had a chat with Bittern. Next time he pokes his head out, let me know right away."

"Of course," Prentiss said.

"I wonder what's taking our guest?"

Prentis rose. "I can check, if you like."

A knock rattled the door.

"It sounds as if that won't be necessary," Lavicius said. "Come in."

The door swung inward to reveal the stout form of Thoren Theratigan, his legs in shackles. He was flanked by Inquisitors.

Lavicius stood and smiled broadly. "Theratigan, my old friend. Please, make yourself comfortable. Prentiss, would you be so kind as to find another glass for our guest?"

The Inquisitors made to follow Theratigan inside, but Lavicius waved them back and closed the door. He gestured absently at Theratigan's shackles. "I'm terribly sorry about those. I'm sure it's all just a misunderstanding, but it's considered bad form to countermand the Primal."

"You needn't worry about that," Theratigan said as Lavicius filled his glass. "Whatever gave those orders wasn't the Primal—unless, of course, your Primal is a demon. Do you mean to say you didn't know?"

Lavicius shot Prentiss a troubled look. That the Primal could have been an imposter hadn't occurred to him. It seemed preposterous, but Theratigan typically knew what he was about—Lavicius had seen him in action during the Histlewick Downs debacle. "Now, there's a perspective we haven't heard. Care to elaborate?"

Theratigan shrugged. "Apparently, the demon who attacked Ordinal Laitrech found the Primal before I had a chance to hunt him down."

"An interesting theory. You do realize accusing the Primal of being an imposter is a very serious—and dangerous—charge. There's very little room for error. Can you prove it?"

"Imprisoned, shackled, and without my equipment? I very much doubt it, which I expect is precisely what the demon was thinking when he gave those orders."

"For the sake of argument, say you were free and had your equipment. Could you prove it then?"

"That depends on the sort of evidence you find convincing. What people are willing to accept as proof is often a deeply personal matter. Even ironclad evidence is useless if you refuse to believe it. That's why, when I take a job, I offer only my professional judgment. What a client chooses to do with that is up to him."

"Let's put it this way. What was the evidence that convinced you?"

Theratigan refilled his glass. "That discussion would take us into the realm of the highly technical and violate any number of closely guarded trade secrets."

Lavicius raised an eyebrow. "I'd like to help you, but I need more than just your 'professional judgment' to go on. In this case, because the Primal ordered your imprisonment, said judgment could be called into question as being, well, somewhat self-serving."

"Look at it this way—if I'm wrong, why would the very person who requested my services imprison me and take my equipment?"

"My dear man, by those criteria, anyone with whom you'd ever had a simple contract dispute would be conclusively proven to be a demon."

Theratigan swirled his glass and admired the bouquet. "Don't take my word for it. Look to your own experience. Is your Primal behaving normally?"

"Also not conclusive. Granted, it's not normal for him to disappear as he has, but neither is it normal for demons to invade the Palace. We have no idea what a normal response should be."

"But if he was so concerned about this demon that he thought it prudent to flee, then why imprison the very person he'd hired to deal with the problem in the first place?"

"Why indeed?" Lavicius said. "Unless, perhaps, he thought the demon hunter was somehow involved."

"Now you're grasping at straws."

"Am I? I imagine the demand for demon hunting is not what it once was. Isn't it possible this entire situation was merely a misguided attempt to drum up business?"

Theratigan laughed. "If I had that kind of power, do you really think I'd waste it trying to outwit the Church? And even if I'd had the poor judgment to try it, do you think I'd suffer you to slap me in chains and run off with my equipment? I repeat—grasping at straws."

The interrogation was foundering. Perhaps a more outcome-oriented approach was called for. Lavicius leaned in close. "If you're so convinced that the Primal is some sort of changeling, then tell me, where is the real Primal?"

Theratigan slapped his knee. "Now you're asking the smart questions. Judging by the demon's past treatment of Ordinal Laitrech, I'd expect the true Primal lies imprisoned somewhere nearby—unless, of course, eliminating the Primal was the main goal, in which case, it may already be too late."

Lavicius turned to Prentiss in alarm. "Has the Palace been searched?"

"We presumed he had left the city. We didn't have any reason to search the Palace."

"See to it right away. Weren't the Primal's quarters under guard?"

"There were two guards with him," Theratigan said.

"Find them," Lavicius said. "I'll need to talk to them."

Prentiss nodded. "I'll attend to it immediately."

"And as for you, my demon-hunting friend, while it may still be premature to countermand the Primal's orders, I think I can arrange for the circumstances of your internment to be a bit more pleasant. Prentiss, could you set him up in his own apartments under house arrest? Oh, and I think we can lose the shackles."

Prentiss bowed. "Of course, Your Ordinence."

"If you're right about this, Theratigan, you may just have earned yourself a fat reward."

"And if I'm not?"

"Let's just say I generally find it's better for morale to focus on the positive."

· · · · ·

Dona held still, not daring to breathe for fear of the blade at her throat. She watched helplessly as a tall shrouded figure deliberately ascended the Nevinander's grand foyer stairway toward her, illuminated only by the brittle light of her gently swaying lantern and an occasional flash of lightning. The figure threw back a hood to reveal Professor Reston's dark features, twisted with exasperation. "Jonas, what do you think you're doing?"

"Isn't it obvious?" Dona felt Jonas's breath hot on her cheek. "This little one's been playing us. How else could the Nevinander woman have been waiting for us in the library? Why else would we find her here, a guest in this house? It all makes sense now."

Reston looked suddenly uncertain. His eyes sought out hers. "Quietly now. Why are you here?"

"I'm looking for your book for you."

"Lies," Jonas said. "She's obviously a guest."

Reston's expression said he thought Jonas had a point.

"I wrangled an invitation," Dona said. "Verone is planning to marry my uncle."

"Ah," Jonas said, "and there's the missing link."

Dona felt a trickle of sweat down her spine. She realized how her presence in Verone's parents' house must look to Reston and Jonas, and how hollow her excuse must sound. Even though the bulk of the Inquisitors had left town, recent fatal attacks involving Phrendonic

Heresy had left the Church on high alert. Dogged inquisitorial pursuit was certain to accompany even the faintest whiff of heresy, which meant the book could be used to destroy him and every member of his secret society. If Verone had indeed stolen it from Reston as he claimed, Verone's engagement to Dona's uncle must seem incredibly suspicious. Yet, Reston wasn't prone to behave rashly. Unbelievable though it might be, truth was her best recourse.

"I only found out tonight, cross my heart. Verone and Rayen met while searching for me—and that was your doing."

Reston stroked his chin. "Perhaps this could work to our advantage after all. Where does Verone sleep?"

"She's not here. Look, why don't we just go to my room and I'll tell you what I know."

"Don't trust her," Jonas said. "It's a trap."

Reston eyed her thoughtfully. "I'm inclined to believe her."

Dona felt a rush of relief, but it was short-lived.

Jonas's grip on Dona tightened. "What?"

"Quiet." Reston said. "You two go first. I'll hang back. If it is a trap, I'll be in a position to turn the tables."

"And if that woman is in there? How do you turn the tables on a Sacrifice?"

"She won't risk burning her parents' villa. Now, go."

"This had better work." Jonas released the pressure at Dona's throat, spun her around, and nudged her forward. She started toward her room, careful to make no sudden moves.

. . . . .

"This is it," she said when they arrived.

"Knock softly," Reston said.

She gave a gentle tap and waited.

"All right, go on in."

Dona stepped inside, followed closely by Jonas, who did a quick scan. The room's lavish four-poster bed and mirrored vanity were just as she'd left them. Satisfied, Jonas leaned back into the hall and beckoned Reston.

Reston pressed the door gently closed. "How well do you know the layout of this place?"

"I don't," Dona said.

"What kind of access do you have?"

"What do you mean by access?"

"Is any part of the premises off limits?"

"I'm a guest," Dona said. "They didn't explicitly state there were places I couldn't go, but social convention dictates that I shouldn't abuse the privilege, don't you think?"

"Even to retrieve stolen property?"

"You forget, this isn't Verone's house. It belongs to her parents—or are you accusing them of being involved in the theft as well?"

"As long as Verone has the book, our position is precarious, since she could use it to out us to the Church at any time. You saw what the Inquisition was capable of. If they get it in their heads we were in any way responsible for those fires, I very much doubt they'll let a little detail like our innocence stop them from exacting righteous vengeance—and they aren't likely to stop with me."

"So you want me to ransack my future aunt's parents' house in the dead of night on the off chance she might have stashed your heretical book here? Is that what you're saying?"

Reston shrugged helplessly. "We've already checked her bungalow. There was no sign of it there."

Jonas rounded on Reston. "Are you out of your mind? When will you get it through your thick skull—she's one of them."

"What other choice do we have? You've seen the size of this place. What chance would the two of us have of finding it stumbling around in the dark?"

"A far better chance than we'll have once you've sent her off to rat us out."

Reston shook his head. "I don't believe she'd do that."

"Are you daft? She was the only person who could have told that woman where in the library to find the blasted book in the first place. It's only by the skin of our teeth we survived, and now, mysteriously, we find her here, an honored guest and on the brink of becoming kin. How much more evidence do you need?"

Dona crossed her arms. "You're a fine one to preach about turn-coats. Or have you conveniently forgotten how you threw in your lot with the very same people who murdered your father and drove your mother to suicide?"

Jonas flinched, but his composure bore the strain. "There's no way we can let her go. She knows too much."

Reston shook his head. "Miss Merinne says she's here looking for the book. I choose to believe her."

"You choose blindly, then. How else could you so completely miss my point?"

"I didn't miss your point, I simply disagree with it. I think Miss Merinne will help us."

"Really?" Jonas said. "Give me one good reason why."

"Alexi. She cares about him."

Jonas considered that for a moment. A crooked smile formed, and he fingered the edge of his knife. "Come to think of it, she does seem inordinately fond of the boy, doesn't she?"

"Put that thing away."

Jonas sheathed the blade. "Suit yourself. I can find it again when the need arises."

"What I meant to say is that if the Church comes for me, likely they'll come for Alexi as well. For that matter, they might well trace the associations even farther back."

Dona sank onto the bed. "I don't get it. Why are you so convinced Verone would use the book against you? Perhaps she wants the copy of the book for herself, or maybe she simply wants to sell it to a collector."

"Either of those alternatives is possible, but given the horrific consequences if we're wrong, can we really afford to just walk away?"

Dona raised an eyebrow. "As opposed to getting caught breaking and entering?"

"If we get caught here, we risk only ourselves, not everyone we ever knew."

"So, what do you want from me?"

"Find the book. Or at least help us narrow down where it could be. As a guest with the run of the house, you have a far better chance of success than Jonas and I have. I won't even ask you to take it. If you find it, let me know, and I'll do the rest."

Dona sighed. "I can't guarantee anything, but I suppose it couldn't hurt to keep an eye out."

"I can't reasonably ask for more. You have my thanks."

Jonas huffed. "When all this comes back to bite you, don't say you weren't warned."

Reston shook his head. "How do you live like this? Never trusting anyone, even your friends."

"That's precisely how I've managed to live, on more than one occasion. You would do well to learn from the example."

"We shall see. Let's get out of here."

.  .  .  .  .

Dominick Everson ran his hand over a week's growth of stubble as he surveyed in the hotel mirror the savagery Verone's ring had wrought across his cheek. He needed to do something soon. What little cash he'd brought with him out of Exidgeon was nearly gone, and even the cheap rooms at the Expatriate in the Artists' Colony were not inexpensive. Still, it was worth it—he was starting to believe he'd given the Inquisition the slip. Even if the Inquisitors had captured Reston and his society, they couldn't turn him over, since they didn't know where he'd gone. Not even Verone had known he'd stowed away in the Nevinander carriage's luggage compartment when the Church Mothers fled the University. Still, he had no delusions. He may have escaped Verone for the moment, but if she had need of him, she'd find a way to track him down.

Only three options presented themselves, none attractive. He could leave town, find someone willing and able to protect him, or make sure she would never need his services again. Leaving town meant giving up his tenured post and his livelihood. Seeking out another of the Phrendonic families to protect him was fraught with risks, since he had no way of knowing who was allied with whom. He even considered groveling to Reston, but he wasn't certain Reston's skills were up to the task. The third option was unthinkable, but the more desperate he became, the more it occupied his thoughts.

Regardless, he would need money, and that meant a trip back to Exidgeon. He'd gleaned from common-room gossip that the Inquisition had finally left the University. Perhaps he could slip in, grab his savings, and get out without being noticed. It was not a plan without risk, but he was increasingly a man without options.

He slipped the last of his coins into one of the many pockets nestled within the embroidery of his "borrowed" Inquisitor vestments. He would have to find a way to replace those soon. The vestments had been instrumental in his escape from the University but were now a liability. The unwelcome stares of common-room patrons often forced him to retreat to his room or take his meals during off hours.

He considered the coins again and sighed. No matter how he counted them, there weren't enough to stay another night. He probably had enough to buy himself a new shirt at the market—something he'd definitely need before risking Exidgeon's gates. Oddly, now that he had the rudiments of a plan, the despondence associated with his fugitive status lifted. He even smiled at the thought of having made Reston dance through his hoops. Maybe he could use a similar strategy to keep Verone in check—perhaps that was overly optimistic, but it seemed worth considering.

He stood tall, assumed a condescending glare, and stepped out of his room. No use wearing the clothes if you didn't look the part. Although it was still early, the common room bustled. Whether the occupants consisted primarily of tourists and patrons in search of artists or Inquisition refugees seeking asylum, he couldn't say, though furtive glances suggested there were a fair number of the latter, since the island's feud with the Church made it a natural refuge. Passing the lobby fountain, he caught the eye of the desk clerk and nodded. He didn't trust that man in the slightest and had therefore tipped him generously. Because he hadn't had any trouble, he allowed himself to believe he'd chosen wisely, even though it had forced him to shorten his stay.

He paused at the front door. The view was bucolic and the air clear and crisp from the evening rains. He stepped into the sunlight, his spirits buoyed by the thought that things might be looking up after all. A quick hop across the river, and he would leave the island behind, grab a new shirt, and blend safely back into the main city's faceless throngs.

As he approached the bridge, he noticed several men stopping people as they tried to cross. Closer inspection revealed they wore the black leather jerkins favored by the Princess's security force. Of course, he was passingly aware of the ongoing dispute between the Princess and the Church, which is why he'd chosen the Expatriate in the first place, but he'd been so focused on avoiding the Inquisition, he hadn't really considered how the Princess's men might view someone dressed as an Inquisitor. No wonder they'd stared at him in the common room.

Turning on his heel, he started nonchalantly back toward the Expatriate, but had taken only a few steps before a voice cried out.

"Hey, you. Hold up."

Everson pretended he hadn't heard and kept walking.

Another voice chimed in. "An Inquisitor, here? Could he be the one the Princess warned us about?"

"That's him, all right. Hey! I ordered you to stop."

Everson broke and ran. Heavily clad as he was, it didn't take long for his pursuers to overtake him. Ironically, out of deference to the status those vestments conferred, they only beat him a little senseless.

# CHAPTER TWO

---

# CHANSONS DE GUEST

*C*eleste threw open the heavy brocade curtains of Ranselard Keep's octagonal tower guestroom and turned to face her patient. She took in the black circles around his eyes. "You look dreadful."

"That's good, given how I feel," Michlos said. "I wouldn't want to give anyone the wrong impression."

She sat on the edge of the bed and put her hand to his forehead. "At least you're not feverish. The Sisters said to watch for that."

Michlos couldn't let his throbbing head distract him. Too much was at stake. He pushed aside the covers "I need to get going. Vane's a menace. There's no telling what he'll do next."

Celeste pushed him gently back down. "You're not going anywhere, mister."

"But Vane—"

"Has been taken care of."

"What? Who…how?"

"Don't worry about that right now. Your job is to focus on getting better."

"But Vane…"

"…is a rogue Santine with resources at his disposal that make him unspeakably dangerous and ridiculously difficult to keep in custody. I know all that."

She said all the right words but obviously didn't appreciate the danger. Blunt contradiction was unlikely to end well. The clock was ticking, but he had little choice. He'd simply have to convince her. "Then you know why I must go."

"Because you're the only person capable of dealing with the likes of him?"

Michlos shrugged, albeit a little self-consciously.

The Princess laughed. "I told you already. It's been taken care of."

Michlos raised an eyebrow.

"You don't believe me."

"He's incredibly resourceful."

"How about I tell you how we dealt with him, and if you can think of any way he could still cause problems, I'll let you go. If you can't, you stay and do as you're told until you get better."

At last, an opening. Surely there were thousands of ways Vane could still wreak havoc. "Oh, very well. Where is he now?"

"In the dungeon, where he belongs."

"Here?"

"Can you think of a better place?"

"But he'll just rust the bars."

"There aren't any bars. His cell has a solid brass door."

"The hinges—"

"Also brass."

"He'll do something to the guards, then get the keys."

"They don't have keys."

"How do they feed him?"

"Through a tiny window in the door at floor level. They slide in the tray. He has to slide it out before they give him another."

"He'll cut the tray in half, place it against the far wall, and repel the other against the door—like I did with the coffin lid."

"Oh, I don't think he'll be landing any spells."

"You have him drugged?"

"Wasn't necessary."

"Then what's to prevent him?"

"The Eye of Moravidos. Since he went to such great lengths to get it, I couldn't bear to separate him from it."

Michlos gaped at her. "You left it with him? He'll find a way to crush it."

"I didn't leave it with him. I just made sure it was well hidden somewhere close by."

"He'll trick a guard into getting it."

"They are under strict instructions to ignore him, and there are always at least two of my most trusted guards on duty at all times. And they are also under strict instructions to steer clear of the cell next door, to which they also don't have a key."

Michlos opened his mouth to speak, but nothing came. No doubt his headache was stifling his creativity. "He'll find a way."

"Perhaps, but that wasn't the deal. The pertinent question is can you find a way?"

"Not at the moment, but I'm still working on it."

She tucked his blankets up under his chin. "Good. That will give you something to occupy you while you're recovering."

"You find this entertaining?"

She grinned wickedly. "If I said yes, would that make me a bad person?"

A knock at the door saved him from having to answer.

"Who is it?" she called.

"Newcomb, your Highness. Sorry to disturb you, but Miss Verone Nevinander and her friend, a Father Cartier, request an audience."

Celeste shot Michlos a significant look. "Tell them I'll be down to see them presently."

"Yes, Highness."

"What does she want?" Michlos asked.

Celeste shrugged. "I expect she's here to apply more pressure for me to reconcile with the Church."

"What's in it for her?"

"Isn't it possible she's merely acting out of concern for a friend?"

"No."

"I know your families have had their differences, but it's been a long time since the falling out. This Verone could be a completely different person from the one you once knew."

Michlos crossed his arms. "As much as you'd like to believe it, people are not caterpillars; they don't just miraculously transform overnight. And, if Verone has turned over a new leaf, you can bet it's only because she wanted something underneath."

"I'd already considered that, but to be honest, I don't see how my reconciling with the Church affects her in the least."

Endearing though it was, Celeste's tendency to expect good faith where it didn't exist was a tactical disaster waiting to happen, particularly where his cousin was concerned. "That's just the way she intends it to look."

"Are you sure you aren't letting the consequences for the Academy cloud your judgment?"

It would be just like Verone to concoct this whole reconciliation scheme for the sole purpose of destroying his alma mater. Perhaps she viewed it as another way to annoy her father, though Alistair had never expressed any particular interest in the Academy. Or perhaps she was striking at Michlos personally for having had the temerity to interfere with Everson's mission to abscond with Dona's book. "I suppose she suggested disbanding the school as well. Grandpa must be turning over in his grave."

"She didn't, actually, but it is a logical extension of the reconciliation. Look, I have to go."

"Just tell me, what tactic did she use to convince you this reconciliation was such a good idea? I can't help if you keep me in the dark."

"An interesting argument. I wonder where I've heard it before?"

Michlos had the grace to blush. "I just don't want to see her hurt you."

"If I can survive an all-out confrontation with Josephus Vane, I'm probably capable of handling a friendly little meeting with your cousin. Now eat your breakfast, get some more rest, and I'll be back to check on you later."

She ducked out and closed the door firmly behind her.

. . . . .

Verone stretched and rubbed her eyes. She'd had a long night, and she wasn't at all certain she could fit a nap into her itinerary, but if the Princess made her wait any longer, Ranselard's cushioned vestibule benches were comfortable enough to be tempting.

Next to her, Cartier fidgeted. "You're sure my being here isn't going to cause problems?"

"This is not the kind of deal you can broker from a distance, and if I'm going to have the wedding here, we need to get things moving."

"And what if we can't get this resolved today? These types of negotiations can take time."

"Then we'll just have to get dispensation. Mum's preparing the invitations as we speak, and I doubt she'll be willing to start over yet another time. Besides, with the Primal's brother performing the ceremony, how hard could it be?"

Cartier raised an eyebrow. "Does he know where he's doing it yet?"

"First things first. I can't tell him until Celeste has formally agreed."

"Until Celeste has agreed to what?" the Princess asked, stepping through the nearest archway.

Cartier leapt to his feet and bowed deeply. Verone rummaged through her leather case, retrieved an envelope, and held it out. "I wanted Your Highness to be among the first to know."

"What is this?"

"It's an invitation. I'm going to be married."

Celeste spent a moment blinking in surprise, then recovered. "Congratulations, Who's the lucky man?"

Verone extended her hand for the Princess to view her ring. "His name's Rayen, and he's tall, dark, and incredibly handsome."

"Oh, it's gorgeous." Celeste's brow furrowed as she examined the stone more closely.

"It's a vintage piece from his mother."

"His mother? Are you sure?"

"That's what he told me. Is something wrong?"

"The style strikes me as much older than that, and…oddly familiar."

Cartier cleared his throat.

"Oh, forgive me, Your Highness. Allow me to introduce Father Cartier. You might remember him from my brothers' weddings."

"Oh yes," Celeste said, "how nice to see you again. Will you be performing Verone's ceremony as well?"

Cartier glanced at Verone. "Well…"

"Regrettably not," Verone said. "Father Cartier has quite a backlog of funerals. As a result, we've had to find a last-minute replacement. That's why we're here."

"I…don't think I follow," Celeste said.

"Well, as luck would have it, Monsignor Goodkin has offered to step in."

"The Primal's brother?"

"You know him?"

Celeste fussed with the invitation. "I know of him, but we've never met."

"Well, once the Monsignor got involved, it occurred to me that this would be the perfect opportunity to work out that reconciliation we talked about. Since the Monsignor has already agreed to perform the wedding, it would be awkward for him to back out."

With a decisive tug, Celeste wrestled the document open. "If he's already agreed, why would he want to back out? And what does that have to do with the reconciliation?"

"You'll note the address," Verone said.

Celeste's jaw dropped. "You aren't suggesting you want me to host the wedding here?"

Verone felt the rush of a strategy in the midst of flawless execution. She'd generated sufficient empathy, now it was just a matter of directing it. "We could always hold it back at the villa, but the more I thought about it, the more it seemed having it here would be a great way to help you move forward with the reconciliation. Not only does this venue provide an incentive for the Monsignor to broach the subject with you, but it also sets a reasonable time frame for resolving the matter—all in a setting of celebration and good cheer. Besides, you've put so much effort into beautifying the courtyard, it seems a shame to deny your friends an opportunity to enjoy it. And lest you think it would be too much trouble, Mum has already volunteered to spearhead the decorating efforts."

"Let's not get too far ahead of ourselves. I know when we last talked, we agreed there were good reasons to move quickly, but circumstances have changed. I therefore think a slow, meticulous approach might make more sense. We don't want to go to all this trouble reconciling just to have it all fall apart again because we didn't take the time to work out our differences properly."

Cartier cleared his throat. "With all due respect, Your Highness, if you are referring to the Inquisition, I'm not sure circumstances have really changed all that much."

"What do you mean? I have it on good authority that the main force of Inquisitors has left town and that the Monsignor is working diligently to repair relations with the Crown."

"There are some wounds so deep that even our fabled Monsignor would be hard pressed to heal them. Obviously, I can't go into detail, but were I you, I would view this lull as merely the calm before the storm."

Celeste crossed her arms. "Is this some sort of scare tactic?"

Verone admired Cartier's technique. A little clumsy, perhaps, but he'd certainly gotten Celeste's attention. And Celeste's ruffled feathers stood no chance whatsoever against Verone's next sympathy bid. "Not at all, Highness. The original reasons for Exidgeon's Inquisition remain unresolved. Not only that, but heretics burned several buildings there, and now they've attacked the Church directly. In fact, one of Cartier's upcoming funerals will be for his caretaker, who was killed in a vicious attack that also took the lives of two others and destroyed the vicarage."

"How do you know they were heretics? Couldn't they just as easily have been robbers?"

"The Monsignor himself concluded as much after an investigation of the crime scene," Cartier said. "Despite his efforts, this situation remains far from stable. Of course, it's one thing if you are not really committed to reconciling—but if you are, wouldn't it be a shame to miss out because of a false sense of security?"

Newcomb stepped through the archway.

"What is it?" the Princess asked.

"A situation has developed. The guards have detained a suspicious individual near the bridge. They would like to know what you want done with him."

"Suspicious how?"

Newcomb eyed Cartier hesitantly. "Well, for one, he was oddly dressed."

"And that makes him suspicious?"

"People dressed as Inquisitors are a rare sight on the island. The guards were concerned he might be someone of special interest. You know, like yesterday."

Celeste turned to Cartier. "Do you know anything about this?"

"You have my sincere apologies, Highness. The Inquisitors were clearly instructed when they arrived that this island was off limits. Perhaps he got lost."

Celeste rubbed her temple. "All right Newcomb. Have the guards escort him off the Island, and make sure he gets the standard warning."

"One moment, Highness," Verone said, "if I may be so bold, so long as you are planning to release him anyway, you could use this as an opportunity to showcase your dedication to making this reconciliation work."

"How do you propose I do that?"

"Perhaps you could hold him a few days so that his release better coincides with the reconciliation. You know, make it a grand gesture. People love that sort of thing."

"And offend the very institution with whom I'm trying to reconcile?"

"Actually, Verone may have a point," Cartier said. "A few days' detention would be a lesser penalty than the Church might bestow for such blatant disregard of instructions, particularly for something this politically sensitive."

"You'd actually prefer we detain him?"

"That's your call. I'm simply agreeing with Verone that a demonstration of magnanimity couldn't hurt, and this one would be relatively painless."

Celeste shrugged. "Very well, then, to the dungeons with him, but make sure he's otherwise well-treated."

"Yes, Highness," Newcomb replied.

"As for the wedding," Celeste said. "It's incredibly short notice, but after all your family has done for us, I would be ungracious to say no—particularly if your mother is willing to direct the decorating."

Verone had, of course, banked on that result, but she was still relieved to hear Celeste say the words. "I can't wait to tell her. Oh, and I suppose that also means we should arrange a meeting with the Monsignor right away."

"I'm willing to meet, but I make no guarantees about reconciling. Much will depend on what he has to say. Understand that while I'm more than happy to provide the location, I won't allow the fate of my kingdom to rest on concerns about the legitimacy of your wedding. Are you willing to take that risk?"

"Happily," Verone said.

"Then I think we are agreed. You may tell the Monsignor that I would be delighted to receive him at noon tomorrow."

"Thank you, Highness. We'll be there—"

The Princess raised an eyebrow.

"—assuming, of course, the invitation extends to all three of us," Verone hastily added.

"I suppose somewhere amidst all these paintings there must be a table that accommodates four," she said. "Until then."

. . . . .

Breakfast was nearly over by the time Dona made an appearance. Her sleep had been fitful, punctuated by half-remembered dreams of wandering an endless maze peopled by unctuous harlequins who drew wicked-looking blades whenever she turned her back. Before she could turn to face them, the blades disappeared, leaving behind only the harlequins themselves, smiling broadly with obsequious disdain.

Nathalie, Olivia, and Dona's mother had already adjourned to the great room to slog through the stacks of invitations awaiting them. Gregory had gone to ready the cart. That left the unlikely trio of Alistair, Miranda, and Rayen lingering at the breakfast table. As usual, Miranda had somehow made herself the center of attention and was animatedly fielding Alistair's rapid-fire questions.

"I could see how Professor Reston might have spirited you away in all that commotion," Alistair said. "What I don't understand is how you got through the University's gates."

"You know," Miranda said. "I'm not really sure I do either. One minute they were this impossible obstacle looming over us, and the next they were lying in ruins. Normally I'd suspect some sort of explosive, but I don't recall hearing anything like that before the gates fell. Maybe the blast was muffled by the gatehouse. Dona, do you know?"

Dona's heart skipped a beat. It hadn't occurred to her to ask Miranda to keep the details of her recent exploits secret, and how the gate had fallen was not something she was eager to share, especially with Alistair.

She yawned and stretched to cover her initial shock. "I'm not sure either. You were closer than I was, and there was a lot going on. Maybe you are just misremembering."

"Could be," Miranda admitted. "Now that you mention it, a huge cloud of dust billowed up once the gates fell. Maybe that hid the smoke."

"Well, the important thing is that you are safe," Dona said, trying to convey a sense of finality. Alistair's curiosity, however, was not cooperating.

"And when you ran into the Ordinal again, he didn't recognize you?"

Miranda shook her head. "I saw him first, and I never gave him the chance to see me. I took a dreadful risk leaving Dona behind like that, but it wouldn't have done her any service to stay and have us both taken prisoner. Besides, Father needed to know right away."

"I think you did exactly the right thing." Dona said. "All's well that ends well."

"It doesn't sound like it ended so well for Mrs. Temrich," Alistair said. "What happened there?"

"There was a big commotion, and one of the Ordinal's men fired into the crowd. Poor Mrs. Temrich was just in the wrong place at the wrong time."

"But what caused the commotion? Foreign dignitaries travel through Trifienne with a retinue all the time without this kind of mishap."

The little beast in the pit of Dona's stomach gnawed fiercely. She couldn't very well tell her uncle's future father-in-law, in the very midst of an Inquisition, that an Ordinal had publicly accused her of being a heretic. The problem was, she suspected Verone had probably seen it. But then, Verone had herself been accused, so she might also hesitate to bring it up.

"I'm not sure," she said. "Maybe the crossbow misfired. Once that happened, there was no controlling the crowd. It was a terrifying experience. I'd just as soon forget it."

"I beg your pardon," Alistair said. "I didn't mean to pry."

The beast nibbled again. Now she felt like she'd been too abrupt with her host. She cast about for some way to compliment him. "Before I forget, I want to tell you how amazing this house is. I've never seen anything so magnificent."

Rayen cleared his throat.

"Oh—except, you of course."

Rayen winked and sipped his coffee.

"Thank you," Alistair said. "I can't take all the credit, of course. The Nevinanders have been working on it for generations."

"There must be all sorts of interesting rooms and spaces still to see. Might we have a tour?"

"I suppose we could fit that in."

Gregory strode in brushing grime from his hands. "Morning Bella. The cart's hooked up and ready. We can leave any time, assuming you're finished getting your beauty sleep."

Dona primped her hair. "You mean you can't tell?"

He peered at her carefully. "You do seem to have stopped snoring."

"That's not what I meant," she said ominously.

"Quite all right. A lot of folk have trouble being understood before they have their morning coffee—it is still morning, isn't it?"

Dona raised an eyebrow. "And here I was thinking it was almost lights out—for some of us, anyway."

"I yield." Gregory said. "I can only keep up that kind of banter for so long. I've only had one cup myself."

"Wise," Dona said.

"Besides," Gregory added, in an aside to Miranda, "she hates it when I let her win."

"Just for that," Dona said, "I'm sentencing you to the ultimate penalty."

"You're taking away my coffee?"

"Worse. I'm making you sing at the wedding."

"Oh, I couldn't possibly. You know how I hate being the center of attention."

"I shudder to think how you'll suffer."

"Do I get one last request?"

"A blindfold, perhaps?"

"I was thinking more along the lines of another coffee." He poured himself another cup. "So, are we ready then?"

"I was sort of hoping to get the tour of the house," Miranda said. "Do we have time for that first?"

Gregory considered, then shrugged. "I don't see why not."

Alistair nodded. "Very well then, let's start right here with the dining room. If you look up, you'll notice ceiling frescoes commissioned by my great grandfather Ernst Nevinander. They were included in the original plans for the main house. According to family legend, Grandmother Nevinander considered them too risqué for polite company and had them whitewashed without consulting anyone. As you can imagine, that didn't sit well with grandfather, and, over her strenuous objections, he paid a small fortune to have them restored. In retaliation, she refused to entertain guests at the house. To mollify her, he built the south wing with its ample great room—you saw it last night. After that, social events at the house took place either there or in the courtyard, weather permitting. For all the years Grandmother ran the house, the dining room was off-limits to visitors."

Alistair's tour took them next to the great room, where invitations were still busily being scribed. Once again, he pointed out noteworthy artistic and architectural details while recounting another old family anecdote whereby Verone's brother Jedidiah got his arm caught for several hours in the mechanism of Grandmother Nevinander's mahogany roll-top buffet, which had been specifically designed to keep small hands away from her precious china. Apparently, Verone had told him she'd accidently dropped his prized magnifying lens down the back, and he'd gotten stuck trying to retrieve it. The lens was never found, but Alistair later noticed a suspicious accumulation of burnt insects populating the corner of the courtyard where Verone had been playing during their frenzied attempts to extricate her brother.

Dona's mother paused her penmanship. "Dona, by any chance do you know the situation at the University?"

"In what respect?"

"Have classes resumed?"

"I very much doubt it. There was quite a mess to clean up after the riots."

"If it wouldn't take you away from your studies, do you think you could stick around a few days and help with the wedding. We're swamped here."

Miranda touched Dona's arm. "I can send word if I hear anything about classes resuming."

"In that case, I'd be happy to help out. What would you like me to do?"

Amanda waved them on. "Finish your tour. In the meantime, we'll talk it over and come up with a list."

Dona nodded, and Alistair ushered them on to the next attraction. Although the kitchens were impressive and the stories diverting, Dona inevitably found her attention straying to places that had the potential to conceal a large book. She lingered long enough scanning the pantry that Miranda came back to look for her.

The pantry, however, was nothing compared to Alistair's study, which sported a multitude of bookcases, cabinets, and cubbyholes. While the others crowded onto the balcony to hear Alistair describe pertinent features of the courtyard, Dona loitered at the rear, stealing glances back into the room for telltale glimpses of red fabric.

A crash of breaking glass from below interrupted Alistair's narrative.

"You all stay put, you hear me?" Alistair said. He dashed back into the study and out through the open door, slamming it behind him.

Inside the study, Miranda wasted no time in applying her ear to the door. Gregory cast about for something to defend them, finally settling on the fireplace poker. Unfazed, Rayen remained behind on the balcony, leaning on the railing and gazing out across the courtyard.

Only moments after Alistair's departure, Dona noticed movement out of the corner of her eye. A thud made her jump.

Miranda started. "What was that?"

Dona snatched up the toppled spyglass from a nearby bookcase before it could roll off the shelf. "Whatever's going on down there, it's shaking the whole house." As she righted the instrument, she felt the bookcase move. She gave the shelf a little tug and the entire bookcase began to swivel out into the room. Before she could investigate further, the bookcase wrenched itself out of her grasp and back against the wall. The spyglass tipped again, and Dona barely caught it in time.

Dona placed it back on the shelf. "Did you see that?"

"See what?" Gregory asked.

"Quiet," Miranda said, her ear still pressed against the door.

"What do you hear?" Gregory asked.

Miranda held up her hand for silence and listened intently. After a long pause, she leapt back, away from the door.

The spyglass toppled again, and Dona caught it just as Alistair threw open the door.

"Sorry about that," he said. He raised an eyebrow at Dona, who still cradled the spyglass.

"You might want to find a more stable spot to store this."

He regarded her for a long moment. "Perhaps you're right," he said at last. "Why don't you leave it there on the desk for now?"

"What happened?" Miranda asked.

"I hope everyone is all right," Gregory said.

"Oh, fine. Everyone's fine," Alistair said. "Succession, it seems, is a messy business. People develop expectations completely out of line with their actual level of entitlement."

*"Reflecting back what she was dealt in kind,"* Rayen muttered.

All eyes turned to him, but he was oblivious, still leaning on the railing, and staring out at the courtyard.

"Miranda and I should really be going anyway," Gregory said. "I still have to get her up to the University, and if I'm going to sing at the wedding, I'll need to come up with a list of music choices for the bride—and I'd like to try to work in at least a couple rehearsals with the musicians."

"I understand," Alistair said. "Shall we?"

He led them back down to the great room. Eloise was busily sweeping up crystalline shards near the fireplace, while Nathalie paced nearby. Olivia sat before the invitation-stacked table filling a glass from a half-empty bottle. Dona's mother sat off to one side looking tense.

"How was I to know you hadn't told him about Alistair's new arrangement with Verone?" Olivia said.

"If you had to bring it up, you could at least have done it gently," Nathalie said. "Damien always was a sensitive child."

Olivia snorted. "If by that you mean he can dish it out, but he can't take it, I completely agree. But he's not a child anymore, and it's way past time he stopped behaving like one."

"You don't suppose he'll do anything rash?" Amanda asked. "I don't think I've ever seen anyone so angry."

Olivia finally noticed Alister and his guests. "Oh, is the tour finished so soon?"

"We'd love to see more," Miranda said, "but Gregory has much to do before the wedding. Thank you so much for letting us stay. We had a marvelous time."

"Our pleasure, dear," Nathalie said. "You'll have to come again when we aren't quite so preoccupied. Will we see you at the wedding?"

"I wouldn't miss it for the world."

# CHAPTER THREE

## OPEN QUESTIONS

Prentiss bowed as he entered the Ordinal's lavish chambers. Though Lavicius pretended such demonstrations were unnecessary, nothing was as effective for staying in His Ordinence's good graces as the occasional demonstration of fealty. "Were your conversations with the Primal's guards productive?"

Lavicius looked up from the notes scattered across his desk. "I'm glad you're here. Perhaps you can help make some sense of this. It seems that both guards, after only a modicum of encouragement, reported the Primal's chambers were visited on the morning of his disappearance by an elderly washerwoman, who, as I understand it, described the Primal's infirmities in some detail."

"I take it there is reason to view the testimony with suspicion?"

"Indeed. Only two servants have that sort of access to the Primal's chamber, and neither admits to being there that morning. More to the point, neither can accurately be described as elderly, and both guards were emphatic that neither was the woman they saw."

Prentiss raised an eyebrow. "Our demon, perhaps?"

Lavicius bit his lip. "I think we have to seriously entertain the notion that Theratigan may have been correct. I also tracked down the guard who was with the Primal on the night of the abduction attempt. According to his account, the demon first appeared as Ordinal Laitrech, and later, as the guard himself, but there was a point at which he looked back and caught the fleeting impression of a wizened old man."

"The demon's true form?"

"I wonder," Lavicius said.

"Are you thinking the demon may also have used that form to gain access to the Primal's chambers?"

"If we presume the demon could impersonate an Ordinal, it is no great leap of faith to believe it could also impersonate the cleaning staff. Which reminds me, would you mind spitting in this jar for me?"

Prentiss chuckled—until he noticed Lavicius wasn't laughing. After an awkward pause, Prentiss cleared his throat. "Certainly, Ordinence, if that is your wish."

Together, both men stared into the jar.

"What's it supposed to tell you?" Prentiss asked.

"I'm not precisely sure. I'll have to pass it along to Theratigan for analysis."

Prentiss couldn't help being amused by Lavicius's paranoia. If there was a threat, he would, of course, presume he was a primary target. Outwardly, though, he merely nodded. "You are wise to be cautious. Were there any other visitors to the Primal's chamber that day?"

"Only the Primal himself and his nephew Thurman, who hasn't been seen since. Theratigan tells me Thurman wasn't present when the Primal fled. I'm beginning to fear the worst."

"Speaking of Thurman, did you get a chance to check for any record of his companion, Father Anton?"

"I did. I located five different occurrences of Anton in the rolls. Three are deceased, one is a young man of 27, and the fifth has been bedridden for several years with a wasting disease."

"So our Father Anton is an imposter as well?"

"It certainly seems likely."

"Which suggests Thurman is either a victim or an accomplice."

"Either way, it makes finding Thurman a priority. Have you found any new leads?"

Prentiss shook his head. "Not with respect to Thurman, but I do have news regarding Ordinal Laitrech. He's left the Chapel."

"Well that should make him easier to monitor at least."

"Not necessarily. He and Bittern commissioned a carriage this morning. They've left town."

"Toward Caprian? Are they following the decoy?"

"I doubt it. The recorded destination was Trifienne."

"Trifienne? Why there?"

"All I can say at this point is they are headed in that direction."

"Wait, isn't that where Armand went? They must be banking that the Primal is on his way there to meet him."

"That theory is as good as any."

"You can't let that happen. If we're wrong about the demon and Laitrech gets credit for rescuing the Primal, it will undo everything we've worked for."

"I'll put someone on it immediately."

Lavicius shook his head. "This situation requires a steady hand and a deep appreciation of all its subtleties. And, since Laitrech must surely have known that I can't leave the city so long as I'm standing in for the Primal, you'll need to see to this personally."

Prentiss nodded. Leaving now would be inconvenient for many reasons, but none was as crucial to his beloved Accipitrines as who sat on the Primal Throne. "I shall leave immediately. Just so there are no misunderstandings, what limitations are you placing on my authority?"

"My dear man, I'm surprised you still bother to ask."

"Unwarranted presumption can undercut even the most solid working relationship. I need to hear you say it."

"Oh, very well," Lavicius said. "You have carte blanche, as usual."

. . . . .

Michlos eyed the Princess dubiously. "You mean someone has actually agreed to marry that woman?"

Celeste positioned a tall stepladder amidst the sea of easels holding all her studio's works-in-progress. "So she assured me. She had a big old ring and everything." She reached for one of the chandelier's glowing crystals but pulled back when the ladder shifted.

Michlos rose from his ottoman. "Here, let me help you."

"Move a muscle, and it's back to bed with you. You're supposed to be resting, not working. Newcomb can help with this."

Michlos settled back. "All right, fine. I do feel obliged to point out that only my nose was broken. Last time I checked, my hands were perfectly functional."

"It had to be quite a blow to give you those shiners. The Sisters tell me you aren't out of the woods yet, and I'm inclined to believe their assessment over yours. The last thing I need is you passing out on me while I'm standing on a ladder."

"What are you trying to do, anyway?"

"I'm taking down the chandelier. It's not the sort of thing you want hanging around when the Inquisitor General drops in for a visit."

Given the combination of Vane's presence and Verone's involvement, that had a particularly ominous sound to it. "Wait, the Monsignor's coming here?"

"I think there's a good chance of it. Verone seems pretty determined to make it happen."

"And you're just going to allow her to force the issue?"

"I haven't promised anything. I merely told her I'd be willing to meet with the man."

"Are you sure that's wise?"

As I recall, I was willing to do the same for you. You didn't seem to think it was such a bad idea then."

Newcomb arrived to steady the ladder, and Celeste removed crystals from the chandelier one by one, wrapped them in cotton batting, and placed them in a chest resting on the ladder's fold-out shelf. Once she finished, she stepped down, brushed herself off, and faced Michlos squarely.

"You're awfully quiet. Are you feeling all right?"

"I've just been considering my behavior. You'd think someone who prizes equity and consistency as highly as I thought I did would have a better track record."

Celeste's eyes twinkled. "Is that what's bugging you? Well I hope you don't spend too much time berating yourself. When it comes down to it, life is little more than a complex dance of competing priorities; you do your best to stay in step, but the when the music changes, of necessity, the dance does too. You'd have to live in a cloister to expect never to change your tune."

"In a way, I wonder if I haven't done just that."

"Lived in a cloister? I think you'd know."

"Maybe not. When was the last time you visited my mother's house?"

"Last March, for Irina's birthday."

"And when was the first time?"

"I don't know. I was very young."

"In all that time, what about the house has changed?"

"Nothing I can think of. At least not since your father passed. Why?"

"That's what I mean. Nothing ever changes there. It's almost as if as long as the house doesn't change, she hasn't really lost him."

"It must have been hard for her to be widowed so young."

"In a way, he took her with him. She's lived most of her life in the past."

"At least she had a reasonably pleasant past to retreat to—not everyone has that luxury."

"It's not a luxury, it's a trap. Her fixation on the past denied her a future."

"Oh, I don't think she did so badly. She did manage to marry off her daughter to the Crown."

"Would it surprise you to know she fought that marriage?"

"You're kidding. Why?"

"Fear of being found out. She argued if the Church ever got wind of the family secret, it would destroy the Monarchy and drag Trifienne down with it."

"Well, that is cause for concern, isn't it?"

"Oh, I agree. Mother always makes a strong logical argument. Indeed, she had little trouble winning me over with it. But in retrospect, that probably wasn't the real reason for her opposition."

"Why do you say that?"

"Think about it. Being the mother of the Crown Princess was an enormous change for her, involving obligations, appearances, and a level of public scrutiny completely at odds with her previous life. It must have been incredibly uncomfortable for someone so strongly rooted in the past. And, fool that I was, I stood with her, castigating Irina for having the temerity to want to make a future with the man she loved."

"Uncomfortable for her or not, what makes you think your mother wasn't acting primarily out of concern for her daughter?"

"If that had been her real motivation, don't you think she'd have given up her little hobby and purged the house of anything incriminating?"

"I'm not sure you're in any position to throw stones there."

"Ironically, I used to privately scoff at all her little anachronisms, but now I discover I am my mother's son after all. Who am I kidding? The Church won the war on Phrendonic Heresy in Caprian years ago, and this supposed mission I'm on to preserve it smacks of little more than knee-jerk devotion to the past. Come to think of it, even my arguments for saving the Academy are probably just rooted in a deep-seated fear of change, which makes some sense when you consider that growing up in a cloister would have been more dynamic than my childhood."

"All this angst because I caught you in a few minor inconsistencies? Need I remind you that not all change is good. In fact, when things are good, it's perfectly natural to want to preserve the status quo. Now, speaking of change, if you'll pardon us sneaking past you, we still have an entire gallery to decrystalize."

Michlos joined them in the gallery. Spilling such personal details was wildly out of character, but once he'd cracked open the door, he couldn't stop himself. "I wouldn't call it angst so much as self-reflection. When I disappoint myself, I generally try to analyze the situation so I can prevent it from happening again. I'll try to be more consistent in the future."

Celest reached for another crystal. "Well, don't bother on my account. I don't make a habit of imposing impossibly high standards on my friends. That's not to say, of course, that I won't point out the occasional inconsistency when I see it. Oh, by the way—you can tell your mother that as much as I appreciate these glowy little gifts of hers, I'm unlikely to need any more, at least until I get things resolved one way or the other with the Church."

"I'll let her know."

"Wait a minute…" She bent to peer intently at the nearest painting. "I knew I'd seen that somewhere before."

"What?"

"The ring in this picture. It's the spitting image of the one Verone got from her fiancé."

"Whose picture is it?"

She turned slowly to face him, her eyes wide. "It's Dreamweaver's."

. . . . .

The Nevinander carriage was every bit as opulent as the villa's foyer. Its button-tufted upholstery and damask draperies were so luxurious Dona was afraid to touch them, but once she did, it took significant force of will to stop. Her hand lingered on a velvety cushion as the coach departed the Nevinander compound for the city beyond. Watching over her shoulder, Dona marveled once again as the resplendent gates swung slowly closed.

In the opposite seat, her mother checked and rechecked multiple shopping lists. "Let me see. White ribbon is not negotiable, but if they don't have gold, I suppose we could substitute silver or a nice contrasting tan. Good lord, I almost forgot wire. We'll need entire spools for all sorts of things, not the least of which is hanging the party favors. It doesn't pay to make them if you can't hang them."

"What are you getting them for a gift?"

"Merciful heavens, I hadn't even considered that. I should have asked Rayen what I was getting them before we left. It would have saved me the trouble of having to think of something on such short notice."

"That's mean," Dona said, snickering anyway.

"I know I shouldn't make fun. I'd like to say I'd been planning for this day for a long time and have the perfect gift lined up, but I'll be honest, I never thought I'd see it."

"It's not like he didn't warn you."

"For years, he warned me. How could I have been so taken by surprise?"

"He means well."

"Tell me, is this going to end as badly for him as I think it is?"

Donna smirked. "Aren't you asking the wrong person?"

Amanda choked back a snort. "Oh, stop."

"He's tougher than you give him credit for. He'll be all right."

"Well it's clearly out of my hands. Until it's time to pick up the pieces, I'll focus on the decorations and mind my own business."

Her mother always maintained a strong façade, but surely a change this drastic would not be easy for her. "Will you be all right without him, do you think?"

"The house will be a bit lonely I suppose."

"You could always move closer to town."

"Rayen's not the only one who's tougher than he gets credit for. Don't you worry about me. I'll be fine right where I am."

There it was, the "tough-old-bird" routine, right on schedule. "I wasn't implying you weren't capable. I just thought you might enjoy yourself more if you weren't so isolated."

"Next you'll have me teetering around in white gloves and a veil, frantically seeking out good works in a desperate bid to give my final days meaning."

"Ma, for shame."

"I'm sorry, but I'm just not ready to think of myself in those terms."

"No one was suggesting you should. In fact, I was thinking this might give you an opportunity to find someone to settle down with. If Rayen can, why not you?"

Amanda held up her hand to show off her ring. "In case you've forgotten, I'm already married."

That ring could have as easily been a sword the way she wielded it to ward off male attention. "Dad's been gone a long time. I don't think he's coming back."

"And what happens when Rayen's little boondoggle goes up in flames and he shows up back on my doorstep?"

"You cross that bridge then. You shouldn't have to sacrifice your happiness to care for Rayen."

"In case you haven't noticed, life isn't always fair. Now, where was I? Oh yes, woven baskets—we'll need at least one for the flower girl, and it wouldn't hurt to get several more, just in case. There will be a flower girl, won't there?"

"You always do that," Dona said.

"Do what, dear?"

"Cut off the conversation when it gets the least bit uncomfortable. No wonder we never talk anymore."

"I thought we were done. Is there something else we need to talk about?"

"Never mind. You'll just get uncomfortable and change the subject again."

Amanda slipped her lists into her reticule and folded her hands in her lap. "All right, you have my full attention. What seems to be the problem?"

Dona sighed. "It's not important." Once her mother assumed that position, she stopped listening entirely and wouldn't rest until she'd fully analyzed Dona's problematic behavior and patiently explained, step by step, how to fix it.

"Well, something is clearly bothering you. For a mother, that's the very definition of important. Out with it—is it trouble with classes?"

Dona shook her head.

"Roommate problems? Money problems? *Boy* problems?"

"It's nothing like that."

"Well, I'm not your uncle; I can't read your mind."

Dona dared to believe her mother might be forthcoming for a change. She did seem genuinely concerned, and, if Dona explained the situation carefully enough, perhaps her mother wouldn't interpret it as amenable to a behavioral solution. The shock of finding her favorite stuffed animal in the caves beneath the college—the same caves where Dreamweaver had rubbed elbows with Chervillian Heretics—had niggled at her long enough. Why had her inherited jewelry matched those of the subject of Celeste's Dreamweaver painting? Why had the Vismort demon in the caves mistaken her for "the Mistress?" And how had an exact match of Mr. Lop Ears found its way into those caves? Too many coincidences to be caused by chance—and her mother almost certainly knew something she wasn't telling.

"If I tell you, you won't cut me off?"

"Of course not. Honestly, where do you get these strange ideas?"

"All right, it's about Mr. Lop Ears."

"The stuffed toy? Are people teasing you about still having one at your age?"

"No, I've just been wondering where he came from."

"I imagine he came from a stack of stuffing and a rabbit hide. Why should that worry you?"

"I mean, to whom did he belong before he came to me?"

Amanda's eyes narrowed. "So, with all that's going on, why, of all things, would that weigh so heavily?"

Odd reaction—Dona must have struck a nerve. "Are you changing the subject?"

"Did Rayen put you up to this?"

"No. Are you suggesting I ask him instead?"

"I'm just trying to understand the basis for your concern. If you must know, the toy came from your grandmother."

"And where did she get it?"

"I have no idea. It came in a trunk of her things your grandfather sent us after she passed away. Now, suppose you tell me what's really bothering you?"

"I saw another stuffed toy just like him."

"You did? Where?"

"When the Inquisition was trying to put down the riots up at the University, we avoided them by ducking into some old tunnels. We found it deep inside those tunnels."

"It's an adorable toy," Amanda said. "I'm sure whoever made it could easily have made more than one. Why should that bother you?"

"This one once belonged to a woman called Dreamweaver."

All colored drained from Amanda's face. "Oh?"

That reaction was hardly one Dona expected. Her mother wasn't merely annoyed—she was afraid. "You know something, don't you? Tell me."

The carriage lurched to a halt.

Amanda sat up and peered out the window. "Well, here we are at the market. Do you mind if we continue this conversation later? We are operating under a pretty strict deadline—"

"You're doing it again. You promised."

Amanda set her jaw and stepped out of the carriage. "I know this runs contrary to everything they hold dear up at that University of yours, but, trust me—there are some things it is simply better not to know. Are you coming?"

Dona climbed out of the carriage, ignoring her mother's proffered hand.

Amanda shrugged and pulled out a sheaf of parchment. "Here's a list of some of the things we need that are likely to be sold by multiple vendors. You get quotes, and I'll take care of buying the things on my list. When I'm done, we can finish your list by heading right to the vendors with the best prices."

"Ma, the Nevinanders are ridiculously wealthy. They aren't going to care if we save them a few coins here or there."

"That's no reason to be wasteful, and neither is that my decision to make."

Dona huffed and took the list.

"Let's meet back here in two hours and see how we're doing."

"Fine," Dona said. Her mother bustled off, a list in each hand.

Still fuming, Dona found it difficult to muster enthusiasm for shopping, particularly since it was now clear she wouldn't even be permitted to do the actual buying. She picked a direction and walked, scanning the list as she went.

"You're going to fly right past and not even say hello?"

Dona nearly dropped the parchment. "Oh, Professor Reston, I beg your pardon. I didn't see you." She eyed her surroundings suspiciously. "Jonas isn't with you, is he?"

"Not this time. I suppose you know why I'm here?"

"You want to know if I've found anything."

He leaned in a little closer. "And, have you?"

"Maybe. We had a tour of the house, and, while I never saw the book, I did find a place where it might have made sense to put such a thing."

"Where?"

"In Mr. Nevinander's study. He has a bookcase that swivels open. When I gave it a tug, though, it snapped back against the wall. I don't know if it was on a spring, or what, but either way, why would you have such a thing unless there was something hidden behind it?"

"Excellent. If you'd be willing to make a rough map, Jonas and I can check it out this evening."

The thought of Jonas and his knife prowling the premises made her shudder. "I'd really rather you didn't. I'll be staying the night again, and there's something that feels wrong about sending you in there while I'm still a guest. Unless, of course, you've found evidence to suggest Verone's parents played a role in the theft."

"I'm not sure we have other options. The longer the book remains unaccounted for, the greater the risk to us all."

Dona sighed. "Well, if someone must go, it makes the most sense that I do it. If I'm caught, I can always say I was retrieving something I left in the study during the tour. I shudder to think what would happen if someone happened across Jonas in the dark."

"He has been a bit more excitable than I expected," Reston conceded. "Even so, I can't ask you to do that. It could be dangerous."

"If they catch you and Jonas, it would be every bit as dangerous. Do you really think Jonas wouldn't give me up to save his own hide? This way, even if I'm caught, and even if they don't believe my explanation, I can count on my uncle to intercede for me, and he's just a few days away from being family to them. Even if that doesn't work, I would still have you to back me up."

"I can't argue with your logic, but I still don't feel right about it. Jonas and I should be able to handle this."

"Please let me try. I'd feel awful if anything happened that interfered with my uncle's wedding, and under these circumstances, I suspect my failure would be far less disruptive than yours."

Reston studied Dona carefully. "You're sure?"

She nodded.

"All right then, come with me."

"Where are we going?"

"A place I know here in the market."

She scurried to keep up. "For what?"

"If you're going to do this, you'll need the appropriate tools."

"Wait—I really need to start my shopping. I only have two hours."

"This won't take long, and I suspect you won't succeed without them."

. . . . .

The Trifienne market was labyrinthine, and although Dona prided herself on being familiar with a fair portion of it, Reston was rapidly heading into a region with which she was completely unfamiliar. The area reminded her of the neighborhood around the Sultan's Respite prior to the fire. It had a seedy and lawless feeling that made the hairs on the back of her neck stand up.

Reston finally approached a small booth tucked back into a dimly lit corner between an apothecary and a fortuneteller. The apothecary was attending to a concatenated series of alembics, each of which spewed a vapor more noisome than the last. The fortuneteller wore an elaborate and colorful costume that shimmered like silk, complete with a multicolored headscarf. She sat at the counter of her booth resting her chin in her hand, but at the sight of them, she grinned broadly, exposing all six of her remaining teeth. Although the smile had something of a predatory air about it, Dona had trouble looking away. She wondered whether this woman could possibly be suffering from the same affliction as Rayen.

The booth Reston approached displayed a collection of finely carved toys, many of which appeared to have working parts. The toy chariots had wheels that turned, and the wooden dolls had jointed arms and legs that permitted arranging them in natural-looking poses. There was even a toy crossbow with little mini bolts so realistic that the obvious risk of a child catching one in the eye made her wince.

The man behind the counter set down his carving tools and greeted Reston. "What can I interest you in today, my friend? I just finished a Shunese puzzlebox. It would make a great gift for the lady."

"Arne, I'd like you to meet my niece, Miss Emily."

Dona wondered briefly who he was talking about until he nudged her.

"Oh," she said, dipping in a shallow curtsey, "pleased to meet you."

"Likewise. The Captain's kin are always welcome here."

"I was wondering, Arne," Reston said, "could we take a quick look at the premium merchandise?"

He lifted the counter. "Come on back."

A small door at the rear of the booth opened into the adjoining building—an old shed, by the look of it. The inside, however, gave a whole different impression. The center of the room was clearly work-space, clean and orderly. Locked display cases arranged around the walls contained a vast array of gadgets, wands, and jewelry.

"Perhaps a trigger ring for the lady?" Arne asked. "The activating mechanisms are as precise and resilient as the settings are beautiful."

Reston shook his head. "Actually, I was wondering if we could see the promise sticks. We need something on the small side, with a dowel and two notches, if you have it."

"Of course. Right this way."

He led them to a bureau, turned a key in its lock, and pulled open the fourth drawer. Notched sticks of every description rested on a bed of red velvet.

He lifted one out for them to see. "Here's a fine little number in clear pine. Two notches and a dowel, just like you asked for, and small enough to conceal in a sleeve."

"How much?" Reston asked.

Arne placed the stick in Dona's hands. "Since it's the lady's first visit, this one's on the house."

"That's very kind of you," Dona said.

"Anything else I can get for you?"

"Not just now," Reston said.

Arne walked them to the door. "Always a pleasure, Captain."

Once away from the shop, Dona paused. "I don't understand. How does this promise stick help me?"

"I'll show you. Follow me."

Reston led her out of the blighted section of the market. He finally located a small bench in a semi-secluded spot near a couple of shuttered vendor stands.

"Will this take much longer? I haven't even started my shopping."

"Just a few more minutes. I promise."

He sat on the bench and motioned for her to join him. "About that bookcase of yours. Did you ever stop to consider that a family such as the Nevinanders might have access to options other than lock and key to protect their valuables?"

"You mean Phrendonic magic?"

"I do indeed. If that's what they're using, how would you propose to get past it?"

"I have no idea, but I bet it requires a promise stick."

"Requires is too strong a word. Such protections can be set up to be interrupted in any number of ways, since the owners will want access now and again, but without knowing the set up, how they're opened is anybody's guess. Fortunately for us, assuming they are using spells to hold the bookcase against the wall, we can narrow the possibilities down to a single category—Kinesis. It's the same category of magic that Everson likely used to swipe your satchel. Fortunately, someone with the proper knowledge can fashion a Diffraction to neutralize the entire category."

"So you're proposing to put such a thing on the promise stick?"

"That's exactly the plan."

"How do I get it from the promise stick to the bookcase?"

"There are several ways. I could cast it as a compound sorcel, but then it would only affect the promise stick and nothing else. Instead, I'll cast it as a displacement sorcel. That will allow the spell to affect things in a radius around the promise stick."

"Such as the bookcase?"

Reston nodded.

"Aren't they going to be upset if I ruin their defense system?"

"If a Kinesis holds the bookcase closed, it would almost certainly have to be Patterned. Otherwise it would only last for about a day. If that's true, then once the Suppression is gone, the Patterned Kinesis should reassert itself. Not only that, but as a radiated effect, such a Diffraction can't actually alter the Kinesis itself—it can only suppress the radiated effect the Kinesis generates—and that's what does the actual work of holding the bookcase closed.

"So you can't get rid of the Kinesis itself?"

"You can, but not with a radiant effect. You'd either have to vest a Dispel directly on whatever the Kinesis is vested on or simply destroy that object instead."

"Am I supposed to keep track of all of this?"

"No. The whole thing is done in three simple steps. Once I'm done here, you'll take the promise stick and keep it hidden. Once you get to the study, you'll break the stick here, at this first notch. That will allow the Diffraction to manifest and neutralize any spells holding the bookcase closed. When you are finished, but before you leave the study, you break the stick at the second notch. That will destroy the Diffraction and allow the Kinesis on the bookcase to reassert itself. Breaking the stick there eliminates all the spells remaining on it. Of course, you probably want to dispose of the scraps discreetly, since it's obvious to anyone in the know the sorts of things a promise stick can be used for."

"That seems simple enough."

"One more thing. You'll want to be on your toes when you break the first notch. The stick will Suppress not just the bookcase, but also any other Kinesis spell within range—it's possible you could set off some sort of trap. That's also why you'll want to break it at the second notch before leaving the study. You don't want to inadvertently affect anything else in the house."

"Oh, great."

"If you prefer, I'm happy to do this myself."

Dona sighed. "No, I'll do it."

"All right then, let's make this."

She handed him the stick. It was the length of her hand with two notches, evenly spaced. A wooden dowel half the length of the stick was inserted into a channel in its side. With some effort, Reston pried it out.

He held up the dowel. "First, the Diffraction for Kinesis." He focused on it intently, mouthing mnemonics.

He took a few deep breaths. "That should do it. I tried to make it fairly strong in case they've pumped up the thrust of the Kinesis. If it's not strong enough, it simply won't work."

"What do I do if that happens?"

"Short of breaking the object the Kinesis is cast on or finding their mechanism for opening it, there's nothing you can do. You'll just have to let me know, and I'll figure something else out."

Despite herself, Dona was intrigued. So, the mark of effective Phrendonics wasn't merely their lists of spells, but the complexity and thoughtfulness with which they applied them. Viewed that way, the possibilities seemed endless. "What's next?"

"Now I put the dowel back in the channel." With a little pressure, it snapped tightly into place. "Next, I attune the dowel to the stick while they're touching each other." He muttered for a moment.

"What does that do?"

"For purposes of vesting spells, it makes the dowel and the stick parts of the same object. That's necessary because I'm going to cast what is essentially a Suppression for Suppression on both things together. The idea is to keep the Diffraction for Kinesis from functioning until you break the stick at the first notch. Keeping the stick non-functional until you need it makes it safer to wander about the villa—on the off chance they have any other Kinesis spells around you don't know about."

"A Suppression for Suppression? Won't that just end up Suppressing itself?"

"Very perceptive. These were initially tricky spells to design for just that reason, but you can get around it by tweaking the effective thrust of the Suppression to make it slightly less than the spell's actual thrust. It's the same sort of thing that determines whether the Diffraction is strong enough to overpower the target Kinesis. Anyway, here you go."

Dona took the stick and looked at it in awe. "How long will it last?"

"If it isn't broken, it should be functional until tomorrow around this time."

"So what does breaking it at the first notch do again?"

"Spells are delicate. If the object they are vested on loses more than 20 percent of its original mass, it breaks the spell."

"Oh, I think I get it. When you break the stick at the first notch, you lose more than 20 percent of the mass of the whole stick and dowel together, right?"

"Exactly."

"And since the stick and dowel together hold the Suppression that keeps everything from working, that spell is broken."

"Correct."

"But, you haven't actually damaged the smaller dowel, and that's where the Diffract Kinesis is, and without the compound Suppression to keep it inactive, it now is free to start working again."

"Precisely so."

"So, the whole purpose of the stick-and-dowel design is to permit you to break one spell while not affecting the other. And the final notch is for breaking the dowel to get rid of that spell too, right?"

"Move to the head of the class. You've really got a knack for this. I've tried to explain it to Tamry four times now, and he still doesn't get it. I confess I only explained it because I thought you'd insist, not because I had any expectation you'd follow. I don't think even Alexi would have caught on this quickly."

Dona rose to Alexi's defense. "I doubt he's ever had quite as serious a need to understand."

"You have a point there, but that doesn't make it any less remarkable."

"Tell me more about the shop. What were all those other things he was selling?"

"You see what you can do with something as simple as a promise stick. It shouldn't take much imagination to work out how other sorts of simple mechanics could be used to generate complex and useful results."

"Like a wand maybe?" Dona had been curious to know how they worked since Tilly had used Jonas's Color Wand to convince Father Cartier to quarantine Ordinal Isrulian.

"Where did you hear about wands?"

"Jonas has one, remember?"

"Oh, that's right. Well, yes, a wand is another example, but it's considerably more complex."

"How does it work?"

"That's way too complicated to go into just now."

"Just in basic terms. I'd really like to know."

"Hmm, basic terms. I guess the essence of a wand is the design of its tip."

"Tip?"

"Yes, it's the end of the wand you touch to something to get the effect you want. "Essentially, you need a means for it to attune to what it touches and a way of Extending the spells that are vested and patterned on it."

"Now you've lost me. Extending?"

"It's another type of Phrendonic effect. Extensions recast spells of a particular category that they are co-vested with. For example, with Jonas's wand, you would need a tip with an Attunement, an Extension, and a Color spell. When you touch the tip to something, it reattunes to that object, provided it's substantially more massive than the handle. Since the Attunement is only on the tip and not the handle, when the tip reattunes, it's not considered part of the handle anymore. Often the handle and tip together will have some sort of Suppression to keep the Extension turned off. When the tip reattunes though, the portion of the Suppression on the tip makes up less than 20 percent of the tip and handle together, and the Suppression on the tip is broken. That allows the Extension to activate and recast the Color spell. Of course, you also need a Charged Reservoir present to power the Extension, which adds a bit to the complexity.

Dona was captivated—even complex magic, it turned out, could be viewed as a combination of much simpler logic puzzles. "Wait—why does recasting the spell on a tip where it's already vested make any difference?"

"Because that tip is also now touching something else it's attuned to. That means when it recasts, it vests not just on the tip, but on both the tip and whatever it's touching. And, that thing very likely makes up more than 20 percent of the total mass of the tip and the object together."

"Ah, I see—that means when the wand is pulled away from the object, the recast spell will stay on the object but be lost from the tip. That's brilliant."

"And, when the Ordinal gave Amberton a haircut?"

Dona rubbed her chin. "Let's see—the hair makes up less than 20 percent of the spell, which means the color on the hair goes away."

"And the spell on Amberton?"

"Stays intact, since he's more than 80 percent of the spell."

"I'm thinking Tamry may want to take you on as a tutor."

If Reston was this impressed by mere comprehension, wait until she tried her hand at application. She was just warming up. "What happens when you—"

"Dona, if you can find time to squeeze me in, I think we need to have a little chat."

At the sound of her mother's voice, Dona realized she was probably late for their rendezvous, and worse, that she hadn't priced anything at all."

Reston scrambled to his feet. "How nice to see you again, Mrs. Merinne."

Amanda stood a few feet off, hunched from the weight of over-stuffed baskets in both hands. She nodded coolly. "And you, Professor Reston."

"I'm so sorry. I seem to have distracted your daughter from her duties. I take full responsibility. It's not every day I get a chance to interact with my very best students socially, and I guess I got a little carried away. Someone so incredibly bright will undoubtedly go far."

Amanda warmed a bit. "Is she really doing that well?"

"I was just telling her I thought she was more on the ball than some professors I know. You should be very proud."

"She's always been a quick study. She takes after my mother's side of the family."

"Well, she does your mother's family credit. Once this mess at the University is over, I intend to recommend her for some prestigious scholarships. That is, of course, with your permission."

"Do you really think she'd have a chance?"

"She does if my recommendation means anything. Now, Dona has made it clear that you both are in a hurry, so I won't keep you. Once more, my sincere apologies."

As Reston disappeared into the crowd, Dona faced her mother. "Professor Reston sure can talk—I didn't have time to get to any price comparisons."

"Well, I suppose you can't really afford to snub someone who is willing to go out on a limb for you like that. We'll just have to do the best we can in the time we have left. What did you two talk about for all that time, anyway?"

"We mostly discussed my immediate future. I have to say, I think he's being genuine when he says he would really like to see me succeed."

# CHAPTER FOUR

# Ob Brothel

Thurman pulled the carriage to a stop, hopped down to tie off the horses, and cracked open the carriage door just enough to see inside. "Are you sure this is the place? It looks like there's been a fire recently."

The old priest poked a nose out. "Oh yes, this is it."

"You sure you don't want me to go with you? This isn't the best of neighborhoods."

The old priest skewered him with a withering look. "Why don't you just stop and think about that for a minute?"

Thurman's face colored. "Or I could just wait right here until you come back, like we planned."

Thurman helped the priest out of the carriage and then climbed inside.

The old priest leaned in behind him. "Make sure you keep this door closed until I get back. We can't afford any missteps."

Thurman nodded and pulled the door shut.

The old priest headed down the block, most of which was taken up by a nondescript squarish building. Upon reaching a side entrance, the priest tried the latch and was pleasantly surprised to find it unlocked. A furtive glance in either direction confirmed the absence of prying eyes. Moments later, the street was empty.

Heavy shutters cast the inside of the building in deep shadow, but the priest could still make out the dim outline of a tall horse cart of the type favored by traveling merchants. Nearby, stacks of fresh lumber, crude sawhorses, and an assortment of woodworking tools were clear evidence of a project in progress, and the acrid odor of stale smoke hinted strongly at its purpose. Near the lumber, a narrow line of light at floor level revealed the location of the door to the adjoining building. Stepping carefully, the priest approached. Women's voices could be heard beyond.

The priest wrenched open the door and rapped on the frame.

Across the room, two women faced each other in alarm. Neither seemed aware the door was already open. The first, who had been washing the wall with water from a wooden bucket turned to the second. "Shelby, honey, be a sweetheart and go see who that is."

Covered head to toe in bits and pieces of the old wallpaper, Shelby did not seem inclined to comply. "Get it yourself. I'm not letting anybody see me like this."

"It's quite all right, ladies," the old priest said. "I'm perfectly capable of letting myself in."

"I'm sorry sir," Shelby said, "we're closed."

"Actually, I was looking to find Jonas Harcourt. Is he here, by chance?"

"Oh, he's upstairs talking to Tilly. Just go on up."

Near the top of the stairs, Jonas's raised voice became audible, and the priest paused a moment to listen.

"I don't care what it says. The whole thing is preposterous. You knew her as well as I. Do you honestly believe Nanna did any of those things?"

"I was young once," Tilly said. "And naïve, and idealistic, and all the other things that go with it. If I'd fallen in with the wrong man, I could easily have gotten in over my head. Why do you find it so hard to believe the same could have been true of Nanna? Good grief, man, you're not even young, and you still get yourself into exactly these kinds of situations."

"Getting in trouble is one thing, but selling out your friends to the Inquisition?"

"How is that any different from what you did to her? And you weren't even being blackmailed."

"I told you, I thought I'd lost them."

"I'm just saying I don't think the story is that far-fetched, except maybe for the part about leaving her child behind. I still have trouble seeing her do that."

"You haven't met him," Jonas said.

The old priest stepped into the upstairs hallway. "Jonas, my old friend, is that your voice I hear?"

The sound of hurried rummaging was his immediate answer. After a few moments, Jonas popped his head out of the room at the end of the hall.

"Father Anton?"

"It's good to see you again."

Jonas flashed a nervous smile. "Likewise."

"Do you have a moment to chat?"

"If it's about that little deal of ours, I can explain."

"Do you happen to have the item?"

"It's not here, but I know right where it is. I can have it for you in a few hours, tops."

"That would be perfect, except for one thing."

"I swear it will only take a few hours."

"And I believe you. It's just that after several days spent carriage-bound, one of my companions has taken ill."

"You'll probably want to get him to the Sisters as soon as possible, then."

"I'm sure it will pass, but if we must wait, surely there must be a more comfortable place for him than the carriage?"

"I'd invite you to stay here," Jonas said, "but as you can see, the recent fire has made most of the building uninhabitable."

"If it's only for a few hours, even one of these rooms at the head of the stairs would be suitable. With the window open and some fresh bed linens, I would be hard pressed to even notice the smell. It will just be a few hours, won't it?"

Tilly appeared suddenly in the doorway behind Jonas, her hands firmly planted on her hips. "If I let your friend stay here, then once Jonas completes this deal, you and your sick friend will leave this place and forget you ever knew him?"

"You must be Mathilda. A pleasure to finally meet you."

"I don't know who you are or how you know my name, and I frankly don't care. Just answer the question."

The old priest met her gaze squarely. "If that is your wish."

"All right then, bring him. Jonas, you go get that medallion of yours and let's get this over with. I have a business to run."

Jonas took a few steps and paused. "You're sure you're all right with this?"

"You should have asked before you involved me. As it stands, the sooner it's over, the better I like it."

"I told you I didn't know—"

"Go!"

"I'll be back as soon as I can." He made his way past the priest and headed down the stairs.

Tilly and the priest appraised each other.

"Well, what are you waiting for?" she asked.

"I was wondering, would it be acceptable for us to briefly move the carriage into the warehouse? He's having trouble walking."

"If you must."

The priest smiled and gave her a little bow. "I am in your debt."

. . . . .

A knock on the carriage prompted Thurman to peer out the window, and then, to open the door. "Are you done in there, because our patient isn't looking so good."

"Not yet," the old priest said. "In the meantime, move the carriage into that warehouse. I've already opened the doors."

Thurman eyed the dilapidated structure with alarm. At this rate, he wouldn't be surprised if they ended up spending the night in the sewer. "Are you serious?"

"Perhaps you'd rather take him up to the University?"

"I was thinking an inn might be nice."

"Given our current cargo, you can bet Lavicius has mobilized that band of ruffians he runs with to stake out all the inns within a hundred miles. I don't know if he was involved in Laitrech's little plot or not, but it certainly wouldn't shock me."

"I see your point. When is he going to wake up?"

"Shortly. I can't wait any longer. He's been going downhill since last night. He needs to move around and eat and drink something."

All Thurman's attention had been focused on spiriting his uncle out of danger. When it finally dawned on him how the man might react upon awakening, his mouth went dry. "What are you going to tell him?"

"I'm not. He can't know I'm involved, at least not until we find your father for backup."

That left only Thurman to face the full force of the Primal's wrath. "But you saved his life. Surely that must count for something."

"I suspect it may take some time before he sees it that way."

At least Thurman could stop worrying about that sewer nap—at this rate, he wouldn't survive that long. "But I don't have any idea what to tell him."

"I guess you'll just have to improvise. It won't be safe for me to be around while he's awake."

"You're not going to just leave us here, are you?"

"Someone's got to figure out where your father is. I don't see you as being the best choice for that."

"How long will you be gone?"

"I'd like to be back before Harcourt arrives with the goods—and he told me it would take him a few hours."

"Harcourt's here?" Thurman was certain he'd explained Jonas's heretical associations. If the Primal didn't do him in, surely Jonas's friends would.

"Is that really so far-fetched? His sister owns the place."

"Wait, you brought us to the brothel? Are you out of your mind?"

The old priest fixed Thurman with a withering glare. "Are you quite finished?"

"I'm sorry," Thurman said. "It's just that several people died here trying to capture him, including two Inquisitors. I doubt they are going to be particularly well disposed to me, or to anyone else from the Church for that matter."

"That is unfortunate, but I'm not always going to be around to clean up your little messes. It's high time you started displaying some of that good old Goodkin ingenuity. If you broke it, find a way to fix it."

"But that could be dangerous."

The old priest sighed. "All the really important missions are. Now, our patient will be waking shortly, and before that happens, I need to be out of here, and he needs to be inside and in bed, so stop dithering, get up there, and drive."

. . . . .

Moments later, the carriage rolled into the warehouse.

Tilly was waiting at the brothel door. She already regretted the deal, even if, by some miracle, it got Jonas off the hook. She felt sullied, and worse than that, somehow disloyal to Nanna's memory. But done was done—there was no turning back at this point. "What took you so long? The bed is already made."

"I'm afraid he's taken a turn for the worse," the old priest said. "He seems to have passed out."

She should have expected the situation would be worse than they'd represented. "If it's gotten that serious, shouldn't you take him to the Sisters right away?"

"We should get him out of this chilly carriage and into a nice warm bed. If that doesn't help, we can always send for the Sisters."

Thurman opened the carriage and hefted the man over his shoulder. "All right, where is this bed?"

"Inside, take a right, and it's at the top of the stairs," Tilly said. "What's left of the door is open and the bed is turned down with fresh linens."

As Thurman carried him inside, Tilly rounded on the old priest. "That man's not just sick—he's at death's door."

"He hasn't been well for some time. That, combined with the motion sickness of the carriage ride, seems to have been too much for him. Once he's had his nap, he'll come around." The priest climbed into the driver's seat.

"Wait a minute," Tilly said. "Where do you think you're going?"

"I have a quick errand to run. I hope to be back before Jonas returns."

A growing sense of panic seized Tilly. What would she do if they abandoned that man in her care and never came back? Her words came out calmer than she felt. "What about your sick friend?"

"I'm sure he's in very capable hands." With a nod, the old priest shook the reins, and the carriage pulled out of the warehouse.

Tilly stalked back inside the brothel and slammed the door. She needed to distract herself before she said something she'd regret. By the time she made it upstairs, her unintended patient was already in bed. She brushed past Thurman for a closer look. "All right, so what am I really dealing with here? Motion sickness doesn't look like this."

Thurman shrugged. "Father Anton seems to think we'll see rapid improvement once he wakes up and has a bite to eat."

"Assuming he wakes up at all."

"The father usually knows what he's talking about."

"For his sake, I pray you're right. Were it up to me, I'd have taken him directly to the Sisters, and even then I wouldn't have held out much hope. You have no idea what's ailing him?"

Thurman shook his head. "He was pretty sick when he joined us. I'm not sure even he knew why exactly."

"You're sure he's not already dead?" She fingered his throat for a pulse. "I guess he's still ticking, at least for the time being. Is there anything he can't eat?"

Thurman shook his head.

"All right, I'll see about making some applesauce. He should be able to stomach that. In the meantime, if he wakes up, holler down, and I'll bring up some water."

Thurman nodded, and Tilly headed back downstairs.

· · · · ·

With Tilly safely gone, Thurman collapsed into a bedside chair only to leap to his feet again moments later when the Primal stirred, his sunken eyes blinking against the light.

"How are you feeling?"

Darron rubbed his forehead. "My head is killing me. Where am I anyway? Did I faint again?"

"Listen carefully, Uncle Darron, you've been out a long time. The demon hasn't been found yet, so it was agreed we should go into hiding to guarantee your safety—at least until you got back on your feet. For your protection, nobody here knows our true identities. While we're here, you're my uncle Dar. Can you remember that?"

"What?" Darron cried. "The Primal doesn't slink away from danger—he faces it head on. Whose ridiculous idea was this? Theratigan's? No, that can't be. You'd never have gone along with it had it come from him. It wasn't Laitrech's, was it?"

Thurman shrugged. He dare not lie directly, but he had no obligation to correct erroneous assumptions, particularly those Darron might find more palatable than the truth.

Darron struggled to get up. "When is that man going to learn I don't need coddling. Well, it's time we put things right."

He didn't make it even halfway to sitting before he sank back down. "I guess I may have tried to move a little too fast, there."

"You aren't well," Thurman said. "We can put things right just as soon as you're feeling up to it, but first, let's get you something to eat to help you get your strength back."

"I thought I heard voices up here," Tilly said from the doorway. "Why didn't you call me?"

"He was a little disoriented," Thurman said. "I was just explaining where he was and how he'd passed out."

"Well, here's a glass of water to start with. The applesauce won't be ready for a while. I'll be back up when it is."

Thurman handed off the cup to his uncle, who promptly spilled it on his chest.

"No, that's not how you do that," Tilly said. She snatched the glass from Darron's trembling grasp. She used her other hand to help him to a sitting position, and held the glass, allowing him only brief sips. "Get me a clean rag. There should be some just outside in the hallway."

When Thurman returned, Tilly lowered her patient and mopped up the spill.

"Bless you, child," Darron said.

"It's been a long time since I've been either," Tilly said. "But you're welcome.

"I thank you too," Thurman said. "If you hadn't helped, he'd be halfway through his bath by now."

Tilly smiled. "It was nothing, really. I should see to the applesauce." She paused at the doorway. "I'm sorry, I missed your name. I'm Mathilda, but everyone calls me Tilly."

"Franklin," Thurman said. "Please, call me Franklin."

· · · · ·

Dominick Everson cringed as the tray slid under the bars of his cell. Though ravenous, he was not yet so desperate that he could force down boiled turnips.

He called out to the departing guard. "Wait."

"What is it now?"

"Has there been any word from the Princess? This is all a terrible mistake."

The guard absently scratched his ample neck beard. "When she gets to you, you'll know…*if* she gets to you."

"Can you take her a message? I have money. I can pay."

"Don't you be lying to Ol' Bart now. He knows what you brought in with you, and there wasn't much in the way of cash."

"I don't have it with me, but I can get it. Once I'm out of here, I can get you however much you want."

Bart laughed and turned his back on his prisoner. "Sure you can. When you get to it…*if* you get to it, if you catch my drift. Ol' Bart's heard that story before, and it always ends the same way."

"I wouldn't do that. Let me prove it. How much would it take just to get a little note through to her?"

Bart reached the door to the cell block. "If she's not wanting to come visit, ain't nothing Ol' Bart's gonna do to change her mind."

"Please. I'll do anything. Just one little note."

Bart eyed Everson and scratched his beard again. "Anything, eh?"

"Well, almost anything…"

"Thought as much." The door clanged behind Bart, leaving Everson with only himself for company.

. . . . .

Thurman woke with a crick in his neck to the sound of nearby conversation.

Tilly was assisting Darron with the last spoonful of applesauce. "Oh, I'm sorry—I didn't want to wake you, but I thought it would be best to get some food in him as soon as possible."

Thurman sat up straight in his chair. "What time is it? How long have I been out?"

"About an hour, give or take. Your uncle really is looking much better. Maybe Father Anton was right after all."

# Oh Brothel

55

Darron's eyes narrowed. "Did you just say Father Anton?"

"Did I get the name wrong?"

Darron glared at Thurman. "Good question. Did she?"

Thurman's plan hadn't anticipated this wrinkle. He laughed nervously and pulled up Darron's sheet. "Maybe we should discuss this after you've had a bit more rest."

Darron pushed his hand away. "Maybe it's time you stopped patronizing me and brought me up to speed."

"You are up to speed. I've already told you everything you need to know."

"Patronize me again, and I don't care who you're related to, you'll find out first-hand why it's unwise to displease a Primal."

Tilly backed slowly away. "I certainly didn't mean to cause a row."

"It's not you," Thurman said. "Sometimes he gets a little truculent after his nap."

"That does it," Darron said. "He threw off the bedclothes and started to climb out of bed.

Thurman tried to restrain him. "Careful. You're not well. You're going to overdo."

"Take your hands off me."

"You need to rest."

"I need to know what's going on here." Then he froze. "Wait a minute. I know who you are. You must have tried again, only this time you succeeded. Unhand me, demon!" Then, abruptly, he went limp.

After a few dumbstruck moments, Tilly reached out to feel for a pulse. "What was he talking about? Did I hear him say he thought he was the Primal?"

Thurman tapped his head with his forefinger. "Senility. Sometimes it gets the better of him. He'll be fine for hours or days, and then, just like that, another episode."

"How horrible. He's lucky to have someone like you to look after him."

"Thanks. It's not always easy, but you do what you have to do for family."

Tilly tugged the blankets up again. "Such a shame—and just when he seemed to be doing so well."

A single rap on the doorframe announced the old priest's arrival.

"How did your errand go?" Thurman asked.

"Quite well. How's our patient doing?"

Thurman fumbled for a Tilly-safe explanation. "He was fine for a while—he got down plenty of water and a whole bowl of applesauce. But then he had another one of his episodes."

"What happened?"

"He declared himself Primal and started calling everyone demons. And then he passed out again. You know, just like he did in the carriage."

"Like in the carriage, you say?"

Thurman relaxed a little, satisfied he'd been understood. "Exactly like that. He could be out for an hour."

Tilly snatched up the applesauce bowl and headed for the door. "It's none of my business, but if I were you, I'd take him to the Sisters straight away. I'll be downstairs if you need me."

Once she was safely out of earshot, the old priest turned to Thurman and raised an eyebrow. "Well?"

"It wasn't me. I told him Laitrech insisted we travel incognito until the demon crisis was resolved, and he seemed annoyed at being coddled but willing to play along. Later, though, Tilly was feeding him and commented how he seemed to be getting better, just like 'Father Anton' had suggested, and he lost it."

"So you used the Signet?"

"I had no choice."

"Well, at least Father Cartier had some good news. The Inquisition has left the University, and Isrulian was sent packing to the Holy City. Last he'd heard, your father was free and making nice with the Crown."

"I didn't know you knew Cartier."

"I don't, but that didn't stop him from getting chatty with a visiting brother of the cloth."

"What about the heretics? Were they caught?"

"I didn't think to ask."

The door burst open. Jonas, breathless but triumphant, held aloft the medallion. "I got it," he said. Then he saw Thurman.

Tossing the medallion aside, he drew his knife. "You know, I've dreamed about this moment many times now, but I never honestly thought I'd get the chance. It's time to atone, brother."

Tilly screeched from the doorway. "Jonas, what are you doing?"

Undeterred, Jonas leapt for Thurman.

Thurman dodged backward but stumbled over the chair. Jonas was on him in a heartbeat. He raised the blade for the *coup de grace*, but the blow never fell. As Tilly gawked, Jonas stiffened, then toppled. Thurman scrambled away.

Tilly rushed to Jonas's side. "What have you done to him?"

"It's not my fault," Thurman said. "He tried to kill me."

The old priest sighed and stooped for the medallion. "Give him an hour or so, and he'll be fine."

"You did this to the old man too, didn't you?"

"I think we've overstayed our welcome," the old priest said. "Come, Thurman. Bring your uncle, and let's go."

"So, you really are the infamous Thurman Goodkin," Tilly said. "How does it feel to murder your mother, I wonder? Compared to that, I suppose kidnapping your uncle is child's play."

"I don't know what you're talking about," Thurman said. "Look, I appreciate your help, and I'm sorry about your brother, but he attacked me."

"Thurman," the old priest said. "Now."

Thurman threw his uncle over his shoulder. The old priest took one last look at Tilly tending to her brother, and with a final shake of the head, turned and left.

Thurman paused at the door. "I'm truly sorry."

Tilly glared after him. "No, you're not. But when you get a chance, ask your father how your mother died. Maybe—just maybe—you will be then."

# CHAPTER FIVE

## GETTING THE MESSAGE

By the time Dona and her mother made it back to the Nevinander villa, Verone had already carted Nathalie and Olivia off to Ranselard to work out the details of the ceremony. Alistair and Rayen were absent as well; they were off to see what Alistair's tailor could do for them on short notice. With almost everyone gone, it was a perfect time to check out the mysterious bookcase in Alistair's study, but Nathalie had other plans. She'd left instructions with Eloise for Dona and her mother to finish the invitations, which were now complete except for the date, time, and address. One look at the mound of stationery on the great-room table, and Dona abandoned all hope of doing anything else until long after her usual bedtime.

Her writing hand was badly cramped and scattered embers were all that remained in the fireplace when Alistair and Rayen wandered in, both uncharacteristically garrulous and reeking of whiskey. Although she held her tongue, Amanda's disapproval was palpable, and she wasted no time in whisking her brother off to bed. Alistair, meanwhile, dropped himself heavily into a chair at the table next to Dona and picked up one of the invitations for inspection.

"Very pretty," he said. "What a waste."

"Excuse me?" Dona asked.

"She'll never go through with it."

"What do you mean?"

"Isn't it obvious? She hates men."

"I don't understand."

"I don't think I can make it any clearer."

"That makes no sense. Even if she were callous enough to be indifferent about what that might do to Rayen, is she really capable of putting her poor mother through all this for nothing?"

Alistair shrugged. "She wants the estate."

"Doesn't she need to marry Rayen to get it?"

"She's banking on getting out of that on a technicality."

"What sort of technicality?"

"That's probably one of those things better left to those intimate discussions between a bride and her intended, don't you think?"

"You aren't suggesting I tell Rayen to ask, are you?"

"That, my dear, is up to you. I will say, though, that your uncle seems to be a decent enough chap." He waved his hand over the invitations. "It would be a shame if he were blindsided at the altar in front of all these guests."

"If you like Rayen so much, why don't you tell him?"

Alistair yawned cavernously. "And betray my daughter's confidences? I'm afraid that would be behavior most unfitting for the father of the bride. Now, if you'll excuse me, I'm expecting another big day tomorrow."

Dona watched in shock as he staggered out of the room. Try as she might, she couldn't fathom what game the man was playing. Why try to force Verone to marry against her will and then go around spreading such rumors? And why had he told her instead of Rayen? He'd put her in the unenviable position of having to decide between telling Rayen a rumor that might cause him to call off the wedding, and not telling him, which might result in Verone making him a very public laughingstock. Absently she ran her fingers over the contours of the promise stick concealed beneath her sleeve. She didn't feel so guilty anymore.

When her mother reappeared, Dona wished her a good night, kissed her on the cheek, and headed upstairs. She listened at her door for telltale sounds that her mother had turned in as well and resolved to wait another half hour just to be sure everyone in the house was sound asleep. As the minutes ticked off, she found herself second-guessing. After all, losing Reston's book hadn't really been her fault. Besides, after her chat with Alistair, she suspected that Nevinander largesse never sprang solely from a sense of *noblesse oblige*. Their true motives were often complex and self-serving, even vaguely sinister. Given that, she doubted her connection to Rayen would afford her as much protection as she'd initially thought, and she wondered if it didn't make more sense for Reston to make the attempt. And for all that, even if she was blowing the dangers out of proportion, she'd never forgive herself if she got caught and Rayen's wedding fell through because of it. Finally deciding that the reward simply wasn't worth the risk, she closed her door and dressed for bed.

But sleep eluded her. She tossed and turned, struggling to make sense of her conflicted conscience. She nodded off once, briefly, only to be rewarded with visions of Jonas, knife in hand, cutting a bloody swath through horrified wedding guests as he searched vainly for the missing book. She sat up in a panic, her hand seeking out the place on her throat that had once felt that same blade.

Jonas, she decided, was a problem. If he were caught with Reston burgling the villa, there was no telling how he would react. She'd already seen him pull that knife of his twice, and once it was on her. Although she had survived, she had no doubt an unfamiliar target would fare less well. If someone were hurt, she'd regret it to the end of her days. She simply couldn't risk allowing that man in the villa again. With a sigh, she lit a lantern, retrieved the promise stick, and stepped into the hallway.

The planks were cool beneath her feet as she tiptoed toward Alistair's study. She felt her heart race each time she approached an alcove, and each time she felt foolish when she passed it without incident. At last, she stood before the study door, steeling herself for what was to come. She tried the latch, almost hoping it was locked. Her heart sank a little when it clicked and the door creaked open. After a quick glance up and down the hallway, she stepped inside and pulled the door silently closed behind her.

. . . . .

Inquisitor Grummon drew the harsh wool blanket more tightly around his shoulders as he stared into the dying campfire, but the chill in his bones was something over which the blanket held little power. Even the rhythmic whisper of the Scandus against the nearby shore couldn't soothe him. As a battalion commander, he was a man well acquainted with the value and necessity of following orders, even those that might seem superficially ill advised. And yet, this was somehow different. He'd grown up in Trifienne, and though he no longer lived here, in many ways he still considered it his home.

As a young man, he'd even witnessed the royal wedding, cheering the Crown Prince's good fortune amidst throngs of well-wishers and marveling at the fairy-tale princess by his side. He also remembered where she was from—once the engagement was announced, it was, for a time, a common practice for young men to sneak up to the mansion on the cliffs to catch a glimpse of the exotic bride-to-be.

As their orders took them far south around Exidgeon and then back north along the river, their destination became obvious. When he finally realized he'd been ordered to apprehend the Crown Princess's family, he broke into a sweat. Presuming there was some mistake, he sent an under-cover envoy back to Trifienne to confirm the orders with someone higher up, preferably Monsignor Goodkin or Ordinal Isrulian. He still awaited the man's return.

A snapping twig caught his attention. He prodded the embers with a stick to coax out a bit more warmth. "You're going to need your rest for the days ahead."

A young man stepped from the shadows. "I couldn't sleep."

"Neither could I."

The man stepped closer to the fire but did not sit.

Grummon made out bruises on the man's face. "What happened to you?"

"I fell."

"Nothing broken, I hope."

"No."

"Lucky."

The man shot an anxious glance upriver. "We're going up there, aren't we? To the Serrola estate."

"What makes you think that?"

"It's a treacherous place. Will you see Father Cartier soon?"

"I don't think so."

The man sighed. "If you do, tell him Vane's a heretic."

"Vane?"

"He'll know."

Grummon watched in silence as the man wandered off through the camp, fading at last into the obscurity of the darkness, the smoke, and the river mist.

. . . . .

Bathed in Dona's lantern light, Alistair's armillary sphere cast a web of shadows that menaced most of the balcony. Although she doubted anyone would be in the courtyard at this hour, she pulled the draperies, just in case. The room was as they had left it—even the spyglass rested where she'd placed it on the desk. A closer examination of the bookcase revealed nothing out of the ordinary, except that now it was stubbornly immobile, defying her every wiggle, prod, or nudge.

She produced the promise stick from a pocket in her nightgown. Mindful of Reston's admonition, she cast about for a safe place. After an extended internal debate, she finally climbed beneath the desk.

Closing her eyes, she snapped the stick at the first indentation.

She was rewarded with a slow squeal of hinge on hinge. Peeking out, she saw the bookcase had rotated out from the wall. She padded over and gave it a tug. It pivoted easily but concealed only disappointment. Behind lay a smooth expanse of wall. She held the lantern close, but there was no sign of anything that could be construed as a latch. She reached out her hand—and snapped it back. Although she'd felt nothing, her fingers had passed right through the surface. She held the lantern close, but there was no indication she'd touched it at all. She examined her hand and wiggled her fingers. Everything seemed normal. She reached out again, and, as before, her hand simply passed through the surface without feeling anything.

She passed her hand with the lantern through. The entire room was plunged into darkness. She pulled the lantern back. Its fire still burned.

She was hesitant to step through—she'd fallen into enough pits of late. Neither did she want to call it quits after coming this far. Maybe she could look through before she stepped? Taking a deep breath, she shoved her face through the wall.

Dazzling colors blinded her. Beyond the illusion lay a windowless chamber lit by brilliantly hued blown-glass globes suspended from the ceiling. The space was divided into separate areas. One contained display cases and storage bins that reminded her of the strange workshop she'd seen with Reston in the market, right down to the types of items displayed. There were boxes, wands, and promise sticks aplenty, trays of jewelry, and numerous objects she couldn't readily identify. Another section contained an assortment of tools for working wood, metal, and glass on a fine scale. The third section truly caught her eye. It contained comfortable chairs, a desk and table, and an entire wall of bookcases. A single display case stood out. Unlike the other storage units, this one held only a single book.

After tapping her toe on the floor, she stepped inside. Careful to avoid touching anything, she approached the display case and squinted through the glass.

She covered her mouth in shock. *He'd been in on it all along.*

. . . . .

As Arerio retreated down the hallway to inform the mistress of his arrival, Alistair had a seat in the parlor. The room was exactly as he remembered it, a fact he found vaguely disturbing. He went over what he had to say before he could leave, but the throbbing in his head wasn't making that any easier. Thankfully, he didn't have long to wait.

"As I live and breathe," Marguerite said.

Alistair stood and faced his sister. "Good to see you too."

"That remains to be seen. What do you want?"

"Why, the pleasure of your company, of course."

"Sarcasm never was your forte."

"I'm serious—but don't worry, it's not for my benefit."

"Give me one good reason why I shouldn't have your sorry ass booted all the way to the bottom of the hill."

"Because that's not the way the great and noble Marguerite treats her guests."

"Guests, no. Beggars on my doorstep—I'm not yet convinced. What do you want?"

"Verone is getting married. She'd like you to attend the ceremony."

"Are you kidding me?"

He pulled an envelope from his jacket pocket. "I have the invitation right here."

She snatched the document, ripped it open, and gaped at its contents. "This says the wedding is tomorrow. How long have you been sitting on this?"

"Not long. I think she was expecting a reply. Can I tell her you'll be there?"

"I don't know. For some reason, I've come to view your family's invitations with a healthy dose of skepticism."

Alistair brightened. *Now to set the hook.* "I take it you'd like me to convey your regrets, then?"

Marguerite's eyes narrowed. "On second thought, you can tell her I'll be there."

Alistair unconvincingly feigned regret. "You're sure? It is very late notice. I expect she'd understand if you couldn't make it."

Marguerite's jaw tightened. "I said I'd be there."

"Whoa—I'm just the messenger. And since the message has been duly delivered, I'll just be on my way."

She watched at the door as he heaved his bulk onto his horse. She was still watching when he disappeared around the bend at the bottom of the hill.

"What do you make of that?" she asked.

Arerio, who had been peering over her shoulder, considered only a moment. "I've heard it said the best way to survive the viper's bite is to avoid setting foot in the nest in the first place."

. . . . .

Dona threw wide Reston's office door. Seated at the room's far end with his back to the window, Reston looked up from writing and waved her in. The narrow space, with its rows of overstuffed bookcases to either side, made most visitors feel like the walls were closing in, but Dona seemed unfazed. She slid the book out of her satchel and tossed it triumphantly on his desk. "Well, I got it."

Reston ogled it in disbelief. "Her father was keeping it for her after all?"

"So it seems. I really didn't think I'd find it—she and her father are always acting like they don't get along. Anyway, there it is, and good riddance. She gathered her satchel. I'd best get going. These invitations need to arrive at the post soon if I want them delivered today, and the wedding is tomorrow afternoon."

While delighted by the book's return, Reston shuddered at the thought of what Verone might do when she realized her plans had been thwarted. "You know, it might be safer for you to skip the festivities. What if they find this missing?"

"They won't. I discovered it in a dusty old display case and replaced it with another book that resembled it. With the wedding coming up, hardly anyone will be at the villa, much less notice the swap. Besides, if I disappear, wouldn't that instantly make me the prime suspect?"

"How soon they notice depends on what they were planning to do with it. I really think you'd be best off staying well away from the Nevinanders for a while."

"And miss my uncle's wedding?"

Jonas burst into the room, slamming the door behind him. "The bloody hypocrite's a heretic."

Reston suffered yet another pang of regret for having brought Jonas on board. His skills were useful, but his temperament was exhausting. "Now what?" Reston asked.

"Thurman Goodkin—he Slept me. Tilly saw him do it."

"Hold on. What on earth were you doing anywhere near Thurman Goodkin?"

"I was trying to rip his miserable throat out."

Reston sighed wearily. If he couldn't be reined in, Jonas's Goodkin obsession was going to get them all killed. "Please tell me you didn't attack him."

"Give me a good reason I shouldn't have."

"Well, for one, the Church has very specific, graphic, rules regarding the punishment of those who lay a hand on the Clergy."

"The monster killed my mother."

"And I sympathize, but I don't think the Church is going to see it that way."

"Maybe they will when they find out he's a heretic."

"And just how do you propose they're going to learn that?"

Jonas paused. "You could tell them. You're a professor. They'll listen to you."

The man had clearly lost his mind. "Hold it right there. I have no intention of making myself any more of a target than I already am."

"But he's guilty."

"I think in this case you'll find that justice really is blind."

"There must be something we can do"

"There is. We can thank our lucky stars they didn't draw and quarter you on the spot. Care to tell me how all this came about?"

"It started when Father Anton showed up at Tilly's place."

"Who?" Dona asked.

Jonas shot Dona a sidelong glance. "What's she doing here?"

Reston patted the book. "She brought me a certain misplaced tome she found up at the Nevinander villa. It seems you owe her an apology."

Jonas grunted. "Well, maybe I was wrong this once, but she was sleeping with the enemy. The whole thing still stinks as far as I'm concerned."

Reston bit his tongue. "So noted. Anyway, you were saying?"

"So, Father Anton was the guy who originally hired me to get the medallion. At first, I assumed the Inquisition was after us again, but he showed up by himself, and he made no threatening moves. I explained about the medallion, and he offered to wait while I retrieved it from Alexi. I was tempted to trust him, thinking maybe I could be done with the whole thing once and for all."

"I thought Alexi gave that back a long time ago," Dona said.

"He was supposed to, but he never did. So anyway, I get the medallion, and then I show back up at Tilly's place, and who should I find there but Thurman Goodkin."

Reston's heart skipped a beat. "She didn't tell him anything, did she?"

"What happened to Father Anton?" Dona asked.

"He was there too, along with some old sick guy they were trying to nurse back to health. So, I see Goodkin there, and I lose it. Next thing I know I'm waking up, it's an hour later, and all three of them are gone. We have him dead to rights. There must be some way to expose him."

That the Church had gotten so corrupt it would commit the selfsame heresies it pretended to ban didn't strike Reston as much of a surprise. There were historical precedents aplenty. "I don't see how," he said. "It's your word against his. For that matter, even if you had indisputable evidence, do you really think it would make the slightest difference?"

"It would if word got out."

"People won't believe it, at least not unless it comes from a far more credible source than either of us."

"It still wouldn't matter," Dona said. "The Church has the option of overlooking heresy used in self-defense."

"He had to learn it somewhere," Jonas said. "And that wouldn't have been done in self-defense."

Dona turned the doorknob. "As fascinating as this conversation is, if I don't get going, these invitations won't be delivered in time."

Reston patted the book again. "Many, many thanks, Miss Merinne. I'll sleep much better tonight knowing this is in safe hands."

. . . . .

When Dona was gone, Jonas took a seat in front of the desk. "Well, you know what they say—if you can't beat 'em, join 'em. When do I get my first lesson?"

Reston's second thoughts extended to the training arrangement as well. Using the Hanged Man's Gambit as a ploy to convince Jonas his Trumps of Doom hand was weak had struck him as so clever he'd been unable to resist, and leveraging the win together with the training offer to encourage Jonas's assistance seemed natural at the time. The irony wasn't lost on him. In retrospect, the Gambit would have been better applied to the whole situation—sometimes losing really was the best way to win. But, even if he was now stuck with Jonas, his cooperation had limits.

"If you're planning to use it in some misbegotten scheme to frame Thurman Goodkin," Reston said, "then never."

"We had a deal."

"Yes, a deal, not a suicide pact."

"Raiding the Nevinander estate wasn't exactly a picnic in the park, either, or are you forgetting what she did to us in the library?"

"I'm not going to argue. If you can't be reasonable, you'll have to get your training elsewhere."

"Fine," Jonas said. "I won't use it against Goodkin."

"Are you willing to swear to that?"

"All right, I swear."

"I don't believe you."

"That's not my problem."

"We'll discuss this again later."

Jonas shrugged. "Fine by me. Anytime you like."

It seemed there would be no getting out of it. Perhaps focusing on a lesson would distract from his misgivings. "Very well, let's get started." Reston opened the book, but something immediately struck him as strange. "Hmm. Well, this could present a bit of an obstacle."

"I already promised. What more do you want?"

Reston paged back to the inside front cover. "It's not that."

"Well, what is it, then?"

Reston looked up, still blinking in surprise. "This is not my book."

. . . . .

"How's he doing?" Thurman asked as the old priest examined their high-profile charge.

Since the reputable inns were suspect, the old priest had bid Thurman to lease them a room at a seedy flophouse. Thurman was grudgingly relieved, since, even though they were filthy, the pallets seemed preferable to curling up on the carriage floor. Unfortunately, morning, and the itchy welts it revealed, told a different tale.

"He's hanging in there," the old priest said. "The stop at the brothel did him some good, but he can't stay like this indefinitely."

Thurman furiously scratched his shoulder. "So why didn't we just take him to the palace last night? Father could have talked some sense into him, and we could have slept somewhere a little less bug infested."

"After you called down a battalion of Inquisitors to invade his city, you'd just waltz in and expect the Crown Prince to treat you like some sort of honored guest?"

Thurman shrugged. While he understood the need for an abundance of caution, this was getting ridiculous. "We had every right to investigate the heresy up at the college. Besides, we're traveling in the company of the Primal. Do you really think he could afford to treat us any other way?"

"Such privileges only exist as long as you maintain the political clout necessary to enforce them."

"Like I said, we have the Primal with us. What more clout do we need?"

The old priest sighed. "A few years of political stability, and this is what happens."

"What?"

"Everyone starts thinking in terms of rights and entitlements. Politics is solely a game of expedience. Political stability only arises when numerous incentives are carefully aligned. Change those incentives, and all bets are off."

Despite the risk of a "back-in-my-day" lecture, Thurman couldn't let it drop. "What are you saying? The Primal doesn't have any clout anymore?"

"I know this might be difficult for you, but for once in your life try viewing the situation in terms of political incentives instead of all that gibberish about rights and entitlements."

"He's the Primal. What incentive could the Crown Prince possibly have other than to stay in his good graces?"

"Were you asleep all last week, or were you just not paying attention?"

Thurman unwisely let himself get rankled. "What was I thinking, presuming the Crown Prince would want to provide the Primal with a decent bug-free bed like that?"

The old priest, arms folded, eyed Thurman for a long moment.

"I'm sorry," Thurman said at last. "I was out of line there."

"Let me spell this out for you. A few days ago, the Primal, who was already reputed to be terminally ill, disappeared without a trace. What incentives do you suppose that gives to people who were considering a bid to replace him?"

"They'll try to find him, of course."

"And that helps them, how?"

"Well, there is sort of a power vacuum as long as he's missing."

"And who do you think will try to fill that vacuum?"

"Ordinal Laitrech?"

"Possibly. Now, if Laitrech does step in, what's his incentive? To locate and reinstate the Primal as soon as possible, even though there's a good chance that by now he's probably aware he was being poisoned?"

"Well, put that way, I don't imagine he'd be very keen on getting the Primal back at all."

"And given that everyone was already under the impression he was terminally ill, what's the simplest way to achieve that?"

Thurman's jaw dropped. "Find him, and finish him off before he reappears?"

The old priest tapped finger to nose.

"And, if Laitrich has the Primal killed, he certainly isn't going to want any witnesses."

"No, I would suspect not."

Thurman waved his hand at their cramped room. "But we have no protection whatsoever here. Shouldn't we seek asylum with the Crown Prince as soon as possible?"

"Should we? Where does the Crown Prince stand on the issue?"

Thurman shuddered as the hopelessness of their predicament finally sank in. "You think he's in on this too?"

"Even if he's not, from his perspective, your uncle's days on the Primal Throne are numbered. Will he really want to risk taking a stand with the lame duck against anyone who has any possibility of succeeding him?"

Thurman still couldn't fathom a world in which his uncle's title held no power. "Oh, please. He wouldn't dare strike down a sitting Primal."

"He wouldn't have to. All he'd have to do is leak our whereabouts to the right person, and he'd make a friend forever."

"But the people would be outraged if the Primal were murdered on his soil. Surely the Crown Prince would never allow that to happen."

"And what makes you think they would ever know?"

"But if you knew we were just going to end up in this situation, why did we bother to do this at all?"

"Because some chance is better than no chance. Now, I need to talk to your father as soon as possible, but not while he's lodging with the Crown Prince. Fortunately, Father Cartier mentioned he will be performing a wedding at Ranselard Keep tomorrow."

"On the artists' island? I thought that was under interdict?"

"It is."

"Then how's he going to perform a wedding?"

"Good question. Maybe he intends to lift the interdict."

"I thought only the Primal could do that."

"I doubt that will prevent Armand if he has a mind to do it. He is a Goodkin, after all."

"I don't understand. The Canon is clear."

"So he'll prevail upon his brother to make the decree retroactive. The important thing is that he'll be out of the Crown Prince's jurisdiction."

"Yeah, well what about the Princess?"

"After years of interdict and given her status, I think it's unlikely she's been in close contact with any of your uncle's current enemies."

"But if the interdict is being lifted?"

"I expect your father will be conversant with the details of the situation. I concede it is still a risk, but nothing we do from here on out is going to be risk-free."

Thurman scratched his leg. "I suppose that means we'll be stuck in this rat hole with nothing to do but scratch ourselves for another whole day."

"Not true. I'm sure your uncle will need changing at least several more times, and you'll need to keep working his limbs to keep them limber."

Thurman was suddenly aware that, despite numerous scriptural examples to the contrary, a newfound appreciation for the bleakness of one's future did little to encourage generosity of spirit. "Isn't it about time we woke him up?"

"And, given how he reacted at the brothel, how do you think that would end?"

"It's just that saving him from being poisoned seems sort of pointless if he dies from the rescue."

"I guess you'll just have to make sure that doesn't happen, won't you?"

"Speaking of the brothel, what did she mean?"

"Who?"

"The woman there. She asked me how it felt to murder my mother. Do you have any idea how she knew?" Thurman wouldn't normally have asked in the midst of such pressing matters but feared if he didn't ask now, he might never get another chance.

The old priest looked away.

"I mean, I've never seen her before in my life. How could she have known my mother died in childbirth?"

"People say things when they're upset. Don't let it get to you. Now, I'll get out of your way and let you tend to your uncle."

"What are you going to do while I do that?"

"I have one more matter to take care of before we can meet with your father."

"And that is?"

"You'll see."

. . . . .

The Monsignor took another sip of wine. "I must say, I never did think much of Ordinal Isrulian's campaign against your charming little island, and I'm delighted you are considering a reconciliation."

Princess Celeste congratulated herself on her choice of venue. Ranselard's conference tower's tall ceilings, aged beams, and scenic views projected precisely the soothing yet serious atmosphere the situation called for. The Monsignor's bearing impressed her. His thoughtful, reasoned demeanor was completely at odds with her previous Church interactions. "If I had been aware that we had supporters in your camp, I might have reached out sooner. What do you suppose the Church will require from our end?"

"Probably not much. The offending artwork is long gone, and Ordinal Isrulian's recent actions will seriously impact any influence he may once have had with the Primal."

Across from them, Verone exchanged a troubled glance with Cartier, who was seated next to her. "The Primal? Does that mean this situation can't be resolved today?"

The Monsignor pondered a moment. "I don't think so. The decision rests ultimately with the Primal, though under the circumstances, I expect he'll be favorably disposed."

"Perhaps we could work out a temporary exception to cover the wedding," Cartier said. "It's pretty clearly too late to change the venue. You saw all the preparations taking place when we arrived."

"I am sorry for the confusion. I only found out about those plans this morning. I do, however, have some ideas how that problem might be resolved without adversely affecting those preparations."

Verone brightened. "So despite the interdict, the wedding will still be valid?"

"I think we can make that work."

Celeste veered back on topic. She needed to stay in control or Verone would hijack the conversation and the only thing they'd resolve is her validity problem. "What about artistic integrity? I trust you know how important that issue is to the Colony. Do you think a reconciliation can be achieved without compromising that?"

"I think that issue can be best managed using a combination of discretion and sensitivity. My brother and I share the perspective that these types of offenses pose little actual threat to the Church as an institution. In our view, the main issue is whether such works are likely to be so offensive or disrespectful that they might reasonably be expected to incite violence. However, I've found over the years that even those at the fringe are far less likely to react violently if they feel enfranchised. Perhaps the simplest solution would be to set up a panel before whom those who are offended can lodge a grievance."

Celeste set down her glass. "How would that work?"

"I envision something along the lines of a three-member panel. You could appoint one member, the Church would appoint a second, and the third would be some individual amenable to both. Grievances could be brought before the panel, and only those works deemed too offensive by a panel majority would be subject to removal. Even if such removals were very rare, the process alone would go a long way toward resolving most situations before they became problematic."

She gave him credit for trying, but his plan was a bit too egalitarian for her taste. She didn't imagine he would have dared pitch such an intrusive approach to the Crown. "Forgive me, Monsignor, but that sounds like a significant abdication of my sovereignty."

"It is. But your stance on censorship is well known. Without at least some Church input into the process, those who file grievances will not feel represented, and the whole arrangement becomes pointless."

"These are all just details, though," Verone said. "Basically, you both agree that a reconciliation would be in your best interests, right?

The Monsignor nodded. "Had it been up to me, I would not have resorted to such a draconian measure for such a trivial issue in the first place."

"Well then, why not just agree to lift the interdict and work out the terms later? What's to be gained by delaying?"

"I would be amenable to that," the Monsignor said, "provided the Princess is committed to resolving our few remaining issues in good faith."

Another subtle and likely unintentional slight. Celeste wondered how Nathan would have reacted, but of course, her interest was merely academic—the Monsignor would never have used that language with him. It wasn't worth raising a fuss, but neither could she let it slide completely. She smiled and topped off his glass. "My dear man, I make it a point to deal in good faith whenever possible."

Cartier backed his chair away from the table. "That's terrific news. I'd stay longer, but I have a funeral to prepare for. Before I go, Monsignor, I was wondering, has there been any progress on the arson investigation? I'd love to be able to tell Garvin's family that his killer will get the justice he deserves."

"I'm afraid not. Phrendonic arson is notoriously difficult to track down. While the nature of the crime is obvious, few identifying clues are left behind if the arsonist is careful. You can assure Garvin's family that we're doing our best."

"What can I tell them you'll do if you catch the perpetrator?"

"Murder alone would be serious enough, but murder by heresy is more serious still. It's been quite some time since anyone's been convicted of that, but since Caprian, the traditional punishment has been death by burning at the stake."

Cartier nodded. "That won't bring Garvin back, of course, but I think his kin will take comfort in knowing that at least the punishment fits the crime."

All heads turned as the conference-room door creaked open.

"I'm terribly sorry," Nathalie said. "But we do have a wedding to throw. Would it be too much trouble to expect the bride to at least try to come up with a dress to wear? The rehearsal is only a few hours away."

.  .  .  .  .

Dona caught up with Alexi at Exidgeon's cafeteria. His injury certainly hadn't affected his appetite. "How's the ankle doing?" Dona asked.

"Only hurts when I walk on it. The crutches help though."

"So you think you can still get around?"

"I'm not going dancing anytime soon, if that's what you had in mind."

"Actually, I was thinking you might like to come with me to my uncle's wedding. The invitation says I can bring a guest."

"Which uncle?"

"Rayen."

Alexi stopped chewing long enough to raise an eyebrow. "The one who has seizures?"

"Don't sound so surprised. He's really a very nice man."

"Who's the lucky bride?"

"That's the odd part. He's marrying Verone Nevinander, or at least that's what the invitation says."

Alexi's mouth fell open. "What?"

"I know it's a little bizarre—"

"A little? Weren't she and Everson your best suspects for stealing the book?"

"She did steal it. Not to worry though, I found it and returned it to Professor Reston not half an hour ago."

Alexi finished his meal and reached for his crutch. "Does your uncle know he's marrying a heretic?"

"I doubt the matter has come up."

"Doesn't that worry you?"

Dona looped her arm through his. "I think if a heretic is going to be my downfall, it won't be the one marrying my uncle."

"I bet you say that to all the heretics."

Dona tousled his hair. "Only the ones who can't run away. Grab your best clothes. You're coming with me to deliver these invitations to the post, and then we're heading up to the Keep for the rehearsal. If we don't leave now, there isn't going to be a wedding. As it is, I have no idea how they expect anyone is going to show. Is Alphonse around?"

"I think so, why?"

"I wrangled an invitation for him and Helena as well. The wedding is going to be held at Ranselard Keep in the Artists' Colony. If we left her behind, I don't think she'd ever forgive me. There are strings attached, though. There is much still to prepare and very little time. Do you think they'd mind helping out?"

"An extra day up at the Keep hobnobbing with a Princess? I somehow think Helena might be able to force herself."

Dona grinned. "I thought so too."

. . . . .

Inquisitor Grummon heard the hoofbeats over the gurgling of the nearby river and the hum of his impatient battalion and burst from his tent. "Any luck?"

The envoy dismounted. "It's complicated."

Grummon held open the tent flap. "Come inside and we'll talk about it."

"Thank you, sir." He sank into a folding chair next to a small table.

Grummon produced a flask from his vestments. "Thirsty?"

The envoy took a long swig. "Thanks."

"So what did you find out?"

"The Ordinal is no longer in Trifienne. Word has it, Count Laslo ran him out of town."

"He ran an Ordinal out of town?" Grummon took his own hit from the flask. "Maybe the situation is more serious than we appreciated. Was there any sign of the Monsignor?"

"He's been staying at the palace. This morning, however, his carriage was spotted crossing the bridge to the Artists' Colony."

Grummond's eyes widened. "In spite of the interdict?"

"Apparently so."

"Voluntarily?"

"I have no way of knowing. I do know, however, that at one time, the island boasted a sturdy prison."

The situation was worse than he feared. "You think they're holding him hostage?"

"I can't rule it out."

Grummon's gut lurched. His superiors would not be pleased. "I've been a fool."

"How so?"

"I balked. Like some miserable trembling acolyte, I waited by the sidelines for an additional pat on the head when I should have been carrying out my orders."

"The orders did seem extreme."

"It's not my place to second-guess. We must pray my dereliction hasn't compromised the mission. The Monsignor's life may be riding on it."

"We don't know he's being held against his will."

"It's the only thing that makes sense. This situation has all the hallmarks of a hostage exchange—except that my cowardice may have just cost us our bargaining chip."

"So you're going to carry out the orders after all?"

"Roust the men. We move before dawn."

"The envoy nodded. "I'll see to it sir." He ducked outside.

For a long while, Inquisitor Grummon sat alone, reliving cherished memories from his youth. When the commotion of the men breaking camp finally filtered in, he sighed and got to his feet. With vacant eyes, he drained the flask and let it fall.

"Saints preserve us all."

# CHAPTER SIX

## MISGIVINGS

e didn't look happy, did he?" Dona said as the Nevinander carriage rolled its way across the bridge to the Artists' Colony.

Alexi grinned. "He's going to be delivering invitations until the cows come home. You can hardly blame him."

"He can't be the only person making deliveries."

"Even if he only had to deliver a tenth of them, it's still a lot. How many of those did you write?"

"I have no idea. My hand prefers I don't think about it."

"The things we do for family. How's your uncle taking the stress?"

"Can you keep a huge secret?"

"If I can't, we're both in serious trouble."

"Not that—it's about the wedding. I'm not sure it's going to happen."

"This sounds like it's going to be juicy."

Dona looked him hard in the eye. This was no time to be flippant. "I'm looking for some advice here. The other night, Verone's father came back from having a drink with Uncle Rayen. Still tipsy, he confides in me that Verone hates men and that she's going to try to get out of the wedding on a technicality."

Alexi nodded. "Yup, that's pretty juicy."

"You're not helping."

"How am I supposed to help?"

"So, do I tell uncle Rayen or not?"

"Do you think what he said was true?"

"If it's true, why would he try to force Verone to marry in the first place?"

Alexi's brow furrowed as he absorbed that. "Wait, he's forcing her?"

"The story I heard is that if she's married by the end of the week, she inherits the whole Nevinander estate."

"And your uncle is aware of this?"

Dona shrugged. One could never be precisely certain what Rayen knew.

"Then why does it matter if she hates men? It's understood she's just marrying him for the inheritance anyway."

"I'm afraid she might ditch him at the altar in front of all the guests."

"It sounds like he'd be better off that way."

Dona sighed. Alexi clearly wasn't following. "He's an incurable romantic. He sincerely believes she's going to be the love of his life. Not only that, but in his mind, he's been predicting this wedding for years. I wouldn't be surprised if what little self-esteem he has left is completely tied up in this one successful prediction. Having it fall through so publicly could crush him."

"So why don't you tell him and let him work it out with her before the ceremony actually happens?"

"But what if her father was lying to me? What if I tell Rayen, he calls off the wedding, and none of it was true?"

"It seems to me if he knows she's just marrying him for the estate, this really isn't that much different."

"It is different though. He thinks they'll grow to love each other. I'd be telling him there's no chance of that happening."

"He thinks that based on his prophesying?"

"I guess so."

"If he really believes that stuff, what's the chance anything you say is going to change his mind?"

"I don't know. Sometimes with him it's hard to tell how much is an act."

"I'd tell him," Alexi said. "If he's going to consent to an arranged marriage, he ought to do it based on all the available facts. If he can't deal with something like this, he's going to have real problems navigating the marriage anyway."

"You're probably right, but that's not going to make it any easier."

"I guess it's just another one of those things we do for family. After all, you'd expect your family would tell you something like that, wouldn't you? Even if it was painful or embarrassing."

Dona snorted. "Tell that to my mother."

"She told you not to tell him?"

"No, this is something else."

"Now what?"

"Well, it's like this. You said you have an ancestor who was a famous general, right? Do you happen to have any other relatives who were maybe crazy or criminal? And if people knew, do you think it would affect how they view you?"

"I doubt it would make a whole lot of difference to people who know you, but it might matter a little if you were dealing with people you'd never met. I think people do tend to expect the worth of the ram shapes the cut of the cloth."

"So, you're saying my mother might be justified if she tried to whitewash our family's dirty laundry by covering up any connections to an infamous relative?"

"With all that's going on right now, why on earth would you worry about that?"

"Hear me out. Do you remember, down in the caves, that place where I almost fell? I think Brent called it the funerarium."

Alexi shivered. "Sort of a hard place to forget."

"Do you remember there was a stuffed animal there? I think you used it to start the fire."

"Oh yeah," he said. "Disgusting, ratty old thing, but it made for decent tinder. So?"

"I have one just like it."

"And?"

"Doesn't that strike you as odd?"

"No, should it?"

"Well, maybe not that by itself, but what about the other stuff? Like when the Vismort mistook me for the Mistress. Didn't you think that was strange?"

"It was dark down there even with the light from the alcoves. I'd think it would be an easy mistake to make."

"You know the Mistress was Dreamweaver, right? Brent told me so."

"So you resemble Phrendonian's niece enough to be mistaken for her in a dark cave—I still don't understand why that matters. Even if you looked identical, the only one who'd ever know evaporated in the caves."

"Not true. There are portraits."

"Of Phrendonian's niece?"

"Yes. I know of at least two. The Princess has one of them in her collection—I've seen it. The resemblance is more than passing."

"Where's the other?"

"I have it."

Alexi shrugged. "That doesn't mean you're related any more than it means the Princess is."

"Yeah, but I also have the jewelry she was wearing in the pictures."

"You have jewelry that once belonged to Phrendonian's niece? It must be worth a fortune."

"I thought of that, but then it occurred to me that there might be spells on them. If I tried to sell something like that and the Church found out, I could get in serious trouble."

"There are spells that can detect things like that. I bet Professor Reston would be willing to have a look if you asked him."

Dona grimaced. "I don't know. Lately he's been a little too close to Jonas for comfort. Did you know Jonas put a knife to my throat?"

Alexi's jaw dropped. "He did what?"

"It's true. Because I was staying at the Nevinanders, Jonas was convinced I was working with Verone to steal Reston's book."

"Well that's just a misunderstanding, right?"

"Maybe, but when someone puts a dagger to your throat accusing you of treachery, you tend to take it personally."

"All right then, if you don't want Reston to test the jewelry, then what about your friend Michlos?"

"He'd probably want to know where I got it. If it turns out this Dreamweaver is related, I'm pretty sure I don't want the Crown to know."

"Doesn't look like you have many other options, unless, of course, you learn the spells and do it yourself." Alexi's grin turned sly. "After all, the jewelry might be dangerous. You'd only be doing it to save lives."

"I'll let you explain that to the nice Inquisitor."

"Suit yourself."

They continued their ride in silence, with Dona watching the passing trees through the carriage window, remembering fondly the breathless, late-night ride along this same stretch of road on the back of Michlos's horse. She could almost see the twisted branches flying past, illuminated by the glare of Michlos's strange hat. And then there was the wonder that was the Princess's chandelier: a source of light so bright and clear that the Princess could use it to paint long after the sun had set. If only the Sultan's Respite had used such lights instead of lanterns, countless lives would have been saved. And what about Brent's vault? If Alexi hadn't been with them, they'd either be dead by now or still be trapped there waiting to die. Even the Monsignor had recognized the necessity of using Alexi's talents. And when Jonas held that knife to her throat, how empowering it would have been to do something, anything, other than just stand there helplessly.

"You know," Dona said, "*you* could always learn the spells."

"And risk another penance?"

"You're right. I shouldn't have suggested it."

"Wait, you were serious?"

"Forget I said anything."

Alexi eyed her sidelong. "You're tempted, aren't you?"

She turned away. It somehow felt as though he'd just stolen a glimpse of her private innermost being and discovered something black and twisted staring back.

"Oh, look," she said. "Here we are at Ranselard Keep."

. . . . .

"What are you doing?" Thurman asked.

The old priest had barred the door to their flophouse room, cleared a space in the center of the floor, and was busily arranging clay bowls in a circle, placing a smoldering punk in each. The space was cramped enough that Thurman was relegated to crouching on a pallet.

The old priest stood back to inspect the symmetry. "Generally speaking, the older the scroll, the more elaborate the ritual. The ancients held a special reverence for these rites—through them they believed they established a communion with the Divine. In those days, Riturgy was viewed as a sacred gift, granted only through a Martyr's noble sacrifice. I doubt those Martyrs ever imagined that one day that sacrifice would amount to little more than an incidental perk awarded to toadying politicos."

The haze of incense was growing thicker, and Thurman's eyes already burned. "Are you using the scroll now? I thought you were using it to bargain with Laitrech."

"I was offering it in return for a chance to examine your uncle. Laitrech is not in much of a position to grant that anymore, is he?"

"I suppose not, but if you no longer need anything from Laitrech, what's the point? Are you going to sell it to the Accipitrines?"

The old priest spat. "Lavicius's thugs? Not on your life."

"Then what?"

"I would have thought it would be obvious. We can't keep your uncle unconscious forever. Of course, the instant he discovers I have Laitrech's Relic, he's going to confiscate it. Without a better understanding of his mental state, I have no intention of relinquishing what little advantage I might have in dealing with your uncle's enemies, and this is how I intend keep it. Now, stand back."

The old priest placed a heavy wooden candlestick in the center of the circle and the medallion from Jonas on top of that. "This first part I've done before. While Laitrech was bringing down the Bastion, I used it to make myself a Relic."

Thurman's brow furrowed. "But you didn't have the medallion then."

"Sorry, I misspoke—I meant I made myself *into* a Relic. As I expected, it wasn't so much the sacrifice that mattered, but the presence of spirit. I must have been correct, because it certainly seemed to work."

"Weren't you worried about what that might do to you?"

"I was desperate. If I hadn't chanced it, once Laitrech passed through the Bastion, I would have been powerless to follow him. Besides, even if it did do something unpleasant, I was banking it would wear off after an hour."

"But it was well over an hour later that you finally went after Laitrech in the Chapel. If it had already worn off, how did you get through the Bastion?"

"I used the old trick of Nullifying my resistance so that it could last all day—the same approach we've been using in combination with the spell from Samulian's Signet to keep your uncle from raising a ruckus. Unfortunately, the wand's effects didn't benefit similarly."

"But how could you do any of this in the first place if you didn't already have a Relic?"

"Contrary to popular belief, Relics are not specific to the bearer. Makes sense when you think about it—otherwise you couldn't pass them from one Ordinal to the next. Since it stands to reason they must simply act in a radius around the Relic, I stood close to Laitrech and used his."

Thurman didn't know if he was more impressed by the brilliance of the deductions or disturbed by the recklessness of the actions based on them. "So, after all this, you're saying that making a Relic is trivial?"

"Not exactly. Acquiring the expertise initially was far from trivial, though once you know how, it's not so difficult. There are two parts that are tough. The first, as I'm sure you are aware, is acquiring an object that has spirit associated with it. The second is making the Relic permanent."

Thurman's pulse quickened. They were already skirting the ragged edge of disaster. If they weren't careful, they'd cross a threshold from which there was no return. "You're going to Pattern it? Wouldn't that be heresy of the worst kind?"

"The Riturgy doesn't contain anything even remotely similar to Patterning. The closest I can come to it is a Hallowing, and that's assuming I'll be able to pull it off."

Thurman wiped smoke-induced tears on his sleeve. "What's a Hallowing?"

"As I said, it makes things permanent. Unfortunately, unlike Patterning, it requires the presence of spirit. As I understand it, spirit normally helps to protect and support an individual's consciousness. A Hallowing can co-opt that property to support various Rites as well, including the Hallowing itself. Once Hallowed, not only does the spirit cease to resist the Rite, it supports it and keeps it from decaying indefinitely. But unlike a Patterning, you can eliminate a Hallowing at any time."

Thurman blinked as he experienced a disturbing epiphany of his own. "But, if that's true, doesn't it mean each of the Relics still has a Martyr still trapped within it?"

"I'm afraid so. In fact, it may interest you to know they were not considered martyrs because they died for their faith. Instead, they made a compact to postpone their salvation in the service of their faith."

"And now their souls are trapped there forever?"

"That wasn't the bargain. The deal was that the Relics would eventually be decommissioned and laid to rest in consecrated ground. The Martyrs consented only to delay their salvation, not give it up entirely. But those terms had been forgotten or ignored for generations by the time I happened across them buried deep within the oldest sections of the Chapel."

"That's outrageous. Uncle Darron needs to hear this—you need to tell him."

The old priest snorted. "That's unlikely to make the slightest bit of difference."

Thurman frowned. "Why do you say that?"

"Because, my dear boy, I already have."

# CHAPTER SEVEN

# TECHNICALITIES

Word had spread through the Colony like fire through a distillery. The grounds before Ranselard Keep teemed with island denizens. As Dona's carriage approached, she heard the calls of vendors hawking wares and the incessant hammering and sawing of booth construction. Many aspiring artists, lacking the wherewithal to build a booth, simply spread blankets on the ground and arranged the fruits of their labors upon them.

"Is it always like this up here?" Alexi asked.

"I don't think so," Dona said. "They must have heard about the wedding."

"They swarm weddings like this? That's a little disturbing."

"This isn't just any wedding. The Crown is invited."

"The Crown?"

"Of course, silly. Verone is a cousin to the Crown Princess—Verone's mother thinks there's even a chance they'll attend. It could be a very long time before many of these people have this kind of opportunity to land a rich patron again."

Alexi's grin turned impish. "Does that mean you'll be royalty? How will I be expected to address you?"

"No more than your ancestor makes you a general."

"I suppose I could start off with 'Your Esteemed Royal Ladyship' and then just see what everyone else does."

Dona giggled. "That's the best you can do? You clearly have a lot to learn about being a courtier."

Landing on his good ankle, Alexi hopped out of the carriage and threw open the door for Dona with a flourish. "That may be, Your Esteemed Royal Ladyship, but in my favor, I am bright, eager, and wondrously good-looking."

Dona took his hand and inclined her head to him as he assisted her down from the carriage. "All worthy traits, 'tis true, but next to useless to us gentle ladies of the court unless accompanied by a properly loose moral character. What say you to that?"

Alexi bowed. "Only that should her Esteemed Royal Ladyship deign to teach me that which I needst must know, she shall find me an apt pupil."

"That's more like it. Perhaps we could be troubled to find a position for you—in the Royal stables."

While Alexi leaned into the carriage to grab his crutches, a man in a plumed hat and a black-and-white-striped doublet approached, swept off his hat, and bowed. "You are expected, Miss Merinne."

"Newcomb, how are you?"

He winked. "My resources are a mite stretched, but I am looking forward to the festivities."

Newcomb escorted them past the exhibitors far more quickly than Dona would have liked. The wedding was still a day away, but the artists had already assembled an impressive collection. Inside the keep, all the artwork Dona had previously seen stacked in the corridors had been cleared, and a small army of staff scrubbed relentlessly to ensure every surface gleamed.

In the courtyard, the Princess and the Monsignor chatted on the dais before her mother's throne. The Princess motioned for them to join her. Dona suspected she must have been watching for Newcomb's outfit—it was the only way anyone could possibly have picked them out from among the work crews, musicians, and servants. The Princess addressed Dona as they approached. "Miss Merinne, a pleasure to see you again."

Dona curtseyed. "The pleasure is all mine, Your Highness. Permit me to introduce Alexi Reysa, my escort for the ceremony."

Alexi bowed.

"Delighted to meet you. By chance, are you any relation to the Count?"

"Only very distantly. We've never even met."

"Well, perhaps if he gets the invitation in time, you'll finally have your opportunity. As for you, Miss Merinne, you'll see I took your suggestion to heart and invited the Monsignor here to dine with me."

The Monsignor raised an eyebrow. "Miss Merinne had a hand in that?"

"Indeed—you came highly recommended."

He gave a formal nod. "Then once again I am in your debt. Your track record is improving—the last Princess you had me meet was somewhat less than enthusiastic."

Dona blushed. "I'm sorry about that."

The Monsignor raised a hand. "Think nothing of it. I was amused, and for her part, I suspect Princess Julienne could benefit from a little religious discourse now and again. And Alexi—good to see you looking so well. How's that ankle doing?"

"Better, thanks. The crutches help."

"Miss Merinne," the Princess said. "I wanted to catch you while I still remembered. Our mutual friend is in residence, and when you find a spare moment, he asked if you could pay him a visit. Mention it to Newcomb when you are ready, and he'll take you to him. Otherwise, you should be able to find your mother over by the musicians. I think she and Nathalie are solving a logistical problem with the stage."

"Thank you, Your Highness. We'll be sure to do that."

The instant she and Alexi were out of earshot, Dona stopped and scanned the crowd.

Alexi squeezed her hand. "So, you've met Princess Julienne too?"

Dona kept scanning. "Just once—at the opera with Gregory. Didn't I tell you?"

"I don't think you mentioned it. Did he introduce you to anyone else?"

Dona shaded her eyes against the sun. "No one. Why do you ask?"

"What are you doing? Your mother's over this way."

"I'm looking for Newcomb. Do you see him anywhere?"

"You aren't thinking of running off before you tell your mother the invitations are posted, are you?"

For such a bright young man, Alexi could sometimes be exasperatingly clueless. "You bet I am. Once Ma sees me, I'll never get away."

"Is this 'friend' really all that important? Who is it anyway? Gregory?"

"You aren't still jealous of Gregory, are you?"

Alexi's ears colored. "I was never jealous of Gregory."

"Oh, really? Then why did you just get all mopey when you somehow got it in your head I was off to meet with him?"

"You mean it's not Gregory? Aren't we expecting him to sing tomorrow?"

"I can think of only one person the Princess might refer to as a mutual friend, and it's not Gregory."

"Oh, it's Michlos."

Dona patted his cheek. "Such a smart boy. Seriously, you're going to have to let go of that jealous streak. It'll eat you alive."

"I'm not jealous—how many times do I have to tell you?"

"Oh, there's Newcomb. Let's try to catch him before he disappears again."

Before long, Newcomb was escorting them slowly up a circular staircase to a tower room. Once Newcomb announced their arrival, they entered to find Michlos standing before the window gazing down at the preparations below.

He shook his head sadly. "For joyously and with both hands shall they relinquish that which sets them free."

"I'm sorry?" Dona said.

Michlos sighed and turned toward his guests. "It's nothing. Just an old verse from a seer long dead."

Dona clapped a hand to her mouth. "Oh, my word—what happened to your face?"

He gingerly touched the bridge of his swollen nose. "Oh this? I had a slight difference of opinion with another Enforcer."

"What did he do to you?"

"It could have been worse—much worse, in fact. Not to worry though, the matter has been satisfactorily resolved, at least for now. I see the two of you've been through some difficulties of your own. Is it broken?"

Alexi shook his head. "Just a sprain."

Michlos nodded. "Still, best to keep your weight off it when you can. Please, have a seat. So, I understand there were some adventures involving our friend the Monsignor?"

Dona and Alexi exchanged glances.

"Sensitive topic?"

"Sort of," Dona said. "There are some things we promised not to talk about."

"Oh?"

"I guess that sounds sort of suspicious, doesn't it?"

"Michlos laughed. "Well, if you're thinking I suspect you of selling me out, let me put your mind at ease. Everything I've seen suggests the Monsignor doesn't yet suspect anything. If he did, it wouldn't make sense for him to try to patch up relations between the Church and the Crown. It's Father Cartier I'm worried about. He's somehow gotten it in his head that my mother is a heretic. He went so far as to send members of the Inquisition to try to take her into custody."

Dona blanched. Such a blatant attack on the Crown meant no one was safe. "So, Cartier knows, but the Monsignor doesn't?"

"Cartier may not actually know, but there's no doubt something makes him strongly suspect."

"But I just saw Cartier and the Monsignor together the other day. If Cartier suspected, wouldn't it be the first thing out of his mouth?"

Michlos nodded. "I've been pondering that myself. It's not like there hasn't been opportunity. Cartier and the Monsignor were both present at lunch with the Princess today, along with one other person. Take a guess who."

"Verone?"

"How'd you know?"

"She and Father Cartier are friends. Besides, is there anything she isn't involved in?"

"What do you mean?"

"Well, let's see—she got her Church group to try to find me when I wasn't lost, she managed to escape from Exidgeon even though it had been taken over by the Inquisition, she stole Reston's book, and we think she was behind Professor Everson's attempts to steal the book three times before that, and to top it all off, now she's marrying my uncle."

"Everson? I'd forgotten about him. Where is he now?"

"I have no idea. No one's seen him since Verone and her Church group left Exidgeon."

"So Verone finally ended up with Reston's book after all?"

"Not exactly. I found it and secretly returned it to Reston."

"Does Verone know that?"

"Not yet—I just gave it back this morning."

Michlos frowned. "You're playing a dangerous game. Verone does not take interference with her plans lightly."

"I think she's more likely to suspect Reston than me."

"I hope you're right—and that Professor Reston is aware of that."

"He is."

Alexi cleared his throat. "If Father Cartier tells people he thinks your mother is a heretic, couldn't that end up reflecting poorly on the Crown?"

Michlos took a deep breath. "Oh, it's a bit more serious than that—it puts the Church and the Crown on a collision course."

"Could that be why Cartier isn't telling anyone?"

"I doubt it. If Cartier were merely trying to cover it up, he wouldn't have sent Inquisitors to apprehend my mother. I'm frankly at a loss to explain it, but I have a sinking feeling Verone may have had a hand in it."

"But that doesn't make any sense," Dona said. "Your mother is Verone's aunt. If Verone turned her in, wouldn't she also incriminate herself?"

"Verone is many things, but self-sacrificial is not among them. I was hoping perhaps you could help explain it."

"How would I know?"

"Word has it you've been staying at the Nevinander villa. That's not a place from which I can easily obtain information. While you were there, did you happen to see or hear anything there that might help put all of this in perspective?"

Dona shook her head. "Verone was almost never there. And what little time she was, she spent fighting with her father about where to hold the wedding. Verone was expecting to hold it at the villa, but when her father heard that the Monsignor would be performing the ceremony, he cut off that option."

"No big surprise there. What about the wedding itself? How did that come about? Verone never struck me as the marrying type."

"That was her father's doing. Apparently if she marries Uncle Rayen, she inherits her father's estate."

Michlos leaned back and crossed his arms. "Really? Now that is a surprise. Verone and her father have always been oil and water. She's the last person I would have expected to inherit."

"Well, he wasn't very nice about it. He gave her only a week to do it, or she doesn't inherit. Not only that, but he also doesn't seem to think she'll go through with it. He told me he thought she was going to try to get out of the wedding at the last minute on a technicality."

"You know, that part makes no sense to me," Alexi said. "If her father's the one giving her the estate, why can't he just refuse to transfer it if she's not married by the deadline?"

Dona tapped her chin thoughtfully. "Could he have been referring to the interdict? Maybe they won't technically be married if they hold the wedding here."

"Given what I know of the Monsignor," Michlos said, "I find it difficult to believe he would perform a ceremony he knew to be a sham. And that still doesn't address Alexi's point—if the marriage is invalid, there's nothing to stop Alistair from simply refusing to transfer the estate."

"Unless they have some sort of agreement," Alexi said. "When my father gets a client who's stuck in a bad contract, sometimes he's able to help by exploiting a technicality."

Michlos's eyes narrowed as he considered the implications. "Alexi, that's brilliant—Verone would never trust Alistair on his word alone, and I very much doubt he'd take her at her word either. Whatever arrangement they have, they almost certainly put it in writing, and if that's true, I suspect that document holds the key to a great many unanswered questions."

Dona sighed. "I suppose this means I'm going to have to go back and rifle through Alistair's study again."

"Perhaps not."

"How else are we going to get a look at it?"

"If there is an agreement, Alistair would have a copy, but Verone would keep a copy as well. Otherwise if things didn't turn out the way Alistair planned, he could just destroy the original and say it never existed."

"But how are you ever going to find it? At least I know where Alistair's study is. I have no idea where Verone would keep something like that."

Michlos started pacing. "What about that leather case of hers? The way she clings to the thing, I'd be surprised if she didn't walk down the aisle with it tucked under her arm."

Dona held up her hands. "Hold it right there—snooping for something in an empty office is one thing, but taking documents from a case she carries with her? She'd discover they were missing almost instantly."

"What if you didn't actually have to take them?"

"I have a good memory, but my detailed recall of legal documents is not that good."

"I have just the thing." From his pocket Michlos produced a silver cigarette case. Flipping it open, he selected a tiny black wand and held it up in the sunlight for inspection. Six glittering gemstones encircled its golden tip.

A chance to finally examine an honest-to-goodness wand in detail gave Dona a secret thrill. "Isn't that gorgeous. What does it do?"

"It collects images. Here, take a look. The gemstones rotate around the tip. All you have to do is line a gem up with the little dot scribed on the tip and then touch the tip to the document whose image you want to capture. It can hold up to five images, one per citrine."

"What about the purple stone?"

"Aligning the amethyst turns it off."

"How do you view the images?" Alexi asked.

"The wand doesn't do that by itself. I'll have to retrieve them later."

Dona marveled at the miniature wand's craftsmanship. "Did you make this?"

Michlos smiled. "I don't have that kind of patience."

"Who does?" Alexi asked.

Before he could answer, the door burst open and the Princess stormed in.

"We've got trouble," she said.

. . . . .

Dominick Everson finished his boiled turnips and threw the tray against the bars of his cell. The idea he might not be free for a very long time, if ever, was finally sinking in.

The noise roused Bart, and soon Everson heard the jingle of keys and the groan of the outer door's ancient tumblers.

"Now then," Bart said, "why all the ruckus?"

Everson hunched in the far corner of his cell and glared.

"I see you've finally been eating your veggies," Bart said. "That's fine and all, but you're going to have to return the tray before Ol' Bart can get you your dessert."

Although Everson had promised himself he would stop responding to Bart's attempts to bait him, hunger overrode his resolve. "There's dessert?"

"Course there's dessert. What do you think we are here, barbarians?"

Everson caved again to his gut's insistent growling. "What is it?"

"You'll see."

Everson slowly made his way over to the tray and slid it under the cell door.

Bart snagged it. "Such a good little trooper you're turning out to be. Ol' Bart'll get you that dessert just as soon as it's finished."

"Finished?"

"Yep. As soon as it comes out of the oven. Oh, and once they're all done with it up at the wedding and all."

"Wedding?"

"Assuming there's any leftovers, of course."

The pitch of Everson's voice rose. "Leftovers?"

"Well—and assuming Ol' Bart ain't hungry or nothing. You wouldn't want Ol' Bart to get grumpy now, would you?"

"Why do you keep lying to me like this?"

"Now that hurts. And after Ol' Bart, out of the kindness of his heart, offers to go out of his way to get you that dessert and all."

Bart had done it again, and he'd fallen for it. "There is no dessert."

"Sure there is. They're cooking it up in the kitchens right now."

"Oh really? Well, if there's a wedding cake, whose wedding is it then?"

"From what I heard, it's some friend of the Princess. Long weird name. I think it was Verna Eviander, or something like that."

Everson gasped. "Verone? It wasn't Verone Nevinander, was it?"

Bart considered that and nodded. "Could have been that, I guess."

"It can't be."

"Sure it could. Didn't Ol' Bart just say so?"

Everson paled. "Who's the groom?"

"Don't know. Nobody's saying nothing about no groom. Hey, you feeling all right?"

But Everson was no longer paying Bart any attention. Instead, he slid slowly down the bars of his cell.

"She found me," he said. "I'm doomed."

. . . . .

Dona, Michlos, and Alexi all gathered at the foot of Michlos's guest bed to see what the Princess brought in with her. Dona recognized it immediately and was surprised when Alexi didn't.

"What is it?" Alexi asked.

"A promise stick," the Princess replied. "One of the servants found her child playing with it in the courtyard. Fortunately, she took it to Newcomb to see if he could find the owner. I shudder to think what could have happened had someone stepped on it."

"Or if the Monsignor had found it," Dona added. "Is it armed?"

"That's precisely what I was hoping Michlos could tell us."

Michlos looked suddenly hopeful. "Does that mean I'm officially off bedrest?"

Celeste raised an eyebrow. "I'm going to have a talk with your sister. I can't believe she's let you go all this time without impressing upon you the dangers of trifling with a princess."

"Fine. Let me see it. Hmm. fairly high quality for a throw-away piece. It's even lacquered. The construction is consistent with production by one of the upper-echelon families, but of course, doesn't prove that. The single dowel and single notch suggest whatever it's armed with is likely to be pretty simple. Let's see, the sorts of effects we'd be most concerned about would be Summonings, in which case we'd expect a Suppression for Summoning as well—and if that's true, it should prove resistant to a color change."

Dona watched with rapt attention as Michlos held up the promise stick and focused. Unlike Alexi, he made the casting seem effortless.

"Hmm," he said. "That doesn't bode well."

The Princess barely dared to breathe. "What does it tell you?"

"It's armed."

"What does it do?"

"I can only easily narrow it down to the category. At very least it's suppressing Summoning. It could do any number of things, including just change color, but the most dangerous options are likely to be things like Darkness or Incinerate. I can't easily do a more detailed analysis for other Categories since the Suppression would interfere with the readout for my Detections. Of course, I can't remove the Suppression because that would allow the Summoning to manifest. Were I you, I would lock this well away from anyone for at least the next twenty-four hours. We can then check it again to be sure its spells have expired."

"This isn't the one that worries me—it's those we haven't found yet. For all we know, there could be twenty just like it scattered around the grounds."

Dona shuddered at the thought of the wedding going up in flames. If there were any chance of that, Verone couldn't possibly avoid calling off the wedding. "You really think there might be more?

"I don't have the luxury to assume there aren't. Is there any way we can check to see?"

Michlos rubbed his chin. "I don't generally play with area-wide Detections—I tend to set them off, which makes them sort of useless. However, if someone else were willing to do the actual scanning, I probably could come up with something. You'll appreciate, however, that such a thing is not something you would want to fall into the hands of say, the Inquisitor General."

"True, Celeste said. "But neither would you want random people to be Incinerated in his presence either—it's the lesser of the two evils."

"Very well, I'll start work on it right away. In the meantime, you might want to give some thought to how it got there. If someone did this deliberately, you'll want to know who and why as soon as possible."

Celeste sank wearily into a chair. "Would Verone try to sabotage her own wedding?"

Dona gasped. "You don't suppose that could be the technicality Alistair was referring to, do you? Something that would cause the wedding to be canceled?"

"I don't know," Michlos said. "But the sooner we find out, the better off we'll all be. Do we know if Verone has chosen her maid of honor yet?"

Celeste shook her head. "I don't think she was planning on one. Rayen doesn't have anyone in town for best man either."

"Perfect. Could you apply some pressure to have her pick Miss Merinne here? After all, it's only fitting that she should be included in her uncle's wedding."

Dona was grateful for vote of confidence but wasn't thrilled by the increased risk to her person. Still, if there was any way she could help her uncle through this mess, she felt obliged to try.

Celeste shrugged. "I can ask, but how does that help us?"

"We have reason to believe Verone may be concealing some answers in that attaché of hers. Let's hope the bride can be convinced that a celebration of 'leather and lace' was not exactly the statement she should wish to make during her little trip down the aisle."

· · · · ·

"Impossible. Absolutely impossible. It simply cannot be done."

The woman who looked up from the sketches was tall, imperious, and beside herself. "Never in all my years have I heard such a ridiculous request. You are all alike. You think you can just sprinkle your money over your shoulder like so much seed, and miracles will instantly sprout in your wake like pretty little flowers."

Verone and Dona's mother stood behind in solidarity as Nathalie tried to smooth the lady's ruffled feathers. "I am sorry about the short timeframe, Madame Rhozhia, but I'm afraid in this case it was unavoidable. What if we simplified the neckline and dispensed with the train entirely?"

"You have heard nothing I've said. Why? Why must I be tested like this? Why must great talent always be rewarded so?"

The Princess strode into Ranselard's expansive sewing room followed closely by Dona and also by an awestruck Helena, whose eyes, when they finally left the Princess to take in the wealth of mannequins, fabrics, tables, and tools, grew, if possible, even wider. Dona lacked context to form her own opinion on the space, but if Helena was impressed, so was she.

The Princess got right to the point. "How goes the dressmaking?"

Rhozhia executed a deep and sustained curtsey. "Your Highness."

The Princess perused the drawings and waved her hand absently. "You may rise. So, tell me about your design."

"The design is irrelevant. They want it to be completed by tomorrow morning. Even with my entire staff, such a design would take at least a week to complete."

"What if you just used this design to make the simplest possible dress? Even without all the sequins, ties, and lace, it would still be quite attractive. If it turns out that it needs anything more, we could always dress it up with some accessories and a fancy veil."

Rhozhia fanned herself with both hands. "Your Highness, I have a reputation to uphold."

"Oh, I understand. You certainly wouldn't want the Crown to witness a substandard product. After all, his entire court will no doubt be talking about this dress for weeks after the event."

The fanning abruptly ceased. "The Crown? The Crown will be in attendance?"

"Yes, of course. The bride is his cousin after all. Not to worry though, I'll see if I can get Nils Calenti to come up with something. He has a reputation for reasonable designs even under trying circumstances."

"Calenti? Bah, that amateur?"

"Well then, no doubt his reputation could stand to benefit from all the publicity. I'll have Newcomb track him down."

The back of Rhozhia's hand rose to her forehead. "Wait—I've just had…an inspiration."

"Does that mean you'll be making the dress after all?"

"And what a dress it shall be. A study in simplicity, the very essence of elegance. It shall be my magnum opus."

"I'm sure the Crown Princess will be captivated. What do you think, Verone? You are the bride after all. Is that what you had in mind?"

"If worse comes to worst, I'll simply wear what I'm wearing now. It fits reasonably well, and it covers everything that matters."

Nathalie harrumphed. "And they said romance was dead."

"Speaking of things that matter," the Princess said, "have you given any thought to your maid of honor?"

Verone shrugged. "I'm trying to get married, not lead a parade."

"The maid of honor isn't just decoration. You'll be wearing an awkward and heavy dress that will be difficult to get out of or around in, and you'll be constantly nitpicked by dozens of little things that will need doing, many simultaneously. A good maid of honor is instrumental to making a wedding work."

"Isn't that what Mum is doing?"

"The mother of the bride has enough other responsibilities. You'll want it to be someone else, preferably someone young, with plenty of energy. A wedding makes for a long and arduous day."

"Oh, very well. Dona, how nicely would I have to talk to you to get you to sign on for the job?"

Amanda brightened, and her head bobbed a series of tight, encouraging nods. "You should consider it, dear. It would make your uncle very happy."

Dona was amazed by how smoothly the Princess had obliquely maneuvered Verone's compliance with the plan. Now, it was on her to accept without seeming too eager. "I'm not sure I can. I don't have anything to wear."

Helena patted her shoulder. "Yes, you will, at least if I have anything to say about it—that is, of course, if her Highness doesn't mind providing some fabric and tools."

"You may have the run of the room," the Princess said. "Just try to stay out of Madame Rhozhia's way."

"Then consider the dress taken care of."

"Well," Dona said, "I guess it beats being the flower girl."

. . . . .

Alphonse trailed Alexi as they crisscrossed Ranselard's courtyard scanning for Phrendonic magic.

"Does the Monsignor know about this?" Alphonse asked.

"No—and he can't. But someone had to do it. The Princess thinks someone might be trying to sabotage the wedding."

"Now you're rubbing elbows with the Princess too?"

Alexi shrugged. "She called us over the moment we arrived. How was I to know she and Dona were pals?"

"Careful there, knight errant. As often as not, folks above your station who seem to take an interest in you aren't looking for friendship so much as someone to take a fall."

"I don't think she's like that."

"Famous last words. Is she carrying around one of these things?"

"If she did, the Monsignor would probably notice."

"Oh? And he won't notice you?"

"Whoops, there it goes." Alexi looked anxiously about, but relaxed when the bride-to-be flew past. "Oh, it's probably her—Michlos thought she might set it off."

"What's it doing?"

Alexi held out the device. To Alphonse it looked like a saltshaker with a marble in it.

"That's it?"

"That's all there is to it."

"How does it work?"

"When something detectable gets in range, the cap attracts the marble like a lodestone. There, see?" He held out the shaker. The marble stayed firmly planted against the lid—for a few seconds. Then it dropped back into the shaker."

"Wait, did it just break?"

"Nope. Verone went out of range."

"So we're just looking for heretics we don't already know?"

"No. The Princess found a dangerous device lying around. We're supposed to use this to sweep the grounds and make sure there aren't others."

"Oh, I get it. We're on garbage detail." He drew his blade. "Fear not. I shall skewer the foul refuse."

Alexi's breath caught. Baring steel at a royal wedding was hardly the best way to escape notice. "Put that away. You want to get us kicked out?"

Alphonse shrugged and resheathed. "So we're expected to grapple the garbage bare-handed?"

Alexi looked about. To his relief, no one seemed to care. "I suppose so. The Princess carried the stick she found without any trouble. I think the goal is to make sure they don't get broken."

Alphonse's hand sprang back to his pommel. "Ah, so we are to *defend* the trash. I'm on it."

"All right," Alexi said. "That does it."

"The sarcasm was too much?"

"No, we covered the whole courtyard. I wonder if we are supposed to check the grounds outside as well?"

"What's the alternative? Scanning the courtyard again?"

"Good point. Let's head out."

Finding the way wasn't difficult. Not only was it a mostly straight shot, but the Princess had also ordered the deployment of a trail of old carpets to keep the constant foot traffic from dirtying her freshly cleaned floors. Two guards in outlandish outfits identical to Newcomb's stood at attention near the entrance. For convenience, the portcullis was left open, and, with a nod to the guards, Alphonse strolled through. With his crutches, Alexi struggled a bit to keep up.

Guards had cordoned off a broad swath of green nearest the keep. Beyond that line, every inch, right up to the edge of the cliff overlooking the river, had been staked out by artists. Several more guards patrolled the area, resolving the inevitable territorial spats as they arose.

Alphonse was immediately drawn to a display of chains, bracelets and baubles. "You wouldn't happen to have any spare change on you?"

"A little. Why?"

"Helena's been admiring the locket you gave Dona. A lot, in fact. I don't think I can pretend to be oblivious much longer."

Alexi rummaged through his pockets. "I suppose that would be a dangerous thing to ignore. Here."

"Thanks."

While Alphonse agonized over the jewelry, Alexi wandered among the exhibits, recalling the occasion of the locket's gift. Dona had still been angry she'd been kept in the dark about the book she'd found in the library and Alexi's involvement with Reston's secret society. He and Reston couldn't possibly have anticipated Everson would waylay her carriage in an awkward attempt to steal the book, but she had every right to be upset. Alexi had used every trick he knew to win her forgiveness, including an exotic dinner at the legendary Sultan's Respite. The locket wasn't just a gift, it was a test. When he made it glow for her—and demonstrated beyond a doubt that magic was real and that he could work it—her eyes widened, not with fear, but at the possibilities. He knew then his decision to force Reston to include her had been the right one. Such a shame the Respite had burned. Celebrating the anniversary of that moment wouldn't be the same without the Respite's outlandish opulence.

One artist was stocking a booth with brilliantly glazed jugs, bowls, and vases. Although Alexi had no intention of engaging in an arms race with Alphonse, he browsed the vases anyway. Things with Dona were going well. Better to keep something on hand, just in case she started pointedly admiring Helena's new jewelry. He'd narrowed the field to a vase and a figurine when he felt a click in his pocket. He ducked around the side of the booth and whipped out the saltshaker. Sure enough, the marble was stuck soundly to the lid.

He held up the saltshaker. "Alphonse, over here."

Alphonse nodded. "No Verone this time?"

"I don't think so—it's hard to tell with all these booths."

"How far away could she be?"

"You saw how it worked before. Maybe ten yards or so?"

Alphonse scanned the possibilities. "That covers quite a few people."

"I know, but I think we can narrow it down if we move around a bit. Try to look like you're browsing."

Slowly wending their way through the crowd, they eventually narrowed the signal to a small booth under a large oak near the cliff. Since the booths all faced inland, they ducked behind one in the row and snuck toward the suspect booth. Partially wrapped canvases stacked against the back of the booth identified the occupant as a painter of island landscapes. Alexi was about to poke his head around the side, but Alphonse grabbed his arm, shook head, and pointed to his ear. Through the back of the makeshift structure, he could hear muffled voices. They sat, and each applied an ear to the wall.

Alexi could make out two distinct voices. The first was smooth and oily, the second wary and indignant.

"Surely even an artiste such as you can appreciate the value of a tenth of the estate," oily said.

"While the three of you split the rest evenly? I may be an artiste, but I do understand simple fractions."

"Your share is discounted because your chances of actually landing the estate on your own are, well, next to nil."

"Isn't that what you used to say about Verone?"

"If you think your chances are better on your own, feel free to decline. It's not like I couldn't find somebody cheaper."

"What did you want me to do?"

"It's trivial, really. Just take this—"

"A party favor?"

"Brilliant. Must be those keen artistic powers of observation. Just make sure to place it among the others so it doesn't stand out."

"That's it? You'd give me a tenth of the estate for that?"

"That's all there is to it. Think you can handle it?"

"All right, what's on it?"

"What do you mean?"

"You don't expect me to believe you'd offer me a tenth of the estate for my decorating skills, do you? What's that thing going to do?"

"Just a little something to disrupt the festivities."

Alexi gasped. No doubt the promise stick was intended to do the exact same thing. It had been no accident.

"Oh, now I understand," the artist replied. "You want me to deliver a little something with my name on it to distract the Inquisitor General. Then if it happens to be a little difficult for me to claim my share of the estate from the inside of a torture chamber, well, it's not like you didn't offer, right?"

Oily chuckled softly. "As delightful as that sounds, the intention was for you to be long gone before anything happens. The idea is to make it look as though the arsonist has struck again."

"Wait—it's got an Incinerate on it?"

"No. The idea isn't to hurt anyone, just delay the wedding. You can pique the Inquisitor General's interest just as easily with Darkness, and, according to several reports, the arsonist has been using that as well."

Alexi's world spun. These men were baiting the Monsignor with Phrendonic Heresy. While that might well delay the ceremony, the repercussions were likely to extend far beyond the island. Reston must be warned.

The artist was having none of it. "If you don't intend for it to get traced back, why not do it yourself?"

"As a matter of fact," Oily said, "I already did it once, but with Verone buzzing about, going back is too risky. As it was, she almost caught me several times. You're on good terms with her, so that wouldn't be a problem for you."

"So why didn't it work?"

"Because when I went in, I hadn't thought of it yet, and all I had on me was a promise stick. Although I put that somewhere where I thought it would get stepped on, so far that hasn't happened. We need something more definite."

"What do you mean, we?"

Oily grew agitated. "Haven't you been paying attention? If this wedding happens, we lose everything."

"You can't lose what you've never had."

"Are you out of your mind? This could be your last shot at happiness."

"You just don't get it, do you? For the first time in my life, I am happy, and I'm not about to risk that, particularly not for a small fraction of what I used to be. Not only that, I wouldn't interfere with what might be Verone's best shot at quelling her demons for anything in the world."

"You're joking, right?"

"I'm afraid this time you're going to have to find someone else to bully. This playmate has grown up and left the playground."

"All right, eight percent. Reg and Jed aren't going to be happy about it, but I suggest you take it, because it's the best offer you're going to get."

Alexi held his breath as he awaited a response.

"Not interested," the artist said at last. "Now, if you don't mind, I have a display to arrange."

"If you're considering holding out for a quarter, you're crazy. Reg and Jed would flay me alive."

"As tempting as that would be to watch, the answer is still no."

"This is your last chance. I won't ask again."

"Goodbye, Damien."

"Very well. Enjoy your smug little moment while you can. You're going to regret this, and mark my words, it will be sooner rather than later."

"The only thing I'm regretting is not having said no sooner. Have a good riddance."

Convinced the conversation was over, Alexi and Alphonse independently came to the same conclusion: it was time to leave. They intended to make their way between the booths and the cliff's edge for some distance before ducking back into the crowd. As it turned out, they only made it a few feet before everything went black.

# CHAPTER EIGHT

## ÐARK ÐEALINGS

Terrified cries drew Michlos to the window of his tower room. In the courtyard below, the rehearsal had just gotten underway. The Monsignor stood in his appointed spot near Rayen and Dona, and Verone was halfway down the makeshift aisle—a pair of ribbons that marked future location of a white silk runner. No one looked at the bride-to-be—all eyes were fixed at a point above and behind her. A jet-black dome had materialized in the green just outside the keep, tall enough to be visible even to those in the courtyard.

As Michlos watched, the Monsignor grabbed his cane and hobbled with remarkable speed toward the disturbance, Dona on his heels. Since Verone faced the wrong way, it took her a moment to realize what was happening, but once she did, she dashed after them. Michlos's heart raced. Not only was there no chance of covering this up, but the Monsignor could be rushing headlong into a trap. He took the tower stairs three at a time, telling himself repeatedly that Vane could not possibly be behind this. Unconvinced, he triggered his Amulet.

. . . . .

When Dona realized Verone was following them, she waited for her to catch up. "You go with the Monsignor. I'll see if I can find the Princess."

Verone hardly paused. "You do that."

Dona watched as Verone and the Monsignor disappeared down the hallway. Then she headed back toward the courtyard. Instead of searching for Celeste, however, she ducked into the little room where Verone had left her belongings and closed the door behind her.

· · · · ·

The dome still loomed as the Monsignor limped across the green. Most who had not fled stayed well back, but occasionally someone would emerge from the blackness, blink at the sudden sunlight, and then scramble away to safety. Wails of terrified artists still emanated from within the dome, some believing they had been struck blind, while others more in tune with recent events feared imminent death by fire.

The Monsignor yanked down the rope that cordoned off the artists. Could their arsonist be to blame? If so, what was the goal? Did this new attack have more to do with the wedding or the artists? Either way, locating the source would be the necessary first step. He beckoned Verone. "Give me a hand with this."

"What are you doing?"

"Laying it around the perimeter. We'll need that to have any chance of finding its source."

The unlikely pair guided the rope along the dome's edge. They'd gotten no more than a quarter of the way around when the darkness winked out of existence.

"I think we got enough," the Monsignor said.

Verone nodded but looked dubious.

He then turned to address the shaken artists. "I am Monsignor Goodkin. Everyone please gather at the keep wall. We'll get to the bottom of this, but it's going to require your cooperation."

The hysteria began to abate. Most were more than happy to comply with the Monsignor's request.

Michlos burst from the gate, breathless, Celeste on his heels.

"Michlos Serrola? Is that you?" the Monsignor asked. He almost hadn't recognized Michlos behind his blackened and swollen features. He wondered what could have caused it—Michlos didn't have a reputation as a brawler. His very presence posed an additional puzzle. He'd understood the Serrolas and Nevinanders were estranged. And yet, the Crown was on the guest list. Perhaps Michlos was attending in his official capacity.

Michlos gave a polite nod. "Monsignor Goodkin." He was still trying to catch his breath.

"I see that once again the Crown is on top of the situation, though, I must confess, the speed of your response is a bit unexpected."

Verone crossed her arms. "I was just thinking that same thing."

Alphonse's panicked cries rose above the murmur of the crowd. "We need help over here. It's Alexi. I think he fell."

The four of them rushed toward Alphonse's voice. As Michlos passed over the rope, he scooped it up and dragged it along.

"No, wait—leave that," the Monsignor said.

Michlos ignored him. "We'll need it to haul him up."

Despite his disappointment at the loss of his only clue to the spell's source, the Monsignor bowed to the more immediate need. He sighed and followed.

Alphonse knelt and peered over the cliff. "Help is coming. We'll have you back up in no time."

Alexi had come to rest on a steep incline ten feet below the edge. He clung to a spindly sapling.

The Princess sidled up and peered down. "What happened?"

"He got disoriented in the dark," Alphonse said. "I think he was trying to catch up to me but got too close to the edge."

Michlos called down, "Are you hurt?"

"I don't think so," Alexi said. "I'm such an oaf."

"Hang on and don't move." Michlos began knotting the rope.

"What are you going to do?" Alphonse asked.

"We'll make two harnesses and anchor them to the booth here, then I'll lower myself using one. Once I've gotten him into the other, you'll pull him up."

"Got it—Um, I don't have to tie any knots, do I?"

Michlos shot him a puzzled look. "I don't think so."

"Good."

The Monsignor had a seat on the grass and watched. After a moment, his hand strayed across something hard and smooth. He held it up to the sunlight. "Hmm, what have we here?"

Michlos paused for a brief glance and stifled a cough. "Looks like a saltshaker to me. Maybe someone's lunch got interrupted?"

"There's no salt in it though—just a marble stuck to the lid."

"A toy rattle for a babe, perhaps?"

The Monsignor slipped the object into his pocket. "Possibly."

Michlos tested his knots. "I think we're ready." He strapped on the first makeshift harness and tied the free ends of both harnesses securely to the booth. He then lowered himself over the edge. Moments later, he reached Alexi.

"No sudden movements, now." Little by little, he tucked Alexi into the harness. He then gave Alphonse the thumbs up."

Alexi climbed over the edge of the drop to cheers from some of the more adventurous artists who had ventured close enough to watch the rescue unfold. Moments later Michlos pulled himself over the edge and was greeted by another round of cheers.

"Well done," the Monsignor said. "Watching you in action, I better understand the high regard your citizens hold for the Crown. They're lucky to have you on their side."

Verone herded them back toward the keep. "Now that the excitement is over, we have a wedding to rehearse."

The Monsignor paused, and everyone else followed suit. "I'm not sure that's such a good idea. If this heretic also happens to be our arsonist, then until we catch him, everyone in attendance is in danger. Once I've had another look at the scene, I'm going to have to interview as many of the artists as possible. I know it's distressing, but in the interests of safety, I think it prudent to postpone."

Verone's jaw tightened. "You can't cancel a wedding the day before it's scheduled. There's too much at stake."

"I'm sorry, but the safety of the guests must be our top priority."

Celeste crossed her arms. "No offense, Monsignor, but may I remind you that the island is still under interdict. While that's true, any investigation, even into heresy, falls under my jurisdiction."

He had overstepped again. The tense history between the Church and the Colony made her understandably sensitive. He made a mental note to use more deference going forward. "My apologies, Your Highness, I did not mean to presume. If you are amenable, I request your permission to conduct an investigation."

"You have it, but only with respect to the physical evidence and the scene. The questioning of witnesses I reserve to my guard. The artists are not accustomed to Church authority and as yet know nothing of the reconciliation plans. Those, I wish to reveal on my own terms, and not before the details have been finalized."

Verone tried herding them again. "Well then, as long as you won't be interviewing the artists, there should be plenty of time to fit in a wedding."

"Not and be able to ensure the safety of the guests," the Monsignor said. "Here's what I can do, though. To get around the interdict, I can perform a small ceremony just off the island. The larger ceremony would only have been a reenactment and reception anyway."

"If that's what it takes to get this done—"

"There's just one problem," the Princess said. "There isn't time to send out cancellations. Unless we put up a roadblock, the guests will arrive tomorrow whether we like it or not. And a roadblock is likely to cause quite a backup—if the attendees are the target, they'd be sitting ducks."

"What do you suggest?"

"What if, once they arrived, we could ensure their safety?"

"How do you propose to do that?"

"Ever heard of the Eye of Moravidos?"

The Monsignor raised an eyebrow. "Dreamweaver's Downfall? The Unassailable Hedge? That's the stuff of legends. I always envisioned it as little more than a plot device invoked by an ancient storyteller resorting to hyperbole to justify the defeat of his otherwise unstoppable villain."

"What if I told you it's real?"

"I don't mean to doubt you, but even if you had a something you thought might be the Eye, how would you truly know?"

"I am satisfied of its authenticity," the Princess replied. "I think it could be used to safeguard the ceremony at least."

"Even if it were real, I couldn't sanction such use of a Profanity."

"Once again, you forget the island is under interdict. But apart from the question of authority, are you saying a Profanity couldn't be used even for the protection of innocent lives? Does the rule admit to no exceptions whatsoever?"

"I didn't say that."

"Besides, how do you know it's a Profanity? As I understand it, the Eye has defied all attempts at analysis. Perhaps it wasn't created using heresy at all. Can you really say for certain?"

This was a new twist for which he was utterly unprepared. "You'd be comfortable with the risk?"

Celeste shrugged. "It's a risk either way. If we use the Eye, and things go awry, at least we tried."

"Let me send for Albert. He may have a better understanding of what we're dealing with."

"By all means—but do hurry. Time is short for devising an alternative. In the meantime, we have a rehearsal to finish."

. . . . .

Despite continued decorating and construction, the rehearsal went off without a hitch. Verone appeared precisely when she was supposed to, Gregory's voice brought tears to the eyes of all assembled, and Rayen got through the entire event without a seizure. By the time it was over, Dona was antsy as a flower girl. The instant she was free, she ducked out of the courtyard and dashed up the stairs to Michlos's room. Alexi and Alphonse were already there, looking uncharacteristically grim.

"What is it?" she asked.

"Verone's brother did it," Alexi said.

"The Darkness?"

He nodded. "We overheard arguing just before it happened. One admitted to dropping the promise stick. He tried to bully the other into putting the darkness in the courtyard, but the other brother refused."

"I'm not surprised. I found the contract. If Verone marries within the week, she gets the bulk of the Nevinander estate. The brothers get nothing."

"Did she leave herself a loophole that could account for Alistair's little technicality?" Michlos asked.

"Yes. For some reason Verone wrote in that Alistair had to personally invite someone named Marguerite, but if this person doesn't show, she can call off the wedding and still inherit the estate. In return, she provided Alistair and Nathalie with documents called 'Inquisitorial Indulgences,' signed by Father Cartier."

Michlos let out a long low whistle. "That would make them effectively Inquisition-proof."

"Why would Father Cartier ever agree to something like that?"

Michlos's jaw dropped in sudden realization. "Because he has bigger fish to fry. Dona, did you get a chance to use the wand on the documents?"

She nodded.

"Can I have it, please?"

She reluctantly slid it from her sleeve. She'd been hoping to examine it in more detail. Once it was safely back in its case, Michlos collected his belongings.

"What are you doing?" Alexi asked. "Is something wrong?"

"I have to go, but I'll be back as soon as I can. Can you fill Dona in on the saltshaker situation?"

"Sure," Alexi said. "Do you still want to warn Verone about it?"

He considered a moment, then shook his head. "I don't have time to plug any more leaks, and if Verone has immunity, she can no longer be trusted. Instead, find the Princess and tell her to make sure the Monsignor's cane stays within his reach while he has that saltshaker. Also, tell her that under no circumstances is she to do anything with the Eye until I get back. Got it?"

Alexi nodded.

"Where are you going?" Dona asked.

Michlos took a deep breath. "Home," he said.

. . . . .

The Monsignor stayed at dinner only long enough to give the benediction and sample the first course—the investigation was simply too pressing. Precious little daylight remained to inspect the crime scene, and hundreds of guests were due to arrive the next morning. He nodded to the guards hovering at the scene. They eyed him warily but suffered him to pass.

First, he unwound a spool of string to approximate the arc he and Verone had marked with the rope Michlos had used to rescue Alexi. Next, he recreated the arc's radius with another string. Though obstacles prevented a precise measurement, he was pleased with the result. He had narrowed the Darkness epicenter to the vicinity of a single booth.

A carriage rumbled to a stop, and Albert emerged. "Ah, there you are. What's this I hear about another incident?"

"You're standing where it happened."

Albert looked around. "The area seems surprisingly unscathed."

"It was just Darkness this time."

"A refreshing change of habit."

"Perhaps not. Have a look at this."

Albert held the object up to the light. "Looks like a saltshaker—with a marble in it."

The Monsignor shrugged. "Had it held salt, or if I hadn't found it in the vicinity of a heretical incident, I probably wouldn't have thought twice about it. Can you think of any use a Phrendonic Heretic might have for such a thing?"

"I've never curated a saltshaker before, but Phrendonic Heretics are endlessly inventive. May I hold onto this while I ponder whether the collection contains something analogous?"

"By all means."

"Now, was I imagining it, or did you imply the lack of a fire at the scene isn't as unusual as it seems?"

"The original incident we investigated at the University involved only Darkness—there was no fire there either."

"You mean the building in the Hathaway compound? I was under the impression that had burned too."

"It did, but that happened in a later incident."

"That's odd. If they wanted to burn down the building, why didn't they just do it the first time?"

"I have a clue that speaks to that. There were pieces of a promise stick at the first incident."

Albert raised an eyebrow. "A promise stick? That suggests a courier, doesn't it?"

"Possibly, although one could also use such a device for instantaneous effect. Sometimes there just isn't time to cast."

"Which do you think it was?"

"I'm leaning toward the courier theory. From my examination of the scene, it appeared that the perpetrator had been attacked unexpectedly by Shoruga's dog. Probably the stick was broken in response."

"Darkness wouldn't deter a dog attack, would it?"

"I doubt it. And someone sophisticated enough to create a promise stick would no doubt realize that, and anyone who had dealt with

Shoruga before would surely have known about his dog. The courier may have been sent there without being warned."

"And yet, he was given a promise stick with a Darkness spell on it? Wouldn't it have made more sense to warn him about the dog and forget the promise stick?"

"Well, the Darkness could have been intended to help evade human pursuit, but it's always a risk because, once you break that stick, you can't see anything either. You'd definitely want to take careful stock of your surroundings before you used it, or you'd end up tripping over something or running into a wall. Against a dog, it would be a huge disadvantage."

"Are you suggesting the courier was set up?"

The Monsignor nodded. "Whoever sent him was either trying to get him killed or was intending to draw attention—or both."

"So the fires may have been set by someone else?"

"I think they must have been. And unless I miss my guess, the attack on the Church was perpetrated by a different person than the arson at the college."

"What makes you say that?"

"At the University, only objects were targeted and there were relatively few injuries, despite the structural damage. At the church, the spell was centered on or near the victims. Someone wanted to be absolutely certain there were no survivors."

"Copycat crimes?"

"Seems likely, doesn't it?" The Monsignor had seen this sort of thing before. An area can seem to be heresy-free for a long time when in reality the heretics have simply become adept at concealing their presence. They proliferate until someone makes a mistake and draws attention, and then the floodgates open. Suddenly everyone feels free to act on their personal vendettas, hoping to pin the blame on the first perpetrator.

"How many heretics are we talking about?"

"No idea. Hmm—now this is interesting. Have a look."

"It's a landscape," Albert said. "Much like the others in and around the booth. Reasonably rendered, I guess, but nothing particularly special."

"No, look at the lower right corner.

"It's signed and dated. That's not unusual, is it?"

"Not of itself. Can you make out the name?"

Albert leaned in close. "My eyes are not what they once were. Looks like it starts with a T. Tha…Thaddeus. Yes, that's it. Thaddeus Nevinander."

"That's what I thought," the Monsignor said. "Maybe it's time we had a little chat with our blushing bride."

# CHAPTER NINE

## PATTERNS OUT OF CHAOS

Twilight had fallen by the time Michlos arrived at his mother's estate. Arerio was waiting for him on the porch.

"Is Mother about?"

"The Mistress has retired to the boudoir."

"Already? It's a little early for her, isn't it?"

"She has an engagement tomorrow. I believe she is attempting to make decisions as to wardrobe. Mistress Veronique will be taking a husband. You may find it interesting to know that Alistair himself delivered the invitation."

"And she's going?"

Arerio shrugged. "The idea appeared to disagree with Alistair sufficiently that I'm afraid she may have felt compelled."

"I suppose I'd better get this over with."

"Shall I announce you?"

"That won't be necessary."

As Michlos passed the family portraits that crowded the stairwell walls, he wondered whether previous generations had been equally headstrong or if his mother's bullheadedness was merely an anomaly. Although his grandfather had been by no means shy, force of will had not been his defining characteristic. Rather, Michlos remembered mostly his overwhelming sense of optimism and the rampant enthusiasm he brought to bear on whatever project he dabbled in. The empty space that once held his grandfather's portrait still jarred him. In a house where almost nothing ever changed, that would have been the last thing he would have expected his mother to part with.

He faced the door to the boudoir, took a deep breath, and knocked.

.  .  .  .  .

Marguerite had laid out several gowns on the settee, each somehow more dramatically floral than the last, and not one of which could have been called stylish even in the decade that had spawned it. Fashion was neither her focus nor her forte. The knock took her a bit by surprise.

"Oh, it's you," she said. "Nice of you to finally drop by."

"I've been indisposed."

"What happened to your nose?"

"I had a little run-in with Josephus Vane."

"When I suggested that you confront him, a round of fisticuffs was not exactly what I had in mind."

"Obviously, me either."

"Where is he now?"

"In the dungeons at Ranselard."

Vane's imprisonment was welcome news, but his Santine training might make him difficult to keep there. "Does Celeste realize what she's dealing with?"

"She's been briefed. She's using the Eye of Moravidos to keep him docile."

"She convinced the Magisters to give it up?"

Michlos shrugged. "I doubt she gave them a choice. You know she's Reconciling with the Church?"

"It's high time. Given recent events, it makes no sense to continue to stick her neck out."

"You approve?"

"Don't get me wrong. Personally, I think it's tragic, but I'm not so blinded by my own biases that I can't appreciate the strategic wisdom. She has the welfare of her subjects to consider."

"It means she's closing the Academy."

"Ah well. It was a noble experiment, but its time has passed. The lack of centralized authority made the whole project unwieldy and unreliable. This whole situation with Vane is a classic example of permissiveness run amok."

Michlos's jaw tightened. "I do not believe that evil is the inevitable result of a diffuse power structure. Need I remind you what happened at Caprian? One could hardly call that hierarchy permissive."

"I know you find it distressing, and I'm not trying to bait you, but sometimes the world changes despite us. When that happens, we need to adapt and move on."

"I'm not here to debate philosophy. I've come because I have information I think you'll find useful."

"Really? What about?"

He flicked open the cigarette case and plucked out the wand he'd retrieved from Dona. "It's all right here."

Marguerite was pleased to see it. "So you do occasionally use the little toys I make for you?"

"All the time. And here's the viewer."

She took the second wand from him. It was plain except for a tiny golden tip much like that on the first wand. She rotated the tip by 180 degrees until it clicked into place. "Ready."

Michlos switched the gemmed collar from the amethyst to the first citrine. An image of a document flared into being, skewered by the viewer-wand's tip.

Marguerite squinted at the text. "Care to summarize?"

"It's a contract between Verone and Alistair."

"You've touched the wand in the middle of the document. Why not in the margin so the wand doesn't get in the way?"

"I guess I forgot to mention that when I lent the wand to Miss Merinne."

"Am I to understand you lent it out?" Given recent events, sharing his talisman collection seemed uncharacteristically reckless.

"I thought it unlikely that Verone would let me anywhere near her personal effects, so we engineered Miss Merinne's selection as her maid of honor."

"What if she'd been caught?"

"I was nearby. I'd have come up with something."

Marguerite sighed. "Well, at least you got it back without it devolving into a total fiasco. Now, what does this say?"

"It transfers Alistair's estate to Verone."

"So the girl won the lottery, did she?"

"Not yet—there are conditions. For the transfer to take effect, she must be married within the week."

"I take it this wedding is not something she's been planning for a while."

Michlos shook his head. "The groom is Miss Merinne's uncle—Verone only met him a few days ago."

Marguerite's eyes narrowed. "So Alistair wasn't sitting on the invitation after all."

"There's more. One of the conditions was that Alistair had to invite you to the wedding personally—and if you don't attend, Verone can call off the wedding but still inherit the estate."

Marguerite nodded. "Oh, I think I understand now. They have a long history of this sort of thing. If one of them wants something, the other always tries to test how much by adding an unpleasant condition. Alistair was probably trying to goad Verone into marrying a stranger because he knew how much she'd hate that. In return, Verone forced Alistair to abase himself to his least favorite person, and his failure to do so would nullify the repugnant wedding requirement. I think he outfoxed her on this one though. Instead of prostrating himself, he presented himself as if he was doing Verone a favor, and that my presence was the last thing he wanted. I'm embarrassed to say I fell for it. What I don't understand is where Verone gets her bargaining power. I can see where Alistair could compel the wedding or withhold the estate, but how could Verone compel Alistair to invite me?"

"That's another of the conditions. Verone wrangled Inquisitorial Indulgences from Cartier."

"Cartier? He's not even an Inquisitor. Where does he get the authority to grant Indulgences?" Clearly there was more going on than was apparent on the surface. They needed a more complete picture to understand what was motivating events, or they would never get ahead of them.

"Apparently Ordinal Isrulian put him in charge of the Inquisition."

"Well, even if he had the authority, why would he grant it to Verone?"

"You can't guess? I thought it would be obvious to you, of all people. I think it's gotten personal."

Marguerite's jaw fell open. "That vicious little harlot. She's the one who ratted me out."

Michlos nodded. "It makes sense based on the evidence."

"And that's how Cartier got my wrap."

"Your wrap? What are you talking about?"

"Didn't I tell you? I found Cartier and confronted him. I was hoping to induce him find the other witness to Vane's heresies, but he was absolutely convinced that I had orchestrated all the recent attacks, including those at the college. He even went so far as to say he'd seen me there and that I'd dropped my wrap at one of the crime scenes."

"That's preposterous. You haven't been to the college in years."

"So I told him. But out of nowhere, he produced my wrap."

"Are you saying Verone manufactured evidence?"

"No. It was definitely my wrap. I wracked my brain to figure out how Cartier could have gotten his hands on it, but now I know. The last time I wore it was on my birthday, when I tried to make my peace with Alistair. Verone took it from me when I arrived, but by the time I left I was so upset, I completely forgot to get it back."

"That would also explain where the bogus invitation came from."

Marguerite rubbed her temples. "So she must have been planning this all along. That means Verone is also behind the events at the college. And now, even if the Church discovers the truth, she has the Indulgence to protect her. What other interesting documents did Miss Merinne discover?"

"I'm not sure—I left in a bit of a hurry. Let's have a look." He turned the gemmed collar on the wand to the next slot. The image of the page skewered by Marguerite's wand flickered and became something else.

"It's just the second page of the contract. Next?"

Again, the page on her wand shifted.

"Looks like Verone's Indulgence," Michlos said. "Next?"

Marguerite nodded, and Michlos rotated the collar again.

"Hmm, this would appear to be Alistair's and Nathalie's Indulgence. Is there anything else?"

Michlos turned the collar once more.

"And this is?" Marguerite asked.

"It looks like some sort of disclaimer. Ah, yes, Verone convinced Cartier to agree that, in return for her aid, the Church would disclaim any interest in your estate, ostensibly to eliminate any conflict of interest."

"How uncharacteristically caring of her. So, what's her real motive?"

"I'm not sure. I really don't see how that helps her. Even if they captured and convicted you of heresy, your estate simply goes to the next of kin instead of the Church."

"I do have a will," Marguerite said. "You and Irina are the primary beneficiaries. You don't suppose she actually cared whether the Church was biased, do you?"

"Not in a million years. It doesn't add up—what are we missing?"

"Any more images?"

"No, there's only room for five. We've seen them all."

"Do we know anything else about Verone's recent activities?"

"Other than the wedding?" Michlos asked. "Wait, come to think of it, we do. She's been pressuring Celeste to Reconcile with the Church."

"Why on earth would she care about that?"

"Maybe this is quid pro quo for Cartier. He's been included in all the discussions. If it goes through, and he's viewed as the primary mover, his reputation with the Church could get quite a boost."

Marguerite shook her head. "I don't buy it. If he convicts the Crown Princess's mother of heresy, his reputation won't need any boosting. How did Verone sell the idea to Celeste?"

"She wouldn't tell me."

"What? Why not?"

Michlos's face reddened. "I think she was a little upset because she thought I wasn't being completely forthright with her."

Marguerite sighed. "Next time you're going to keep her in the dark, you might consider keeping her in the dark about it. All right, let's try a different tack. If you were Verone, how would you convince Celeste to Reconcile?"

"Let's see. I'd know about the Inquisition, since I would have been the one to usher it in. If I really wanted her to Reconcile, I'd probably point out that it might be better to be on good terms with the Church if there's an Inquisition going on next door."

Marguerite waved her hand. "Not good enough. If there's an all-out Inquisition going on at the College, the island would at most be incidental. You'd have to go through Trifienne to even get to it, and there's no way the Crown would ever permit that."

"Unless they somehow got the Crown out of the way."

"How?" Marguerite asked. "Nathan would never agree to sacrifice the island. He views Celeste as family."

"Well, what if the Inquisition really got out of hand? At some point it could even threaten the Crown. I'll be honest—ever since I heard about Vane trying to cart you off, I've been worried about how that would affect the Crown. If they can convincingly use you to brand Nathan as a heretic, it would almost certainly destroy his popular support. Not only that, but it would be a great recruiting tool for convincing other states to join a crusade against him. If that were to happen, then if I were Celeste, I'd really want to be on good terms with the Church. She'd still have nothing to fear from Nathan, but she'd have a much better chance of sparing her island from the turmoil if he fell."

Marguerite blinked several times in shock. "You know, I think you were wrong before."

"About what?"

"About this whole situation being personal."

"You don't think her outing you as a heretic is personal?"

"No. I think it was simply a very deliberate means to an end. Think of it this way. If I am gone, and Nathan falls, what happens to my estate?"

"Assuming there's any kind of orderly transition, it should still pass to the next of kin."

"And if Nathan falls, and I'm taken as a heretic, do you suppose you, Irina or her children will be in any position to make a claim on that inheritance?"

"If it turns out like it did at Caprian, we'd be lucky to survive at all."

"And then who inherits?"

Michlos rubbed his chin. "I suppose Alistair would be next in line."

"But if Alistair has already passed his estate on to Verone, an inheritance might well be considered part of that."

"You mean Verone would inherit?"

"It would be the ultimate indignity for Alistair. Verone could potentially accomplish in a few short months what he couldn't in twenty years—reuniting the entire original Nevinander estate. That's why she needed the disclaimer."

Michlos's brow furrowed in thought. "But that still doesn't explain the push for reconciliation."

"Oh, I disagree. You put your finger on it when you said there would need to be a smooth transition of power for Verone to inherit. If Nathan fell, and particularly if he fell due to allegations of corruption from his wife's heretical influence, who, from Verone's point of view, would be the best candidate to replace him?"

Michlos's breath caught. "Of course. Celeste is a distant enough relative of Nathan's that she could escape the heresy allegations, but she's close enough to have a legitimate claim on the throne. Not only that, but she's on good terms with Verone, which, from Verone's point of view, makes Celeste a vast improvement over the status quo."

"Now, let's assume none other than the same humble priest, whose tireless efforts brought the evil heretical Crown Prince and his family to justice, promoted Celeste for the position. Recall, she would be fresh from a reaffirmation of her loyalty to the Church through a nice official reconciliation."

"I warned Celeste not to trust that woman."

Despite the inconvenience, Marguerite admitted a certain grudging admiration for her niece's plan. Risky, yes, but its breathtaking scope and multiple moving parts would have made it impossible to decipher without access to the documents. "Fortunately, we were alerted to the danger in time to make sure it doesn't happen. Now, which of these gowns should I wear tomorrow?"

"You aren't still planning to go? Need I remind you that Verone is expecting you, and she's gone to extraordinary lengths to frame you. She's even recruited the Inquisitor General to officiate. She won't miss this opportunity to turn you over to the Inquisition. In fact, given that her whole plan hinges on you, I think it would be best if you left town."

Marguerite considered for a long moment. "Oh, all right. I've been meaning to visit the bazaar in Azelon for some time now. I'll leave tomorrow."

"Thank you, Mother." He leaned down to give her a peck on the cheek. "I was expecting you to make that much more difficult than you did."

Marguerite frowned. "You always make me out to be such an ogre. You see, I can be quite reasonable—provided your request is equally reasonable."

"How could I have ever doubted it."

"Now, promise you'll be especially careful untangling this mess. Because, if we're right about this, once I'm out of the picture, you're the next logical target."

. . . . .

"I can't breathe," Verone cried.

"Bah," Madame Rhozhia said, "I haven't even pulled the lacings yet."

"This isn't fashion, it's torture. I think we'll have to make do without the corset."

"Nonsense. Fashion is torture. Those who pretend otherwise aren't designing gowns, they're peddling rags. Now hold still while I try to create at least the illusion of a waist." Rhozhia yanked the laces taut and tied them off. "And, voila. What do you think?"

"I think I'm going to be sick."

Rhozhia pulled up a chair. "You'll get used to it. Here, have a seat."

Verone struggled to sit. "I don't think I can do this."

"Do you want a gown, or do you want a tent?"

"A tent sounds really nice."

"Arms up." Rhozhia ran a tape around her midsection and checked the measurement. "If you think the corset is tight, wait until you try the shoes."

. . . . .

Across the now-cluttered sewing room, Helena draped Dona with various fabrics to see how they worked with her complexion.

"I won't need to wear a corset, will I?"

"Not unless you keep moving when you need to stay still. I was thinking of a nice little structured cropped jacket with three-quarter-length sleeves over a floor-length gown with stark white petticoats. If you happen to have them with you, you could use your opera gloves for dramatic impact. What do you think of this crimson?"

"You can't dress a bridesmaid in in crimson—it will compete with the bride."

"That's the idea."

"But the maid of honor is supposed to blend in."

Helena snorted. "And the fancy designer is supposed to design her own stuff too, but that isn't happening either. So far, she's looked over my shoulder five times. She criticizes everything, I come up with, then she steals my ideas and uses them."

"Well, maybe she's just trying to make sure the two dresses share a common theme."

"If by 'common theme,' you mean she's making the same dress, only in white."

"It can't be that bad."

"No? Here's the sketch for my initial design. Now, look at what she's squeezing Verone into."

"Hmm, there is some resemblance, isn't there? On the brighter side, it might actually be attractive when it's done."

"And if it is, that harridan will get all the credit. That's why, once she got far enough along to be committed, I decided to just start over. I didn't want to be publicly accused of copying myself."

"Will you get this done in time?"

"I'll be up all night, but I'll get it done if it's the last thing I do."

"What happened to her other design?"

"Even simplified, it was too complicated. She would never have finished."

"Well, your new design looks pretty complicated too."

"I'll manage. Unlike some, I'm used to doing my own stuff—I don't have a whole boutique of seamstresses doing my work for me."

Nathalie poked her head in. "Is everyone decent? The Monsignor is wondering if he could steal Veronique away for a few minutes."

"I'm afraid not," Rhozhia said. "If you expect a masterpiece in the ridiculously short timeframe you've given me, I simply can't have any more interruptions."

"Could he talk while you work? I get the impression he thinks it's important."

Rhozhia waved dismissively. "Nothing is more important to a wedding than the dress. He's free to talk, but I can't guarantee she'll remain decent throughout, and I'm in no position to wait until a lull in the conversation to take a crucial measurement or fit a vital piece."

"I see," Nathalie said. "Perhaps I'll find a nice screen for him to sit behind while you work."

"As you wish. Now, if you'll excuse me, genius calls."

Moments later, Nathalie lugged in a woven triptych emblazoned with brilliant green peacocks and positioned it near Verone. Next, she ushered in Albert and the Monsignor and sat them behind the screen. Dona crept a bit closer. She wanted to be certain to catch anything important.

Verone fanned herself as she gulped for air. "Are you sure this will get better? If it doesn't, I'll never make it through the ceremony."

"Poppycock—you'll be radiant, and radiance begets endurance. Stand up."

"Thank you for agreeing to chat with Albert and me," the Monsignor said. "I know how pressed for time you must be."

"Think nothing of it, Monsignor," Verone wheezed. "What did you want to talk about?"

"Albert and I were investigating the scene of the latest attack when we came across an interesting piece of evidence, and we were wondering if you could possibly help explain it."

"Me? I'm not sure why you think I'd be able to help with something like that, but I'm happy to give it my best effort."

"I appreciate that. When we were last at the scene, did you notice anything out of the ordinary? Maybe something one might consider unusual or coincidental?"

"I'm sorry, Monsignor, I was so concerned about that poor young man, I didn't pay much attention to anything else. Thank goodness he wasn't hurt."

"Yes, fortunately Michlos Serrola was there to help. I'm getting a little too old for those sorts of rescues. So you didn't notice anything special about the booth near the scene?"

"I'm afraid not, but I confess I'm a little scattered at the moment. What did I miss?"

"Do you happen to know a Thaddeus Nevinander?"

"Thad? Of course. He's my brother."

Dona stifled a gasp—how had the Monsignor learned of Verone's brother so quickly?

"Are you close?" the Monsignor asked.

"Not particularly. I see him maybe a few times a year. He's an artist, and he spends much of his time here on the island. He specializes in landscapes, I think. Why do you ask?"

"Lean forward," Rhozhia said.

"Would you recognize his work if you happened across it?"

"Oh, I don't pay much attention to that sort of thing. Thad got all the artistic ability in the family. I have trouble drawing a stick figure."

"When was the last time you saw him?"

"A week or so ago. Once in a while I take him some lunch. He doesn't eat as well as he should."

"All right," Rhozhia said. "We can loosen the corset for a bit."

"Did you happen to notice anything special about the booth right by where the young man fell off the cliff?"

"I didn't, but then, I wasn't really paying attention. I suppose, given all of these questions, that it must have had something to do with Thad. Was it his?"

"It had his paintings all over it."

Verone exhaled lavishly. "Oh, that's so much better."

"Sit," Rhozhia said. "This part will take a while."

The Monsignor pressed on. "Can you think of any reason the heretic might have targeted your brother's booth out of all the booths on the green for working this afternoon's mischief?"

A long pause from the other side of the screen prompted Albert and the Monsignor to exchange glances.

"Miss Nevinander?"

Verone sighed. "I take it, then, that Father Cartier hasn't spoken to you?"

"Father Cartier? No. If he had, what would he have told me?"

"He has a suspect who may have been involved in the arsons. Given the sensitive nature of the situation, he asked me not to say anything until he assembled his case."

"If it's so sensitive, why did he see fit to tell you?"

"He asked if I'd be willing to help with the investigation. I agreed to do it, but only because I couldn't possibly believe he had the right person. I presumed I'd just be helping to exonerate her."

"And now you're not so sure?"

"I don't know what to believe anymore. I don't want to think ill of anyone, but this latest incident feels personal—like it was deliberately calculated to cause the greatest possible disruption to my wedding plans. By agreeing to help Father Cartier, could I have made myself a target?"

"Whom does he suspect?"

"You remember how my cousin Michlos showed up so quickly after the incident? Well, Cartier's prime suspect is his mother—my Aunt Marguerite."

The Monsignor gasped. "The Crown Princess's mother?"

Dona was equally shocked. Rather than help the Monsignor solve the problem, Verone was leveraging her brother's plot against her to further her own twisted goals. Perhaps that made sense, though. Even if Verone were aware of her brother's perfidy, to protect the rest of her immediate family, Dona could see her keeping that information from the Monsignor.

Verone continued playing the ingenue. "I told Father Cartier I didn't believe it for a minute, but he was adamant. He said he'd seen her at one of the fires and that he'd found her wrap at another."

"How did Father Cartier intend for you to help him?"

"I'm not sure. I barely know the woman. She and my father have been estranged for twenty years. I don't know what the fight was about, but it must have been serious. She's been something of a recluse up at her estate ever since."

"How would your father have reacted if he'd discovered his sister was practicing heresy?"

"He'd have been horrified, but that doesn't mean that's what happened. Families have spats all the time. That doesn't make them heretics."

Dona found the subtlety of Verone's technique alarming. She connected all the dots and then weakly denied their logical conclusion. Had Dona not known better, she would probably have fallen for it.

The Monsignor pressed on. "Can you think of any reasons your aunt might hold a grudge against the Church?"

"As I said, I hardly know the woman. You might want to ask Father Cartier though. I think he might have mentioned something about sending some Inquisitors to ask her a few questions. Maybe he's heard back from them."

"I'll do that," the Monsignor said.

. . . . .

Lit by a handful of lanterns instead of the great crystal chandelier, the Princess's studio acquired a gritty and neglected feel at odds with its former splendor.

Michlos tossed his riding cloak on an ottoman among the canvas-bearing easels scattered throughout the space. "I hope I'm not late. I got back as soon as I could."

The Princess tried to hide her displeasure, but a certain coolness of tone crept in despite her intentions. "There's been a change of plan."

"Oh? Has there been another incident?"

"You might say that. Dona overheard a conversation between Verone and the Monsignor, and Verone has upped the ante. She's told the Monsignor that Cartier has evidence to suggest your mother could be the arsonist."

Michlos swallowed hard. "She told him about the wrap?"

She noted with some satisfaction that he at least had the grace to blush. "So, you knew about that? Do you have any idea how awkward it looks that you showed up so unexpectedly after the incident this afternoon when your mother is a prime suspect?"

"I only just found out about it myself. Verone planted it."

"You just found out about the wrap, or that I found out about it?" She made the question seem uncomfortably rhetorical.

"Look, I'm not keeping things from you. I only learned about the wrap tonight. We think Verone is trying to force a showdown between the Crown and the Church, and she's using Mother as the catalyst."

"Don't you think that comes across as a little far-fetched?"

"Brazen, perhaps, but Verone is nothing if not brazen. We think she's worked out a scheme whereby she stands not only to inherit her father's estate, but my mother's as well, but for her to do that, the Crown must fall."

The Princess set her jaw. "What is this fixation you have with your cousin and apocalyptic conspiracy theories? I'm sorry, but I find it really hard to believe that everything she has ever done is somehow calculated to lead to the downfall of all civilization. We already know she wasn't responsible for the situation this afternoon. She was in the middle of the rehearsal. Isn't it possible that once in a great while, things actually happened for the reasons she said they did?"

Michlos blinked in shock. Slowly, he drew himself up. As he did so, the subtle traces of all the endearing little traits that made him so uniquely Michlos, the very things she'd been trying so hard to coax from him for so long, withered and withdrew to a place beyond her power to reach. Only cool formality remained.

"My apologies. It was presumptuous of me to waste the royal time with such idle speculation. In the future, if it pleases your Highness, I shall strive to be considerably more circumspect."

"Oh Michlos, don't do this. We both know I'll need your help to make it through tomorrow. It's only a matter of time before the Monsignor will want to see the Eye of Moravidos, and I'm not going to have the first idea what to tell him."

"In that case, may I humbly suggest your Highness consider canceling the wedding. Perhaps if you're lucky, the ensuing chaos will distract the Monsignor from pursuing the matter."

Had Michlos's injury addled his brain? It wasn't like him to invent far-flung excuses to cover his shortcomings or overreact when called on them. "I know you think it was a terrible idea for me to mention the Eye, but you are not a head of state involved in negotiations with the Church. Too many people knew—I couldn't take the chance that word of it would reach the Monsignor. This way, if we do manage to hammer out a reconciliation, it will be with full disclosure."

"And yet, you weren't worried he might find out you'd thrown an Inquisitor in your dungeon?"

"Oh, for goodness' sake, I forgot all about him."

"You forgot about Vane?"

"Not him—the other one."

Michlos sank onto the ottoman. "Wait, there's another one?"

"The guards caught an Inquisitor skulking about the island while I was meeting with Verone and Cartier. I was going to evict him, but they both argued for holding him for a few days to make a grand gesture of releasing him. But the Monsignor needed no such encouragement, and I forgot all about him."

"What are you going to do with him? That is, if it's not too presumptuous of me to ask."

"When the wedding is over, I'll evict him like I originally planned."

"I take it that means you're not cancelling the wedding."

"Verone isn't exactly my favorite person either, but I'm not so cruel that I could cancel her wedding on the eve of the event."

"Would it change your mind if you knew she was planning to call it off at the last minute anyway?"

"Dona told me all about the contract with Alistair, and if Verone ultimately decides to call it off, that's her business. And she might surprise you—you didn't see how she beamed over the ring."

"I'll wager the only thing she was proud of was the way she contrived to get your Highness to do her bidding."

A stiff knock rattled the door, and Newcomb poked his head in. "The Monsignor is asking after you, Highness. He would like to settle the matter concerning the Eye of Moravidos."

"Tell him I'll be there presently."

"Very good, Highness."

The Princess shot Michlos a sidelong look. "If you have any suggestions, now would be the time."

"If Your Highness is serious about offering up the Eye for inspection, you'll first need to make certain Vane is in no position to cause any trouble."

"And how do I do that?"

Michlos sighed and grabbed his cloak. "I guess I take care of it, don't I. I'll need the key."

"To the cell with the Eye?"

"To both."

She reached beneath her collar, caught hold of a silver chain, and drew it over her head. Two brass keys dangled from it. "Will you need backup?"

"I'll take Newcomb. He can bring you the Eye when we're finished. Under the circumstances, you probably wouldn't want to be seen with me."

He took the keys and turned to leave. She stopped him with a hand on his arm. "I'm sorry I snapped at you."

"Your Highness is too kind."

She chose to take it as a good sign that he didn't slam the door on his way out.

# CHAPTER TEN

## EYE PROBLEMS

During their descent into the musty stone passages of the old prison complex, Newcomb seemed to sense Michlos needed time to ruminate and allowed the conversation to die. Although grateful he didn't have to strain to make small talk, Michlos couldn't help adding that fact to the growing list of evidence that he was losing his touch. In his prime, he would have controlled his reactions so completely that no one, not even his mother, would have had the slightest inkling that anything was amiss. Still, it was a minor lapse compared to his misjudgment with the Princess. He had allowed himself to become so wrapped up in his enthusiasm for the elegance of his speculations and the expectation of her approval that he failed to monitor how she was reacting. It was only after her outburst that he realized how ridiculous his conspiracy theory must seem to her. What had gotten into him? He would never be so lax with anyone else. If that wasn't bad enough, he'd then let his own reaction betray him. From long experience honing the skill with his mother, he considered himself expert at letting criticism appear to roll off. He was mortified; he'd behaved as badly as a jilted schoolgirl. What must she think of him now?

"We're almost there," Newcomb said.

"You know what to do?"

Newcomb patted the crossbow he carried. "I've got you covered."

"If anything goes wrong, you'll probably only get one shot. Make it count."

Newcomb opened the door to the cell block. "I hope it doesn't come to that."

"So do I."

Newcomb directed the two guards to take one of the lanterns and step outside to keep watch. They looked puzzled but complied. Meanwhile, Michlos peered between the brass bars in the little window at the top of the door. He felt a pang of guilt as he imagined what it must be like to be held in such conditions indefinitely. Death might be preferable.

Vane, however, seemed unperturbed. Clothed in a simple white tunic, he sat cross-legged in the center of the cell facing the door, his eyes closed, his back erect, his breathing deep and regular. As Michlos watched, his eyes slowly opened and then closed again.

"Ah, the Forkhead Serpent. No doubt you've come to chat."

"That depends," Michlos said. "Have you anything to say?"

"First, let me congratulate you on your apparent good health. I was given to believe you were no longer with us."

"So sorry to disappoint you."

"On the contrary. I'm delighted."

"Pardon me, if I find that difficult to believe." Michlos gave a subtle nod, and Newcomb inserted the key in the lock of the adjacent cell. The door squeaked a little as it inched open.

"It would seem to suggest the charges against me are, shall we say, a tad exaggerated."

"The charges against you are unlikely to matter much. You're not in Trifienne. On this island, the Princess's word is law, and I seriously doubt the she's planning to give you a public trial."

"Oh yes, the Princess. Regrettable that she happened by when she did, isn't it? Now she's inadvertently run afoul of a very powerful organization. If I were her, I might want to reconsider getting embroiled in this."

"Even if the Church knew you were here, given the nature of your crimes, I don't expect you'd want them to intervene on your behalf."

Vane laughed quietly. "What makes you think I was referring to the Church?"

Michlos's hackles rose. "Are you threatening her?"

From the corner of his eye Michlos saw Newcomb emerge from the adjacent cell. He held up something small and glittery, nodded, slipped it into his pocket, and readied his crossbow. Then he backed toward the cell-block door.

Vane held up his hands and smiled innocently. "What could I possibly do to her while I'm like this? I'm just saying that there are some people who might not take kindly to my incarceration here, people who might not be so troubled by my purported crimes. If they aren't put through the bother of having to track me down, they might be inclined to forgive and forget. And they will find me. Witnesses were present at my abduction—word will get out."

Newcomb reached the cell-block door, gave Michlos a nod, and ducked through.

Michlos counted silently. Casting before the Eye was out of range would be a disaster, since it would accomplish nothing other than to tip Vane off. He'd activated his Amulet as a backup, but Vane's eyes were open and on him now. There was a small chance if Vane figured out what he was doing, he might be able to cast first. The Amulet would block anything other an attempt to overpower it, but since Vane had overpowered his Amulet once, he already knew how much effort was needed. To make matters worse, unlike Vane, he was currently in no position to overpower his own Amulet since he was already spent from his exertions on the saltshaker, the Monsignor's cane, and his examination of the promise stick. He would have to risk turning it off.

"You expect her to believe there's an institution out there more formidable than the Church?"

Michlos started mnemonics immediately on finishing his question and switched off the Amulet just as he was about to complete them.

"Not at all," Vane said. "It's just that the Church is hampered to some degree by—"

Faster than Michlos thought humanly possible, Vane sprang up. He dove and rolled toward the wall near the door. If he had been even a fraction of a second faster, he'd have made it out of sight before the spell landed. As it was, by the time Vane's body crashed against the wall, it was already limp.

Vane's skin flickered momentarily green as Michlos made certain the spell had landed. There was too much at stake to assume Vane's inactivity wasn't just an act. Satisfied, he called Newcomb back.

"Stand here with the crossbow aimed while I go in. If he moves, you know what to do."

Michlos used the key and swung open the brass door. Then he wriggled his hands into a pair of gloves and retrieved a small box from his pocket. He flicked open the box to reveal a plain silver ring. With his gloved hand, he slipped it onto Vane's finger.

Michlos relocked the door. "That should do it, but we must make absolutely certain the Eye is back in place before this time tomorrow."

Newcomb nodded.

Michlos was, if possible, even less chatty on the way out. Why hadn't he anticipated Vane's attempt to dodge? Had Vane gotten out of sight before Michlos's spell landed, he could have shrouded the whole area in darkness or worse, and Michlos probably wouldn't have had sufficient resources left to counter it. He really was losing his touch.

. . . . .

Seated at the table that filled most of the tower conference room, Celeste gnawed her lip as Albert peered through his jeweler's loupe at the Eye of Moravidos. She'd been considering Michlos's preposterous words, and, to her dismay, she couldn't pinpoint any inconsistencies. If he was right, much depended on the outcome of the next few hours—the slightest misstep in this politicized heretical maelstrom could spell disaster.

Next to Albert, the Monsignor shrugged and glanced apologetically across the table at Verone, her mother, and the Princess. "Albert," he said. "So far we know it's astounding. We also know it's amazing and incredible. But what we really need to know is whether it's genuine."

Albert frowned. "That's a trickier question. I'd need to determine its specific gravity to eliminate the possibility that it's been faked. Assuming the stone is genuine, the next question is whether it's the Eye of Moravidos. All I can say without consulting my library is that this gem is consistent with the reports—as best as can I recall them. The Eye was reputed to be an extremely large, nearly flawless, 12-ray black star sapphire, which this certainly seems to be."

"Yes, but is there any way for us to test whether it's functional?"

Albert grinned. "That's the corundum conundrum, isn't it? I've been waiting all night to say that."

The others chuckled politely, but the instant he went back to his loupe, they exchanged dubious glances.

"But have you solved it?" the Monsignor asked.

"There's really nothing to solve. The Eye is a passive piece. There's no triggering, adjusting, or breaking required to activate it. It just lies there doing nothing, unless you attempt Phrendonic magic nearby. Then it blocks all radiant forms of that magic in a ten-yard radius."

Verone sat up and eyed him intently. "What does that mean?"

"Basically, it blocks spells," the Monsignor said.

Albert raised a finger. "Not precisely. A radiant Hedge alone would block new spells from vesting across space within its domain, while a radiant Suppression alone would block radiant effects that had already been cast, such as a Darkness, from taking effect wherever the effects overlapped. Neither the radiant Hedge nor the Suppression would prevent a spell from being Extended, however. Thus, for example, one could still theoretically use Extension-based artifacts within the radius, provided, of course, they didn't have a radiant effect."

"But it could block a Darkness spell like the one we saw this afternoon, right?"

Albert nodded. "If it works as reported. But I don't see an easy way to test it, short of using a device with a radiant Phrendonic effect near it, or failing that, finding a cooperative Phrendonic Heretic willing cast something within its area of influence. I don't suppose any of us has a cooperative Phrendonic handy?"

Again, Albert laughed at his own joke, and again, those present eyed each other uncomfortably, but this time, the glances exchanged were uncomfortable for a very different reason; each of them either was—or did.

"What about the reports that the Eye cannot be overpowered? Do you suppose there's any truth to them?"

"According to legend, Hassett Bey used the Eye to keep Dreamweaver imprisoned beneath these very halls until her sentence could be carried out. She was among the most skilled Phrendonic Heretics ever known. If the Eye was the means of her imprisonment, there is likely some truth to those reports. Of course, it's also possible Bey didn't rely solely on the Eye. For all we know, he may have kept her drugged. Then, as now, drugging was not an uncommon practice for imprisoning Phrendonics."

"So the provenance seems right anyway. At least it's not wholly improbable that the Eye would surface here."

"Oh, not at all. Based on the historical accounts, this would be the first place you'd look."

Verone shifted in her seat. "On any other evening, I'd be tickled pink to participate in a drawn-out theoretical discussion, but I'm getting married tomorrow. I need to know—are we having the wedding here, or aren't we?"

The Monsignor sighed. "A ten-yard radius?"

Albert nodded.

"That won't protect even a significant fraction of the courtyard."

"No, but it would cover the wedding party."

"That wouldn't prevent someone from creating a disruption to one side, though. We were lucky this afternoon. It's a miracle no one was hurt."

"But we still have no idea why it happened," Verone said. "The Darkness may have nothing to do with the wedding. Nothing untoward has happened since. Isn't it possible whoever is responsible accomplished his goal and moved on?"

"No other incidents occurred on the island until the day before your wedding," the Monsignor said. "We can't ignore the possibility that you were specifically targeted."

"That may be, but if you're truly convinced Aunt Marguerite is behind this, why not take advantage of the situation? You're the Inquisitor General—as long as she's planning to attend the wedding anyway, why not just intercept her on the way and prove it one way or the other?"

At the mention of Marguerite's name, Nathalie's eyes met hers, and Celeste saw her own alarm reflected there.

"And if she wasn't responsible?"

Verone shrugged. "Then I probably wasn't the target. And if it turns out she was responsible, which I sincerely doubt, you'll have your suspect in custody, and the wedding can proceed without any risk of her meddling."

The Monsignor weighed the Eye of Moravidos in his palm as he considered. "Your Highness, would you mind terribly if I were to borrow this until tomorrow morning? I promise to have it back to you in plenty of time for the wedding."

Celeste blinked. "I'm not sure that's such a good idea. Apart from its historic significance and its value as a gemstone, it's practically a royal heirloom. If anything were to happen to it…"

The Monsignor held up his hand. "If for any reason I am unable to return it, the Church will compensate you for thrice its value as a gemstone."

The Princess swallowed hard. "It's just that if it's all that Father Albert says it is, it's probably priceless."

"It's also probably a Profanity. If so, it would be subject to confiscation once you reconcile with the Church. Do me this favor, and I'll see to it that the Church makes an exception in this case. You do still want to reconcile, don't you?"

The Princess swallowed again and glanced toward Verone, who had been watching their exchange with a smug little half smile that made her want to kick herself for ever having doubted Michlos.

"Of course, I do. "And of course you may borrow the Eye."

"Excellent. Then, for the time being at least, the wedding is on."

Verone grinned and nodded her thanks.

The Monsignor held up the Eye. "Thank you for this. I'll see to it you don't regret this favor."

The Princess smiled politely but couldn't imagine him making good on that promise; she had already started regretting it before she'd even agreed.

. . . . .

Although Nathalie and Olivia had outdone themselves festooning the grand ballroom with lanterns, favors, and silk banners, it still had a dank and oppressive feel, attributable in some measure to its original incarnation as a prison mess hall. Two lanterns were lit at one end of the expanse, creating a tiny guttering island surrounded by a sea of shadows and half-seen shapes. On one side sat the Monsignor, on the other, his good friend, Albert, Curator of Profanities.

"That's quite a tale," Albert said. "Such a pity you had to part with the Morgatuan. A Chervillian artifact that's also a Phrendonic Profanity would have been quite an addition to the collection."

"Not to mention all those Chervillian texts," the Monsignor said. "There were enough there to endow a small library."

"What of this demonic Vismort? Is he likely to pose a threat?"

The Monsignor shuddered. The fact that such a creature could exist kept him awake at night. "Assuming he's able to materialize again. The frustrating thing is, without breaking my word, I can't warn anyone. Was I wrong to make the deal? Should I have tried to make it out without the Bursar's help?"

"A pact with Chervil is always a deal in the dark."

The Monsignor looked away to cover his blush. He knew he'd done the right thing—made all the correct logical choices—but discussing them here, without context, and in the comfort and safety of Ranselard Keep, those decisions somehow felt like failures. "There were more lives at stake than just mine."

"I'll grant that the moralities are complex. I'll have to ponder it for a bit. In the meantime, why don't you tell me your plans for the Eye. Are you really thinking to intercept the suspect on the way to her niece's wedding?"

"About that, did you think there was anything odd about the bride's comments tonight?"

Albert shrugged. "I thought her suggestion bordered on impertinent, but, given that her whole wedding was in jeopardy, I was inclined to overlook it."

"What struck me was her willingness to implicate her aunt as a suspect. I don't usually get someone to give up a name until after at least several hours of interrogation."

Albert grinned impishly. "That's because you don't use the rack."

"Now you sound like Isrulian."

"Ooh, I withdraw the comment. So why do you think she's so eager to offer up her aunt?"

"I can think of several possibilities. The simplest is that she is just unusually frank with her opinions. That wouldn't be inconsistent with what little I know of her, although she does strike me as bright enough to realize that merely casting these sorts of aspersions can have unpleasant consequences for even an innocent suspect. A second possibility is that she may hold some sort of grudge against her aunt, which seems unlikely, given that she claims to have had little contact with her. Finally, she may be trying to misdirect suspicion from herself or someone close to her."

"Her brother, perhaps?"

"Possibly, although there is another candidate." The Monsignor took a wedding invitation from his pocket and placed it before Albert on the table. "Does this name ring any bells?"

"Theratigan—isn't that the surname of our demon hunter? I thought he was the last surviving member of that family."

"Looks like my father may have missed one."

"But the groom was in no better position to cast the Darkness than the bride was."

"True enough, which makes it a perfect alibi. Maybe too perfect. I'm sure I don't need to remind you that Darkness can also be created with a device."

"So you suspect she's throwing suspicion on the estranged aunt to divert attention from her groom?"

"Or the brother. I've met Marguerite Serrola. Even if she were a heretic, she doesn't seem the sort to engage in random acts of arson. Nor can I discern a solid motive for her where either the previous incidents or this afternoon's Darkness would make any sense, particularly given her ties to the Crown. Of course, I could just be missing too many pieces of the puzzle."

"So how will you proceed?"

"Perhaps it's time I learned a little about landscape painting."

"Hasn't the Princess forbidden you to interrogate the artists?"

"She didn't say I couldn't browse their wares."

The door at the far end of the ballroom squeaked open, and Alexi peeped in. "You wanted to see me, sir?"

The Monsignor rose. "Alexi, come in. I'd like you to meet Father Albert Graves, Curator of Profanities."

"Good to meet you."

The Monsignor pulled out a chair. "Have a seat."

Albert cleared his throat. "So, I suppose you're wondering what the title means? The Church has long maintained a collection of heretical artifacts. However, during the Inquisition at Caprian, so many such items were confiscated that Armand's father, who was Inquisitor General at that time, decided that someone needed to catalogue and preserve the inventory. I've been known as 'the Curator' ever since."

Alexi nodded, but apprehension lined his forehead.

The Monsignor placed a hand on Alexi's shoulder. "I've called you here because I've happened across a way for you to complete your penance."

Alexi's eyes widened and darted to Albert.

"You needn't worry about Albert. He already knows what happened in the caves, but he's sworn to secrecy. He's my Confessor, you see, and I know of no one who is more trustworthy."

Albert snorted. "You can't have been Confessor to three generations of Goodkins and not be able to keep a secret."

"What would I have to do?"

"First, were you responsible for what happened this afternoon out on the green?"

"You mean the Darkness? I don't know how that's done. Even if I did, I still wouldn't do it while standing on the edge of a cliff."

The Monsignor nodded. "I had to ask. Next, I'll need you to promise that nothing we discuss tonight will go beyond this room."

"Not even to Dona or Alphonse?"

"I'm afraid not. This information is too sensitive. Lives may be at stake. Will you agree to that?"

"I guess so. What do you need me to do?"

The Monsignor plucked a candle from the centerpiece on the table in front of him. "I need you to light this up."

Alexi reached for the table lantern.

"No, not that way. The way you did it in the caves."

Alexi eyed Albert again. "Are you sure?"

The Monsignor nodded. "I'm sure."

"And that will satisfy my penance?"

"I may ask you to try it several times, but once that's finished, as far as I am concerned, your transgressions will be expiated—you can start over with a clean slate."

"Why the change of penance? I thought you wanted me to help find the arsonist."

"That hasn't changed. With luck, your assistance here tonight will help bring the arsonist to justice."

Alexi shrugged. "Seems simple enough. I'll do it."

"Excellent." The Monsignor laid the candle on the table.

"Now?"

"Now would be perfect."

Alexi focused his attention on the candle, his mouth working silently.

Nothing happened.

Alexi rubbed his neck. "I don't understand—that should have worked."

The Monsignor exchanged a significant look with Albert. "Perhaps you're just out of practice. Why don't you take a deep breath and try again?"

There was still no effect.

"I'm sure I got it right that time."

"Perhaps I'm making you nervous. I'll give you some space, and you can try again. How does that sound?"

"I don't think that's the problem. You can kind of tell when it works and when it doesn't. It should have worked both times."

"Let's try it anyway." He grabbed one of the lanterns and headed for the other side of the ballroom.

"All right, but I don't think it's going to matter."

"Humor me."

Albert remained where he was, transfixed by the demonstration.

"Now?"

"Go ahead."

Alexi tried a third time.

The demonstration was interrupted by a distinctive "click" from somewhere nearby. Albert looked about, frowning.

"Any luck?" the Monsignor asked.

"I'm not done yet." Alexi concentrated again, and the entire candle flared to light."

The Monsignor headed back toward the table. "Well done."

He'd taken only a few steps when another click echoed through the chamber. Albert scowled, lifted the tablecloth, and peered underneath.

The Monsignor shook Alexi's hand. "Consider yourself absolved, my friend."

"I don't understand. What did I do?"

The Monsignor picked up the candle and snapped it in two. Its light was extinguished instantly. "You helped me solve a puzzle I couldn't solve any other way. I'd tell you more, but for your safety, I'd rather not involve you any more than I already have. Suffice it to say, I am very grateful for your cooperation."

"Are we done then?"

"We are. Remember, not a word to anyone—not even Miss Merinne."

Alexi nodded.

"Sleep well. I'll see you tomorrow."

As Alexi left scratching his head, the Monsignor opened his palm to reveal the Eye of Moravidos. "Convinced?"

Albert nodded. "Your approach was a bit unorthodox, however. I'm not sure your father would have approved. Phrendonic Heresy is seductive. He would have said the knowledge wasn't worth the risk."

"My father said a great many things with which I don't agree. The exception exists for a reason. Besides, it was your suggestion."

"You can't blame me for that. How was I to know you actually had a heretic at your disposal? And granting absolution on condition he commit even more heresies? Your father wouldn't have been quite so forgiving."

"And look where that approach got him."

"You might instead want to reconsider this new approach of yours. Exception or no, I doubt Darron, even at his most indulgent, could afford to condone some of the things you've done here tonight. I shudder to think what he would do if he found out his Inquisitor General was allowing known heretics to walk free, technicality or no."

"Then we must see to it he never finds out."

"Is the young heretic really worth the risk?"

"He gave himself up in part to save my life. Could I do any less?"

"I see. In that case, I think I am ready to bestow your penance."

The Monsignor bowed his head solemnly. "I am ready, Father."

"So long as the young heretic's slate remains clear of further heresies, you are to see to it that he comes to no harm from the Church for his past misdeeds."

The Monsignor looked up in surprise, but Albert's expression made it clear the matter was not open for debate.

Reluctantly, he bowed his head once more. "By your grace and upon my soul, it shall be done."

# CHAPTER ELEVEN

## OPENING DOORS

Dawn was still a distant blush as the two men made their way down the hallway toward Reston's office. One was Reston himself, looking tired, disheveled, and a touch annoyed. His companion, by contrast, was uncharacteristically animated and awake.

Reston stifled a yawn. "I appreciate that finding their carriage in the dark wasn't trivial, but it changes nothing. Thurman Goodkin is simply not someone I want to tangle with. There's no point in pursuing the matter any further."

Jonas eyed him archly. "Not even for a share of the reward?"

"No one is going to offer you a reward for proving Thurman Goodkin is a heretic, unless, of course, you view an extended stay at an exotic location, complete with thumb screws and iron maidens, as somehow rewarding."

"I'm not talking about proving Goodkin is a heretic. I'm talking about rescuing the Primal."

Reston ran his fingers through a pillow-inflicted cowlick. Managing Jonas had devolved into a more-than-full-time job. "All right, I can see you've put a fair bit of effort into concocting this one. As long as I'm now awake, I may as well hear you out."

"I was talking with Tilly last night. The sick old man they were with let slip during his argument with Thurman that he was the Primal."

"That's it? That's the best you can do? You really expect me to believe that while he was sick, the Primal decided to take a little unannounced side trip to Trifienne accompanied only by his nephew and some old priest? I suppose next you're going to tell me his stay in a decrepit flop house reflects his urgent desire to see how the little people live."

"Not at all. His stay in the flop house is just more evidence that the Primal is being held against his will."

"By his own nephew?"

"Doting relatives don't typically use Phrendonic Heresy to keep their loved ones in check. I know that's what he did because he did it to me too. It makes sense when you think about it. Thurman claimed the man was his uncle, and it's well known his uncle is the Primal. He also tried to convince Tilly that the old man was senile, but the only evidence was that he seemed to think he was the Primal. Unless you believe Thurman is treating a senile uncle to a luxury vacation among the roaches and the bedbugs, he must be staying there because he has something monumental to hide. I've spent all night thinking about it, and there simply isn't a more plausible explanation."

"That rationale reeks of wishful thinking. Would such a bizarre explanation really seem so attractive if it didn't involve catching Thurman Goodkin in a punishable offense?"

"It's not just me, Tilly thinks so too."

"If you're so convinced, why don't you simply turn the matter over to the Constable and claim your reward?"

"Because the Constable isn't going to believe me. Just because there isn't a better explanation doesn't mean it still doesn't seem far-fetched. Besides, the best evidence against Thurman is his use of heresy. I know what I'm talking about on that score, but I'd really prefer not to have that conversation with the Constable."

"So what are you suggesting? A daring rescue in which the two of us steal a doddering invalid away from an old priest and the Primal's nephew? What if it turns out he didn't really need rescuing?"

"It doesn't have to be anything quite so dramatic. I thought maybe you could just Sleep them and ask him."

"And if he says thanks, but no thanks, I've just committed a blatant act of heresy against a member of Primal's family. I think I'll pass."

"But if this works out—"

"I'm not willing to risk it and that's final. Whoa, what happened here?"

Reston's office door had fallen inward and was lying on the floor.

Reston bent to inspect the damage. The hinges, knob, and lock were missing, and little piles of brownish powder dotted the floor beneath where they had been.

"Rusted," he said. "Stay here."

He hopped over the door and scanned his desk for the book Dona had left him, but, of course, it was gone. In its place lay a hastily scrawled note:

> *Reston,*
>
> *I was here, and you were not. Happily, I retrieved the book without your help. Consider yourself dismissed.*
>
> *Bainbridge.*

For a moment Reston was relieved, not only at his luck at having missed the Widow Bainbridge, but also because she had apparently let him off the hook without appreciating the subtle differences between the book on his desk and the one she had intended to confiscate. Then it occurred to him how she might react if she discovered her mistake. He shuddered, realizing there was a very good chance the situation had just become a matter of life or death—he had to find that book, and fast.

"What is it?" Jonas asked from the hallway.

Reston crumpled the note in his fist. "Trouble."

"Verone again?"

"Sure looks that way, doesn't it? This time, she leaves me no choice."

"What are you going to do?" Jonas asked.

"I'm going to crash a wedding."

. . . . .

Nathalie breezed into Verone's Ranselard guest room, breakfast tray in hand. "Knock, knock, dear. Rise and shine. You've got a busy day ahead of you."

Verone's eyes popped open in alarm. "What time is it?"

"Late. Madame Rhozhia has been clamoring after you for over an hour now. I don't think I'll be able to keep her at bay much longer."

"I need to speak with the Monsignor."

"You're too late. He left on an errand half an hour ago."

"Did he say where he was going?"

"No, and it has me worried sick. What were you thinking, sending him after Marguerite like that?"

Verone's little half-smile appeared. That was excellent news, indeed. "You really think that's where he went?"

Nathalie placed the tray in front of her daughter. "I wouldn't be surprised. He was very vague about the whole thing. If you've gone and messed up this wedding, I'll never forgive you."

Verone examined the tray. "What's this?"

"A muffin and some fresh milk. Rhozhia was emphatic that you were not to have a large breakfast."

"Not the food." She held up a sealed parchment. As she did so, she caught a whiff of roses. "Is this scented?"

"Oh that. It's from Rayen. He wanted to bring it up here himself and slip it under the door, but I was not about to risk letting him see his bride before the ceremony. We have more than enough to worry about without tempting fate."

Her heart fluttered as she cracked the seal. Had Rayen decided to call off the wedding? Perhaps Alistair had gotten to him. Or maybe he'd had one of his visions. "He didn't have another seizure, did he?"

"Not that I'm aware of. What does it say?"

"It looks to be some sort of poem. You're sure he didn't have a seizure?"

Nathalie craned her neck for a better look. "I don't think so. Oh, that reminds me. He made me promise to tell you that this wasn't so much about what he'd seen, as what he felt."

Verone pressed the note against her chest. "Mum, please—this is private."

"Oh, be that way, then. Deprive your poor old mother of the opportunity to share a tender moment with her daughter."

"There's nothing tender about snooping."

"All right. I know when I'm not wanted. I'll be downstairs, then. Hurry down, though, won't you? Last time I saw her, Rhozhia was beginning to froth."

Once her mother was safely out of the room, Verone unfolded the parchment:

> *Today we lie as two apart*
> *The separate longing of each heart*
> *Compelling that the twain shall meet*
> *And, in their joining, be complete*
> *With each now whole, not just a part*
>
> *And where did longing get its start?*
> *In verse? In song? Perhaps in art?*
> *Or was it born of brash deceit:*
> *Today we lie?*
>
> *Regardless of the course we chart*
> *Or how we try to dodge love's dart*
> *Or otherwise our fates to cheat*
> *It's with your heart mine longs to beat*
> *Though in the end you may depart*
> *Today we lie*

As she read, a solitary tear crept down her cheek.

. . . . .

The approach to the Serrola estate from the south was rocky and windswept. The nearby river had eaten through the limestone to create steep cliffs, and the path was treacherous for man and horse alike. Inquisitor Grummon was relieved to finally catch a glimpse of the mansion's distinctive cupola. Bathed in the early morning sun, it lit their way like a beacon. He gave the signal to unfurl the Inquisition's standard—the white rose of purity emblazoned above the Church's entwined serpents. Heartened by its appearance, the trailing Inquisitors redoubled their pace, making short work of the remaining climb. When at last they arrayed themselves in position on the estate's grounds, Grummon and his standard bearer advanced on the mansion's wrought-iron gate.

Arerio waited for them on the other side, his tuft of white hair ruffling in the breeze. "May I help you?"

Grummon took a step forward. "I have been charged in the name of the Inquisition to take Marguerite Serrola into custody. She stands accused of heresy, arson, and murder."

"You are aware, I presume, that the person so named happens to be the mother of the Crown Princess of Trifienne, wife to the Crown, on whose lands you currently stand?"

Swallowing his personal misgivings, Grummon persisted. "The Church is under no obligation to treat with temporal authorities in its pursuit of heretics, regardless of whom they call kin."

"It's not the power that I question—it's the wisdom. Pursuit of this matter without consulting the Crown could be perceived as an act of war. Think carefully, sir. Is that truly your goal?"

"I have my orders. Bid your mistress to present herself."

"And if she should decline?"

"As a courtesy to the Crown, I will allow her one hour to prepare. If she fails to appear by that time, we shall use force."

Arerio sighed. "Very well. I will relay the message."

. . . . .

The sprawling green before Ranselard Keep once again teemed with expectant artists lying in wait for potential patrons of the royal persuasion, or, failing that, at least rich ones. Questioning by the Princess's guards had uncovered no leads regarding yesterday's incident, and, for most, this wedding opportunity was too good to let a little heresy ruin it. As the Monsignor browsed the booths, the quality of the work on display impressed him. Apparently, competition was a potent muse.

The booth of Thaddeus Nevinander was much as it had been the previous evening, except the last of the paintings were unwrapped and on display. Thin and angular, the booth's occupant bore little resemblance to his sister, except for his hair color. Instead of coming forward to ply his wares, he hung back and eyed the Monsignor with suspicion.

The Monsignor pointed to a landscape of the sun setting over the river. "Would you mind telling me a little about this one?"

Reluctantly, Thad moved to where the Monsignor stood inspecting the painting. "I did that one from the crest of a hill in the center of the island. It made for a spectacular angle."

"So I see. Do you do all your work on the island?"

"Most of it. I haven't really needed to go any farther afield. There are so many vastly different scenes to be had here, often within just steps of each other."

"Do you only do landscapes?"

"Mostly. I find landscape subjects to be somewhat more cooperative and far less critical than portrait subjects. That doesn't mean I won't do them, though," he added hastily. "Were you looking to have one done?"

The Monsignor laughed. "I'd do the art world no favors by imposing this mug on it. I was just noticing that you share a last name with the bride, and assuming you're related, it occurred to me you might be missing an opportunity to paint the wedding portraits."

Thad snorted. "I'd rather starve. As fond as I am of my sister, I'd never do her portrait. If I painted her accurately, she'd accuse me of making her look fat, and, if I tried to somehow slim her down, she'd tell me it didn't look anything like her. Either way, I lose."

"I see your dilemma. Will you be attending as a guest, then?"

"I'll try to drop in, at least for the ceremony. There probably won't be much action out here while that's going on anyway."

Establish a connection, then begin the interrogation. That approach had always served the Monsignor well. "You know, I think I may have met your Aunt Marguerite on some of my past visits to the Palace. I imagine she'll be attending? It would be nice to renew our acquaintance."

"I wouldn't count on that."

"Really? Why not?"

"She and Dad had a falling out years ago. The two halves of the family haven't interacted much since then."

"I'm so sorry. It must have been pretty serious to have gone on for so long."

"Yeah—it was about the inheritance. Dad put in quite a few years working for Grandpa in the family business, while Aunt Marguerite ran off and got married. Then, when it came time to pass on the estate, instead of giving Dad credit for all his years of hard work, Grandpa simply split it down the middle. It got pretty ugly."

"Was that the only reason for the falling out?"

Thad shook his head. "The two of them never really got along growing up, either. From what I've heard, Aunt Marguerite was Grandpa's favorite, and she spent a lot of time belittling everything Dad did, or at least that was Dad's take on it. I'm not sure how much stock you can put in that, though. Knowing what I know of him, I doubt he was much of a joy to have for a brother either."

"I suppose Verone was outraged at the injustice of it all?"

Thad snorted. "Amused, more like. She and Dad don't get along any better than Dad and Aunt Marguerite did. The two of them have gone for years at a time without speaking."

"That's odd. I thought that despite his failure to show for the rehearsal, he was still planning to give her away during the ceremony."

"Thad shrugged. "They must have made up. All I know is that a couple weeks ago, you'd have been hard pressed to get the two of them in the same room. Now it sounds as if she's going to inherit everything."

"He's not going to split the estate? That hardly seems fair."

Thad shrugged. "Doesn't bother me. I'm doing what I love to do, and I make enough to get by. The last thing I need is more familial entanglements."

*And now, the money question.* "So everyone is happy with that arrangement?"

A faraway smile crept across Thad's face. "Oh, lord no. It's driving my brothers crazy."

The rumble of an arriving carriage brought Thad back to himself. He blinked and looked suddenly uncomfortable. "Uh, I should probably see to finishing up my displays."

The Monsignor turned to catch a glimpse of the vehicle, curious whether it carried someone he might recognize. He was shocked to discover it did—Thurman was driving.

. . . . .

*Swit-swish, swit-swish, swit-swish.* Dominick Everson awoke from troubled dreams to the monotonous sound of straw against stone. Apparently, Bart had chosen today to sweep the cellblock. Everson watched him silently until he could stand it no longer. At some level he realized he was asking for trouble, but he couldn't help himself.

Maddening though he was, Bart was his only link to the outside world, and more, his only form of human contact. "What are you doing?"

"Don't you go worrying about that now. Ol' Bart's going to take good care of you."

"That'll be a refreshing change of pace."

"There you go again, hurting Ol' Bart's feelings when he's only got your best interests at heart."

"What's the occasion? Judging from the clouds of dust you're kicking up, it's clearly not like you to tidy up often."

"It's a surprise."

Everson eyed him askance. "What sort of surprise?"

"The kind Ol' Bart was told not to say nothing about." He leaned toward Everson, and, with a conspiratorial smile, added "Want a hint?"

Everson crossed his arms. "Oh, why not."

Bart picked something out of his beard and studied it intently. "Ol' Bart's feelings are still feeling a mite tender. Maybe if you was to say something nice, he'd be more inclined to let something slip."

Everson rubbed his eyes with his palms. He'd been duped again. "There isn't any surprise, is there?"

Bart shrugged. "Suit yourself."

Bart went back to his sweeping, while Everson sat sullenly in the far corner of his cell trying his best to ignore him.

*Swit-swish, swit-swish…* It went on interminably.

"All right, *all right*," Everson said. "You're doing a great job cleaning up around here. I really appreciate it."

Bart beamed. "There, that wasn't so hard, now, was it?"

"Look, I played your little game—now what's the hint?"

"I thought you just told Ol' Bart you didn't believe in surprises."

Everson massaged the bridge of his nose until he calmed enough to force an apology through clenched teeth. "I'm sorry I doubted you."

"Well, in that case, if I was you, I'd be getting myself ready to see some visitors."

A great weight lifted from Everson's soul. "Is it the Princess? Did you give her my message?"

"What message?"

"The message I had you write down for her yesterday."

"Oh, you mean this one?" Bart produced a crumpled scrap from his pocket. "Nah, Ol' Bart ain't had a chance to do that yet."

"I knew it—you're just doing this to torture me. There won't be any visitors and there never was a surprise." He slumped in the far corner of his cell, determined this time to ignore his tormentor no matter what.

To Everson's relief, instead of trying to provoke him further, Bart just shrugged and carried off the pan of dirt. Unfortunately, he reappeared after only a few minutes, unrolling a length of carpet before him. When that roll ended, he came back with another carpet and proceeded to unroll it right up to the edge of Everson's cell.

Bart wiped his hands on his pants. "There. Now at least when your guests don't visit, they'll have a proper place to not stand during the ceremony. The rock floor of a jail cell just ain't a fitting place for the feet of a lady and a clergyman."

Everson's resolve failed him yet again. "Ceremony?"

"Yep, but make sure you don't forget—if they ask, you didn't hear nothing about no ceremony from Ol' Bart."

Everson's mind raced. Could Verone be planning to force him to marry her? The whole idea struck him as preposterous—this had to be another one of Bart's irritating pranks. But as he considered the matter more carefully, a vicious seed of plausibility took root. How could Bart possibly have known enough about his history with Verone to concoct such an elaborate scam? He rubbed the scar on his jaw as he replayed in his mind her threat from the day she slashed his face and left him for dead on his office floor:

*"Rule number three: there is no quitting, not now, not ever. Let's just say I don't take rejection well."*

The more he pondered, the less ridiculous it seemed. She could hold his freedom hostage to force him to comply with the ceremony. If that didn't work, she could threaten to tell her priest friend that he was impersonating an Inquisitor. He knew himself well enough to realize that either of those threats would probably suffice, and he had a sinking feeling Verone knew it too. And then, marriage certificate in hand, she could simply leave him here to rot in his cell while she took possession of everything he'd ever worked for. The thought chilled his blood. With cold resolve he vowed to stand and fight—no way would he allow that evil woman to destroy him.

Bart continued chatting while he aligned the carpets. "If you talk nice to Ol' Bart, maybe he'll see if he can find you a pretty flower or something for your collar." Then, he gave Everson a puzzled look, shook his head twice as if trying to clear it of unpleasant thoughts, and collapsed.

Everson closed his eyes and worked his way through another set of complex mnemonics. When at last he opened them, the bars of his cell had crumbled. Looking about, he nodded in satisfaction.

Stepping over the bars' rusted remains, he leaned down and turned out the pocket where Bart kept the ring of keys that would free him from the rest of the prison.

More rust was all he found there.

# CHAPTER TWELVE

# epiphanies

Alexi was miserable. He kept telling himself he should be relieved now that his score with the Monsignor was settled, but all he could think about was the difficult position that left him in—Dona and Alphonse had promised to help him with a penance that he couldn't tell them he'd already completed. Even worse, he'd asked Dona to go with him to see the Monsignor, and she would no doubt expect him to provide a full account. Telling her he couldn't tell her would not be tolerated with grace.

He munched a buttered biscuit as several more people filed into the Ranselard dining room. To his relief, he didn't know any of them. The only person he recognized was Father Albert, nodding off after a sizable breakfast. Alphonse, who had gotten up early to help with the final decorations, had wolfed down breakfast and gone to clean up and change clothes. Alexi was about to do the same when he heard that oddly familiar clicking sound. Albert started and sat up, blinking.

Moments later, Verone appeared. She greeted several well-wishers and chatted briefly before heading into the kitchens. The association between Verone and the clicking sound immediately reminded Alexi where he'd heard it before, but he wasn't the only one having an epiphany—for when it clicked again a few seconds later, the saltshaker rested squarely in the palm of Albert's hand.

. . . . .

Thurman's carriage bounced to a stop beyond the entrance to the keep, and by the time the Monsignor caught up with him, the horses were already tethered.

"Welcome to the island."

Thurman grinned. "I see you escaped house arrest." He shot a glance at the keep. "Or did they just transfer you here to do your time?"

The Monsignor hugged his son. "I'm afraid Ordinal Isrulian has very little influence at Ranselard. Now fill me in—what's this about Darron being poisoned?"

A new voice chimed in. "Why don't we wake him, and you can ask him yourself."

The Monsignor whirled to discover the old priest leaning out of the open carriage. He couldn't believe his eyes. "What are you doing here?"

"Saving your hare-brained pig-headed brother's life—and he's made it none too easy."

The Monsignor gaped. His presence on the island was even more unexpected, and far more fraught with complications. "He's here?"

"Since Laitrech was the one doing the poisoning, I couldn't very well leave him behind, could I?"

Are you sure it was Laitrech?"

The old priest dangled Laitrech's Relic from its chain. "I did the Diagnosis myself. It's a wonder Laitrech didn't use this thing to do him in instead. It would have been a lot less traceable, but then, I suppose even murderers must draw a line somewhere."

"You stole his Relic?" Though he doubted there was applicable canon, the idea of absconding with an Ordinal's relic struck him as somehow sacrilegious.

"He should never have been given it in the first place."

The Monsignor embraced the old priest as well. "As usual, you are irascible, incorrigible, insubordinate, and reckless."

"You forgot incognito."

"It's no wonder Darron had you sent away. But despite everything, it's always good to see you. I'm afraid to ask, but now that Darron is here, what do you plan to do with him?"

"Getting him here was the plan. Now you can convince him that Laitrech doesn't have his best interests at heart."

"Wait—if he doesn't already know that, how did you get him to come?"

"Fortunately, he slept most of the way."

The Monsignor eyed the old priest, and turned to Thurman, who smiled innocently and shrugged. He let it go. Sometimes it was wiser not to ask, and given current circumstances, Darron was his top priority.

"I suppose I'd better get this over with. Is there anything else I should be aware of?"

"There is one thing. If he should start going on about some demon or other invading the palace, you might want to suggest that whole thing was blown way out of proportion."

"Are you saying there was a demon in the palace?"

"No, I'm telling you there wasn't. Some people simply got the wrong impression."

The Monsignor's head throbbed in anticipation of the headaches he now suspected awaited him, both here, and back at the Holy City. "Speaking of the palace—if Darron is here and Laitrech is in doubt, who's in charge?"

"How should I know? I had more than enough trouble rescuing him from his supposed friends without trying to manage his chain of command."

"So, he just disappeared?"

"Pretty much. How else were we supposed to do it? We had no idea who else was involved in the plot."

The Monsignor sighed. "Need I point out that whoever takes charge as acting Primal will have vast resources at his command? If that person happens to be Laitrech or a co-conspirator, I sincerely doubt he will be content to wait idly by for his beloved Primal to simply reappear."

"I'm aware of that, but as dire as that sounds, it's better than just letting Laitrech finish him off at his leisure. Now at least he has a fighting chance."

"I hope you're right, but I see a whole lot more potential here for fighting than chance."

"That could be said of almost any situation that's not properly managed. After all, look at what Thurman and I accomplished with very little fighting at all."

The Monsignor sighed. "That's because you've left the real fighting to me. I wish I had the luxury to put this off, but I don't. Thurman, make sure no one comes near until I have this resolved."

The Monsignor stepped into the carriage. He shook his brother gently to rouse him.

Darron's eyes opened, then widened.

"So you're in on this abduction as well?"

The Monsignor smiled. "Some would call it a rescue."

"A rescue typically involves a willing participant. I never asked for this."

"You didn't ask to be poisoned, either. Would you really have preferred that?"

"So the demon has gotten to you as well, has it?"

"Tell me about this demon."

"It tried to abduct me from the palace. It had taken Laitrech's form and ordered a guard to carry me. Then, before we made it outside, the foul thing shifted form to that of the guard who carried me. Before it fled, it tried to convince me I was being poisoned."

"Why did it flee?"

"I don't know. Perhaps Theratigan had done something to frighten it."

"Theratigan? He was with you?"

"Not at the time, but he'd had the run of the palace. It's possible he laid a trap or did something else to scare it off. I don't know."

Mention of the demon-hunter's name gave the Monsignor a slim hope that someone capable might still be minding the store. Perhaps he had been the one to determine Darron's demon was fictitious. "Has it occurred to you that the demon may have been telling the truth?"

"You would have me take the word of a demon over that of my most-trusted advisor?"

With Darron, it was more effective to lead him to his own conclusions. "No, I would have you trust what the evidence tells you."

"What evidence?"

"That of your own eyes and flesh. How do you feel?"

"If you must know, I'm feeling stiff and bruised, and I'm still weak."

"But what of the headaches and nausea? Last time I saw you, they were debilitating."

"They do seem to have receded for the moment, but any disease may have periods of remission."

"Consider the timing. Did the remission by any chance begin once Laitrech no longer had access to you?"

"Perhaps they were just side effects of the medications."

"Possibly. but isn't it also possible they were the intended effects?"

"Now, why would Laitrech intend something like that?"

"You know how ambitious Laitrech is. Do you really think his goal in life is to play nursemaid to an old man?"

"Is it impossible to be both ambitious and honorable?"

"No, but when a crime has been committed, one typically examines all the potential suspects for motive and opportunity. Laitrech is low on the pecking order as Ordinals go. Yet, with your support, he might have a chance to succeed you. Without it, he could wait his entire life and never get the chance. Your death from natural causes could take years. He had motive, and he might well be the only one who had opportunity."

"That assumes a crime has been committed. You have no proof of that."

The Monsignor sighed. "Actually, I do. Our very own Father Anton claims to have Diagnosed you."

Darron snorted. "I don't see how. Whether you know it or not, for that to be true, our dear Father Anton would have needed a Relic."

"Apparently that wasn't a problem."

"Whose? Oh wait—Laitrech's?"

"So it would seem."

"And where is our dear Father Anton now?"

"You can deal with that later. Right now, we need to come up with a plan. We have no idea who's running the Palace, but if I'm right about Laitrech, he'll be looking to quietly finish what he started."

"And if he's innocent?"

"Then the worst that happens is you were a little overcautious. Wouldn't Laitrech himself advise you the same way?"

Darron rubbed his chin. "I suppose you have a point. What did you have in mind?"

*Progress.* The Monsignor sighed inwardly in relief, though he still found it disturbing that mentioning Laitrech had been required. Unfortunately, he hadn't thought far enough ahead to have a plan in mind, and he had another issue hanging over him that required his immediate attention. "Before we start on that, I have a small favor to ask."

"I thought we didn't have time for distractions?"

"I agree, but this will save me considerable time today that I think could be better spent elsewhere. Could you lift the interdict on the Artists' Colony in Trifienne? I've already done the groundwork, and Thurman should be able to draw up the papers."

"How is that going to save you time?"

"I'm scheduled to perform a wedding there this afternoon. It will save me the trouble of having to repeat it somewhere else."

"Fine. I don't know why I ever humored Isrulian on that boon-doggle in the first place. If you need to make it back there by this afternoon, how far away are we?"

A deafening fanfare of horns and trumpets blared just above the carriage from the ramparts of Ranselard Keep, followed by a crier's formal announcement of the arrival of the Crown of Trifienne and his retinue.

"Oh, not far," the Monsignor said.

· · · · ·

Michlos cursed the maze of prison tunnels beneath the keep. The Princess had agreed it would be wise to refresh Vane's ring to be sure he stayed out of commission until the ceremony was finished or the Monsignor returned the Eye. Yet, because Newcomb was pulled in so many directions, Michlos had, stupidly in hindsight, volunteered to do the job alone. Now, armed only with a lantern and ring of keys, he was having difficulty remembering the combination of doors and corridors that led to Vane's cell. He'd already doubled back to the entrance twice, but he kept missing a turn somewhere. Deep into his third try, he was relieved to see the flicker of another lantern reflecting off the wall of the corridor ahead. Male ego be damned—this time he would ask for directions.

"Hello? I was wondering if I could get some help finding my way?"

The reply was not swift, but it came: "Sure, but can you give me a hand with this first?"

"I'll be right there." As he got close, he caught his toe on the edge of a carpet extending under the cellblock door.

Michlos fussed with the lock "What's this carpet for?"

When the door creaked open, he discovered a half-naked man lying just inside. His finger twitched to activate his Amulet, but he was a moment too late. Lethargy sapped his will and drained his strength until, unable to fight it any longer, he fell. The last thing he saw before darkness claimed him was a strangely familiar face looming over him. But by then he was too far gone to trouble himself with trying to place it.

. . . . .

A slamming door brought Michlos to his senses. He guessed he'd only been out for a minute or two. One of his mother's protective trinkets was turning out to be much more useful than he ever would have imagined; this was the second time it had revived him from an unexpected magical attack.

As he lay in darkness, the image of his attacker still lingered in his mind's eye. *Everson.* Clearly that shoulder of his hadn't been as injured as he'd let on.

He activated one of his rings, feeling with satisfaction the cool breeze it generated as the hilt of the rapier formed in his hand. He followed with a flurry of whispered syllables, and the rapier flared alight. Next, he activated his Amulet, cursing himself for not having done so when he'd first entered the dungeons.

To his dismay, his keys were gone, but to his relief, the half-naked man next to him still breathed. The rusted remains of the cell-block's bars made it obvious how Everson had escaped. And discarded vestments identified him as the second Inquisitor the Princess had been holding.

A tug on the cellblock door revealed Everson had locked it behind him. Flicking open his cigarette case, Michlos selected a small cedar wand. He applied the wand's ivory tip directly to the lock, but nothing happened. Then he remembered his Amulet. Once he switched that off, the tip bored through the cast-iron lock like butter. He paused a moment to clear the rust from the hole and continued until the door swung open.

He was already well into the hallway when he remembered his hapless cellmate. Although torn by the urgency of apprehending Everson, he returned to the cell, where he set a lucifer to his lantern and placed it within the fallen man's reach. Then he was off down the hallway once more.

. . . . .

His dress coat still unbuttoned, Alexi raced down the stairs and out into the courtyard as fast as his ankle and crutch would permit. He'd wasted time searching for Michlos. Now the Crown had arrived, and he still wasn't ready. He was relieved to see Alphonse waiting for him, even if he did make wearing a dress coat look like the most natural thing in the world.

"How much time do we have?"

"Not much," Alphonse said. "They're already gathering on the green—maybe five minutes."

"Where are we supposed to stand?"

"I think we line up on either side of the courtyard for their entrance. As citizens of Trifienne, we go to one knee as the Crown passes."

"What about the girls?"

"I imagine they'll curtsey."

"No, I mean, where are they?"

Alphonse pointed to a disturbance across the courtyard.

Dona's scarlet-and-white gown made her a focal point, and she clearly knew it. With a queen's bearing she glided through the crowd, and all along the way people stepped out of her path. Their eyes followed her long after she'd passed.

Alexi stood transfixed.

Alphonse beamed with pride. "My Binky made that." He grabbed Alexi's arm. "Come on—we'd better hurry."

They caught up with Dona as a second fanfare announced the royal procession. Helena and Miranda joined them moments later. Although Helena's eyes were glazed from lack of sleep, that didn't stop her from appreciating all the attention Dona's dress was generating. Miranda, bedecked in her cranberry outfit, seemed somewhat less enthusiastic.

Dona held out her arms and twirled for Alexi. "Well? What do you think?"

"You look absolutely stunning."

Dona coyly adjusted his lapel. "You don't look so bad yourself, Mr. Reysa."

Alphonse put an arm around Helena and squeezed. "Looks like someone has truly outdone herself."

Helena eyed the dress. "It does look good, doesn't it? Let's just hope it holds together long enough to make it through the ceremony. I had to take a few shortcuts."

"Alexi, where were you?" Dona asked. "I was worried you were going to miss the procession."

"Looking for Michlos. You haven't seen him, have you?"

Dona shook her head. "We've been tied up all morning with this dress. Is there a problem?"

"Maybe—I saw Father Albert with the saltshaker."

"What? Is he still with the Monsignor?"

"No, and as you might guess, he seemed particularly interested in it this morning—right about the time Verone stopped by for breakfast."

Miranda put her hands on her hips. "All right—what am I missing?"

"I'll tell you later," Dona said.

"You'd better. Ever since our escape from Exidgeon, I've been feeling left out."

"We'll fill you in—I promise."

"Shh," Helena said. "Here they come."

Princess Celeste emerged to enthusiastic applause and took her place on the dais before her mother's throne.

On her cue, the musicians opened with Trifienne's anthem, and the Crown Prince appeared, in full military dress, arm in arm with the Crown Princess, resplendent in a green velvet gown.

Dona nudged Alexi. "Notice the resemblance?"

Alexi nodded. "I do now. Speaking of which, wasn't Michlos supposed to be here for this?"

"I don't know. He's been keeping pretty much out of sight."

As the Crown Prince and Princess passed them, the men knelt and the women curtseyed.

By the time Alexi and Alphonse regained their feet, the Crown's daughters had come into view. The first two were accompanied by escorts, but the third made her entrance solo. Her pout suggested she had no great fondness for weddings.

"Ah, Princess Julienne," Miranda said. "The inevitable cloud in an otherwise perfect day."

"Have you met her?" Dona asked.

"I've seen her at functions. That was more than enough exposure."

"I think I told you I once had the pleasure."

"Oh, that's right. And Gregory's here too. This just might get interesting."

"Keep an eye on him in case he needs help."

Miranda patted Dona's arm. "Don't you worry—I'll look after him."

Helena eyed Julienne with grudging admiration. "My, but she does know how to work a dress, though, doesn't she?"

"What do you mean?" Dona asked.

"Just look at her. In a courtyard chock full of royalty, everyone has eyes only for her."

"Oh really?" Dona said. "Alexi, is that true?"

"Well, she is gorgeous—"

"She *is*, is she?"

"—but I have everything I could ever want right here."

Dona took his hand and leaned up to bestow a quick peck on his cheek. "Oh, that's so sweet."

Alexi was pleased with the result. He was learning that navigating a relationship involved knowing when a compliment was required and how to deploy it to best effect.

Julienne suddenly squinted at Dona with keen interest.

Miranda noticed first. "Don't look now, but I think you've caught the royal eye."

"I see. Maybe it's time I gave her a little lesson on how to really work a dress."

She acknowledged Julienne with a smug smile and a small curtsey. Then she held out her arms and twirled, just as she had for Alexi. While still meeting the princess's gaze, she leaned back into Alexi.

"Don't just stand there, hold me," she stage-whispered.

Alexi wrapped his arms around her. "So, what's this all about?"

"Let's just say I have a little score to settle. Even if we are tied as far as the gowns are concerned, from the perspective of someone like Julienne, no doubt I'm still way ahead."

Alexi turned questioningly to Alphonse, but he only shrugged.

Miranda smiled knowingly. "It's a girl thing."

Alphonse shot Miranda a sidelong look. "We men favor the sword for resolving our differences. It's safer."

Julienne moved on with the remainder of the retinue to the royal marquee, and, with a final fanfare, the procession was over. Dona turned to leave.

"Wait—where are you going?"

"I'm the maid of honor. I'm supposed to be helping Verone, remember?"

"But what about Albert?"

"Stay with him until either Michlos or the Monsignor shows up. Try to steer him away from Verone, and I'll try to do the same with her."

Alexi nodded. "Oh, one more thing…"

"Yes?"

"You really do look stunning."

She grinned, blew him a kiss, and was off to find the bride.

. . . . .

Arerio stiffened as he peered out the window. "They're approaching the gate."

"So I see," Marguerite said.

She was seated on the second-floor balcony of the great hall. Through tall gothic windows she could see the Inquisition forces arrayed beyond the gate. On the table before her was a small pillbox, its lid flipped open to reveal a tiny white tablet.

"And to think, after all I've done to forestall this day, of all places, it should start here."

"They'll expect a response."

"I don't have one."

"We need only delay them until the Crown gets wind of this."

"They know that. Do you think it coincidence that the Inquisitor General agreed to officiate at Verone's wedding? No doubt keeping the Crown distracted was part of the plan. We've been outmaneuvered at every turn, and they're not about to give up their advantage now."

"Is that it then? Is it time to open the vault?"

She shook her head. "I can't only think of my own welfare. What happens here will have repercussions for Irina, Nathan, and perhaps all of Trifienne for years to come."

"What's the alternative?"

"The alternative is what you see on the table before you. The great and powerful Marguerite swallows the bitter little pill and fades into history. The Inquisition learns nothing, the Crown does what it must to distance itself, and Verone is denied delivering her vicious little *coup de grace* to her father's ego."

Arerio looked dubious. "You think the Church will be satisfied with your corpse?"

Marguerite shrugged. "They don't have any evidence against anyone else. They'll presume I was overcome by guilt for all my evil deeds and took the coward's way out. Case closed."

"And what about Verone? Do you really think she'll be content to leave it at that?"

"Michlos is on to her now. He should be able to keep her in check."

"Speaking of Master Michlos, is he aware of this so-called alternative?"

Marguerite raised an eyebrow. "What are you getting at?"

"If I may speak plainly?"

"By all means. It would be nice for a change to hear your opinions before you run off to share them with Michlos."

Arerio winced but held his ground. "Were he in your shoes, he would not choose the easy way out."

"You think this is easy?"

"By comparison? Yes."

"By comparison to what?"

"To taking a stand."

"I don't have that luxury."

"How could you even consider sacrificing yourself for, of all things, preserving the status quo? The only thing you accomplish by dying is empowering your oppressors. If even you could not stand against them, who else would even try?"

"I don't wield that kind of influence."

"That's not true."

"Even if I did, I would never use my son-in-law as a pawn like that."

"Then use him like the king he is. He's no coward, and neither is your daughter. When he joined this family, he knew the risks, but he chose to do it anyway. How do you suppose it will affect them when they realize their marriage drove you to take your own life?"

"That's not the reason." She said it with conviction, but in her heart, she knew Arerio was right.

"Absent that marriage, the Marguerite I know would never dream of capitulating to the enemy on her doorstep. If self-sacrifice on behalf of those you love is such a noble cause, you do them no favors by denying them the opportunity to do the same for you. You'll only saddle them with guilt they'll carry to the end of their days."

"You would rather have me selfishly plunge the kingdom into war?"

"Phrendonic Heresy is endemic in Trifienne. If the Church continues to insist on suppressing it, your sacrifice merely delays the inevitable. If there must be war, better it comes now while Trifienne's leadership is strong."

Marguerite paled as she considered the implications. "That's not my decision to make."

"And neither is the timing of your death. If war comes, it will be because the Church brings it, not because you chose to live."

Before she could reply, a volley of crossbow bolts collapsed the hall's soaring windows in an avalanche of glittering shards.

Marguerite cringed in horror at the devastation. Then, eyes narrowed and jaw tight, she rose to her feet.

With an odd combination of apprehension and relief, Arerio braced himself for her response. "It would seem the Inquisition grows impatient for your answer."

She snatched the pillbox from the table and snapped the lid shut. "They should be more careful what they wish for."

# CHAPTER THIRTEEN

## CIRCUMVENTING THE DEFENSES

Dominick Everson swore under his breath. This was the third time he'd passed this same spot. Light flickered off the damp stone walls down the tunnel to his right, and he could hear the distant murmur of low voices. Last time he'd gone straight ahead, and before that he'd taken a left. With his lantern oil getting low, he couldn't afford any more mistakes—he would have to brave the corridor with the voices.

He crept down the passage. Peering around a corner, he saw that the light emanated from a small window near the top of a door inset into the passage wall. The voices were louder now, but still too low to understand. Was the door the way out or just another dead end? He steeled himself, sidled up to the window, and craned his neck for a peep.

His heart sank—it was another cell block. Unlike the others he had seen, the cells of this block were carved from bedrock rather than assembled from iron bars. Heavy brass doors cut off the stone cubicles from the rest of the world. It struck him that two of the keys he carried appeared to be cast from the same material as those doors.

Two guards, one bald, one lushly bearded, spoke in hushed tones. "He's still sleeping—hasn't touched his food."

One turned toward him. "Who's out there?"

Everson probably could have put both guards to sleep before they got the door open, but that approach would get him no closer to the exit—he needed them awake to find his way. Instinctively, he resorted to a technique he used when he hadn't adequately prepared for lecture—he made up something plausible and said it with authority.

"I'm here for the prisoner."

The guards exchanged suspicious glances.

The bald guard frowned. "The prisoner is not to leave his cell without the express authority of the Princess."

The other guard, however, stroked his beard thoughtfully. "Or did you mean you were here about the prisoner's ring?"

Everson seized on the new information to change course. "Obviously, I'm here about the ring."

"What happened to the guy with the shiners?"

Everson held a brass key up to the window. "He asked me to cover for him."

"What took you so long?"

"He's terrible at giving directions. I don't suppose you guys could direct me to the entrance?"

The second guard chuckled sympathetically as he unlocked the door. "Yeah, the tunnels take a little getting used to. We're not allowed to leave until our shift ends, but you do what you need to, and I'll draw you a map."

"That would be splendid. Which one is he in?"

"The middle one. Did you want us out in the hallway for this?"

"That shouldn't be necessary."

As leery as he was of the guards, Everson really wasn't thrilled by the thought of entering the cell of a high-risk prisoner without backup. Through the little window in the brass door, he could see the prone form of a man.

"Looks like he's dead."

"He's still breathing," the bald guard said.

"Well, so he is. This should only take a moment."

As quietly as possible, Everson slipped the brass key into the lock and turned it. Simultaneously, the guards aimed their crossbows at him.

His heart leapt to his throat. "Did I do something wrong?"

"You're fine," the bearded guard said. "We need to be ready if he makes a break for it."

Everson steadied the door as it swung open to minimize any squeaking. The last thing he wanted was for the prisoner to wake up. Of course, he had no idea what he was supposed to do with the prisoner's ring, and neither could he ask without giving himself away. His best option was simply to take it, since that's probably what the guards expected, assuming the prisoner had stolen it. As gently as possible, he slipped the ring off the man's finger. It came off so easily it must have been at least a full size too big—which confirmed it probably didn't belong to him. Everson smiled, mentally congratulated himself on his powers of deduction, and slipped the ring into his pocket. Finally, he backed out of the cell and went to lock the door once more—when it occurred to him that if such an important prisoner happened to escape, it was a fair bet the guards would divert all their resources to catching him, possibly to the point of ignoring less-important escapees. Blocking the guards' view, he relocked the door, and, in the same fluid motion, unlocked it again.

"All done."

"Hold on," the bearded guard said.

Everson froze, terrified he'd made a misstep.

"Your directions."

Praying they couldn't tell how fast his heart was racing, Everson mustered the calmest smile he could. "Oh, I almost forgot."

The guard handed him a ragged scrap of paper. "Here you go."

"Thanks," he said as they opened the door to let him out.

. . . . .

Albert placed a crisp white stole about the Monsignor's neck. Fortunately, Cartier kept his spare vestments in the church rather than the vicarage, or they would have had to improvise. "Will Darron be attending the ceremony?"

"He's not up to it yet. A public appearance is the last thing he should be doing right now."

"Where is he, then?"

"The Princess was kind enough to provide him with a suite of rooms. He can watch the ceremony from his window."

Albert draped an embroidered chasuble over the Monsignor's head. "What do you suppose is going on back home?"

"I wish I knew. If Laitrech has seized control, he'll have strong incentive to ensure Darron doesn't return—he'll have no trouble appreciating the potential repercussions of the Primal's miraculous recovery. If that isn't bad enough, instead of sending Isrulian back to Darron for censure, we will have sent him right into Laitrech's hands, complete with trumped-up tales of my insubordination and his ridiculous heresy accusations against me. No doubt before this is over, the so-called demon in the palace will end up being my fault as well."

"Speaking of heresy," Albert said, pulling the saltshaker from his pocket. "Do you remember this? Turns out it is a Profanity after all. Every so often, the marble will get stuck to the lid."

"What do you mean, stuck?"

"Let me rephrase. Not stuck, attracted. It can be resting on the bottom and when it triggers, it will fly right up to the lid."

"What activates it?"

"I haven't figured that out yet. There seems to be no rhyme or reason to it. Sometimes it does it when I'm moving around, and other times I can be sitting completely still."

"When did you first notice this?"

Albert scratched his head. "I think I first noticed it last night—during the young man's demonstration."

The Monsignor leaned closer. "Think carefully. Do you remember when during the demonstration?"

"I don't, exactly. I just recall trying to watch and being distracted by the noise. I didn't even know what was making it."

"Is there any chance it responded to the demonstration itself?"

"I don't know. I guess it's possible."

The Monsignor was staggered by the implications "That's not a possibility we can ignore. We may have to call in Alexi for another demonstration."

"Are you sure that's a good idea? I should think that encouraging the young man to commit additional heresies would be the last thing you'd want to be involved with."

The Monsignor sighed. Perhaps he had more in common with Darron than he was willing to admit—sometimes doing things the right way was annoyingly inconvenient. "That's a good point. Well, keep an eye out for what—or more likely who—changes nearby when it activates. Maybe we can figure it out that way instead."

"I'll certainly keep my eyes peeled."

. . . . .

The lock on the door to Marguerite's cellar was large, complicated, and entirely for show. She touched one of her rings, and the door swung inward.

"After you."

Arerio found himself in a workshop littered with construction projects in various stages of completion, all of them covered with a layer of dust—and all of them otherwise exactly as Spiros had left them all those years ago. But Marguerite was not here to reminisce. Once inside the workshop, she took the lead again, passing the wine cellar and the root cellar until she stood before the subcellar door. Another touch of her ring and this door yielded as well.

The air grew stale as they descended a narrow stairwell, but they did not lack for light—every few feet, glowing crystals were set into the walls an inch above the floor. The center of the chamber below boasted two effigy-bearing sarcophagi, only one of which had been sealed. Marguerite paused as she neared them.

"If I don't make it through this...."

"I'll be sure to remind Master Michlos."

She pulled her eyes away from the sarcophagus and continued past. "There it is," she said.

At the far end of the chamber, a small cast-iron door was inset into the stone of the wall at chest height. As with the door to the cellar, it bore a complicated lock.

"This one actually requires a key. I pity the thief who tries to rust his way through it."

Once again, she touched a ring. With a tiny whoosh of air that stirred Arerio's tuft, the key appeared in the lock. She turned it and pulled open the cast-iron door to reveal a heavy brass plate.

As she grasped handles wrought into the plate's sides, Arerio heard multiple "ka-chunks." With some effort she slid the plate out of the vault and set it aside. The instant she released it, thick brass pegs popped out of slots around its frame.

Arerio took a closer look. "The pegs hold it in place?"

"They do. I'm rather proud of that. Go ahead, touch it."

He placed his hand on the plate and looked up questioningly.

"Now watch as I do it."

The instant she touched it, the plate's pegs retracted in unison. "Anyone else would have to force their way through."

From the open vault, she retrieved a lacquered wooden chest, which she tucked under one arm. "Got it. Let's head to the cupola."

Arerio raised his eyebrows. "Does that mean you aren't planning to give them the courtesy of a warning?"

Her mouth tightened but did not speak.

Arerio persisted. "Mistress?"

With a snort, she capitulated. "Oh, very well. Tell them if they remove themselves from the premises at once, I am willing to overlook their unprovoked attack on my residence. However, any further acts of aggression, including trespass, will be deemed a declaration of war and will be met with lethal force. There, satisfied?"

Arerio bowed. "I am. I'll meet you in the cupola once I've delivered the message."

. . . . .

Alexi kept watch outside the anteroom where the Monsignor prepared for the ceremony until his ankle finally objected. Since Albert was with the Monsignor, and more importantly, the Monsignor's cane, Alexi breathed easier. He sat on a courtyard bench in plain sight of the anteroom door, firmly resolved that any further disasters wouldn't be his fault.

"Excuse me, is this seat taken?"

"No, go ahead," he said reflexively. Only after he'd spoken did he look to see who was joining him. He leapt to his feet. "I'm so sorry. I meant to say 'go ahead, Your Highness.'"

Princess Julienne's laugh was low and musical. It reassured Alexi that she had not taken offense.

She eyed him with an expression of polite curiosity. "Are you waiting for someone?"

"Not exactly."

"Well, I certainly didn't mean to disturb you." She patted the bench next to her. "Sit. You were here first."

Alexi's gaze flitted toward the anteroom. The door was still closed. "All right."

Julienne took a small vial from her clutch and dabbed a touch of its contents on each wrist and behind each ear. She held out her arm. "It's jasmine. What do you think?"

Alexi had never smelled anything quite like it. "It's lovely. It reminds me of a cool breeze on a summer evening."

"You, sir, have a way with words. You must be a poet."

"I'm no poet, but I do like to write. I'm studying to be a professor."

Julienne nodded appraisingly. "I could see that. You have a look of quiet authority about you. What will you be a professor of?"

"History, I think."

"Impressive. So you're a man who likes to take the long view of things. Tell me, how will your students address you?"

"Oh, my apologies, Highness. I'm Alexi. Alexi Reysa."

Julienne raised an eyebrow in delighted surprise. "Reysa? I bet you're related to the Count, aren't you?"

Alexi blushed. "It turns out I am."

"All this, and nobility too. Tell me, are all the Reysas so tall?"

Alexi nodded. "My brother is taller still."

"Does he also have your dimple?"

"I don't have a dimple."

"You do. It shows up every time you smile. Has no one ever pointed it out?"

"Where?"

"Right here." She touched his cheek with a jasmine-scented fingertip. The sensation made Alexi shiver.

"It's adorable. I'm shocked no one has mentioned it before. Perhaps some other feature is distracting them. Do your girlfriends focus on your eyes instead? They are an incredible shade. I'd say almost a burnt sienna, if it weren't for the flecks of emerald."

"I only have one girlfriend, and she doesn't tend to get distracted by my features."

"Only one? Is it customary for the Reysas to be betrothed at such a tender age?"

"Oh, I'm not betrothed. It's just an understanding we have."

Julienne bit her lip in puzzlement. "If it's not a betrothal, then how does this 'understanding' work?"

"It's not complicated or anything. It's just that while we're seeing each other, we aren't seeing anyone else."

"I see. She must be very special then. Who is this lucky lady?"

"Dona Merinne. I think you may have met her once."

"Now that you mention it, I do recall meeting a Dona Merinne recently. I think it was at the opera. But this surely can't be the same person."

"I'm pretty sure it is."

"No, it can't be—that is, unless the understanding between the two of you is not reciprocal."

"What do you mean?"

"Well, this Dona Merinne spent most of the opera engaged in a passionate embrace with a certain tenor by the name of Gregory De-lauren. Perhaps you've heard of him? I remember it distinctly, since they were in a box very near my own. I did my best to ignore it, but their behavior was so distracting I ended up leaving the performance early. I can't have been the only person to have seen it, and anyone who had would surely remember."

Alexi shifted uncomfortably. "That can't be true—Dona assured me the two of them were just friends."

Julienne laid a sympathetic hand on his arm. "I'm sorry. Perhaps your interpretation of your 'understanding' differs from hers?"

Alexi glowered. "I doubt it."

"Well, maybe this is for the best. Someone with all your options would surely benefit from a bit more time playing the field. After all, there are plenty of good honest women who know how to appreciate a man of quality, and you, sir, deserve nothing less."

The furrow in Alexi's brow deepened. Dona was one of the most forthright women he'd ever met. Julienne's accusation made no sense. She must be mistaken. "I don't believe you."

"Oh, now I see I've upset you, and that really wasn't my intention. Perhaps I did get it all wrong. Maybe it was a different Dona. I never should have said anything. You aren't cross with me, are you?"

Confronted by her quivering lip, Alexi felt as if he'd scolded an innocent puppy. "It's not your fault."

"It is so my fault. I can never seem to figure out when to keep my big mouth shut. No wonder people get so exasperated with me. Now you're angry too, and I feel just terrible. Please, let me try to make it up to you. As a history buff, no doubt you appreciate art as well. Let me buy you something."

"Oh, that's really not necessary."

"Please? It would mean so much to me."

"But the wedding is about to begin."

"We have at least an hour yet, and there are all sorts of artists right outside. That should be plenty of time. Besides, I would really love to see the exhibits, but my father wouldn't approve of me wandering out there unescorted. If I don't go now, I won't get the chance. You'd be doing me a huge favor."

Alexi glanced back toward the anteroom. With the wedding coming up so soon, it was almost inconceivable that Albert and the Monsignor would go anywhere else before he got back. He stood and smoothed his jacket. "All right, but I need to be back in half an hour."

Julienne brightened and slipped her arm beneath his. "I can't thank you enough." Gently, she steered him toward the green. "So, what do you do when you're not rescuing fair damsels in distress?"

Alexi played it coy. "Well, when I'm not off slaying dragons, I tend to split my time between overthrowing tyrannical overlords and competing in tournaments—I love a good joust."

She patted his arm. "I think I know just what you mean."

# CHAPTER FOURTEEN

# UNINVITED GUESTS

Michlos finally arrived at the prison entrance after Rusting his way through half-a-dozen locks. Since the former mine rarely held prisoners anymore, no one was stationed there, and it took a while to find someone with a set of keys. When he did, the man was unwilling to part with them without authorization. Michlos didn't have time to argue. He hoped the floor was more comfortable than it looked, or the chap was likely to wake with quite a backache.

Heading back into the prison, he finally recognized the turn he'd been missing and took it. Though Everson was still a problem, Vane was more pressing. He was nearly halfway to Vane's cell block when he noticed lantern light reflecting off the walls of the passage ahead. In the split second it took to confirm his Amulet was active, the lantern went dark. He'd stumbled across Everson after all. Michlos forged ahead, hoping to overtake the man before he could disappear into the maze.

He arrived at the intersection of two corridors and held his rapier aloft. There was no sign of his quarry beyond a whiff of smoke from a snuffed lamp. He decided to pursue—it would be far easier to renew the spells on Vane's ring with the key to Vane's cell. Failing that, he would need to work out a different mechanism or recast the Sleep every hour until the Eye of Moravidos was returned. Perhaps Everson could be reasoned with.

He cleared his throat. "Everson. I have a message from the Princess. If you return the keys you've taken, you are free to go."

An echo was the only reply.

"I know you can hear me. The Princess asked me to apologize. You were imprisoned by mistake. If you're worried about your heresies, don't be. No one was hurt, and heresies don't matter on an island under interdict. There's no need to hide. Simply bring me the keys, and you can be on your way."

Michlos sensed movement ahead.

"It would appear your friend Everson doesn't trust you." Josephus Vane stepped into the rapier light, his expression pensive, his hands tucked behind his back as though he was engaged in a philosophical discussion. "But I would be delighted to accept your offer in his stead."

Michlos ducked back out of the intersection. Since Vane had not been the least bit shy about revealing himself, he had to assume Everson had been the one to extinguish the lamp; he now had two adversaries. Best to keep both in front. Since Vane had plenty of rest, overpowering Michlos's Amulet wouldn't be a problem. Why hadn't he already done so? Could he really be so cavalier as to risk everything for the pleasure of gloating?

"The offer wasn't open to you."

Michlos's mind raced. Either Vane was loath to use up all his reserves this early in his escape, or he'd already used some of those resources and felt overpowering the Amulet would use more than he could afford.

"And why not?" Vane asked. "Don't your assertions apply equally well to me?

"Hardly. You tried to kill me."

"And yet, here you stand with only a minor bruise to show for it. Were I your friend Everson, the similarities of our situations might well cause me to doubt your sincerity."

Michlos blanched. Vane was trying to recruit Everson as an ally. Perhaps he hoped to persuade Everson to overpower Michlos's Amulet for him. "Give it up, Vane. Everson's not stupid enough to fall for that. This is between you and me."

"So what's it going to be? Spells at twenty paces? Who can cast faster do you suppose?"

Michlos was tempted to take that bet. He'd had a knack for that sort of dueling during his academy days, but while Everson remained in hiding, he didn't dare. Nor could he trust Vane not to cheat. Casting faster would do him no good if Vane already Suppressed for what he cast, and he'd had plenty of time to prepare. In retrospect, that's probably what saved Vane from the effects of Michlos's ring during their previous encounter.

"No?" Vane asked. "Well, I guess it's just me against you and that rapier of yours. Are you really the sort of man who attacks an unarmed opponent?"

"I'm not falling for that again." Michlos said it with more conviction than he felt. He couldn't use the blade to advance on Vane without passing the intersection, and that would risk putting Everson at his back. He had a sinking feeling there might not be a good way to resolve this impasse.

With one hand, Vane whipped out a crossbow and aimed it at Michlos's chest. "Fortunately for me, I expected as much."

With that, he pulled the trigger.

. . . . .

Given Verone's insistence that her older brothers play no part in her wedding, Newcomb had defaulted to the role of usher. For a time, Nathalie stood by to ensure he had a grasp of where everyone was to sit and the appropriate way to address each guest, but her hovering was unnecessary. Protocol, it seemed, was his particular specialty. Once Verone and Dona arrived, Nathalie joined them and Dona's mother in the room across the hall from the Monsignor's antechamber. Alistair was there as well, in black tails and a burgundy double-breasted waistcoat that was almost colorful enough to rival Dona's gown. He leaned back in his seat, watching in smug amusement as the women fussed over his daughter.

Verone was in a foul mood. Although her dress was unusually plain, the silhouette was quite flattering. Yet, she was more concerned that it was cumbersome, restrictive, and overly warm. Nathalie flitted about, mopping Verone's brow and sneaking in touches of makeup whenever she let down her guard.

For her part, Verone focused primarily on the strenuous act of breathing. Despite the risk of being seen, she insisted the windows and the door be thrown wide. Dona had no sooner complied than a stifling cloud of tobacco smoke wafted in, which had the effect of turning the already hyperventilating bride's complexion an even paler shade of green.

Amanda touched her daughter's arm. "Dona, could you please deal with that."

"Be right back." A brief respite from the room's toxic atmosphere would be welcome, even if it meant getting closer to the source of the foul-smelling smoke.

Once in the courtyard, she spied a gentleman in an ill-fitting dress coat near the open window. His graying hair was crudely slicked to one side, and he sat alone, puffing contentedly on a pipe. She recognized the pipe before she recognized the man.

"What are you doing here?"

Jonas languidly blew a smoke ring. "Nice party. When do we eat?"

She cast a nervous glance toward the open window. "Come with me, sir."

He got to his feet. "I thought you'd never ask."

She led him across the courtyard to a semi-secluded spot behind the musician's stage and rounded on him.

"This wedding is by invitation only."

"But I have an invitation." He pulled a wrinkled sheet of paper from his pocket and smoothed it against his chest.

She snatched it out of his hand. "This isn't even your name. In fact, it's not even for the right location. These were supposed to have been thrown away."

Jonas shrugged. "One man's trash…"

"Never mind that, why are you here?"

"I tagged along with the Professor."

"He's here too?"

Jonas inspected his nails, then rubbed them on his lapel. "Fortunately, he knew someone with a spare invitation. Oh, he has a message for you."

"Couldn't it wait?"

Jonas shrugged again. "Could have as far as I'm concerned."

"Well, what is it?"

"He thought you might want to know that book you gave him was not his." Jonas smirked as Dona struggled with that revelation.

"What are you talking about? It was an ancient leather-bound book with *Practical Phrendonics* scribed right across the cover. How many books like that does he think there are?"

"Probably on the order of one per family. I wonder how long it will take for Alistair to realize he's been robbed of a treasured family heirloom."

Dona's eyes widened. "Are you saying the book I gave Reston actually belonged to Alistair?"

"I didn't have a chance to read the dedication, but I'd say it's a fair bet."

"We have to return it before he finds out."

"It's a little late for that. Someone's already Rusted Reston's office door clean off its hinges and made off with it."

"What? Who even knew he had it?"

"The Professor seemed to think your Auntie Verone might have some ideas about that. Since you two are on such good terms, maybe you should ask her."

"That doesn't make any sense. Not only is there no way she could have known Professor Reston had the book, she hasn't left the keep since I delivered it to him. Where is he now?"

"He's wandering around somewhere. I think he's hoping to find his book while Verone is distracted."

"You have to find him and tell him to stop."

"I can suggest it, but he seemed pretty set on it."

"You don't understand—the Monsignor is officiating."

"At a Nevinander wedding? How did that happen?"

"Look, I don't have time to go into details, but right now the Monsignor's people have a device that could detect him if he tried any funny business."

"What about Thurman? I don't suppose he's here too?"

"Thurman? I certainly hope not."

"Pity. If the Monsignor really does have a way to detect 'funny business,' I'd love to find a way to get him to check out his son."

Strains of instrumental music quieted the murmuring crowd.

Dona glanced wildly about. "They're starting. And I'm not in position. Oh no—the Monsignor's already part way down the runner."

Albert took a seat near the back as the Monsignor stiffly processed toward the dais.

"What do you know," Jonas said. "Thurman is here."

"Where? I don't see him."

"Neither do I, but there's Father Anton, and the two of them are traveling together. You can bet he's not far off."

"Father Anton? Where?"

"Near the back. Next to the other priest, the one who just sat down."

"So that's the mysterious Father Anton. He isn't exactly young, is he? I wonder—"

"He's ancient, but still sharp."

Rayen entered next, in black tails and a cerulean waistcoat. The music soared.

"Now I really have to go," Dona said. "Make sure you tell Professor Reston no funny business. And for heaven's sake, put out that pipe."

.  .  .  .  .

Dona returned to find Alistair and Verone still sniping at each other.

Verone fanned herself frantically. "We are starting early because we're ready and because I don't know how long I'm going to make it in this corset."

When you set a time for a ceremony, you need to stick to it no matter what," Alistair said. "Anything else is rude to the guests."

Verone smirked despite her discomfort. "You aren't by chance referring to any particular guests, are you?"

Alistair grumbled, but refused to take the bait.

"Well, as long as said guests arrive in time for the vows, you have nothing to worry about. If I were you, though, I wouldn't hold my breath."

"If I'm footing the bill for this," Alistair said, "it's starting on time, and not a moment sooner."

"Actually, it looks far more likely that I'll be footing the bill, and I say we start early."

"You'll be walking down that runner by yourself then."

"Enough!" Nathalie shrieked.

Alistair and Verone both gaped at her. A murmur rippled from the guests outside.

A fist on either hip, Nathalie stared down first her husband, then her daughter. "Let's get one thing straight right now. I don't give a damn who's paying, and at this point, I don't even care who's getting married. I sweated blood for this ceremony, and it's going to start when I say it starts. Either of you have a problem with that?"

Verone and Alistair shook their heads.

"Good. Then sit down, shut up, and wait for my cue."

Father and daughter exchanged astonished glances and sank slowly into their chairs.

Still shaking her head, Nathalie caught Amanda's gaze. "Nevinanders," she said.

# CHAPTER FIFTEEN

# house of cards

The cupola perched atop the Serrola mansion was a recent addition, as evidenced by its stylistic clash with the older architecture. Marguerite had only grudgingly consented to its construction, and she had since spent a lifetime regretting it. The last project Spiros had ever undertaken still filled the space, although Marguerite kept it covered by a great canvas tarp because, even after all these years, she still couldn't bear to look at it. One of the cupola walls was entirely taken up by a folding door that opened out onto the widow's walk, while the other three walls each bore large latticed windows that provided panoramic views of the grounds and of the countryside for miles around. To the northeast, Trifienne's spires glittered in the sunlight. To the southeast, the jagged plateau that held Exidgeon University lorded over the surrounding farmland. Beyond the grounds to the west, the limestone cliffs gave way to the mighty Scandus river. Less than half a league north and west, the island that held the Artists' Colony rose from those waters. At the very southern tip of that island loomed the squat towers of Ranselard Keep.

Marguerite had no time to admire the view. By the time Arerio trudged up the steep stairwell and through the trapdoor, she was seated at a small table. The tabletop contained a series of rectangular indentations numbered from zero to twenty-one, each inset with its own tiny brass plaque.

"How did it go?" she asked.

Arerio sighed. "As you expected. Their leader said to tell you if you presented yourself immediately, he would personally guarantee your safe conduct to the Holy City."

Marguerite snorted. "How generous. Did he also offer to personally guarantee my safe branding, torture, and execution?"

"I'm afraid he was a bit vague on the details."

"How about we discourage him from clarifying?"

She reached into the chest she'd taken from the vault, retrieved a small wooden box, and flipped open the lid to reveal a deck of playing cards. She fanned them in her hand.

Arerio blinked. "Is that Master Spiros's deck?"

Marguerite nodded. "Trumps of Doom. How he used to love that game. He spent a small fortune having these made. When he passed, I chose to believe he wouldn't mind if I adapted them for a slightly different purpose. Would you care to have a look at what they're up to?"

Arerio went to the window. "They have someone fussing with the lock at the gate."

Her eyes narrowed. "I have just the trump for that. Everyone is out of the house, correct?"

"They are. The staff was given extended time off last night after you announced your intention to leave for Azelon."

"Excellent." She plucked the Star card from the deck and placed it face-up in its appointed slot. "There. What's happening now?"

"He's collapsed. It looks like they're attempting to revive him."

"That should keep them busy for a while. In the meantime, why don't we see to our defenses? First, a little privacy would be nice." She slid out the Hermit card and placed it in its slot. The instant she did so, the sunlight streaming through the windows dimmed.

"They're pointing up at the house," Arerio said. "What did you do?"

"It's an illusion. Various parts of the house, including this cupola, are now surrounded by translucent silver spheres. Because they are translucent, some light can get through, which means that we can still see. To those outside, though, it will look like the house has been enveloped by gigantic mirrored bubbles. While the sun shines, you can watch them without fear of being seen."

"Wait, it looks like they've just lost another man to the gate."

She nodded. "It should have Charges for several more, assuming they are foolish enough to keep touching it with their bare flesh."

"Get down!" Arerio shouted.

He dropped to the floor and Marguerite slid under the table as bolts and arrows smashed through the windows.

"They're firing indiscriminately," Arerio said. "Do we have a defense against that?"

Marguerite fumbled for the Chariot card. "Maybe this will help." When she slipped the card into its slot, heavy steel blinds shot up from the sills to completely cover the windows. A few arrows bounced harmlessly off before Arerio risked an inspection.

"Well, that seems to do the job."

"You can adjust their angle to see out as necessary. If they shoot again, just close them. Or are they giving up?"

Arerio adjusted the blinds. "A few are still shooting, but they're also conferring at the gate. What's our next move?"

"We wait. Our cards are on the table, figuratively as well as literally, for everyone—including the Crown—to see."

"Surely it's only a matter of time before the Crown sends a force to deal with these interlopers."

Marguerite rifled through the rest of the deck. "We can't count on that. Nathan has the welfare of his subjects to consider. Now that we've declared ourselves heretics, if he comes to our aid, he declares himself as well. I think the best-case scenario is for the Inquisition to expect they will come and clear out before that can happen."

"And if they don't?"

"Let's pray it doesn't come to that. But if it does, I still have a few cards up my sleeve."

· · · · ·

The instant Michlos glimpsed Vane's crossbow emerging, he threw his arm across his chest and activated another of his many rings, squinting against churning gusts of air as a wooden buckler coalesced in his hand. It had no sooner appeared than Vane's bolt implanted itself near the edge, splitting it down the middle. The two halves fell, disintegrating in twin billows of roiling mist that evaporated before they reached the floor.

Vane threw back his head and laughed. "For your sake, I hope that trinket of yours has another charge." He began to reload.

A quick rundown of his options told Michlos he had only one clear choice. He turned and ran.

Heart pounding, he rounded a turn before Vane reloaded, but the distance to the next security gate was too great. He'd never make it. He activated his Amulet, followed by the ring he'd used to cloak the Sultan's Respite in Darkness. He dropped the ring and dashed for the gate.

Vane stepped into sight, raised the crossbow, and took aim. "Fish in a barrel."

But before Vane pulled the trigger, he was plunged into Darkness. Michlos had moved far enough beyond the ring to remove it from his Amulet's influence.

As Vane cursed, Michlos frantically tried one key after another on the gate. The sixth worked. He leapt through just as Vane emerged. The crossbow sang, but the bolt grazed the gate and skittered harmlessly away. Before Vane could reload, Michlos slammed and locked the gate. Another gate blocked the way forward, but passages to his left and right were clear. Desperate to avoid Vane's line of sight, he slipped to the left and plastered his back against the wall.

The gate rattled. "Damned Amulet. Guess I'll need keys after all. Well, no matter. Perhaps I can sweet-talk your friend Everson into sharing."

Vane's footsteps retreated. Michlos counted twenty and poked his head around the corner, hoping for an opening. A bolt struck next to his head, spewing sparks and chips of stone.

Now he definitely had an opening. Switching off his Amulet, he stepped in front of the gate and mouthed mnemonics, but before he could finish, Vane ducked into the Darkness. Michlos reactivated his Amulet and ducked away. Losing track of Vane was a disaster; there were likely multiple routes to the prison exit, and his amulet couldn't block them all. When Vane finally found the way out, Michlos had to be there waiting. It pained him to admit it, but Everson was on his own.

. . . . .

Arm in arm, Julienne led Alexi through the artists' displays. As she passed, the artists dropped what they were doing to attend her. Often, they presented whatever Julienne lingered near as a gift, and she looked to Alexi to see if it struck his fancy. Since Alexi didn't feel right about taking their work for free, he invariably shook his head, and they moved on.

"We should probably head back," Alexi said. "The wedding is about to start."

Julienne pouted. "But you haven't let me buy you anything."

"It's kind of you to offer, but I don't really need anything."

Julienne peered up at him through dark lashes. "This is art. I know you don't need it, but I was sort of hoping you might value it anyway as a gift from a friend. Isn't there something you'll let me get you?"

"Well, if you put it that way—"

"What would you like?"

"I don't know anything about this stuff. Why don't you pick."

She took him by the hand. "I have just the thing. Come with me."

She guided him to a small booth with an extensive display of fine jewelry and pointed to a large gold ring with a bold squarish stone "May I see this one."

The proprietor, a wizened old lady, bowed and opened the case. "An honor, Your Highness. The ring is 14 carat gold, and the stone is a composite of carnelian, onyx, and jade, with each mineral lending its unique color to one of the three diagonal stripes. While it is an attractive piece, if Your Highness prefers, I do have rings of greater value."

Alexi was quick to intervene. "No, this one's really nice."

Julienne beamed. "Go ahead, try it on."

Alexi held up a bejeweled finger and nodded. He still felt terrible about taking it but feared if he didn't, Julienne would find something even more expensive.

"Then we've found our gift." Julienne turned back to the proprietor. "How much?"

"Please, Highness, take it as a token of my esteem."

"Nonsense. I can't give as a gift something I received as one. Oh, I see there's a tag on the slot." Julienne patted Alexi's hand. "I'm afraid you're going to have to turn your back for a moment."

"But—"

"No buts and no snooping. You're not allowed to know how much I spend on a gift for you."

Grateful that he wasn't robbing the artist, Alexi turned his back.

"There, all done. Now, let's see how it looks."

As Alexi faced Julienne, something in the distance caught his eye.

"What's that?" He pointed across the river. "Over there. Is that a mirror? If it is, it must be huge."

Julienne's jaw dropped. "That's Grandmother Serrola's house. Father needs to know about this. Come with me."

Taking his arm, she led him back toward the keep as quickly as his crutch would allow.

·　·　·　·　·

Dominick Everson crept down the hallway after the man with the crossbow, guided by the reflected light from the swordsman's glowing rapier, now well around the corner. The directions the guard had given him told him this was the way out. But he wasn't quite to the corner when everything went completely dark.

Had the crossbowman caught up with the swordsman? His answer came in the form of cursing from the crossbowman, who, by the sound, was not far ahead. He paused, listening. The distant jangle of keys was followed by a crossbow discharging. He backed off. How was he to escape with these bickering madmen drawing all that attention? Footsteps receded farther down the passage. At last, he could risk a light. Since he had no lucifers, he whispered mnemonics to make his lantern glow. To his surprise, the lantern did not cooperate. In the distance, bars rattled. Echoing words from the crossbowman chilled his blood:

*"Guess I'll need keys after all. Well, no matter. Perhaps I can sweet-talk your friend Everson into sharing."*

Panic surged. He had nothing to defend against a crossbow. Still utterly blind, he backed away. Then, his lantern erupted unexpectedly with light. He could now see the corridor behind him, but the corridor ahead remained shrouded. He dashed back to the intersection and heaved the lantern down the right-hand passage. Then, he padded back toward the high-security cellblock, feeling his way along the wall. He stopped abruptly. Where the door had been, all that remained was an open doorway.

Everson felt his way around until he found the body of one of the guards. The man still breathed but didn't respond to shaking. He found a coin pouch in the man's pocket and took it. After a bit more rummaging, he located the second crossbow. If he could find bolts, he'd have at least a fighting chance. He decided to risk another light, but at that moment, he heard footsteps. With nowhere else to turn, he scampered to the brass-doored cell and slipped inside. He pulled the door ever-so-slowly closed and backed up tight against the wall next to it.

Light flared through the door grate as footsteps entered the cellblock. They meandered a bit, at one point pausing just outside his cell. Sweat trickled down Everson's back. He wracked his brain for something that could save him. Verone hadn't taught him Darkness, and that probably wouldn't protect him in such a small space anyway. Even if he could see his target well enough to use Sleep, by the time he'd finished casting, the man's crossbow would have finished him. The shadows shifted. Was he peering through the grate? Everson tensed every muscle. He dared not even breathe. If he died here, would his poor old mother ever learn of it? How would she survive without him?

Just as he felt his lungs would burst, the footsteps retreated. After several long moments, Everson worked up the courage to peer through the grate. The light faded down the passage he had not yet explored. He waited a bit longer and then cast his own Light on a coin from the purse. Clenching it in his fist, he used the little radiance that escaped between his fingers to scan the room. Both guards were still there, as was the crossbow, but all the bolts were gone.

His hopes for the crossbow dashed, he was at a loss. These passages interconnected. The crossbowman had gone the other way, but that didn't mean they wouldn't cross paths again. With luck and his scribbled directions, he might reach the exit before the other two. If he didn't, he stood no chance—their ruckus would draw every guard in the place. Regardless, he forged ahead. What other choice did he have?

· · · · ·

Dona smiled charmingly as she stepped onto the bridal runner, but inside, she was seething. The ceremony would have been the perfect time to sneak another peek into Verone's leather case. When last she'd looked, it contained a giftwrapped package she presumed was an early wedding gift. In hindsight, it was precisely the same heft and dimensions as Reston's book. Stuck in the ceremony, she was missing a perfect opportunity to get it back. She wanted to tell Alexi to check, but he was nowhere to be found.

A sudden commotion drew her eye. Two people scurried along the courtyard wall faster than was proper, one leading the other by the hand. Alexi's crutch gave him away instantly, but it took a moment to place the leader—until she recognized the gown. At that moment, Dona caught her toe on the runner and nearly tripped, drawing concerned clucks from nearby matrons. She paused, took a breath, and composed herself. She reached the dais without further incident, keeping a baleful eye on Alexi and his escort until they disappeared into the royal marquee.

"Are you all right?" the Monsignor whispered.

She nodded self-consciously and stepped into position.

Verone appeared, and the musicians commenced the bridal march. Arm in arm with her father, she carried a profusion of red and white roses that perfectly complemented her simple off-white dress. Rayen flashed an earnest grin, and her sour look softened. When he followed up with a wink, she even managed a hint of a smile.

As Dona gathered up Verone's bouquet, Nathalie, seated in the front row, let out a sob. Next to her, a teary-eyed Olivia patted her shoulder. Once Dona was back in position, Alistair placed Verone's perfectly manicured hand in Rayen's. Sporting a sidelong half-smile, he clapped Rayen on the shoulder. "Best of luck, my boy." With that, he took his appointed seat next to Nathalie.

The Monsignor opened his mouth to speak, but a disturbance at the royal marquee stayed his tongue—the Crown and the Crown Princess dashed along the courtyard wall, with Alexi and Julienne tagging along behind. Leaving their seats at the start of a ceremony was highly irregular, and the crowd's reaction reflected it. The Monsignor couldn't have been heard over so much hushed chatter if he'd tried.

Verone's sour expression returned in full force. "Oh, not again."

At last, Princess Celeste rose from her mother's throne and called for quiet. Seeing the royal couple leave the courtyard, she called for a ten-minute recess, after which, she assured the guests, the ceremony would resume whence it had left off. She cued the musicians, who resumed playing introductory music.

Dona caught sight of a familiar face working his way through the crowd. Thurman eventually made it to a spot just behind the dais, and the Monsignor leaned down to hear his report.

"It's heresy—and on a grand scale."

"Where?" the Monsignor asked.

"Across the river, but close enough that His Primacy easily saw it from his window. He's more than a little dismayed. He thinks he can ill-afford this kind of disturbance given everything else on his plate. He wants to know what you're going to do about it."

The Monsignor sighed. "I suppose I should start by having a look. Here, take The Eye of Moravidos, and stand right here until I get back."

Thurman shrugged. "If you say so."

The Monsignor turned to Verone and Rayen. "I'm so sorry for the delay. I'll be right back once I find out what's happening."

. . . . .

Albert and Father Anton joined the Monsignor as he left the courtyard.

"What's the status of the saltshaker?" the Monsignor asked.

Albert reached into his pocket. "Active for some time now. Oh wait, I guess not anymore."

"Have you figured out the mechanism yet?"

"Not yet. It's active too often to be triggered by only one thing."

"Out of curiosity," the old priest asked, "where are we going?"

"Outside," the Monsignor said. "There's been a sighting of Phrendonic Heresy across the river."

Arriving at the gate, they saw that many of the artists had arrayed themselves along the cliff to witness the spectacle—the Crown and Crown Princess were among them.

"What do you make of that?" Albert asked.

"It's an illusion, all right," the old priest said. "An interesting twist on the usual Darkness ploy."

The Monsignor's gaze drifted from the illusion to the Crown Prince. For a moment their eyes met. Nathan's brow furrowed and his gaze darted away.

"What do I make of it?" the Monsignor asked. "I think we may have overstayed our welcome."

"Why do you say that?"

"Because if I remember correctly, that's the home of Marguerite Serrola, the Crown Prince's mother-in-law. If I had to guess, I'd say this is probably not something the Crown would have chosen for us to see."

. . . . .

Arerio peered through the blinds. "They're up to something."

Marguerite looked up from her trumps. "Oh? Now what?"

"They've given up on the gate, but now several groups are gathered along the fence. It looks like they're trying to scale it in multiple spots."

"I suppose I should have played this one sooner." She selected the Moon card and dropped it into its slot.

Arerio's eyebrows shot up. "You certainly were thorough. Every inch of fence is covered, and then some."

Marguerite smiled faintly. "I find it wise to keep my enemies in the dark, though I don't often get the chance to do it quite so literally."

"It does seem to have discouraged them."

"Have they all pulled back yet?"

"I can't tell."

"That's the problem with that card. Once they get over the initial shock, they could start using it to conceal their activities. Here, let's make absolutely sure."

She pried the card back out of the slot.

Arerio moved from one window to the next. "I guess they must be pretty leery of anything Phrendonic, even the harmless stuff. Not a one of them stayed anywhere near that fence."

"Excellent. Perhaps we should reward their wise behavior with a glimpse of what might have happened had they been more cavalier."

She dropped the Sun card into its slot.

Even through the blinds, Arerio had to shade his eyes. "My word. How many Incinerates was that?"

"Leave that to me."

The bars beneath Everson's hands heated and crumbled. He nearly lost his balance. The bars blocking the other passage disintegrated as well.

The nearness of death made him oddly cavalier. "A little warning would have been nice."

"Consider yourself warned."

"You aren't planning to do that at every gate we come to, are you?"

"No, you are. So if there's something you'd rather didn't rust, I suggest staying well away from it for the next hour or so. Now, get moving."

. . . . .

"Looks like you boys have company," the old priest said. "I'll leave you to it."

The Monsignor cringed as he noticed the Church banner on the carriage bouncing its way up the road toward Ranselard Keep. It sailed past the artists' makeshift booths and pulled up next to the Monsignor, cutting off his view of the Crown as well as the conspicuous heresies unfolding across the river. He braced himself as the coachman leapt down and threw open the carriage door.

Laitrech smiled as he emerged into the sunlight. "Armand, what a relief. Cartier said you might be here, but one never knows with you."

The Monsignor nodded curtly. "Ordinal Laitrech and Ordinal Bittern. How unusual. To what do we owe the honor?"

Laitrech glanced at Albert. "Perhaps we should continue this conversation privately. It's about your brother."

"Anything you have to say to me can be safely said in front of Albert."

"So I once thought, but recent events suggest that level of trust may no longer be warranted. I must insist."

The Monsignor sighed—there wasn't time to argue. "Albert, could you please inform the bride I may be delayed."

Once Albert was gone, Laitrech continued. "Your brother is missing. It's not clear whether he left by his own devices or under duress. We were hoping you could help us track him down. He is not a well man."

The Monsignor's brow furrowed. "If my brother is missing and you are here, who's minding the store?"

"Ordinal Lavicius convened an emergency Convocation Ordinalis and got himself voted temporary executive powers."

"That's unexpected. I thought you were the heir apparent."

"There were some unfortunate circumstances surrounding the Primal's disappearance, including the theft of my Relic. That, and my imprisonment in the Chapel may have given the impression I was not fully in control. I'm afraid Lavicius exploited that."

The Monsignor's jaw fell open. "Your Relic was stolen while you were in the Chapel?"

"I'm afraid so. As embarrassing as that was, it does narrow the range of suspects."

"So, you suspect an Ordinal?" The Monsignor took that as good news—at least they weren't after Thurman.

Laitrech shrugged. "I can think of one in particular with plenty of motive, but I have no idea how he induced Albert to cooperate."

"Surely you aren't accusing Albert."

"He was the last person I saw in the Chapel before I lost consciousness, and he came alone. If Lavicius can get to Albert, there's no telling how far he will go. If the Primal isn't found and returned immediately, Lavicius will have all the time he needs to consolidate power. Can we rely on your help to find your brother and return him to his rightful place on the Primal Throne?"

Their suspicion of Albert was still a puzzle. Had he been involved, the Monsignor would surely know. "Out of curiosity, what were the circumstances of Darron's disappearance?"

"It began with erratic behavior. He claimed a demon tried to abduct him. He even went so far as to call in that demon-hunter Theratigan to search the palace. However, when Theratigan failed to turn up any evidence to support those outlandish claims, your brother ordered him confined to the Interrogation Chamber and fled the Palace. While his paranoia could be a consequence of his illness, given Albert's unsettling complicity and the swiftness of Lavicius's bid for power, it's possible some concern for his safety was warranted."

"If that's true, wouldn't it be dangerous for Darron to return?"

"We'd have to take steps to ensure his safety, but return he must, unless, of course, you favor the idea of a Church reborn according to Lavicius's twisted vision."

"One every thirty feet along the entire fence. I hope they appreciate the favor I did them by not using that card first."

"You would have slain a quarter of their force. Could you really bring yourself to do such a thing?"

She had wondered that herself. In some ways it was probably foolish to tip her hand, especially since the Sun effect would take a while to recharge. Perhaps subconsciously she was sparing herself the temptation of using it later in self-defense. She did feel a certain sense of relief now that the temptation was gone. "Let's hope they heed the warning and maintain a healthy distance. In the meantime, I hope they're not afraid of the dark."

She removed the Sun and replaced the Moon. In response, the archery barrage resumed.

"If you've rattled them," Arerio said, "they seem determined not to let it show."

"What are they doing now?"

"They're fighting fire with fire. They've just unloaded a volley of flaming arrows into the roof."

Marguerite fanned the remaining cards. "Intending to smoke us out, eh? Let's see… Ah, here it is, Temperance." The card settled into its slot. "How does it look out there now?"

"I can't see what's happening above us, but the arrows on the lower roofs have snuffed out. That hasn't discouraged them from sending more, though."

"Remember, the spheres prevent them from seeing their targets. They may not realize they aren't making progress."

"Wait, there's another group to the south. They have a horse hooked up to a cart, and they're wheeling it this way."

"What type of cart?" Marguerite strode over to the blinds. "That's no cart, it's a catapult."

Arerio blinked. "They can travel with a catapult?"

"Small ones, yes. They carry the parts and assemble them on site. That's probably why we haven't seen this one sooner."

"What card do you have in that deck to deal with those?"

Marguerite's expression was grim. "I don't."

. . . . .

Inch by inch, Dominick Everson groped his way along the prison passage wall. The coin he clutched offered no solace—its light was immediately eclipsed by the velvet blackness engulfing him. Then, just as he was beginning to suspect the Darkness went on forever, light leaked through his fingers. Holding the coin high, he glimpsed the metal bars of a security gate at the end of the passage. He pulled out his keys and dashed for the gate, daring to believe he'd escaped his crossbow-wielding pursuer—those bars had balked the man once before.

"That's quite far enough, Mr. Everson. Hands where I can see them, please."

Everson froze not five feet from the gate. Raising his hands, he turned slowly. The darkness vanished to reveal the man with the crossbow. The weapon was loaded and aimed in his direction.

"You followed me."

"Of course," Vane said. "I just needed to get far enough away so you'd come out of hiding. Now, if you don't mind, I'm going to need those keys."

The prospect of being trapped in the dungeons of Ranselard with only Bart for company made Everson uncharacteristically bold. "I need them too."

"This crossbow says my need is greater."

"But I can help. I know the way out."

"I was counting on that—but if I don't have those keys in my hand soon, I may change my mind."

"You swear you won't leave me behind?"

"Cross my heart."

He tossed the keys to Vane. "Since you have the weapon, once you get the door open, I think it would be best if I just hang back and give directions."

"I have a better idea. "Why don't you turn around and put your hands against the bars."

Everson felt the walls closing in. "You promised."

Vane leveled the crossbow.

He leaned against the bars. "But I did what you asked."

"Here's how this is going to work. You'll go first, and I'll follow at a distance."

"But you have the keys."

"Well, if I should happen across him, I'll convey your concerns, but as you well know, he has a mind of his own. If my brother is convinced he's better off somewhere else, there may not be much I can do. Now, if you'll excuse me, I have a wedding to finish."

Laitrech's lip curled in frustration. "That's it? We came all this way, and that's the best you have to offer?"

"Contrary to popular belief, I am not my brother's keeper."

"We were hoping you might know where we can find him."

"After all this time playing his nursemaid, surely you know him as well as I do."

A distant echoing crash forestalled Laitrech's reply. "What was that?"

The Monsignor shrugged.

Laitrech turned to look, but the carriage blocked his view. When he waved, the driver pulled away to reveal the ongoing heresies at the Serrola estate in all their splendor.

Laitrech stood blinking, his mouth agape. "Oh, my lord."

. . . . .

"They've struck the carriage house," Arerio said. "The carriage will be a total loss. I'm sorry. I know how much you treasured it."

Marguerite's mind churned in search of alternatives. "We're going to lose a lot more if we can't disable that catapult. Their aim can't be that bad; it was a warning shot."

"Can you Incinerate it?" Arerio asked. "Even if the catapult survived, the operators might not fare as well."

"It's beyond my range. And even if it weren't, killing Inquisitors is out of the question. If Nathan were blamed for it, such a crime could end up turning even his own people against him. No, if I could reach it, I'd sooner shroud it in darkness. Let them try to aim it then."

"What about vesting the Darkness on an arrow and shooting it at the catapult? You could diffract for Summoning up here so that the Darkness didn't take effect until the arrow was well on its way.

"I could, but the Diffraction would also eliminate our mirrored spheres."

"You'd only need to have it in effect long enough to cast the Darkness and shoot the arrow. Surely the blinds would hold long enough for that."

"I don't suppose you recall where Spiros kept his bow?"

Arerio pondered for a moment. "I believe the last time I saw it, it was in the carriage house."

"Figures. Do you recall if there were others anywhere in the house?"

Arerio shook his head. "I expect Master Michlos took his with him when he left."

The house shuddered.

Arerio peered through the blinds. "A direct hit. I can see into the parlor through the hole in the roof."

Marguerite shook her head and pulled out the pillbox. "We can't fight this. It's just a matter of time before they target the cupola."

"Then we must be gone before that happens."

"Gone where? The entire estate is surrounded."

Arerio tugged at the tarp concealing Spiros's invention. "We'll simply have to go over their heads."

"What are you doing?" Marguerite snapped. "Leave that alone."

Arerio pulled away the tarp to reveal a light but sturdy wooden framework covered in places with stretched fabric. Marguerite turned away, tears welling. "Why are you doing this?"

"It's our only chance, and I mean for you to take it."

"But the thing doesn't work. Spiros gave his life proving that. Why would I choose to plummet to my death on the cliffs? The pill would be so much easier."

"I was there. It failed only because he couldn't work up enough speed for the launch. You can fix that. Now, help me, before it's too late."

"But it can only carry one. I can't save myself by throwing you to the jackals. If one of us is to go, it should be you. This whole thing is my fault."

"We can both go, but I need you to start helping now."

"What should I do?"

"There, on the wall opposite the door." He pointed. "We need something evenly spaced across the studs. Four spots should do it—two above and two below the windows. Then you'll need to cast Repels on each."

Marguerite scanned the room. "The tarp," she said at last. "I can cut it into strips."

"Excellent idea. I'll need a strip as well."

She activated one of her rings, and a knife appeared in her hand. She sliced the tarp until she had four roughly even pieces about three-feet square, and another larger one for Arerio.

Arerio inspected his strip and then held it out to Marguerite. "Could I get an Attunement on this please?"

"Decay or instantaneous?"

"Instantaneous."

"Of course." She passed her hand over it. "About these squares," she said. "How do I affix them to the wall?"

Arerio began threading his fabric through the framework along the front of the wings. "I don't know, but make sure they are positioned over the studs."

She dragged the chair to the wall and climbed up on it. With one hand she held up the canvas to the wall, and with the other she plunged the knife through it deep into the stud. She produced another knife and repeated the process until all four strips were skewered into position.

The house rocked.

Marguerite risked a peep through the blinds. "My boudoir!"

"Quickly, bring the chair. Climb into the harness."

She dragged the chair to the framework, but before she climbed up, she rushed to the table. Reaching into the chest, she retrieved a small rectangular case. "I can't leave these—they were a gift from my father."

"Hurry, they're reloading."

She climbed the chair and crawled into the harness.

Arerio pulled open both folding doors.

"You realize they'll riddle this contraption with arrows the minute it leaves the cupola, right?"

"Maybe not," Arerio said. He dragged the chest over and placed it in the center of the doorway. "We'll need two more of your silver spheres."

She nodded. "I think I understand."

He kicked the chair aside. "Start with the Repels—three on each square should do it."

She targeted each of the canvas squares in turn.

"Now the spheres."

Twice more the sun dimmed. "I'm ready. Now, where will you ride?"

He reached up to her. "Take my hand."

Despite growing misgivings, she did as he asked. "This won't work—I can't carry your weight."

"Yes, you can. Suppress Evocation."

Her breath caught. "On what?"

"You know very well on what. Hurry, we don't have much time."

"But we don't know what that will do."

"It's time we found out."

Though her heart recoiled, there was no other choice. Her mind danced through the mnemonics required to Suppress Evocation.

Arerio shuddered in surprise, then erupted in a billowing mass of greasy smoke. Where he had once stood, clothes lay strewn across the floor. A plain gold band glittered in her palm. Blinking back tears, she clenched her fist and focused on the next task.

The chest shot out of the cupola, across the widow's walk, and into the air. As the edge of its sphere passed her, the mirrored surface blocked her view. She heard, rather than saw, a host of crossbowmen let fly their bolts. Before they could reload, Marguerite focused her attention on the strip of wing-woven canvas. An instant later, she and her dead husband's final invention burst from the cupola and launched into the space beyond. Over the roaring wind, the crash of splintering beams reached her as the catapult stone found its mark and the cupola crumpled behind her.

# CHAPTER SIXTEEN

## BY ALL MEANS, MAKE AN APPEARANCE

As the delay dragged on, the heat of Thurman's stare became unbearable, and Dona was forced to excuse herself from the dais. She told the bride and groom she needed water and promised to bring some for Verone, who still struggled for breath against the confines of her corset. When Dona reached the keep, however, she ducked into the anteroom. To her relief, Verone's leather case still held the giftwrapped package.

"What are you doing in here?" Dona's breath caught. It was not a voice she recognized.

In a heartbeat Dona changed her plan and slipped Verone's entire case into the satchel she'd used for the invitations.

She turned and smiled sweetly. "Just fixing my hair." She snapped the satchel closed and extended her hand to the man in the doorway. "I'm Dona. I don't believe we've met."

"Damien. I'm Verone's brother."

"I should have guessed. You have your mother's looks."

Damien's eyes narrowed despite the compliment. "Thanks."

"Well, I should get back to the ceremony. No telling when they'll start up again."

Dona sidled past him into the courtyard. Once safely away, she paused to wait for her heartbeat to slow to its usual pace. After a moment, she caught sight of Miranda's golden curls and excused her way over to her.

"Shouldn't you be up on the dais?" Miranda asked. Next to her, Alphonse and Helena looked equally surprised.

"As soon as I get some water. In the meantime, could you keep track of this for me?"

"Sure." Miranda placed the satchel beneath her seat.

By the time Dona arrived back at the dais, Verone lay stretched across a chair, panting. Rayen fanned her devotedly with a wedding program.

Dona passed her the glass.

"Thank you. Is there any sign of the Monsignor?"

"Not yet. I'm sure it won't be long now, though."

"Can you please see what's keeping him?"

"Of course. I'll be right back."

．．．．．

The approaching cacophony took Michlos by surprise. Apparently, Vane hadn't pried Everson's keys away after all. Instead, he must have decided to simply rust everything in his path. Judging by the groans of collapsing catwalks, he had reached the main gallery. The passage reverberated with the tones of partially rusted bars and beams dropping en masse from gates and infrastructure. Vane was using the strategy Michlos had rejected earlier as too dangerous; there was no telling what all that infrastructure supported.

Concealed behind an upended table, Michlos waited in the antechamber that held the prison's main gate. All his plans relied on inactivating his Amulet, if only for a few moments. The flaw in those plans was now obvious: once Vane's Rust spell reached him, turning off his Amulet for even an instant would allow it to destroy the gate. Of course, he'd previously rusted his way through the gate's lock, but since Vane didn't know that, Michlos was hoping to use it to slow him down. Once Vane got in range, the only way for Michlos to use his skills to protect the gate would be to overpower his own Amulet, and if that didn't work, he'd have no resources left.

A dim pinkish light appeared. It bobbed its way down the center of the gallery toward Michlos, chunks of disintegrating metal cascading around it. Michlos reluctantly resolved to overpower his amulet despite the risks but aborted his mnemonics when something about the way the figure moved seemed off. Vane was given to swaggering, but this person was hunched and furtive.

After a moment, Everson's sour face resolved in the pale light filtering through his clenched fist. He didn't slow until he reached the gate's bars, at which point he ogled them uncomprehendingly. "Why don't they rust?"

Michlos poked his head up and waved him back. "Get away from that gate."

Everson's eyes widened in recognition. "Let me out!"

"Not while Vane is a threat. Now, get back."

"Please, help me. He has a crossbow aimed at me."

"Vane's behind you?"

Everson nodded.

"How far back?"

"I don't know. Please, don't let him kill me."

"The Rust spell," Michlos said. "Is it yours?"

Everson shook his head.

"But it's vested on you?"

He nodded.

Michlos groaned. Once again, Vane's plan was devious. So long as Everson remained at the gate, Michlos and his Amulet had to stay there to keep it from being destroyed. And Everson wouldn't leave so long as he thought Vane was aiming a crossbow at him. He was stuck.

Somewhere in the darkness, Vane cleared his throat. "Ah, there you are, Serrola. And here you had me thinking you'd run all the way home to mother."

Michlos peered over the edge of the table. "It's hopeless, Vane. You can't shoot me, and, as long as I'm here, you can't get out. It's just a matter of time before the Princess sends help."

Vane snorted. "Yes, but how much time?"

"Doesn't matter to me. I've got all the time in the world."

"Maybe you do, but I wonder, can you say the same for your friend here?"

The crossbow hummed. Everson howled, clutched his leg, and dropped. The lighted coin flew from his hand, rolled beneath the gate, and collided with the upturned tabletop before finally coming to rest.

"You have a choice," Vane said. "You can open the gate and try to save him, or you can wait for reinforcements while he bleeds to death.

What's it going to be?"

Michlos scooped up the coin and ducked back behind the table. He slipped it into his cigarette case to douse the light. Next, he unscrewed the rapier's pommel, and the entire weapon evaporated. In utter blackness, he felt his way to the gate. Crouching low, he caught its edge and eased it open, hoping that Everson's screams would cover any sounds it might make.

A bolt whizzed over his head.

"Think you can get it unlocked before I get lucky?" Vane asked.

Michlos grabbed one of Everson's legs and dragged. He prayed he could get him through the gate before Vane reloaded. Everson yowled and squirmed until Michlos touched his hand with a ring. Michlos allowed the gate to crash closed as he dragged Everson's limp form toward the table, desperate to reach it before Vane took another shot.

Instead, the gate flew open as Vane crashed through it—but Michlos was no longer there. Leaving Everson behind the table, he felt his way up the broad stairway that led to the Keep. Then, he froze. He heard Vane fumbling with the crossbow again.

Seizing his chance, Michlos switched off the Amulet and snapped open the cigarette case, bathing the scene in light. Vane's momentary distraction as the gate disintegrated gave Michlos a substantial lead on his mnemonics. Recognizing the danger, Vane tossed the crossbow aside and threw himself at Michlos.

The two men tumbled over each other down the steps. The cigarette case, the coin, and numerous small wands scattered. Michlos got in a swipe with his ring, but to no avail. Vane twisted him into a painful hold. With a growing sense of despair, Michlos realized he didn't have the strength to break free. Vane wrenched him to his feet and roared in triumph—until a new voice cut him off.

"As fun as that looks, Ol' Bart is thinking the two of you ought to call it quits and put your hands in the air." Garbed in ill-fitting Inquisitorial vestments, Bart had set his lantern to one side and had the crossbow at the ready.

Vane whirled, putting Michlos between him and the newcomer. With his considerable strength, Vane then shoved Michlos headlong into Bart. By the time they disentangled, Vane had fled up the stairway.

"Do you know who I am?" Michlos asked.

Once Bart got a good look, he nodded.

"Find Newcomb. Tell him Vane escaped. Also tell him the other Inquisitor has been shot and needs help right away. He's over there behind that table. Got it?"

Bart nodded again. "Where are you headed, then?"

"I'm going after Vane."

.  .  .  .  .

The first thing Dona noticed as she stepped out onto the green was the Monsignor standing near the artists' booths with two men dressed as Ordinals. The three of them stood as if spellbound, staring off into the distance. Following their gaze, she saw a great silver globe floating high above the river, drifting in lazy circles that brought it ever closer to the keep. With each pass, it lost altitude until, after several minutes, it skimmed the water's surface. When at last it splashed down, still a fair distance from shore, the illusion faded to reveal a framework of wood and fabric carrying a single bedraggled passenger.

The Crown Prince stripped off his coronet and shirt and sprinted along the riverbank cliffs. Arriving at an outcropping that extended over the river, he leapt headfirst off the edge in a dive that parted the waters below with only the barest hint of a splash. A collective gasp arose from the onlookers. After a breathless moment, his head broke the surface, and a great cheer rose up from the crowd. He swam to the fallen craft with strong, sure strokes. A few minutes later, he assisted the shivering passenger along the steep path that led up from the riverbank.

"Just who is this heretic?" Bittern asked. "And why would the Crown Prince risk his life for her?"

The Monsignor rubbed his temples. "That, gentlemen, is the Crown Prince's mother-in-law—the inimitable Marguerite Serrola."

When Marguerite made it to the green, Irina was there to wrap her in a cloak and usher her toward the keep. The Monsignor wordlessly met the Crown Prince's defiant gaze as they passed. Princess Julienne and Alexi followed, but Alexi was apparently so distracted by the Princess that the two of them were almost on top of Dona before he noticed her. When he finally did, she was standing before him with her arms crossed, wearing, she hoped, an expression that could wither stone. She noticed with some small satisfaction that he had the grace to blush. Without a word, she turned and stalked back into the keep.

. . . . .

"What's going on out there?" Verone demanded. "What was all that applause? Has no one told them the wedding is supposed to be happening in here?"

Still seething from Alexi's perfidy, Dona spoke before she considered the consequences. "Marguerite Serrola arrived in a huge floating silver bubble that landed in the river. The artists were applauding the Crown Prince's dive into the water to rescue her."

Verone beamed with delight. "Marguerite is here? Did the Monsignor witness all this?"

Verone's reaction jarred something in Dona's memory. She'd just taken away the excuse Verone needed to call off the wedding, but despite that, the woman was smiling ear to ear. Perhaps the escape clause wasn't about getting out of the wedding so much as ensuring Marguerite attended—which meant her uncle was even more of a pawn than she'd first imagined. If she could get Rayen to see that the specter of heresy would forever haunt the scions of House Nevinander, maybe he would have the sense to call off this charade before it was too late.

Dona shot a sidelong glance at her uncle. "Not only did the Monsignor see it, but two Ordinals were with him. One of them even referred to her as a heretic."

Behind the dais, Thurman's ears perked up. "Ordinals? Which ones?"

"I don't know. The only other Ordinal I've ever seen is Isrulian."

"It makes an enormous difference. Were they old or young?"

"They both seemed old to me."

Thurman huffed in exasperation. "I need to go look. If my father returns before I do, tell him I'll be right back."

Dona nodded, more than happy to give him any excuse he needed to leave.

"Speaking of fathers," Verone said, "does mine know his sister has arrived?"

Dona eyed Rayen again. "I don't know, but I doubt he'll be pleased when he finds out. Now that the Church views his sister as a heretic, his whole family will be suspect."

Despite the transparency of the attempt, Dona's warning was clearly lost on Rayen, who, true to form, stared fixedly off into space with barely enough presence of mind to continue fanning his fiancé.

"He isn't having a seizure, is he?" Verone asked.

Dona shrugged.

"Well at this rate, if he doesn't, I will. What does it take for a girl to get a little attention at her own wedding, anyway?"

Dona sighed. "I'll see what I can do."

"Tell the Monsignor that if it's not too much trouble, I'd prefer to be married before the reception."

As Dona stalked down the runner through the restless crowd, she spied Thurman ahead and slowed her pace. The memory of him pointing and crying 'heretic' was etched in her brain. It wasn't a scene she was eager to repeat. She suspected he'd let the matter drop only because he didn't want the Monsignor finding out the circumstances of his meeting in the Respite, but she couldn't rely on that supposition. Farther ahead, the Monsignor appeared, clearly returning, and she relaxed.

But, just as Dona concluded the wedding was on track again, Jonas leapt from the crowd. "Thurman? Is that really you? Why, as I live and breathe, it's Thurman Goodkin, my long-lost brother." Arms thrown wide, Jonas rushed at him.

Thurman blanched and shrank back, but Jonas had already built considerable momentum, too much to sidestep. Thurman raised his arms to protect himself, but undeterred, Jonas wrapped him in a bear hug and lifted him off the ground. "It's so good to see you again."

Thurman yelped and batted him on the head with his signet. Jonas wavered and stumbled, taking Thurman with him.

The Monsignor rushed to help. In moments Thurman was back on his feet. Jonas, however, remained splayed across the runner, unresponsive.

The Monsignor bent for a closer examination. "What's wrong with him? What did you do?"

Thurman broke into a sweat. "He attacked me. You saw him."

"It looked more like he was greeting you. Who is he, anyway?"

The old priest stepped forward. "That is Jonas Mapleton Harcourt."

The Monsignor's eyed the fallen man in surprise. "Francesca's son?"

The old priest nodded.

Thurman eyed his father incredulously. "You mean, you know him?"

The Monsignor shook his head. "I only know of him. He's the son of one of the leaders of the Caprian Heretics."

"See. He was attacking me."

The old priest raised an eyebrow at the Monsignor. "Don't you think it's time he knew the truth? If you don't tell him, I will."

"The timing is a little awkward," the Monsignor said.

The old priest stooped to examine Jonas. "The timing is always awkward. Hasn't this little deception of yours caused this family enough anguish?"

"Well, we are in the middle of a wedding," Thurman said.

"Shut up, Thurman."

Thurman reddened, but held his tongue.

"All right," the Monsignor said. "Thurman, I've been meaning to tell you for some time now…"

The old priest tapped a toe. "Get to the point."

"Oh, very well. Your mother didn't die in childbirth. That was a little white lie meant to spare your feelings."

"How does that spare my feelings?"

"The woman abandoned you the day you were born," the old priest said. "Some people might find that traumatic."

"She could still be alive?"

The Monsignor shook his head. "Sadly, she recently passed."

"You mean all this time I could have known her?"

The Monsignor shook his head. "I didn't know where she was. I only found out after she was gone."

"You didn't know, because you didn't look," the old priest said. "I've known for quite some time, but I foolishly promised to let you tell Thurman in your own time."

"Who was she?" Thurman asked.

"Francesca Harcourt," the Monsignor said. "She was this man's mother as well."

"You mean, he really is my brother?"

"I'm afraid so."

"He has a sister too, doesn't he."

The Monsignor nodded. "Mathilda Harcourt. Of course, that makes her your sister as well."

Thurman swallowed hard. "My mother—did she by any chance also live at that brothel?"

The Monsignor paused for a moment that grew long enough to become uncomfortable. "We can talk about all this later, once we've attended to your brother. Will he be all right?"

"He'll be fine," the old priest said, "though he might be unconscious for a while. We should move him someplace less conspicuous."

"I need to know," Thurman persisted. "Did she live at the brothel?"

Thurman's repeated reminders of the senseless tragedy of Nanna's final lullaby fueled Dona's rage and made her reckless. "She did until she was killed in a Church-led raid a couple weeks ago."

Thurman turned to the Monsignor. "Is that true?"

The Monsignor looked away. "I would have spared you this."

The color drained from Thurman's face. "So Mathilda was right. I caused my own mother's death."

"Unintended consequences often burden those of us called to serve through leadership," the Monsignor said gently.

Dona snorted. "Called to serve? You might want to ask him what those Inquisitors were looking for in that raid."

"I fail to see how this is any of your business, young lady," the old priest snapped.

"It's my business because I was there. I saw first-hand the disregard for their property, their dignity, and ultimately, their lives…and for what?" She rounded on Thurman. "Go ahead. Tell your father what was so important that your mother had to pay for it with her life."

"Thurman," the old priest said, "you're the proud son of a house of Primals and Ordinals. You don't need to take this abuse. I think it's time we went someplace where people are more a little more appreciative of the sacrifices we make for them."

The Monsignor stayed them with a raised hand. "Actually, I'd like to hear his answer."

The old priest gaped at the Monsignor. "The boy just lost his mother."

"Yes, and I'd like to know why."

Thurman massaged his temples. "They were only supposed to collect on a debt."

"Harcourt owed you money?"

Thurman paused, and then shook his head. "This is not a matter appropriate for public discussion."

"Grave robbing never is," Dona said.

The Monsignor's eyes widened. "Grave robbing?"

"If you're so concerned about it," the old priest said, "I suggest you talk to Laitrech. He authorized the transaction."

The Monsignor turned on the old priest. "You mean you were in on this too?"

The old priest shrugged. "I thought the Harcourts could use the money."

The Monsignor struggled to maintain composure. "First, I have a wedding to perform. Then, the three of us will have a little chat in which the two of you are going to tell me exactly what's going on here. And then, I'll decide whether this matter warrants appointment of an independent investigator."

Albert pushed his way through the crowd and spied Jonas, who still lay sprawled on the runner. "What happened here?"

"A misunderstanding," the Monsignor said.

Albert kneeled to examine Jonas. After a few moments he rose, his brow furrowed with ill-concealed anxiety. "Exactly what kind of misunderstanding are we talking about?"

"Thurman mistook this man's overly familiar greeting for an attack. Defending himself, he hit him in the head. I saw it happen—it didn't look like he was hit that hard."

"Are you saying Thurman did this?"

The Monsignor nodded. "You look troubled. Are you all right?"

Albert seized Thurman's hand. Samulian's Signet glittered on his finger. "And where did you get this?"

"Father Anton gave it to me."

Albert eyed the old priest. "Oh, did he? Armand, we need to talk."

"We're having a meeting right after the wedding. Can it wait until then?"

Albert slipped on a pair of white gloves. "All right, hand it over."

Thurman sheepishly removed the ring, and Albert tucked it away in a cloth pouch. Then he nodded to the Monsignor. "Now it can, but don't put it off any longer."

"What was that?" the Monsignor asked.

"We'll talk about it later. What happened to Laitrech and Bittern?"

"I told them the wedding was by invitation only. I also reminded them that there were security concerns because of the Crown's presence and that they might want to try back at a better time."

The old priest chuckled. "I bet that didn't sit well."

"No, it didn't, but I'm not about to give them access to Darron under these circumstances. My biggest fear is they'll just wait it out, since I'm sure they suspect he will try to contact me at some point."

The mass of gawkers parted to reveal Verone, her veils thrown back and a fist on each hip. "I hate to be a bother, really I do, but if this wedding doesn't resume this instant, I am removing this corset."

Newcomb pushed his way past her, accompanied by two guards and a stretcher.

"My sincere apologies," the Monsignor said. "Perhaps now that this situation is in capable hands, we can pick up where we left off." Raising his voice, he addressed the crowd. "If everyone would please take their seats, we can try this one more time."

As people shuffled back to their places, Nathalie cued the musicians. The wedding march blared once more, silencing the well-mannered attendees, drowning out the rest, and putting everyone on notice that the wedding was finally moving forward again. Once the Monsignor was in position, he signaled for quiet and waited for the Princess's cue. When she nodded, he began.

"Ladies and gentlemen, I'd like to welcome you all to this ceremony to join Veronique Nevinander and Rayen Theratigan in holy matrimony. Before we begin, let me address an issue that has no doubt been troubling some of you. I assure you all that despite the delicate diplomatic relationship between the Church and this island, the Primal himself has bestowed his blessing on this union. Let there be no doubt as to its validity."

As the Monsignor launched into the scripted portions of the ceremony, Dona scanned for any sign of Alexi or the royal harlot pretending to be his friend. Instead, a figure in a simple white tunic caught her eye as he stepped out from the keep. At first, he seemed startled by the commotion in the courtyard, but, when his gaze lit on the Monsignor, he smiled. It was not, Dona decided, the sort of smile to warm the cockles of the heart. To her amazement, he changed course and stalked down the runner toward the dais. His pace quickened, but only slightly, when Michlos burst out of the keep behind him. The Princess rose from her mother's throne to signal the guards, but still the man pressed forward.

At the dais, the man dropped to one knee and bowed his head. His voice thundered through the courtyard. "Monsignor Goodkin, I formally request asylum from unjust persecution."

The Monsignor paused to squint at the supplicant. "Vane? What are you doing here?"

"I seek the protection of the Church. I have uncovered the identities of powerful Phrendonic Heretics who would silence me before I can unmask them."

Dona expected Verone to be furious, but she was tolerating this latest interruption with uncharacteristic grace. Her little half-smile even put in an appearance.

Guards with crossbows converged on the dais.

"It's all right," the Monsignor told them. "I know this man."

The guards did not stand down.

The Monsignor addressed the Princess. "Is this really necessary? He is an Inquisitor."

The Princess was unmoved.

"The heretics are wily and influential," Vane said. "One can hardly blame Her Highness for being cautious."

"Your Highness, I beg you, have your men lay down their arms," the Monsignor said. "Don't permit this provocation to become a tragedy."

Still, the Princess hesitated. "If what this man says is true, the crossbows may be a necessary precaution until we can get him somewhere more secure."

"On the contrary," the Monsignor said. "Crossbows are unlikely to afford much protection against such heretics. But, if you consider the matter for a moment, a far more effective alternative may suggest itself."

"Oh, how clever of you to remember. We can use it to escort Mr. Vane to a safe place and revisit the issue once the ceremony is complete."

Vane rose. "Monsignor, the heretics could have spies anywhere. There's no safer place for me right now than at your side."

"In case you haven't noticed, I am trying, against all odds, to perform a wedding here. If you are really that concerned for your safety, my son Thurman can accompany you."

"If I am killed, my evidence against Marguerite Serrola dies with me."

"Oh, Marguerite Serrola, is it? If that's all the evidence you've got, you're at no greater risk than most of the people here."

Vane raised an eyebrow. "In which case, I guess there's no compelling reason for me to leave after all."

"Not necessarily," the Princess said. "This is a private ceremony. Admission is by invitation only. Since the Monsignor is of the opinion that you aren't in any significant danger, the guards will escort you out."

"If I may, Your Highness," the Monsignor said, "I humbly request Inquisitor Vane be permitted to stay. As Inquisitor General, I have an obligation to hear him out. I am happy to vouch for him, at least until the ceremony is over."

Verone chimed in. "Rayen and I have no objections."

The Princess frowned deeply. "Very well, but make sure he remains well protected for the duration of his stay. Should any heresies befall him, I shall be most displeased."

The Monsignor nodded deferentially. "Thank you, Highness." He then beckoned Thurman to the dais. "Stay with him at all times. You are not to let him out of your reach under any circumstances. Understood?"

Thurman nodded.

Sparing a glance at Michlos leaning casually against an out-of-the-way statue, the Monsignor continued, his voice so low Dona could barely make it out. "I don't know what's going on here, but we're in over our heads. Before this ceremony is over, I want the two of you to sneak out, find Darron, and get him as far away from Trifienne as possible."

"Where?" Thurman whispered back. "The Holy City isn't safe."

The Monsignor said something into Thurman's ear, and he nodded. Then, Thurman and Vane seated themselves in a pair of empty chairs on the groom's side.

As the Monsignor apologized for the interruption, the Princess resumed her seat. To Dona, she seemed unduly restless. Her eyes, which kept straying back to Vane, conveyed an abundance of alert concern. On anyone else, she'd have called it fear.

# CHAPTER SEVENTEEN

# I DO'S AND DON'TS

Professor Reston shook his head as guards hauled Jonas out of the courtyard on a stretcher. *You just couldn't let it go, could you?*

The ceremony had resumed, and Reston was no closer to finding his book than when he'd arrived. He toyed with leaving Jonas to his fate but abandoned that strategy once he considered how much damage the man could cause if interrogated. Hoping he wasn't as obvious as he felt, he tagged along after the stretcher. No one questioned him, even after several corridors, a set of stairs, and entry into what had to be the Keep's infirmary. The room had several beds stationed along the wall, all of which faced the courtyard through gothic-arched windows that held clear glass. Heavy curtains dangled from a stout rod along the wall. They were all pushed aside, allowing the light to stream in.

Two amber-clad sisters tried gently to rouse Jonas, but when that failed, they inspected his scalp for signs of trauma. They'd barely begun when he opened his eyes and sat up, giving both Sisters quite a scare.

"Jonas, what are you doing up here?" Reston asked. "You're missing the ceremony."

Jonas leapt off the stretcher and grabbed Reston by the shoulders. "Tell me the Monsignor caught him this time. It was perfect—he had to be blind to miss it."

Reston removed Jonas's hands from his person and shook his head. "It's like I told you. Some wrongs simply don't have a right."

"It happened right in front of him."

Reston pointed at the windows. "Look for yourself."

Jonas rushed over and peered out.

"That bastard. He's just sitting there like nothing happened."

"Officially, I'm sure nothing did. Now, can we please go back downstairs?"

Guards rushed in with yet another stretcher. "Coming through!"

Apparently convinced Jonas no longer needed them, the Sisters ministered to their new charge. Reston was ushering Jonas out the door when the new patient suddenly struck him as familiar.

A doubletake confirmed his suspicions. "Hold up a second. That's Everson."

"Really?" Jonas said. "What are the chances?"

"Hmm. Maybe we're getting somewhere after all."

The Sisters' quick examination revealed a crossbow bolt protruding from his calf—but they were still puzzled by his lack of responsiveness. He wasn't especially pale, and there were no other signs of shock. They began searching his scalp for evidence of trauma.

Jonas stroked his chin. "You don't suppose…"

"I was just thinking that myself," Reston said.

Engaged as they were in examining their patient, the sisters didn't notice Reston's muttered counterspell, but Everson's sudden anguished wail was harder to miss.

"Maybe that wasn't such a good idea after all," Jonas said.

"I need to talk to him. I can't do that when he's asleep."

"You can't do it while he's screaming, either. Can't you do something for his pain?"

Reston shrugged. "I'm a magician, not a doctor."

"Well, if they chloroform him, he won't be terribly chatty, either."

Reston strode to Everson's bedside. "How's the patient doing?"

Everson groaned. "Reston, is that you?"

"I'm here, Dominick."

Everson latched on to Reston's arm. "You've got to save me. I'll do whatever you say, but don't let her get me."

"Slow down. Who shot you?"

"Some guy named Vane, but I just got in his way. It's Verone—"

"Your girlfriend?"

"She's not my girlfriend. She made that up as a cover. She was teaching me stuff you weren't willing to."

"In return for what?"

"Errands."

"What kind of errands?"

"She was never very clear on that."

"Was pursuing Miss Merinne and the book one of these errands?"

Everson nodded. "She threatened to turn us all over to the Inquisition if I didn't do what she said. I had no choice."

"What else did she have you do?"

"I made one other delivery, but that's it. I swear."

One of the sisters gently interrupted. "We are going to remove the shaft from his leg. He'll need chloroform."

"Please, just one more minute," Reston said.

She nodded. "But no longer."

Reston turned back to Everson. "What did you deliver?"

"A package. I don't know what was in it."

"Who was it for?"

"One of the Hathaway Scholars. Shoruga, I think. The Darkness wasn't my fault. She tricked me—told me to break the stick if I ran into trouble. How was I supposed to know it would do that?"

"Are you saying she deliberately tricked you into bringing the Inquisition down on us?"

Everson nodded.

"Why?"

"I swear I don't know. Will you take me back? I can't marry her, she'll kill me."

"Marry her? What are you talking about?"

"The wedding—she's going to blackmail me into marrying her."

"I can reassure you there. She's getting married right outside that window as we speak, but not to you. Unless she somehow gets rid of groom number one in the next few minutes, I think you're safe."

"Wait, you mean she's not after me?"

"Sorry to disappoint you."

The Sister raised her eyebrows, and Reston nodded for her to proceed.

Everson finally seemed to relax a little. "Who's the poor schmuck?"

"Miss Merinne's uncle."

The Sister laid a white cloth across Everson's mouth.

Jonas nudged Reston. "Don't forget the book."

"Oh, that's right. Everson, where would she keep the book?"

"The book? I don't know—I never got it."

"No, but if she had gotten it, where would she keep it?"

"I don't know," Everson said groggily.

"I'm sorry," the Sister said. "We can't wait any longer. Would you gentlemen please step outside."

One look at Everson convinced him there was no point in arguing.

"Um, that probably wasn't one of those situations where you wanted to save the best for last," Jonas said.

"This from the man who bets his life that the Inquisitor General will declare his own son a heretic?"

The sister pointed at the door. "Gentlemen, outside!"

. . . . .

Dona could not remember a more uncomfortable wedding. The only person who wasn't on tenterhooks was Rayen, but that was hardly reassuring. Verone was breathing in great gasps, no doubt wondering if she would make it through without fainting. In the front row sat Verone's father, his keen eye fixed on his daughter in a constant vigil for signs she was starting to crack. Michlos stood far in the back, exchanging helpless glances with the Princess, who struggled to look regal despite the dread in her eyes. Even the Monsignor seemed to find it difficult to keep his mind on the task at hand. His attention periodically wavered from the ceremony to his son, and then to one of the squat towers that loomed over the courtyard. Dona didn't even need to look to see how her mother was faring. She would be biting her nails in fear that Rayen was on the brink of another seizure.

And then the music started. Dona knew in a heartbeat this was not the selection listed in the program, and from the sudden silence of the crowd, they did too. The melody soared on the wings of Gregory's flawless tenor, simple and in its own way, haunting:

> *He lived, an aimless man alone, who pined to not*
> *be on his own*
> *But fate had dealt a cruel hand, or so it seemed*

*He dreamed, and in the dream revealed, a sign to say*
*his fate was sealed*
*Though not how others understand, but as he'd*
*dreamed*
*And as the lonely years flew by, he felt the fateful*
*day draw nigh*
*You smiled, and all at once he knew, it was upon him*
*And now you're standing at his side, about to be his*
*lovely bride*
*To him, a perfect dream come true, not just a fond*
*whim*
*He'll prize the life you'll both create, he'll thank his*
*lucky stars for fate*
*And when it is his turn to go, he will go smiling*

Verone raised an eyebrow at the man standing next to her. "I take it this is your doing?"

Rayen smiled shyly. "I know ceremonies aren't your cup of tea, but I wanted to surprise you with something special, so if you ever find yourself looking back on this day, you'll smile. Are you upset?"

A strange expression came over Verone's face. Had it been any-one else, Dona would have thought she was blinking back tears. "It's lovely."

"Will you smile, do you think?"

Verone turned away.

Rayen took her hand. "I'm so sorry. I would never have done it had I known it would upset you."

Verone stiffened at his touch. She slowly turned to stare at the hand that now held hers.

In the front row, Alistair's triumphant little half-smile reappeared.

Verone took a deep breath and set her jaw. Trembling, she placed her other hand deliberately over Rayen's. "That's the single sweetest thing anyone has ever done for me. How could I possibly be upset?"

Rayen beamed. "So, you will smile?"

And then, she did smile. "Every single day." She squeezed his hand. "Let's get this done."

Back in the audience, Alistair's smile suddenly faded.

. . . . .

"Very well then," the Monsignor said. "Please turn to face your friends and family."

Hand in hand, Verone and Rayen obliged. In looking out over the crowd, Verone's eye fell on her father, and she permitted herself a smug little grin. As satisfying as her father's discomfort was, she found her gaze suddenly drawn to Damien sitting next to him. Instead of the transfixed look of horror she'd anticipated at this, the penultimate moment of his disinheritance, his rapt attention was fixed somewhere on the battlements.

"Today," the Monsignor said, "Verone and Rayen ask your love and support as they begin the journey of their lives together. While they look forward to being there to help each other along the way, they know that, as with any journey, there will be times when they must depend on the charity of others. Can they rely on you to be there for them in their times of need?"

Despite the crowd's lackluster response, the Monsignor forged ahead. "Rayen, do you take Veronique to be your wife, to love and to cherish, in sickness and in health, until death do you part?"

"I most certainly do."

Verone followed Damien's line of sight to figure out what could possibly be so fascinating. And then, she saw it.

"Veronique," the Monsignor said. "Do you take Rayen to be your husband, to love and to cherish, in sickness and in health, until death do you—"

In an explosion of tulle and white silk, Verone launched herself at Rayen, knocking him to the dais. As a result, she occupied the space where Rayen had just been as the dart struck her, penetrating deep into her corset. She looked at it in shock and sank to her knees. Instantly at her side, Rayen laid her gently down. Nathalie shrieked and dashed up toward her, with Alistair right behind.

"There," the Princess cried, pointing to a man on the battlements. "Don't let him escape!"

His cover blown, the assassin brazenly pulled a notched stick from his doublet and snapped it in two. He wailed as a searing flash of heat and light engulfed him. Five times the broken stick flared. When it was done, all that remained was a smoldering corpse.

In the courtyard, frantic guests mobbed the exit. On the dais, Rayen rocked Verone, who had gone as pale as her dress, while her parents, Dona, and the Monsignor gathered round.

Alistair had gone rather pale himself. "Well, I guess this means the wedding is off. Such a pity."

"Not so fast," Dona said. "Shouldn't that be up to her?"

"She doesn't seem to be in any condition to finish."

"Wait," Rayen said, "she's trying to say something."

Weakly, Verone beckoned Alistair closer, and then closer still. When at last he drew near enough to feel her fading breath on his cheek...

"*I do*, you bastard." Then she shuddered and lay still.

. . . . .

"Now what?" Reston asked.

Although the hallway had no windows, cries from the courtyard made it plain something untoward was happening.

"I have no idea," Jonas said, "but it might be better if we didn't stay to find out."

"I think you may be right. Downstairs and to the left, I believe."

"Where are the stairs anyway?"

"Around the next corner."

"I don't suppose there's a back entrance?"

"From a prison? I doubt it."

"Well, we are a little out of place here. The less we stand out, the less likely someone will try to scapegoat us for whatever's going on."

Reston huffed. "Good thing you've kept such a low profile, then."

"Shh." Jonas ducked into a room stacked floor-to-ceiling with works of art. "Quick, in here. Someone's coming."

"Are you always this paranoid?"

Jonas yanked him in and clamped a hand over Reston's mouth until footsteps on the stairs finally quelled his objections.

A familiar voice echoed down the corridor: "They put him up here, since it's so close to the infirmary."

Jonas's lip curled. "Thurman."

"Is he ill, then?" Thurman's companion asked.

Reston didn't recognize the voice. "Who's with him?"

Jonas whispered, "no idea."

"Not ill," Thurman said. "Poisoned. We think Ordinal Laitrech was behind it—we had to sneak him out of the palace."

"Is Laitrech in charge, then?"

"We didn't stick around to find out, though my father did just meet with some Ordinals outside. I imagine he's got a better idea what's going on back home than I do."

"Which Ordinals?"

Thurman's response was muffled as he and his companion ducked into one of the many rooms that lined the corridor.

Jonas smirked. "I told you it was the Primal."

So Jonas had been right after all. Reston hardly viewed that as cause for celebration. It probably meant Jonas would need even closer watching. "Don't get any harebrained ideas."

"You mean like crashing a wedding officiated by the Inquisitor General to steal a heretical text?"

"You know what I mean. Now, get moving. The coast won't stay clear for long."

Jonas stepped back into the hallway.

Reston paused to listen. "The commotion is not letting up."

"Maybe we can lose ourselves in the confusion."

"For that, we'd need to arrive sometime before it's over."

Jonas shot Reston an exasperated look. "It's called stealth. If we just run willy-nilly through the hallways, there's no telling what kind of hot water we'll get ourselves… Whoa!"

Jonas stopped short of colliding with Michlos, who stood, arms crossed, at the top of the stairs.

"What are you two doing here?"

"Dona invited us," Jonas lied. "Didn't she tell you?"

"Must have slipped her mind. Since you're here, I could use your help."

"Actually, we were just on our way out."

"Ignore him," Reston said. "What do you need?"

"A diversion. I need to get Vane away from Thurman."

"Who's Vane?"

"A rogue 'Enforcer' masquerading as an Inquisitor. He and Thurman came up these stairs just moments ago."

Jonas sucked his teeth. "Hmm—does Thurman know this?"

"I very much doubt it."

"So, I suppose it would be a bad thing for him to take this Vane person to meet the Primal then, wouldn't it?"

"What? Are you trying to give me nightmares?"

"Actually," Reston said, "I think he's saying Thurman is doing precisely that. We overheard Thurman coming up the stairs. According to him there's been an attempt on the Primal's life, and they brought him here in secret. He's hiding out on the other side of that door."

Michlos shook his head. "That can't be true—I'd have known. She never would have kept that from me."

Jonas raised a hand, listening. "Somebody's coming."

Reston herded them back into the storage room with time to spare—Nathalie's gut-wrenching sobs gave ample warning of the wedding party's approach. Newcomb led, bearing the front of Verone's stretcher. Rayen bore the other end, and various members of the wedding party trailed solemnly behind.

Jonas peeped through the crack in the door as the entire procession disappeared into the infirmary. "Was that Verone they were carrying?"

"I'm afraid so," Michlos said. "She took an assassin's dart intended for her groom."

"At her own wedding? I was no great fan of the lady, but…"

"Who would want to hurt Miss Merinne's uncle?" Reston asked. "A more innocuous man I've never met."

Michlos shrugged. "Pick a Nevinander. Verone was set to take possession of her father's estate upon her marriage."

Jonas whistled softly. "The whole estate?"

Michlos nodded.

Jonas scratched his head. "If they were going to do him in, wouldn't it have made more sense to do it before they were married?"

"I expect that was the plan, but it seems Verone had other ideas."

"How can you be so sure?"

Michlos eyed Jonas quizzically. "About what?"

"About the supposed plan. Maybe the uncle wasn't the intended target after all. I can think of several people who stand to benefit quite handsomely from things turning out exactly the way they did. In fact, I'm beginning to think we've been seriously underestimating our sweet, innocent little Miss Merinne."

"I swear," Reston said. "If you caught a man stealing candy from a baby, you'd find a way to blame the child. How many times must we go over this? Miss Merinne is a victim here."

"You mean because she suddenly finds herself in line to inherit the entire Nevinander estate? Would that I could be so victimized."

Down the hall, a door burst open. Thurman backed through the doorway, nodding. "Yes, Your Primacy. I'll see to it immediately."

A raised voice pursued him. "And while you're at it, tell him I am not about to waste my second chance cowering in some god-forsaken monastery in the middle of nowhere."

"I will, Your Primacy."

"Also tell him I'm through with his excuses. I will elevate him to Ordinal, and this time, he will accept."

"Yes, Your Primacy."

"And don't be all day about it."

"I'll bring him right back, I promise." The door slammed.

Thurman planted his face in his palm and sighed. Then, he headed down the stairs.

"It seems you have your distraction," Jonas said, "courtesy of the Primal himself."

Michlos blanched. "Did Vane leave with him?"

"Nope. He must still be in there."

"Figures."

"What? Are you worried the Primal will protect him?"

"Let me put it this way. Vane has a history of brutally murdering people and making it look like someone else did the deed."

Reston's jaw dropped. "You don't think he'd kill the Primal?"

"I really wish I could rule it out."

Jonas shrugged. "Isn't that what Enforcers do? Besides, given the blood on the Primal's hands, Vane could hardly have found anyone more deserving."

"You don't get it." Michlos said. "What if he were to frame the Crown for it?"

"Why would he?"

"To forever bury his secret. If the Crown becomes the enemy, accusations we level against him as a heretic become completely self-serving."

Jonas waved dismissively. "So what? It's not like you'd be willing to give him up. He'd just turn right around and point the finger at you."

"Oh, we certainly wouldn't give him up willingly. But the Inquisition has a knack for getting around little obstacles like that."

"But he wouldn't reveal your secrets either—it works both ways."

"Normally I'd be inclined to agree, except for one picky little detail. Less than an hour ago, in the middle of the courtyard, in front of the entire wedding, that's exactly what he did."

# CHAPTER EIGHTEEN

# ONE LAST CHANCE

The Sister held the dart up to the light. "It looks to be of Drewor make—crude, but effective. I have no way of knowing what toxin it held, and there are precious few for which any treatments are known."

Nathalie dabbed her eyes. "There must be something we can do."

"We can make her comfortable and hope she's strong enough to pull through. But it does not look hopeful."

The old priest stepped forward. "May I?"

"Of course."

The old priest examined the dart carefully and abruptly snapped it in half, then sniffed one of the broken ends and frowned. "Sjigela. The Drewors brew it from a rare mushroom. It has a distinctive musky scent, and in this form, is highly toxic. Dispose of this carefully."

"But is there a treatment?" Nathalie asked.

The old priest paused a moment. "Possibly."

"Then what are you waiting for?"

"You do understand—it may not work."

"What are her chances if we do nothing?"

The Sister shrugged. "Judging by her current symptoms, I would guess slim at best."

"Then do it."

The old priest raised an eyebrow. "I cannot guarantee there will not be…complications."

"She's dying," Nathalie said. "Whatever the complications are, they can't be worse than that."

"Very well, but before I begin, I have two conditions. First, since the lady is his relative, I shall require the express consent of the Crown Prince—in person."

"I'll drag him up here bodily if I have to. And the second condition?"

"For something this experimental, I dare not proceed without the Primal's blessing."

"But that could take days. She won't last."

"Nonsense. The Primal is somewhere in the building. I saw him this morning."

"If he's here, I'll find him."

Rayen touched Nathalie's shoulder. "I'll go. You should stay with her."

"No," Dona said. "I'll go. You both should stay in case there's any change."

"Alistair can go with you," Nathalie said, looking around. "Wait, where has he gone?"

"He wasn't with us when we came up the stairs," Dona said. "I'll just go."

"Do hurry," the old priest said. "She doesn't have much time left."

. . . . .

"What do you mean it's not here?" Alistair said. He had no time for excuses. Too much of a delay, and Nathalie would surely notice he was missing. "She had it with her this morning, and she certainly wasn't carrying it during the ceremony. It must be here."

"And I'm telling you it's not." Damien said. "As you can see, it's a tiny room. I've searched it twice. There aren't that many places it could be."

"Well, if it's not here, someone else must have gotten to it first. Who would be so low as to steal the bride's belongings on her wedding day?"

"How about that vagrant husband of hers? Probably couldn't wait to get his filthy hands on her stuff."

Alistair shook his head. "Not the type. Besides, he never left my sight all morning."

"How about the girl then? The maid of honor. Wasn't she the vagrant's niece or something? I caught her snooping around in here when I fetched your reading glasses."

"There's no way she could have concealed it up on the dais."

"No, but when she left the room, she was carrying a satchel."

"A satchel? How big?"

"Big enough to hold Verone's documents and then some."

"What could she have done with it?"

"What all women do when they can't watch their own bag—have a friend watch it for her."

Alistair needed those documents. "Would you recognize this satchel if you saw it again?"

"I think so."

"I can think of several people she might have left it with. She's friends with the tenor who sang during the ceremony, but she also pals around with the constable's daughter. There's also the girl who made her dress for the ceremony, and I think she has a boyfriend as well. They should all be around here somewhere."

"How am I supposed to find them in all this chaos?"

"Start with the tenor. He can probably lead you to the others—and Damien?"

"Yes?"

"Just so there's no misunderstanding—everything rides on this."

. . . . .

Dona found Princess Celeste supervising a mostly empty courtyard littered with upended chairs as her guards struggled to extinguish a fire ignited by the assassin's immolation. She welcomed Dona with a sympathetic hug.

"I'm so sorry about all of this. How is Verone doing?"

"Not well. The Sisters hold out little hope."

"This is my fault. I should never have permitted the wedding to go forward. It's not like we weren't warned."

"You can't blame yourself for the misdeeds of others—that's how they win."

"Look around and tell me they haven't."

"They haven't—at least not yet. That's why I'm here. Father Anton says he may have a way to counteract the poison, but he needs the consent of both the Crown and the Primal."

"Who's Father Anton?"

"The old priest who was sitting next to Father Albert during the ceremony."

"And why would an old priest have any more expertise treating poisons than the Sisters do?"

"I have my suspicions. Besides, the Sisters have all but given up on her. This may be her only chance."

"And Nathalie is going along with this?"

"She sent me."

"I must warn you, the Primal is not well—the Monsignor asked he not be disturbed."

"I can't imagine he wouldn't make an exception to save a life."

"Let's talk to the Crown first. His party is still in the marquee. Then we can swing by the Primal on the way to the infirmary. This way."

Dona tried to remain patient as Celeste strode across the courtyard. She understood it was unbecoming for a Princess to break into a run in front of her subjects, but she had hoped the pressing nature of the situation might merit an exception.

Although engaged in a heated discussion with Count Laslo and the Crown Princess, the Crown rose to receive Celeste.

"My apologies and my condolences." Nathan said. "I am personally mortified by today's events and the role my family played in them."

"It's not your fault," Celeste said.

Irina welcomed the Princess with a warm embrace. "I think you should know before you judge too harshly that my mother's unconventional arrival was precipitated by an unprovoked attack on her estate. The mansion was destroyed, and she barely escaped with her life."

Celeste's jaw dropped. "Who would dare?"

Nathan and Irina exchanged troubled glances. "The Inquisition, or so it would seem," Nathan said at last.

Celeste went ashen. "It's to be war, then?"

"Try as I might, I'm having trouble envisioning any other reasonable alternative."

"So Michlos was right. When he tried to warn me, I scoffed at him."

"He knew about this? What did he tell you?"

Marguerite strode through a door at the back of the marquee. "Most likely Michlos told her that Verone was behind a plot to overthrow the Crown."

Nathan's jaw dropped. "Verone? Why would she want to do that?"

"We thought she was trying to put herself in line to inherit my estate. If so, things worked out less well than she'd hoped. It seems such a lot of trouble to go to for a pile of rubble."

"Mother, shouldn't you be resting?" Irina said gently. "You've had quite a shock."

Marguerite waved her off. "Oh, I'm fine. I was just a little chilled."

"Speaking of Michlos," Nathan said, "where is he?"

Celeste shrugged. "I suspect he's keeping an eye on Vane—at least, I hope he is."

Marguerite raised an eyebrow. "Down in his cell, you mean?"

"No—Vane escaped, and the Monsignor granted him asylum. Didn't you see? It happened right in the middle of the ceremony. Once again, Michlos had the right of it, and I foolishly overruled him."

Nathan looked shocked. "The Monsignor granted a heretic asylum?"

"Vane's been masquerading as an Inquisitor. I'm sure the Monsignor has no idea he's a heretic, and since Vane saw me at the Academy, I couldn't very well be the one to call him out."

"Never mind that," Marguerite said. "Where is he now?"

"I don't know. I lost track of him when Verone was attacked. And then the fire broke out. He could be anywhere."

Dona could contain herself no longer. "I don't mean to be impolite, Your Highness, but we don't have much time."

Celeste sighed. "The situation has become substantially more complex, but I suppose you're right. We should at least give Nathan the option while it still remains open."

"Option for what?" Nathan asked.

"Verone still lives, but the Sisters believe it is just a matter of time. An old priest thinks there may be a way to save her but is unwilling to proceed without your permission."

"After everything she's done? I'm afraid she's on her own."

Irina touched his arm. "Are you sure you want to make this decision out of anger? Remember, much of what we think is happening is based only on conjecture. We don't truly know the extent of her involvement or what her intentions were. What if it should turn out you were wrong?"

"Even after all she put your mother through?"

"Mother has lost only things. Things can be replaced."

Marguerite bristled. "As usual, your mother doesn't see things as being quite so simple."

"You agree then," Nathan said. "We should wash our hands of that woman."

"I didn't say that. As convinced as I am of Verone's complicity, there's a part of me that would regret never being able to look her in the eye and ask the question 'why.'"

# CHAPTER NINETEEN

## TANGLED WEBS

Jonas grumbled as he inspected one of several doors to the suite of rooms occupied by the Primal. Rarely had he felt more useless or expendable. While Reston was sent off to find some guard named Newcomb to bring help, Jonas was instructed to check the other doors to make certain they were locked. Ostensibly the task was calculated to cut off alternative avenues of escape, but Jonas knew better—it was clearly intended to get him out from underfoot. Not that he particularly minded actually being expendable, but the perception was beginning to rankle.

Once he'd established all the doors were locked, there wasn't much else for him to do, which suited him fine. This wasn't his fight anyway. What did he care what happened to the Primal or the Enforcer? No matter how grisly their fates, both had it coming. Sadly, the only person who never seemed to get what was coming to him was Thurman, and Jonas had finally learned his lesson there. How could he have been so naïve as to expect the Church to have the integrity to enforce anything, even heresy, against one of its own?

A low murmur from the other side of the door distracted him, but he couldn't make out the words over the courtyard noise. He pressed his ear to the door, but still couldn't hear well enough. The sounds were too low to be coming from the next room, but they had to be coming from somewhere within the Primal's suite. After a quick glance down the hallway, he slipped a pick into the lock. When it clicked, he nudged the door open a crack. As expected, the room was deserted. He slipped inside.

Judging by the harpsichord, he'd found the music room. The airy space featured a regiment of instruments, including a large harp and several basses. A glass-faced cabinet displayed a generous assortment of woodwinds. Every inch of wall bore canvases with musicality-themed scenes or still lifes.

The murmuring was louder here, and Jonas spied another door, slightly ajar. Mindful not to make the slightest rustle, he padded over and peered through the crack.

Although he'd convinced himself the old man with Thurman and Father Anton must be the Primal, it was still a shock to recognize him resting peacefully in one of the Palace's lavish four-poster beds. It was also odd, since it had only been a few minutes since the same man had supposedly sent Thurman off with strict instructions to bring someone right back. As they'd surmised, the Primal was not alone. At the foot of the bed, an imposing man in a white prisoner's tunic paced and muttered.

"Damn you, Serrola," he said, "I know you're out there. What are you waiting for? If this is going to work, you and that damnable Amulet of yours need to show up before Goodkin gets back."

Jonas's mind raced. So Vane was expecting Michlos. That didn't bode well. Not daring to breathe, Jonas leaned over for another look.

Oblivious, the rogue Enforcer continued his muttered soliloquy. "Perhaps you need a little encouragement to help you along. Yes, a little encouragement might be just the thing." Vane snatched up a poker from the fireplace.

Jonas by no means considered himself to be squeamish, but he pulled back from the door just the same. A series of muffled thuds filtered through the crack—the thought of what that could mean made him queasy.

To his amazement, he heard Vane chuckle. Then a door flew open, and Michlos's voice rang out. "It's over Vane. The Princess's guards will be here any moment."

Jonas steeled himself for another look. The Primal lay unscathed, but the padded arm of a nearby chaise was a tattered shambles.

Vane smirked. "Then they are at least one moment too late." With lightning speed, Vane cast off the poker and snatched up a slender taper. In one fluid motion, he snapped the taper in two and tossed the pieces into the fireplace. Turning, he dashed out onto the balcony.

"Heretics!" he cried. "Heretics are attacking the Primal."

As Vane leapt on the balcony's rail and crouched to spring into the courtyard, Jonas threw wide the door and let fly his knife. The blade only grazed Vane's shoulder, but the distraction proved disastrous. Vane misstepped and plummeted sideways off the edge. Jonas winced at the unwelcome realization that the sound of his landing was not unlike that of a poker striking overstuffed upholstery.

Michlos rushed to the Primal and placed his fingertips against his throat. After several seconds, he sighed in relief. "He still lives. I thought I'd delayed too long. What was that noise?"

Jonas nodded toward the damaged chaise. "Your man Vane apparently harbored a deep-seated hatred of fine furnishings."

"I take it at least one door wasn't locked."

Jonas shrugged. "It wasn't while I was using it."

"Good. Then there's nothing standing in the way of your using it again."

Jonas bristled. He'd been dismissed one time too many today. "Trying to take all the credit for yourself, are you?"

Michlos ogled Jonas in disbelief. "Credit? I don't think you understand. Not half an hour ago Vane stood in the middle of that courtyard and proclaimed I was a heretic. Now he lies injured or dead somewhere beneath that balcony. This isn't going to be about credit—it's going to be about blame."

"Then lucky for you I'm here to be your alibi. The Primal was already asleep before you got here. You couldn't have done it. In fact, you saved him from the one who did."

"Vane Slept him? Are you sure?"

"Look at him. How else could he have snored through all this? Besides, he sent Thurman off only moments ago. It's not like he's had a whole lot of time to be tucked in and get comfy. Do you have a better explanation?"

Michlos nudged the old man to rouse him, to no avail. "I'll need to Dispel it before the Monsignor gets here. Otherwise they'll think I'm responsible."

"But asleep, he proves your innocence."

"I wish it were that simple. They only know Vane as an Inquisitor, not a heretic. Are they more likely to trust you, or him?"

Jonas knew all too well how that would play out. "I see your point. Well then, what are you waiting for?"

"Check the courtyard. Make sure Vane is still there. I dare not take down my Amulet if he's still a threat."

Jonas strode toward the balcony. "What's this about an Amulet?"

"It's a protective device—it blocks Phrendonic spells in my vicinity, which is why I can't wake the Primal until I deactivate it."

"If this Amulet is so good at blocking spells, why is the Primal still asleep?"

"Because that spell is already vested."

"And Vane knew you had this thing?"

"He did. Why do you ask?"

"Because he mentioned it just before you barged in. He said he was going to need you and your Amulet to show up soon if his plan was going to work." Jonas peered into the courtyard. "Well, it looks like a solemn crowd has gathered below. Apparently, he's still down there."

"That doesn't bode well."

"I thought you wanted him out of commission."

"I was referring to this plan of his. Think carefully. Did he mention any other details?"

"Look, I didn't even know what an Amulet was at the time. And now that he is where he is, why does it even matter?"

"Because he's an insidious weasel. He did this to me before, too."

"Did what?"

"Found a way to use my Amulet against me. I bet that's why he Slept the Primal."

"Why?"

"Because he knew I'd have to Dispel it and that I'd have to take down the Amulet to do it. And I bet that explains the candle, too."

"The one he threw in the fire?"

"He must have used spells on the taper to keep whatever trap he set inactive until I showed up. He probably expected to be far away by the time I got around to springing it."

"Well, now that you know what to look for, how do you fix it?"

"That's the insidious part. So long as the Amulet is active, I have no way to detect the trap, but taking the Amulet down could very well set it off."

"I have a better idea," Jonas said. "Why don't we just get out of here?"

At that moment, the Monsignor stepped into the room. "I'm afraid, gentlemen, no one will be going anywhere."

The armed guards who piled in behind him drove home the point.

.  .  .  .  .

Princess Julienne poked her head into the hallway. "You can come in now."

She extended her hand as Alexi approached, and he took it. With a playful smile, she drew him inside.

Alexi scanned the guest room with a puzzled expression. "Where's your grandmother? I thought she was resting."

Julienne took a seat on the bed and patted a spot next to her. "And I thought she'd never leave."

"Where'd she go?"

"She'd never admit it, but Grandmother can't stand being out of the loop for even a minute. I presume she's off to insinuate herself into some high-level conversation. And, given everything that's happened today, there will no doubt be talk aplenty. She could be gone for hours. Aren't you going to sit?"

Alexi hesitated. "Now that your grandmother is doing all right, I should probably get back to the ceremony."

"Oh, I suppose you wouldn't have heard. The ceremony is over."

"Already? Dona is going to kill me."

"Whatever for?"

"I'm supposed to be escorting her—I was already in trouble when we ran into her at the portcullis."

"You were assisting the Crown. Surely she won't begrudge you that?"

"You don't know her."

"And from the sound of it, I wouldn't want to. Tell me, does she terrorize everyone like this, or just you?"

"I'm not terrorized."

Julienne stood and rubbed his shoulders. "Your muscles tell a different tale. You're a mass of knots."

"I don't like failing to measure up to expectations."

"Whose expectations? Hers or yours?"

"Mine."

"So, it was your idea to come here today?"

"No, it was hers, but—"

"Then you did her a favor by consenting to be her escort, right?"

"Technically, I suppose."

She pressed her thumbs into the tension at the base of his neck. "How's that? Too hard?"

Alexi sighed contentedly. "No, that's…really good."

"Here, have a seat so I can get some leverage."

Alexi sank onto the bed.

"Anyway, if she really were Miss Right, she'd evoke a whole series of emotions different than the ones you describe. She'd be someone who loves you just the way you are, not the way she expects you to be, someone with whom you could relax, someone you could have fun with just by being yourself."

She leaned in closer.

"She'd also be someone who found you completely intoxicating and wasn't afraid to tell you so."

Alexi's eyes fell closed as Julienne's nimble fingers banished the knots from his shoulders. Her breath was hot across his cheek, the scent of jasmine, overpowering. His pulse throbbed in his ears.

Slowly, she traced the line of his jaw. When her fingertips reached his chin, she urged his face to hers. Her voice fell to a husky whisper. "She would ache to abandon all she is and all she'll ever be to lose herself in you."

Her lips caressed his. He reflexively leaned closer.

"And I would give anything to be her right now."

Hungrily, she pressed herself against him as they fell back across the coverlet. He trembled as her jasmine-scented hands worked their way ineluctably down his back, her lips devouring every inch of his face with an animal urgency.

As much as he yearned to succumb, something niggled at the howling in his mind. He strove to ignore it, to convince himself it was insignificant, that he could deal with it later, but the more he tried to shrug it off, the more insistent it became. At last, with a sigh, he sat up.

"What's wrong?"

"I can't do this."

"For a few minutes there, you were doing just fine."

"I told you. Dona and I have an understanding."

"Ah yes, the one with the exemption for persons named Gregory. Or perhaps it's an exemption for tenors in general?"

"She's not like that."

She rubbed his arm. "Fair is fair. If she can have an exemption, why can't you? Did I mention I'm a pretty respectable alto?"

"This is not about her. I'm not the kind of man who goes back on my agreements. I'm sorry, but I can't continue this unless I break it off with Dona first. I know you think it's foolish."

She sat up. "Actually, I'd call it noble. She truly doesn't deserve you. How long will it take, do you suppose? To break it off with her?"

Alexi stood. "As long as it takes for me to get to the bottom of this 'Gregory exemption.'"

"What would you have me do? Call sworn witnesses? I could do that."

Alexi shook his head. "This is something I need to hear from them."

"I understand. Go to them then."

He turned to leave, but she took hold of his arm. "Just one more thing. As incredible as you are, I do have my pride. I'll wait for you a little if I must, but I won't wait long."

. . . . .

Nothing in the courtyard looked anything like Alexi had expected. To the north, guards scurried about battlements marred by a broad swath of scorched stone that trailed tendrils of smoke. Most of the guests were absent, and where they had once been, chairs lay scattered and upended, the grass beneath trampled and muddied. To the south-west, a tight group had gathered beneath a balcony, some pointing upward, others staring solemnly at something on the ground. Neither Dona nor anyone else from the wedding party was in evidence. The only area of the courtyard that wasn't somehow surreal was the musicians' stage, because the traumatized occupants still carried their instruments. Determined to get to the bottom of Julienne's accusations once and for all, Alexi hobbled off in that direction.

He finally found Gregory chatting with a male guest behind the stage. Since the accusations against Dona weren't exactly fit for public consumption, particularly not among those with whom she now might find herself rubbing elbows, he let Gregory finish with the man first. While he waited, he climbed the stage and took a seat in an empty chair. Though he didn't intend to listen in on Gregory's conversation, he wanted to be close enough that no one else could cut in front of him. But upon hearing Dona's name, he was all ears. He quietly slid the chair closer.

"I'm sorry," Gregory said. "When it comes to any information about Dona, no matter how trivial, I've learned my lesson the hard way. I have no comment."

"Come now," the man said in an oddly familiar voice. "She's my sister's niece. That makes her family."

"Yeah," Gregory said, "and last time it was the kindly professor who wanted to sponsor her for some big scholarship. I spilled my guts thinking I was doing her a huge favor, but I ended up causing a whole lot of trouble."

"I'm simply trying to locate some of my sister's missing belongings," the man said. "Since Dona was the maid of honor, I'm just wondering if she handed them off and then forgot. They were in a brown satchel. She didn't happen to leave it with you, did she?"

A light dawned in Gregory's eyes. "Oh, now I know what this is all about—no wonder you can't ask her yourself."

Alexi finally placed the voice—it belonged to the man who had threatened the artist just before darkness had shrouded the green. He struggled to recall the name. Damien, was it? He winced at Gregory's tone—the man was not someone to be trifled with.

"I don't know anything about a satchel," Gregory said, "but I can certainly let her know you're looking for one. In fact, why don't we go find her together? I'm sure she'd be delighted to discover how much interest her new family has taken in her."

"In case you hadn't heard," Damien said, "my sister is at death's door, and last I knew, Dona was there helping out as best she could. I really don't think that kind of distraction would benefit either of them right now."

Gregory suddenly looked less sure of himself. "What's in this satchel that's so important?"

"Just some legal documents and Verone's personal things. Not that it's really any of your business."

"You're not looking for a book?"

Damien shrugged. "Should I be?"

Gregory's ears flushed. "Oh, I'm terribly sorry. I mistook you for someone else."

"So have you seen it or not?"

"I haven't. Did you check with her mother?"

"She doesn't have it. Is there anyone else she might have left it with?"

"You could try her roommates. I'm pretty sure they're around here somewhere."

"I'd love to. Do they have any distinguishing characteristics?"

"Miranda would be the easiest to spot. She wears her hair in blonde ringlets and is dressed in red and black. If you're lucky, she'll be toting a brown satchel."

"Yeah, right. Thanks for the helpful tip. I'll be sure to keep an eye out for that."

As Damian stomped off, Alexi stood and waved.

"Gregory, you got a minute?"

Gregory looked up. "Sure. I'll be right there."

Alexi dragged over another chair. "Have a seat."

"How's Dona holding up?"

"I don't know. I haven't seen her in a while. What happened here, anyway?"

"You didn't see?"

"I was helping the Crown with something. By the time I got back…"

"Someone tried to kill Dona's uncle, but Verone pushed him out of the way and took the dart herself. They're saying it was poisoned."

"Seriously? Did they catch the assassin?"

"Not exactly. That scorched patch of battlement is where he blew himself up."

"He's dead?"

"As a doornail. Rumor has it Verone isn't far behind."

"Yeah, I overheard your friend say that. Did they complete the ceremony before the assassin got her?"

"That's what they're saying. Apparently Verone managed to choke out the words just before she lost consciousness—and he's not my friend, by the way."

"Then what are you doing sending him after Miranda?"

"He's just trying to collect his sister's things."

"I'll bet he is—those legal papers he mentioned transfer the entire Nevinander estate to Verone. If they ever see the light of day, your friend inherits nothing."

Gregory blanched. "You don't think he'd be a threat to Miranda, do you?"

Alexi scratched his ear. "Let me put it this way—you know the little distraction we had during the rehearsal?"

"You mean the Darkness?"

Alexi nodded. "That was all him."

"He's a heretic?"

Several of the nearby musicians started and glanced nervously their way.

"Keep it down," Alexi said. "You want it getting back to him that you know?"

Gregory lowered his voice. "They're saying heresy killed the assassin too."

"How convenient for whoever put him up to it."

"Surely you don't suspect her own brother?"

"He had motive and opportunity."

"Great—I've done it again. When will I learn to keep my mouth shut? Well, looks like it's up to me to stop him. If I can find Miranda before he does, maybe I can keep him from finding her. Listen, Alexi, thanks for the heads up." He slapped Alexi on the shoulder and leapt off the stage.

"Wait, I need to ask you something."

Gregory called over his shoulder as he hurried away. "I've got to find Miranda. I'll catch up with you later."

Alexi's first instinct was to follow, but his ankle prevented him from jumping, and he'd never be able to keep up anyway. He threw his crutch on the stage and watched helplessly as Gregory disappeared into the keep.

# CHAPTER TWENTY

# PRIMAL FEARS

Getting the chatty royals to move had taken repeated reminders of Verone's urgent plight. If Dona thought she was annoyed by the time she had finally herded them into the keep from the courtyard, she had only to wait. When Celeste mentioned the Primal's presence would be required, the trip to the infirmary became truly exasperating.

Nathan stopped in his tracks. "The Primal is here?"

"Since this morning," Celeste said. "I had no idea he was coming."

Nathan turned to Irina. "In that case, it would be best for your mother to stay behind."

"I'm sorry," Marguerite said, "have I suddenly become invisible?"

Irina placed a hand on her mother's arm. "Nathan is simply saying that, given the manner of your arrival, the Primal may find your presence a bit…awkward."

Marguerite was undeterred. "Given that he excommunicated Celeste and has had this Island under interdict for years now, I should think it will be awkward regardless."

"He's going to lift the interdict," Celeste said. "At least that was my understanding as of this morning. I suppose that outcome could now be in doubt."

"Come now, don't you find the timing of this wedding and the attack on my estate a tad coincidental? Surely this was all a ploy to keep you and Nathan occupied long enough to give the Inquisition a chance to make off with me."

Nathan crossed his arms. "No offense, but if the Primal is behind all of this, he's one lousy strategist."

"At the risk of being obvious, the plan nearly worked."

"By capturing you, he would only have succeeded in trapping himself in hostile territory."

"Yes, but with a high-profile hostage. Perhaps he deemed that sufficient collateral to ensure your cooperation."

Dona huffed. "You know, if we rescue Verone, you can ask her all of these questions directly, but if we keep arguing, you'll likely lose the chance."

"The young lady is right," Irina said.

Nathan nodded. "Fine, but I really think it would be safer if your mother stayed behind."

"Your opinion is noted," Marguerite said. "Shall we?"

Irina clasped Nathan's hand. "Hasn't she earned the right to hear the truth?"

"Please," Dona said. "We may already be too late."

Nathan sighed. "Oh, very well, but I will do the talking, understood?"

"Of course," Marguerite said. "You are the Crown, after all."

Arriving at the top of the stairs, Celeste paused at the sight of several guards loitering down the hall."

"What is it?" Nathan asked.

"The Primal. You go on ahead. I'll be there momentarily."

"Are you sure you wouldn't like me to—"

"No need, thank you. I am perfectly capable of managing my guests, official or otherwise." Celeste darted down the corridor.

Dona threw open a door. "The infirmary is right over here."

The Sisters had accomplished much since Dona left. Verone had been stripped of her dress and corset and transferred to a bed. Tapestries had been hung from hooks in the ceiling to afford some privacy. She lay pale and unmoving. Rayen sat by her side holding her hand.

Nathalie looked up from her hovering and fussing. "Nathan—thank heavens."

"I'm so sorry, Nathalie. How is she doing?"

"Not so well. They don't think she has much longer. Were you able to locate the Primal?"

"Celeste went to find him. I don't think he's far off."

Nathalie faced the old priest. "The Crown is here. He says the Primal is on his way. Can we get started?"

"I dare not begin without the Primal's blessing. There's too much at stake."

One of the Sisters placed an ear on Verone's chest. "Her breathing is ragged. If someone is going to do something, it had better be soon."

Nathalie turned to Nathan. "Isn't there something you can do?"

Nathan shrugged. "I have no jurisdiction here. You need either Celeste or the Primal."

Nathalie resumed pacing. "Where are they?"

"I think the Primal is just down the hall," Dona said.

"Down the hall? Then why isn't he here already?"

"The Princess mentioned he was ill."

"Ill? Well, maybe he needs us to make this a little easier, then. Rayen, would you be so kind as to grab one end of that stretcher?"

"Certainly." He raised Verone's hand momentarily to his lips before grabbing the stretcher.

"I'll get the other end," Nathan said.

"Dona?" Nathalie asked. "Do you know where he's hiding?"

"I can take you to where I think he might be."

"Fair enough. Lead on."

Dona stepped into the hallway, followed by Nathalie and the men with the stretcher. As Marguerite fell into line behind them, Nathan balked. "Hold on, where do you think you're going?"

Marguerite smirked. "Are you kidding? I wouldn't miss this for the world."

·  ·  ·  ·  ·

Celeste pushed her way through the guards into the Primal's apartment. Several guards near the Monsignor stood with crossbows leveled at Michlos and Jonas, who faced the wall side by side, arms in the air. Nearby, the Primal lay, seemingly asleep.

"What's going on here?"

The Monsignor leaned wearily on his cane. "I was just asking Mr. Serrola that same question."

Wild-eyed and out of breath, Thurman appeared in the doorway. He forced his way through the crowd to the Monsignor. "Is he all right? Please say he's all right."

"He appears to be resting," the Monsignor said, "but I'm concerned this commotion hasn't awakened him."

"He's alive then? Because when they said Vane was dead, I feared the worst."

"Vane's dead?"

"I think he hit his head in the fall, but before that, I heard him cry out that heretics were attacking the Primal."

"And where were you? I remember distinctly telling you that under no circumstances were you to leave Vane's side."

"That wasn't my fault. His Primacy ordered me to fetch you. I objected, but he was in no mood to negotiate."

The Monsignor approached the bed and gave the Primal a gentle shake. When there was no response, he turned to Celeste. "Your Highness, we have two suspects in the murder of Josephus Vane, and quite possibly an assault on the Primal. I am compelled to request that you take them into custody until such time as they can be properly extradited."

"You're asking me to incarcerate the Crown's brother-in-law?"

"I know it's politically sensitive, but what other choice do I have?"

"But we don't even have diplomatic relations."

"The interdict and excommunication have been lifted. The Primal signed the decree this morning."

"But we never discussed the conditions."

The Monsignor shrugged. "He didn't require any."

"This is crazy. What reason would Michlos have to be involved in any of this?"

"Please, Your Highness. You were at the ceremony. Vane publicly accused Michlos and his mother of heresy. Few doubts remain as to his mother's guilt. As for using heresy against the Primal, his motive could be as simple as wanting to keep him from witnessing the attack on Vane."

"That's all just speculation. I'm sure he can clear this up if only you give him a chance."

Thurman gaped at her. "I don't believe what I'm hearing. You aren't siding with these heretics, are you?"

The Monsignor closed his eyes and sighed. "Shut up, Thurman."

Thurman glared but complied.

"Your Highness, I sincerely hope you're right. In the meantime, we must assume they are dangerous heretics to be locked away until the truth of the matter is known."

"It's not that simple. We don't have the facilities to safely imprison heretics here."

"I beg to differ," the Monsignor said. "Thurman, do you still have the Eye?"

"The what?"

"The gem I gave you down on the dais."

Thurman reached into his pocket. "Oh yes—here."

"Thank you. Now, Your Highness, I'm sure I don't need to remind you that, with the aid of this little device, Hasset Bey imprisoned Dreamweaver herself within these very walls. If it worked for her, it should more than suffice for these two."

Jonas glared over his shoulder. "As long as we are so eager to lock up dangerous heretics, let's not forget Thurman here, who has used Phrendonic Heresy against me twice now, most recently in Your Highness's very courtyard. He's also used it against the Primal, I might add."

Thurman's eyes widened as he finally recognized Jonas.

The Princess cocked her head. "Really?" She turned to the Monsignor. "Is this true?"

"Don't listen to him," Thurman said. "He's trying to distract you from the real threat."

The Monsignor crossed his arms. "Thurman?"

"Dad, please, don't make me answer that."

The Monsignor turned away from his son, his mouth tight. "Apparently, Your Highness, there are to be three prisoners. I trust you can accommodate them all?"

"We were only trying to save him," Thurman protested.

Jonas's eyes narrowed. "Like you tried to save yourself from being greeted in the courtyard?"

Nathalie pushed her way into the room. "Excuse me. I hope we aren't interrupting anything but even if we are, it can wait. If we are going to save my daughter, we need the Primal to come this instant. Is that him?"

"I'm afraid the Primal is in no condition to help anyone at the moment," the Monsignor said.

Nathalie nodded. "We heard he might not be feeling his best and took that into account." She poked her head into the hallway. "Bring the stretcher."

Guards parted as Rayen and Nathan trotted in, the stretcher suspended between them.

"He's not just ill," the Monsignor said. "He's unconscious. We suspect these accused heretics may have ensorcelled him."

Nathalie put her hands squarely on her hips. "So what are you waiting for? Prince Charming? Have them remove it."

The Monsignor shook his head. "It's too dangerous. While they might do as I ask, there's an enormous risk they'd do something else entirely. I hope you understand—as someone who survived Caprian, I don't dare risk the Primal's life by requiring heretics to commit additional acts of heresy."

Dona followed the stretcher into the room. "Monsignor, did I just hear you say you would never ask a heretic to commit heresy—even to save a life?"

The Monsignor greeted her with a sardonic smile. "Ah, Miss Merinne, I should have guessed. When an ethical dilemma presents itself, you are never far behind. Don't be too quick to judge. Risk is a fickle partner. Just because you might happily choose to live with it yourself doesn't mean you can ethically impose it on someone else."

"No offense, Monsignor," Nathalie said, "but I don't see how the decision is yours to make. Last I checked, Celeste was in charge here."

"Actually, the interdict was lifted this morning, and matters of heresy lie squarely within Church jurisdiction."

"I don't believe this. My daughter is dying, and you're quibbling about jurisdiction?"

"Nathalie has a point," Nathan said. "The Church may have jurisdiction, but they have no enforcers here, and Celeste is under no obligation to obey them. Ultimately, it's her decision."

"Doesn't matter who decides," Thurman said. "They'll never remove that spell. They'd just be proving their guilt."

Marguerite appeared in the doorway. "Oh, for crying out loud. If that's all that's preventing us from saving the girl, I'll do it."

Michlos shot his mother an incredulous look, but his tone was measured. "Mother—what are you doing?"

"Apparently you haven't been keeping up. The Inquisition destroyed my house this morning. In the process of saving my life, I was forced to use a little heresy. Since my deep dark secret's already out, I have nothing to lose by waking His Primacy."

The Monsignor's jaw dropped. "Wait, the Inquisition did what?"

"I guess that's what I get for supporting you in your little struggle with Ordinal Isrulian," Nathan said. "I don't know what you were trying to achieve, but I have no intention of standing idly by while the Church attacks members of my family without warning or provocation. If its war you want, it's war you'll get."

"I swear I didn't know anything about this. Thurman?"

Thurman held up his hands. "Don't look at me—it wasn't my doing."

The Monsignor turned to Nathan. "I don't have any idea why those Inquisitors singled out your mother-in-law, and the Church is certainly not trying to start a war with Trifienne. But I'll be honest, her heresy is going to be a problem, not just with the Church, but with the leaders of nearby states. Given how they suffered for similar offenses, Caprian, particularly, will likely be out for blood. I doubt they'll allow the Primal to just overlook it."

"Marguerite," Nathalie said, "are you going to wake him, or must I find somebody else?"

Marguerite raised an eyebrow at Celeste. "Well?"

Michlos lowered his arms and faced his mother. "You can't. We think Vane planted a trap."

"Trap?" the Monsignor bleated.

Marguerite ignored him. "What sort of trap?"

"I'm not sure, but given what I know of Vane, it's likely to trigger as soon as I take down my Amulet. So, unless you overpower it, you won't be waking the Primal anytime soon."

"Correct me if I'm wrong," Celeste said, "but doesn't the Eye of Moravidos trump an Amulet?"

"It does," Marguerite said. "And I doubt I'm going to be overpowering that. If I'm going to make the attempt, the Eye will need to be taken out of range."

"Oh no you don't," the Monsignor said. "If there's any threat to the Primal, the Eye is staying right here."

Nathalie got a wild look in her eye. "Oh, if they need it to leave, Monsignor, trust me, it's going."

The Monsignor gulped and took a step back.

Marguerite produced a rectangular box. "It's all right, Nathalie. I have a better idea." She unlatched the box and flipped it open to reveal a large assortment of wands.

Nathalie eyed the wands with awe. "Those aren't—"

"Father's Patterning wands? Indeed, they are."

The Monsignor gasped. "Patterning wands? Your Highness, you mustn't allow her anywhere near the Primal with those Profanities. She'll make his condition irreversible."

"Relax," Marguerite said. "It's not the Patterning wands I'm after. Sometimes when you Pattern a spell, you need to do it while the effect is suppressed. If you've ever tried to Pattern a Darkness spell, you'll know what I'm talking about. So, over the years I've added quite a few Suppression wands to the collection. Ah, here it is."

Marguerite turned to Celeste and held up a wand. "Looks like it's up to you. Shall I?"

"Your Highness," the Monsignor said, "I urge you to consider the welfare of your people. What will happen to them if, by your leave, the Primal is murdered by heretics?"

Celeste took a deep breath. The room fell silent as she considered Marguerite's wand and the Monsignor and the Primal in turn. At last, she spoke.

"Monsignor. I urge you to consider the welfare of your soul. What will happen to it if this woman's daughter dies because of your dogmatic conviction that a doctrinal difference of opinion is conclusive evidence of malicious intent?"

The Monsignor blinked in surprise. "I don't think you understand—"

The Princess raised her hand, and the Monsignor fell silent. She nodded to Marguerite. "Do it."

The Monsignor grimaced and looked away. Marguerite stepped forward and touched the wand to the back of the Primal's hand.

Nathalie bent over him. "Wake up, Your Primacy. We need your help."

The Primal stirred and opened his eyes. "Who are you?"

"I'm Nathalie Nevinander. My daughter is dying, and we need your blessing to save her. Will you help?"

"How did you get in here? And who are all these people?"

"They are friends and relatives of Mrs. Nevinander's daughter," the Monsignor said, "and they include the Crown of Trifienne and the Princess of this island, whom you met this morning."

The Primal squinted at the crowd. "I'm not exactly prepared to receive heads of state at the moment."

"I beg you, Your Primacy," Nathalie said. "My daughter doesn't have much longer."

"Oh, very well. Where is she, and what's her affliction?"

"She's just down the hall in the infirmary. She was poisoned. We heard you weren't feeling well, and we brought you a stretcher, if that helps."

"Miraculously, my strength seems to be returning of late. I can manage without."

As the Primal threw back the coverlet, Thurman extended his arm. "Here. Lean on me."

The Primal stifled a yawn. "Thank you, Thurman. Hmm, I must have been very tired. I don't generally sleep fully clothed. Now where is this infirmary?"

"Right this way," Nathalie said.

"Wait," Michlos said. "We still haven't disabled the trap, and I have no idea where it is. If Vane put it on the Primal directly, and he leaves the protection of the Amulet, that could trigger it."

"We don't even know there is a trap," Celeste said.

"Vane's behavior makes no sense at all unless there is."

"Trap?" the Primal said. "What's this nonsense about a trap?"

The Monsignor nodded toward Michlos. "Mr. Serrola, here, is of the opinion that Inquisitor Vane was a Phrendonic Heretic and that he has placed some sort of dangerous trap here."

"I can confirm Vane was a heretic," the Princess said. "And I've learned to take Michos's concerns very seriously. If he says there's a danger, I believe him."

"The difficulty, of course," the Monsignor said, "is that Mr. Serrola and his mother appear to be heretics as well."

The Primal froze. "I presume there's a very good reason they haven't been taken into custody?"

"We don't have the manpower to do it ourselves. I've placed a formal request with the Princess to do so, but so far she has neglected to act on it."

"In case you haven't noticed," the Princess said. "They've been trying to help you. But if you prefer, I'll happily take them both into custody, take back the Eye, and leave you to your own devices. If there is a trap, good luck dealing with it on your own."

"Help me out here, Armand," the Primal said. "Is this all hogwash, or is there really a trap?"

"The Monsignor locked eyes with Michlos, who returned his gaze unflinchingly. "I cannot rule it out," he said at last.

The Primal addressed Celeste. "Fine. I'll allow them to see to this trap, but I suggest you mind them well. Since you speak for them, their behavior shall be on your head. If they betray me, you will share their fate. Now, shall we see to this lady's daughter?"

"Thank you, Your Primacy," Nathalie said. "Follow me."

As Nathalie and the Primal pushed through the guards, Michlos caught the Monsignor's attention. "Go with him. Keep the Eye near him. The trap could be on him, his clothing, or on anything he's carrying. If he sets anything down, pick it up and keep it with you. Understood?"

The Monsignor nodded.

"Hurry, before he gets out of range."

The Princess assigned several guards to travel with the Primal. Several more she quietly sent to see to Vane. By the time she finished, only Michlos and Jonas remained.

"Coming?" she asked.

"I can't," Michlos said. "The trap may have been cast on something in this room. If I leave, who knows what might happen."

"But I might need you. Can't you just leave your Amulet behind?"

"They're not designed that way. It only works while I'm touching it. It's a way of keeping it from being useful to an adversary."

"Would that be true of a prototype too?"

"What do you mean?"

Celeste held up a ring with a faint blue gem. "Magister Treust gave this to me when he learned I was planning to confront Vane. He called it a prototype." She pressed the gem, which flushed blood red.

"There—that means it's working."

Michlos blinked in surprise. "I suppose he wouldn't have given it to you if you couldn't use it. Try putting it down."

She placed the ring on the nightstand next to the bed. The gem's color did not waver.

"Looks like I can go with you after all. Let's hurry. I'd like to be there in case the Monsignor misses something."

They were already well into the hallway before they realized they'd left someone behind. "Jonas, are you coming?"

Back in the suite, Jonas stood at the nightstand turning the Amulet over in his hand. "Be right there." With a twisted grin, he slipped the ring into his pocket and scurried after them.

# CHAPTER TWENTY-ONE

# Tbe (Dotber of Invention

I feel like a walking target here," Helena said. "It's so exposed."

"That's the point," Miranda said. "Dona can't leave Ranselard without passing through this vestibule. If Alphonse doesn't find her first, we'll catch her on her way out. Besides, almost everyone in any hurry to leave has already left. Now sit down and stop pacing. You're making me nervous."

"You saw that man burst into flames. How can we be sure we won't be next?"

"Calm down. He probably did it to himself. According to Daddy's notes, heretics are known for that."

"I don't know—the other guests practically climbed over each other to get out of here."

"Yes, but they don't have access to Daddy's notes." She slipped a package out of Dona's satchel. "Here, come help me unwrap this."

Apparently, no secret was too small for Miranda to snoop. "That looks like a wedding gift. Unless there's something you're not telling me, I doubt it's intended for you."

"Aren't you the least bit curious what's inside?"

"What if Dona catches you? She's probably supposed to be keeping it safe for Rayen and Verone."

"This will only take a couple seconds. It's just a little string, paper, and sealing wax. Once I have a quick peep, I'll have it wrapped right back up good as new. In the meantime, if you're not going to help, at least keep an eye out."

"All right, but if you get caught, don't blame me."

Miranda peered inside. "Oh, I should have guessed. This isn't a wedding gift at all. It's Dona's book—the one she made all the fuss about. She can't even attend a wedding without bringing her school-work with her. She probably thinks she's really clever hiding it from us like this."

"Oh no. Put it back. Quick!"

Miranda slid the book and wrapping back into the satchel. "Is she coming?"

"No, it's Professor Reston. You don't suppose Dona invited him as a way of currying favor, do you?"

Miranda shook her head. "Dona's fixated on her grades, but she prefers to earn them. He must know someone else in the wedding."

"Hello Professor," they said in unison.

"Hello ladies."

"Dona didn't mention you were coming," Miranda said. "Did she invite her other professors as well?"

"Actually, I didn't receive my invitation through Miss Merinne, and, if there are other Professors here, I doubt Miss Merinne invited them."

Miranda favored Helena with an 'I-told-you-so' smile, which Helena pretended to ignore. "Have you heard anything about when classes are going to start up again?"

"Not yet, but the way things usually work at the college, you'll probably hear before I do. Are you waiting for a carriage?"

"No, we're waiting for Dona. We thought she could use some company on the way home."

"I'm sure she'll appreciate that. Well, it was good to see you two."

"And you, Professor," Miranda said. "Have a good day."

Reston had just started down the hallway to the Keep's portcullis when Gregory slid to a halt in front of Miranda.

"He hasn't found you yet, has he?"

"Who? You mean Professor Reston?"

Reston paused at the mention of his name.

"No, this was some other guy. He's looking for that satchel."

"Again?" Miranda asked. "Why is everybody so interested in Dona's stupid extra-credit project?"

Reston whirled just in time to see Gregory collapse.

Miranda tossed the satchel aside and rushed to his aid. "Are you all right?"

Helena felt his wrist for a pulse. "What happened? Did he faint?"

Miranda gently shook him. "I don't know. He's not waking up."

Helena cast about for something or someone to help them. "What are we going to do?"

"What seems to be the trouble here?"

Miranda looked up into the concerned eyes of a ruddy-faced gentleman. "I don't know. He fainted, and I can't seem to wake him."

"Is he prone to this sort of thing? Perhaps he overdid it during the ceremony."

"I don't think so—at least, if he is, this is the first I've heard of it."

"We should get him to the infirmary. Why don't you two find a guard? I saw them running around with stretchers earlier today. Maybe they can bring one. I'd be happy to sit with him until you get back."

Miranda looked hesitant.

The guest smiled reassuringly. "Don't worry, I'm the bride's brother Damien. We'll get him through this. After his stirring performance in honor of my sister, it's the least I can do."

Helena grabbed Miranda by the arm. "There might still be guards in the courtyard. Let's go."

The instant they were out of sight, Damien scooped up the satchel and rummaged through it.

Reston leaned casually against the hallway wall. "I don't believe that belongs to you."

Damien didn't even look up. "Mind your own business."

"Gregory," Reston said, "get up."

"You're wasting your breath."

Gregory stirred. "Professor Reston? What's going on?"

At the sound of Gregory's voice, Damien stopped his rummaging.

"Gregory, get out of here," Reston said. "Now."

Gregory stumbled toward the courtyard.

"Not that way—back this way. Out of Ranselard. Get back to town."

"But—"

"Go!"

As Gregory dashed down the hallway, Damien faced Reston, muttering under his breath. Reston deftly sidestepped into the chamber that held the portcullis control mechanism. Damien spat a curse and scanned wildly for cover of his own. Nothing seemed promising.

Reston popped his head back out into the hallway. "Drop the bag, and we can pretend none of this ever happened."

Damien clutched the satchel more tightly. "What are you, a Santine? Have I been Noticed or something?"

Reston didn't answer. Instead he mouthed mnemonics of his own. Damien followed suit, but Reston finished first. The satchel shot upward out of Damien's reach, plastering itself against a sign that welcomed guests to Rayen's and Verone's nuptials. The satchel's contents spilled during the ascent, and Damien was pelted by perfumes, kerchiefs, coins, papers, party favors, and footwear. A sheaf of wrapping paper was the last to settle, grazing Damien's ear as it floated lazily past. He batted it away in frustration.

Reston's book landed near Verone's attaché at Damien's feet, but he was too intent on resuming his interrupted spell to notice. Reston was forced to duck out of sight once more. When he peeped out a few moments later, Damien was gone. He sidled down the hall toward the book until he arrived at the vestibule. He peered inside, but there was still no sign of his foe. Though scant yards from his book, he still held back. Seeing no movement in any of the room's other exits, he glanced up at the satchel, still mashed against the sign. A moment later, it let loose and plummeted to the floor.

And there it was—a subtle shift in the shadows at the mouth of one of the other corridors—Damien was waiting for him. No matter, Reston had already protected himself against the most obvious threats. He briefly considered grabbing the book and making a mad dash for the portcullis, but then he recalled that Miranda and Helena would likely be back any minute with guards, and there was no telling how Damien might react. Still, the first half of the plan seemed like a reasonable start.

. . . . .

Damien peered around the archway with growing impatience. He'd almost stepped out to begin a spell when the satchel dropped, but fortunately recognized the ruse in time. He couldn't wait forever, but neither could he risk exposing himself to his adversary. Come to think of it, he was more than a little boggled that he even had an adversary. Someone must have reported him to a Santine, but who? And then it hit him—Thad. That simpering artsy brother of his must have turned him in. The more he brooded on it, the more it made sense—and the more outraged he became. When he noticed his hands were shaking, he took a breath and forced himself to focus. With a Santine after him, he couldn't allow rage to cloud his reason.

*Think, Damien.* How do you get those papers and get out of here?

And then it dawned on him that he didn't need the papers at all. A smirk crept across his face. Two simple spells and he'd be free, and he didn't even need to see the Santine to do it. But he did have to be certain he was far enough away. He stole back down the hallway, counting off paces as he went, giving himself ample margin for error. Even from this distance, the bottom edge of the welcome sign was still visible. He completed the first spell with a low chuckle, but his mirth was interrupted by a gasp as the Santine appeared beneath the sign and snatched something from the floor.

*Yes. It was perfect.* The Santine would never escape in time. Feeling an incredible rush of triumph, Damien Charged the Incinerate and chortled exultantly as the vestibule blazed with sinister light. Pausing only long enough to toss off a salute in the direction of his erstwhile opponent, he fled down the corridor, leaving the flickering aftermath behind him.

. . . . .

"I might have known," the Primal said. "Something's always afoot when you're lurking about. So what are you really after?"

The Primal faced the old priest, Rayen, and Nathalie over Verone's infirmary bed. Near Verone's head, a Sister tracked her vital signs. Verone's entourage, including the Crown, the Princess, the Serrolas, and the Merinnes loosely circled the scene, gawking in anticipation. Thurman, Albert, and the Monsignor hovered next to Darron, prepared to steady him should the need arise.

"It's exactly as I said," the old priest replied. "The technique is unconventional, and I merely want your blessing before I make the attempt."

"Oh, spare me. We both know you don't give a damn about my blessing."

"In case you haven't noticed, we're talking about a close relative of the Crown of Trifienne here. If the treatment doesn't work, I'd like it on record that I was acting in an official capacity. That way you can't just disclaim any involvement and hang me out to dry."

"For the first time in history, you're asking my permission before you do something that's politically sensitive? I'm dying to know— why the sudden change of habit?"

The old priest glanced at the Sister. "How's she doing?"

The Sister shook her head.

"There's no time left for debate. It's now or never. The Crown has already consented. Do I have your blessing, or don't I?"

The infirmary went suddenly silent, and Darron felt every eye in the room fixed on him. He searched the Monsignor's face for guidance, but the look in his brother's eye made it clear that he was on his own. In the end, it was Nathalie's pleading expression that moved him, against his better judgment, to favor the old priest with a brusque nod.

. . . . .

Rayen shifted as the old priest lifted Verone's arm. "Let's pray it's not too late."

With an enigmatic smile, the old priest produced a two-handled wand and, with a flourish, applied one end to Verone's flawlessly manicured hand.

The infirmary occupants heaved a collective gasp as the hand shriveled and contorted with age.

"Stop," Nathalie cried. "You're killing her."

The old priest ignored her.

Dona was the first to notice. "Father Anton—she looks just like you."

"Uncanny, isn't it?" the old priest said. "Sister, if you would be so kind, how's she doing now?"

Tentatively, the Sister placed her ear against Verone's chest. "I don't believe it. Her breathing is strong again. Or should I say his?"

"Good question," the old priest said.

The Sister snuck a quick peek beneath Verone's blanket. "Nope—it's definitely 'her.'"

"What have you done to her?" Nathalie cried.

Marguerite snorted. "Looks like heresy to me. And tainted heresy at that. Not that I'd have any reason to know, of course."

"Don't worry," the old priest said. "The effect is temporary."

Albert crossed his arms. "It seems Thurman wasn't the only one taking liberties with the Profanities collection. Why didn't you tell me?"

"Would you have let us take them if we had?"

"Of course. It's just a matter of obtaining the proper dispensations."

"And that's why I couldn't tell you. By obtaining the dispensations, you would have been warning precisely the person we needed the Profanities to circumvent."

The Primal cried out in astonishment. "That was you."

"This close," the old priest said. "I was this close to spiriting you out of Laitrech's clutches when the damnable spell wore off."

"Why did you bother? I suppose you couldn't stand the thought that Laitrech might actually do me in before you'd had a chance to ruin me first."

Michlos turned to his mother. "I'm not sure I understand. Shouldn't the copy be an exact match of the template? How can the gender have changed?"

The old priest snorted. "Ruin you? Allow me to point out that, as usual, it's taking everything I've got to keep you from doing that yourself. I've pulled every string I know to narrow your options to the only one with any chance of saving your Primacy, and still you refuse to see it."

"As I said," Marguerite whispered to her son, "I'm no expert—but I'm inclined to agree with you."

"Perhaps I'm equally dense then," Nathan said, "but I don't see how any of this has the slightest impact on the status of the Primacy."

Dona's eyes widened as the situation suddenly crystallized in her mind. "Oh, I think I do."

Silence fell as every head in the room turned her way. Dona's mouth went dry as she realized whom she addressed.

"It's all right, Dona," Celeste said. "I've been impressed with your intuition in the past. I, for one, would be delighted to hear what it's telling you now."

Dona took a deep breath and locked eyes with the old priest. "Correct me if I'm wrong, Father, but this really isn't about what you've done, is it? It's about who you are."

The old priest regarded her for a long moment. "And why ever should that matter?"

"Maybe it shouldn't, but it does. Just ask Jonas here. Since he was merely an innocent child at the time, maybe it shouldn't have made the slightest difference to him that his father was found guilty of heresy, but it did, didn't it? And what about the Crown—do you think he's the least bit concerned how his mother-in-law's circumstances will affect his reign? Why should it matter to him? He didn't do anything wrong. For that matter, you could even ask my mother…"

Dona's mother was apoplectic with alarm. "Dona, sweetheart, don't you think it would be better to let these fine people work this out among themselves?"

"It's all right, Mrs. Merinne," the Monsignor said. "She hasn't revealed anything we didn't already know. I assure you, as a family, the Theratigans have long since atoned for any past misdeeds."

Michlos's brow furrowed as he considered Dona's words. "While I see your point, I think you may have overstated your case. The connection between mere priest and Primal is far more tenuous than that between father and son, or even mother-in-law and son-in-law."

"I agree," Dona said. "But I'm not arguing that the relevant connection is between priest and Primal, even though on some level, maybe it really should have been." She faced the old priest. "In fact, you aren't even really a priest, are you?"

The old priest returned Dona's gaze with an air of patient amusement. "As a matter of fact, I'm not. Tell me, what gave it away?"

"There were lots of little things that made me suspect, particularly your name, but I think what clinched it for me was the tone you took with the Primal. Even the Monsignor is more deferential, and he's his brother. Well, that and his conviction that your use of heresy had just ruined him, even though you were using it to save a life."

"I still don't follow," Michlos said. "If Father Anton isn't a priest, then what's his connection to the Primal?"

Dona shrugged. "Isn't it obvious? He's his mother."

"Of course," the Princess said. "It's not Anton, it's Antoin*ette*—you're Antoinette Barget. I should have recognized you from your portrait."

"That's Antoinette Goodkin, if you please. It took some doing to acquire that name, and I'd just as soon see the achievement recognized."

The Primal paled and sank onto a nearby stretcher. "Ruined. I am so ruined."

"Good lord, Darron," Antoinette snapped. "Get hold of yourself. You're embarrassing me."

"Great. Not only has she ruined me, but now I'm embarrassing her. Tell me, just how does one embarrass a cross-dressing clergy-impersonating heretic?"

Antoinette's eyes narrowed. "I've been taking notes, but I won't be able to give you a complete list until you've finished. You still don't get it, do you? Laitrech tried to murder you, Lavicius has usurped your throne, and you're worried about whether someone's mother is a heretic? Hold on a second while I add that to the list."

"Mother, please," the Monsignor said, "he hasn't been well."

"So don't just stand there and cluck like a mother hen. Help him."

"I was. I tried to move him quietly to someplace safe, but he had other plans."

"This is my fault," Antoinette said. "I should have married smarter. Does no one else comprehend what a godsend the revelation of this woman's heresy is to us?"

"In case you haven't noticed," the Primal said, "I'm not exactly in any position to make threats."

"So you're out of sticks. Have you considered carrots? What do you suppose is the Crown's number one issue with the Church right now? Is this really so hard?"

"Are you suggesting I grant the mother-in-law an indulgence in return for the Crown's support?"

"It certainly sounds like someplace to start, doesn't it? In the alternative, you could go to war with him over his mother-in-law's heresies, assuming, of course, you can find a plausible way to reconcile that with the remarkably similar sins of yours truly. I'll be blunt. If you don't immediately get at least one state to back your bid to reclaim the

Primacy, you may as well crawl into Armand's hidey hole and stay there until they either find you or you die, which is pretty much the same thing. And guess what? No other state is going to back someone they view as a lame-duck Primal with only a few months left to live."

The Sister raised her hand for silence as she listened once more to her patient's chest. "Her breathing—it's ragged again."

"What's happening?" Nathalie asked. "What's wrong?"

"If I had to guess," Marguerite said, "I'd say the poison hasn't had a chance to assimilate. If that's true, then switching bodies didn't alter the poison, it merely started the poisoning process over again. In hindsight, you might have been better off choosing a body that was a little less frail."

"I've wasted too much time," Antoinette said. "I'll need to do it again. Any volunteers?"

Rayen stepped forward. "Whatever it is, I'll do it."

Antoinette looked him up and down. "You'll do." She pulled out the double-handled wand once more. "Hold this right here, but don't touch any other part of it."

Rayen did as he was told without hesitation.

"Now, touch the other end to her hand."

As he did so, the body under the blanket shuddered and shifted once more. This time, however, the hand resting on the blanket was Rayen's.

Marguerite stood transfixed "Simply amazing," she breathed. "Wherever did you get that?"

"It's called *Vis-à-vis*," Albert said. "It's one of the oldest pieces in the collection. According to legend, it was created by Dreamweaver herself, but of course we have no way of verifying that." He shot Antoinette a sidelong look. "Until quite recently, we had no idea what it did, either."

Antoinette caught hold of a cord around her neck and pulled from her vestments a silver pendant in the form of intertwined snakes.

The sight of it caused the Primal to stir. "That's Laitrech's Relic, isn't it?"

She shot him a long-suffering look.

The Primal rubbed the back of his neck uneasily. "Well, just so you know, we're going to need that back when you're done with it."

"Fine. Now, if you're quite finished, I'm going to request that you and everyone other than the patient's mother and husband retire elsewhere. I've never attempted to counteract a poison under such unusual circumstances before. I'll need to concentrate."

Alistair chose that moment to breeze in. "How's she doing?"

Nathalie rounded on him. "Where have you been?"

"I got distracted. It took me a while to find where you went."

Nathalie's jaw dropped. "Distracted? In case you hadn't noticed, our daughter is dying. What could possibly have distracted you from that?"

"Well I'm here now. So, where is she?" He froze as he realized Rayen appeared to be in two places at once. "It seems I may have missed something."

"That's her on the bed," Nathalie said. "They're trying to gain time to eliminate the poison."

"I see. So it's true what they say—I haven't so much lost a daughter as gained a son-in-law."

Nathalie ogled her husband in disbelief. "Alistair!"

Rayen's angry cry cut off Alistair's half-hearted apology. "Get out of here."

Alistair turned in shock, but Rayen was as surprised as anyone—that is, until the patient sat up in bed and pointed toward the door. "I want you out of here this instant."

Alistair drew closer. "Verone, is that you?"

Verone pulled up the blanket as though it might afford some protection. "Stay away from me."

"Verone, it's me, your father."

"This kind of agitation can't be good for her," Antoinette said.

Alistair faced Antoinette. "What have you done to her? Why doesn't she recognize me?"

Verone pulled back. "I know exactly who you are."

Alistair reached out to touch his daughter's altered face. "It's all right. Daddy's here. Everything's going to be fine."

Verone eyed Alistair's hand as though it were a deadly asp. Then, her eyes rolled back. Her borrowed body thrashed in uncontrolled spasms.

Antoinette lowered the Relic and took a step back. "This isn't supposed to happen."

Amanda muscled past Alistair. "Rayen, help me keep her on the bed. Dona, keep her head from hitting anything."

"How can I help?" Nathalie asked.

Amanda dodged a flailing arm. "We've got this—but she'll probably be thirsty when it's over."

Celeste put her hand on Nathalie's arm. "You stay right here. I'll have someone bring water."

Nathalie nodded and resumed her vigil at the foot of the bed.

The seizure ended as abruptly as it had begun. Dona stepped back to make room for Rayen, who pulled out his kerchief and tenderly dabbed the froth and sweat from Verone's transformed face.

Antoinette raised an eyebrow at Amanda. "I take it from your prompt response that Rayen is prone to seizures?"

"Yes, I'm afraid he is."

"It would have been nice to know that. At least we can guess it's probably not something going awry with the treatment. Unfortunately, it's cost us precious minutes. I need to get started immediately. So, all of you—if I haven't already asked you to stay, out with you."

As the people nearest the door filed out, the Primal caught up with the Crown. "We need to talk."

"Total repeal," Nathan said.

"Excuse me?"

"The Edict of Caprian—it needs to go."

"The one defining Phrendonic Heresy?"

"That's the one. Total repeal is a necessary precondition for any negotiations."

The Primal bristled. "You know I can't do that. Temporal authorities lack the power to dictate Church doctrine, and for good reason."

"Then the two of us will likely have that in common, won't we?"

As the last to leave, Dona heard animated conversation between the Crown and the Primal continue far down the corridor. She paused at the door for one last look at Verone and Rayen. Antoinette was in the midst of invoking the Relic, while Nathalie fretted at the foot of the bed. Rayen was at Verone's side clasping the hand that now looked so like his own.

Verone's eyes suddenly popped open, and her borrowed jaw dropped in awe. "Such...clarity..."

Rayen patted her hand. "Believe me, I know."

She smiled up at him. "You're here." She sounded almost surprised.

"For as long as you'll have me."

She squeezed his hand and nodded in wonder. "So I saw."

. . . . .

In the throes of gathering his compositions and tossing them wildly into a cart, Thaddeus Nevinander glimpsed a flash in the Keep's entrance. His heart sank. He'd been present when Verone had fallen to the assassin's dart and had witnessed the assassin's immolation. Instead of rushing to his sister's aid, he'd been among the first to flee. He was convinced he'd made the right decision. If Damien had been capable of that, there was no telling how much farther he'd go—the entire courtyard could have erupted in flames at any moment.

And yet, he couldn't shake the memory of his mother's anguished cries or the image of his sister's shocked expression as she sank to the dais. He almost managed to convince himself the worst was over—that everyone would be fine and that he wasn't really the spineless coward he perceived himself to be. And now, this. If Damien had been so desperate to inherit that he was willing to do Verone in, what was to keep him from doing in the rest of the family as well? Now that Alistair had passed Damien over, what was to prevent him from being next on Damien's hit list? And why stop there? Once Alistair was out of the way, maybe their mother could be convinced to split the estate, but why risk it? Why not just eliminate all his competition, winner take all? And, of course, he could conveniently blame everything on the mysterious heretics plaguing Trifienne. He winced at the mental image of his mother bursting into flames.

"Damn it."

With a resigned sigh, he turned from his cart, steeled himself, and trudged grimly toward the Keep.

He caught hold of the tenor's arm as he tried to fly past. "What's going on?"

"Don't go in there," Gregory said. "The Professor is fighting the bride's brother, and he's a heretic."

"Which brother?"

"He said his name was Damien. He's trying to make off with the documents for Verone's inheritance."

"Oh, is he? We'll see about that."

More determined than ever, Thad approached the entrance to the Keep and peered inside, fearing to find a field of corpses. But despite a wide swath of scorched and smoldering furniture and several small, but rapidly growing fires, there was not a corpse in sight. He shielded his face against the smoke with a handkerchief and sidled down the corridor, keeping an eye out for any sign of his brother. Arriving at the vestibule, he scanned for victims or witnesses. Seeing neither, he muttered a few words, and the fires abruptly died. At his feet lay Verone's distinctive leather case, charred and still smoldering. As he stooped to examine it, he noticed a line on the floor scribing a broad semicircle centered on the arch he'd just entered through. Although the remainder of the room was scorched, the floor within the semicircle was unscathed. Scattered items lying within that semicircle were similarly intact, including several sheets of paper. Not daring to believe his luck, he scooped them up. When a quick glance confirmed his suspicions, his worried expression gave way to a self-satisfied smirk. Clutching the papers to his chest, he scampered back down the hallway and out of the Keep.

Moments after Thad passed the door to the room housing the portcullis mechanism, Reston poked his head out. Once Thad was safely out of sight, he tucked his precious book under his arm and followed in his footsteps.

· · · · ·

"Miranda, no!" Alexi cried.

"Gregory's in there," she said, disappearing into the smoke-filled corridor.

"Come back—you'll suffocate."

Alphonse dashed after her. "I'll get her."

At that moment Miranda appeared at the entrance, a kerchief over her mouth. "It's not so bad. The fire seems to be out now. Are you coming?"

"I'll come," Alphonse said.

Helena raised her hand. "Me too."

Alexi's ears reddened, but he was relieved Miranda was safe. No one seemed to have a proper appreciation for the danger they were in.

"It's not only the fire that worries me—there's also the person who started it."

Alphonse drew his blade. "You're our best chance against someone like that—assuming he gets past me, of course."

Cursing his own lack of sense, he felt his resolve buckle. "With any luck, the guards will be there before it matters anyway."

The going was slow, not only because of Alexi's ankle, but because, despite the skylights, the lingering haze made it difficult to see and hard to breathe. When they finally arrived at the vestibule, Miranda rushed in despite Alexi's admonitions. "He's gone."

"That makes no sense—Damien was only after the papers."

"Or out to destroy them," Alphonse said. "No document would have survived what happened here."

"Forget the stupid documents," Miranda said. "Where's Gregory?"

"Where did you last see him?" Alexi asked.

Miranda pointed to a spot next to the remains of Verone's attaché. "Right here."

"Then he wasn't here when the fire happened. The floor is evenly scorched—if he'd been there, he'd have blocked it."

"Then where is he?"

"Verone's brother probably didn't have any reason to hurt him. Maybe he woke him up and sent him on his way."

Miranda crossed her arms. "We can't just assume that."

The Princess appeared from another corridor, accompanied by Newcomb and several guards, two of whom carried a stretcher. "What happened here? And where's the patient?"

"I don't know," Miranda said. "When we got here, the room was scorched and both Gregory and Damien were gone."

"I see," she said. "Newcomb, search the Keep and the grounds. If you find either of those two, bring them to me. The rest of you make sure this fire is completely out. Drench anything in the room that emits so much as a whiff of smoke. I need to get back to the negotiations, but don't hesitate to disturb me for anything important."

Alexi picked up the charred leather case. "Looks like he got what he came for."

Celeste's eyes widened. "Isn't that Verone's?"

"I think so. It used to hold the documents specifying that Verone stood to inherit the Nevinander estate, contingent on her marriage. Now, as you can see, it holds only soot."

"What are you suggesting?"

Alexi shrugged. "Damien seemed pretty determined to find the satchel, and now it's destroyed. As far as we know, he was the last person to see it."

"There must be some way to tell whether he's to blame." Miranda said.

The Princess shook her head. "As I understand it, this sort of thing is difficult to prove short of having an eyewitness. Even then, it depends on whether you believe the witness or the accused."

Alexi knelt to examine the floor. "Perhaps we're in luck, then. See this arc? The floor is scorched on one side and unaffected on the other."

"Doesn't that just signify the edge of the spell?"

"I don't think so. The arc is turned the wrong way for that."

"What does that mean?" Miranda asked.

"It means there may have been a witness."

. . . . .

Guards hoisting a stretcher burst into the infirmary. "We've got another one. Don't think he made it, but you're the expert. Where do you want him?"

The Sister led them past Verone's bed to the far side of the infirmary. "Over here."

"Josephus Vane," Antoinette said. "Such a pity. I understand he was quite the rising star."

"What was he even doing here?" Nathalie asked. "He wasn't on the guest list."

"Looks like we'll never know."

Verone still spoke with Rayen's lips. "I'll be sure to ask Vane when when I see him."

Nathalie sputtered at the implication. "Don't talk like that. You're going to be just fine. Isn't that right, Antoinette?"

"We've definitely made some progress, but I've never done this before. I can't say for certain how she'll respond when the spell reverts."

"I'm not talking about the poison," Verone said, "I'm referring to Damien. he wasn't watching me during the vows—he was watching the battlements. He was expecting the assassin."

"Oh, honey," Nathalie said, "Damien's a little put out at the moment, but he'll get over it."

"Mum, he nearly killed me. Mark my words, he'll try again, and next time, he won't leave anything to chance."

"I'll talk to your father if it will make you feel better," Nathalie said. "He'd never stand for such a thing."

"He probably goaded him into it."

"Don't say such things. I know you two have had your little spats over the years, but, deep down, he loves you."

"Mum, how can you possibly still believe that?"

"Because I know him. He'd never do anything to hurt you."

"I don't know quite how to tell you, but you may not know him as well as you think."

"What are you talking about?"

Verone swallowed, pausing a moment to steel herself. "Mum—please, sit down."

Nathalie paled and sank into her chair. "If this is about another of your fights—"

"It's not, Mum," she said. "You know it's not."

Nathalie looked away. "He's a good man." Tears began to well.

"It happened during the lessons. You remember, the ones in the secret room. I was eight years old."

Nathalie's hands shook. "He said he needed to teach you your heritage."

"And so he did, but it didn't stop there. I never told you because he said he would hurt you if I did. And later on, I thought I'd be hurting you if I did. I'm only telling you now because I don't think you appreciate what he's capable of. So long as he and Damien have it in for me, my days are numbered."

Nathalie rocked on the chair and wept openly. "I'm so sorry. I should have protected you."

"Mum, it's all right. There was nothing you could have done. But maybe you can help protect me now."

Nathalie stopped rocking and squarely met Verone's gaze. "Tell me how."

Before Verone could answer, her features flickered and shifted once more, reverting to their original form. Her jaw slackened and her eyes dimmed, and she fell back against the pillow, unresponsive.

# CHAPTER TWENTY-TWO

# REQUIEM

The chapel associated with the infirmary was a holdover from the Keep's prison days. Despite the interdict, the Princess never had the heart to decommission it. Even without formal Church recognition, the chapel's heavy dark-wood beams and guttering candles still afforded a measure of solace to the grief-stricken. The room was now nearing capacity as everyone outside the infirmary with a stake in Verone's welfare waited for word of her condition. Alistair sat near the front, staring silently into the candlelight. Dona sat next to her mother on the far side of the room from Alexi and Alphonse. She occasionally skewered Alexi with a withering glance but looked away if he noticed. Miranda and Helena sat halfway between them in the center of the room, unsure even what the argument was about. Jonas sat near the back fidgeting with his pipe—he had yet to find the temerity to light it up.

All heads turned as the door opened and the Princess swept in. "Have we heard anything?"

"Nothing yet," Amanda said.

"Well I have some news. The Crown and the Primal have come to an agreement. The Crown will support the Primal in his bid to recapture his throne. In return, in addition to other concessions, the Primal will repeal the Edict of Caprian. The Inquisition is officially disbanded."

"What will happen to the Monsignor?" Dona asked.

"Sounds like he'll be promoted to Ordinal whether he likes it or not."

The Monsignor appeared in the doorway. "That point is still subject to negotiation. Is there still no word?"

"Not yet," Alexi said. "Wait, does that mean heretics will be able to use their talents with impunity?"

"Of course not, but it's become obvious that our current methods are woefully ineffective. Instead, I'm proposing an entirely different regulatory framework based on temporal law to keep abuses in check. For example, one could use the Phrendonic arts to commit arson, and although such a use would no longer be considered heresy, it would still be considered arson and punished appropriately. As I envision it, the difference is that now we'll also be able to use it ourselves both for investigating such crimes and for protecting ourselves while we're doing that. More importantly, benign uses such as creating light will be universally permissible, which I expect will be a vast improvement over lantern light. Of course, this arrangement is all contingent on Darron regaining his throne, which may take some doing."

From behind, Albert gave him a nudge.

"Oh, that reminds me—if I agree to do this, I'm going to need a capable and trustworthy assistant. Alexi, could I perhaps interest you in an offer of employment?"

Alexi's jaw fell open. "Me? Are you serious?"

The Monsignor grinned. "Indeed I am."

"I would be honored."

Dona crossed her arms and muttered. "Well, isn't that just typical."

The room went suddenly silent, and after a puzzled moment, the Monsignor finally turned to see Nathalie, wan and vacant, standing next to Albert in the hallway.

Alistair finally broke the silence. "How is she doing?"

Instead of voicing an answer, she shook her head. Even that seemed to take overwhelming effort. Without a word, she turned and trudged back toward the infirmary.

Alistair brushed past the Monsignor. "Nathalie, wait."

Her eyes blazed. "Don't you touch me."

Alistair stopped short. "What's wrong? What did I do?"

"You know full well what you did. Fortunately, she was lucid right up until the end, and in her dying moments, after all these years, she finally told me."

"Told you what? What has she accused me of this time?"

"The room—she told me about the room. Oh Alistair, how could you?"

Alistair went completely white. "That's not possible. She promised she would never do that to you. Dammit, I made my peace with her."

"Well, I'm glad for that at least. You have until tomorrow night to remove your personal effects from the villa. Until then, I'll thank you to do your best to avoid me."

Tears streamed down Alistair's face. His jaw trembled. "Nathalie, you can't mean that. All those years—we made a life together. I...I love you!"

Nathalie regarded him coolly. "How sad for you."

Alistair sank to his knees and reached out to her. "Please, I beg you. Don't do this. I'll do anything."

"It's too late. I only wish…"

"What do you wish? Say the word and I'll do everything in my power to make it come true."

"I wish there was some way I could have known all those years ago that I was as wrong as I could possibly be."

Alistair bowed his head and wept.

Nathalie touched the Monsignor's sleeve. "I know it's an imposition, but would you be willing to officiate at the services? Since you performed their marriage, it would mean a lot to Rayen."

The Monsignor dabbed his eyes. "Of course."

"I'd like it to be simple—just family. I don't have it in me to plan another event."

"When would be a good time?"

"As soon as possible—tonight if you're willing. I expect to have quite a few challenges during the next few days. There's an open spot in the family crypt, so at least we won't have to worry about that."

"I'll begin preparations immediately."

"Bless you, Monsignor."

After one last lingering look at the man whom, despite everything, she still loved with all her heart, Nathalie turned, made her way back to the infirmary, and closed the door behind her.

. . . . .

Lavender clouds hovered against a violet sky by the time Verone's memorial service finally coalesced in Ranselard's courtyard. A cold breeze stirred the vacant throne's matrimonial nosegays, and much of the space was still littered with toppled chairs and discarded programs. While few of the wedding guests had risked returning to what they now referred to as "that accursed place," Cartier had arrived an hour or so earlier in the company of the Venerable Assembly of Church Mothers. Fresh from Garvin's funeral, the news of Verone's passing only served to deepen Cartier's despondence.

Despite their grief, the Church Mothers were predictably industrious once they determined that Nathalie was in no condition make the necessary arrangements, and the courtyard bustled with their activity. They laid Verone in her wedding gown atop the same dais where she and Rayen had spoken their vows, amidst a profusion of white roses commandeered from the wedding decorations. Since a casket had been unavailable on short notice, the flowers served to conceal a stretcher they used in its stead. When they'd discovered the wedding musicians had disappeared, they organized an impromptu choir and improvised elegies in three-part harmony, which, in short order, gave way to something a bit less musically ambitious and considerably more aesthetically pleasing. Arerio somberly circled the courtyard with a long-handled wick, setting alight lanterns hung that morning in anticipation of a jubilant reception.

Nathalie was among the first to arrive. She had requested and received a black veil from the Princess. While it lent solemnity to her otherwise festive gown, it did little to conceal the anguish in her eyes. Mercifully, she was not alone. Her sister Olivia guided her to her seat, followed closely by Rayen, Amanda, and Dona. Once Nathalie was in place, the Crown and his family, including Marguerite and Michlos, emerged from the marquee and positioned themselves in the row immediately behind her.

Catching sight of Marguerite, Cartier sank low in his chair in a transparent attempt to be less obvious. Uncertain of his status with Dona, Alexi played it safe and sat farther back with Alphonse, Helena, and Miranda. The Princess quietly settled in near the Crown and his family. Jonas fidgeted in the very last row, hoping that Reston was still somewhere about, but suspecting his 'plus one' had ditched him. Eventually, Antoinette emerged and found a spot in the back near Jonas.

Alistair's continuing absence caused some consternation, since the Monsignor was loath to begin before he arrived. At last, Albert spoke softly with Nathalie, and, after only a moment, stood and nodded for them to begin.

The Primal stepped forth, swinging before him a heavy thurible they'd found in the chapel cupboard. Clouds of incense swirled about him as he ritually cleansed the way for his brother, whom he'd volunteered to assist. When the two men arrived at the dais, the Primal waved the thurible at all four cardinal directions and then had a seat off to one side.

Concealed in the darkness of a second-floor tower window, Prentiss finally saw his opening. From a long sleek box, he selected precisely crafted parts by their feel alone and deftly fit them together. He didn't hurry. He never hurried.

A late arrival turned several heads, but only briefly, since the limping figure with the crutches clearly didn't fit Alistair's description.

Alexi smiled reassuringly as the man negotiated a seat—he was now keenly aware of the challenges that crutches posed during a ceremony. His expression quickly became one of shock.

He nudged Alphonse. "That's Everson."

Alphonse glanced briefly and shrugged. It was then Alexi recalled Alphonse wasn't privy to the details of Everson's involvement in recent events, and he found himself missing Dona. Only a few feet from him, she might as well have been a continent away. When he tried to catch her attention, she studiously avoided eye contact, but she did spare an occasional glare for Julienne, who spent much of the service glancing back at Alexi to smile fetchingly.

It wasn't long before heads turned again. This time, Newcomb padded over to confer with the Princess. Before long, Michlos was involved as well. After several minutes, Newcomb left, and Michlos followed on his heels.

Up in his window, Prentiss wound the crank on the newly assembled apparatus. In moments, he would be ready.

By the time the Monsignor pronounced the final benediction, even Nathalie was scanning for Alistair, but there was still no sign of him. Olivia finally voiced what everyone was thinking. "He's probably at the villa clearing out everything of any value. The sooner we get back there the better."

As the assembly broke up, Cartier approached the Monsignor, fully aware that he'd become the object of Marguerite's rapt attention. Even now, she followed his every move with a calculating eye.

"Monsignor, could I have a word in private?"

The Monsignor hesitated. "How long will it take? We'll be leaving for the Nevinander crypt shortly."

Upstairs, Prentiss raised his contraption to eye level as the Primal finally came into view.

The Primal put a hand on Armand's shoulder. "That was nicely done."

"I appreciate that. Darron, have you met Father Cartier?"

"The man responsible for the reconciliation? I don't believe I have."

"May I present my brother, the Primal."

Cartier bowed low. "It's an honor, Your Primacy."

"You have my thanks, Father," the Primal said. "If you hadn't initiated this reconciliation, things might have gone very differently today. You laid the groundwork that made our new treaty with the Crown of Trifienne possible."

"New treaty?"

Tucked away in his tower perch, Prentiss raised an eyebrow and momentarily relaxed his trigger finger.

Cartier lowered his voice. "You are aware the Crown's mother-in-law is a heretic, right?"

"That did present a bit of a challenge initially, but we got past it."

"How do you get past something like that?"

"Simple. I repealed the Edict of Caprian. I'm not one to let dogma stand in the way of progress."

Upstairs, Prentiss gasped.

"What? Won't people be outraged?"

"At my disbanding of the Inquisition? I think you may be overestimating their devotion to the finer points of Church doctrine. Armand, how much time do we have before we head to the crypt?"

The Monsignor glanced over at Verone's stretcher. "They still need to load Miss Nevinander's remains into the carriage."

The Primal nodded. "Father Cartier, it was a pleasure to meet you. If you'll excuse us, I have an important matter that requires my attention."

"I think Father Cartier wanted to speak with me privately," the Monsignor said.

Cartier raised his hands and took a step back. "No, it's all right. I've figured out what I wanted to know."

Up in the tower, Prentiss had already completed disassembling his contraption.

"All right then," the Primal said. "Armand, could you round up Albert and 'Father Anton' and bring them to the dais?"

"They can't have gone far. I'll be right back."

As the Monsignor stalked off, Cartier approached Marguerite.

"I take it that conversation didn't go quite as you expected," she said.

Cartier sat heavily in the chair next to her. "That's an understatement. My sincere apologies. Never in my wildest dreams would I have imagined there could be multiple heretics in play."

"It wasn't wholly your fault. Verone was a maestro of misdirection. Say, when last we met, I don't think I emphasized enough how sorry I was for your loss. I know it won't bring him back, but perhaps you can find some solace in knowing the person responsible has paid a steep price for his crimes."

"If that's true, it appeals to my sense of justice, but does nothing to assuage my guilt. I had a momentary brush with power that went directly to my head. I was so giddy I lost sight of the many blessings I'd already been given, and to disastrous effect. The saddest thing of all is that if I'd just taken the time to think, I'd have realized that I never wanted it in the first place—I already had everything I needed to be happy."

"I envy you that. It's been a long time since I've felt that way."

Cartier held up his own leather case. "She gave me this, you know."

"She had expensive taste."

He opened the case and removed a floral wrap. "I believe this belongs to you."

She stood, and he draped it over her shoulders. "Thank you. I've missed it. It was a gift from my late husband—he was so very fond of flowers."

Back up in the tower window, nothing now remained to indicate that anyone uninvited had ever been there.

# CHAPTER TWENTY-THREE

# RECONCILIATION

Alexi leaned against the stone wall outside the keep's front gate as Dona, accompanied by her mother and Rayen, passed by on their way to Nathalie's carriage.

"Hey," he said. "I need to ask you something. Alone."

"We'll wait in the carriage," Amanda said.

Once they were out of earshot, Dona raised an eyebrow. "Well? What is it?"

"Why did you lie to me about Gregory?"

"What about him?"

"You told me you were just friends."

"I don't believe this. I was teasing before, but you really are jealous, aren't you?"

"Have you ever noticed how you tend to avoid answering difficult questions by changing the subject?"

"I didn't change the subject—I got to the point. You're jealous of Gregory, so you're taking it out on me by publicly cavorting with the royal harlot. You're embarrassing yourself far more than you are me."

"Oh, so that's what this is all about. Well, for your information, I didn't look for her—she found me."

"So I was right. You are cavorting with her."

"So what if I am? How would that be any different than what you did with Gregory?"

"I didn't do anything with Gregory."

"That's not what Julienne says, and she's not the only one who saw it, either."

"You call her *Julienne?*"

"Ooh, now look who's jealous. I'd keep a close eye on that if I were you. It'll eat you alive."

"Wait—you're talking about the opera, aren't you."

Even though arguing with her was maddening, he couldn't let it go—he missed her too much. But that didn't mean he could stop himself from pushing her buttons. Maybe even that was part of the attraction. "Go ahead. Change the subject again. That's how I know when I'm near the mark."

"I'm not changing the subject. What happened at the opera with Gregory—that was all an act. Besides, what business is it of yours? That was before you were even in the picture."

"It's not the opera I'm worried about. It's the encore."

"I already told you, there's no chance of that. In fact, the only reason there was anything to see is because Julienne was there to see it."

"Let me guess—you were trying to show the harlot how it's done?"

Her eyes narrowed. "Judging by the cloying scent of Julienne's perfume, it appears she has you for that."

"I'll have you know I was a perfect gentleman."

"Right. Nothing says 'gentleman' like smudged lipstick on the lower lip."

Alexi rubbed his mouth with his thumb and looked at it in shock. "I can explain."

"You really don't have to. I know how aggressive she can be. That's what I was trying to tell you—she did the same thing to Gregory at the opera. He was so afraid she was going to drag him off into the bushes that he asked me to pretend we were dating, but even that didn't put her off. I only managed to rescue him by using the Monsignor as a distraction."

"So, you're saying she's only feigning interest in me to get back at you?"

Dona shrugged. "You have a better explanation?"

"Oh, I think I can be pretty compelling when I put my mind to it."

"Really? Are you saying you put your mind to it?"

"Well no, but if I had…"

"I won't argue that—it worked on me, didn't it?"

Even her coy smile was like the sun emerging from behind a cloud. Alexi grinned in return. "Now that you mention it, I guess it did."

"Look, I should have known better than to use you to taunt her like that. I never dreamed she'd be so publicly brazen—not that it matters anymore."

"What do you mean?"

Dona turned away. "You've just taken a job with the Monsignor. You're going to be off living in palaces and seeing the world. You can't afford to be tied down by a lowly college student. I'd just be a millstone around your neck."

"That's not true."

"I should have seen it coming. The women in my family have a long history of losing the men in their lives. You just never think it's going to happen to you."

"Are you crying? Aw, don't do that. You haven't lost me. We can work this out." Her tears were every bit as potent as her smile. He couldn't stand to see her like this.

"I should go. They're waiting for me."

"Hold on—I have an idea. Tell your mother to go on ahead. Then go up by the cliffs and wait for me."

"Alexi, let it go. I can't ask you to stay, and once you're gone, it's never going to last. You'll promise to write every day, and at first you will, but eventually the letters will reduce to a trickle, and then to nothing. I can't live letter to letter. That's not a life."

Alexi gently brushed the tears from her cheek. "For once could you please stop trying to make sense of everything and humor me? I have something I want to show you."

"But—"

"No buts. Now go on. I'll meet you up on the cliffs in a few minutes."

"Oh, all right, but I don't see—"

Alexi raised a warning finger. "No buts. And be careful. That place can be treacherous in the dark."

. . . . .

After a brief stop at her mother's carriage to send them on without her, Dona wandered over to the cliffs. The wind had come up as the sun had set, and she drew her little coat close against the chill. She paced along the cliff's edge as she waited, coming at last to the outcrop of rock whence Nathan dove to Marguerite's rescue. For a time, she watched the whitecaps crash against the shore below. Fingering Alexi's locket, she wondered what had possessed her to agree to this. Fast and clean. Wasn't that the best way? If she wasn't careful, Alexi would make it slow and messy—and yet, here she was.

A footfall made her turn.

"It's colder up here than I thought," Alexi said. "Here."

He draped his dress coat over her shoulders. Then he wrapped her in his arms and together they gazed out over the river.

She suffered a pang of regret as she reveled in the warmth of his embrace. "Thanks, that's much better. What did you want to show me?"

"The moon. I think it's full tonight."

Despite her misgivings, she smiled. "Why, I think you're right."

"There. You did it again."

"Did what?"

"You smiled. You know I live for that."

She felt another pang—sharper than the last. "You'll get over that eventually."

"You underestimate your charms."

She smiled again, this time slyly. "I'm not saying it will be easy."

He shook his head. "It's not going to happen."

She faced him. "Alexi, be reasonable. Neither of us wants a long-distance relationship."

"I guess you're right. That would never work."

Shivering there in the moonlight in his crisp white shirt, he looked so vulnerable and forlorn that she almost lost her resolve. "So, you know what we have to do then, right?"

"I think so."

"Putting it off will only make it worse. You know that."

"I guess—so this is it then. And you want me to be the one to do it?"

She tried to reply but struggled to hold back tears. She could only muster a quick nod.

"All right then, here goes."

He took her hand and dropped to one knee. "Dona Merinne, you are exasperating, brilliant, and beautiful. I love you madly and I want you always by my side. Marry me, and I swear I'll find a way to make the Monsignor agree to take us both." He opened his hand to reveal a ring with a diamond that almost made the moon look small. "Please say yes."

"Dear lord, where on earth did you get that? You came by it honestly, right?"

Alexi smirked. "Julienne was so eager to give me a token of her esteem, I didn't have the heart to refuse her. I trust she will be delighted to hear I was able to exchange it for something I could really use."

Dona was so shocked she didn't know whether to laugh or cry. "This came from her?"

"Fitting, isn't it? Now, speaking of things I could really use, an answer would be nice. Holding this position is getting awkward, and it's freezing out here."

"You really think the Monsignor would go for that? Taking me along, I mean?"

"If you say yes, I don't see how he could say no."

Dona's smile turned sly. "And while we're at it, what's all this nonsense about my being exasperating?"

"Given that I'm still down here waiting after asking ever so nicely twice now, I should think that would be self-evident."

"At least you can't claim you didn't know what you were in for."

"Is that a yes?"

"Oh, Alexi, of course it's a yes. Now get up off your knee and kiss me."

"Wait, are you crying again?"

She grabbed his collar and pulled him close. "Just kiss me."

· · · · ·

As Verone's stretcher was carted away from the dais, Antoinette approached the Primal, the Monsignor, and the Curator, who were seating themselves after rearranging the chairs among the broken blooms left behind. "All right I'm here," Antoinette said. "Now what's all this fuss about?"

"Thank you for coming," the Primal said. "Could you please take a seat next to Armand? Albert, you too. Where's Thurman?"

"Sulking I think," Albert said. "He seemed a little put out that he might actually have to suffer some consequences for his unauthorized use of Profanities."

Antoinette huffed. "Shame on you, Armand. How could you threaten him like that? He helped save your brother's life, and at significant personal risk, I might add."

The Monsignor sighed. "As Inquisitor General, I don't have the luxury to play favorites, particularly in the face of a tacit admission of guilt. In due course, his offenses would have been investigated, and any mitigating circumstances would have been accounted for. Anything less would ruin the legitimacy of the office."

"Yes, heaven forbid we sully the reputation of an institution that poisons its leader and engages well-known thugs to do its unofficial dirty work."

"Every institution has its bad apples. That doesn't mean we should sink to their level. Besides, as you'll no doubt recall, the Church had its fair share of ethical challenges while Father was Inquisitor General too."

"And Ordinal, and even during the brief time he was Primal," Darron pointed out. "Fortunately, Thurman's issues are all moot now that the Edict of Caprian has been repealed. Can we please get back to the matter at hand?"

Antoinette rubbed her temples. When it came to brevity, both of her boys took after their father. "And just what is the matter at hand?"

"Ascendency. As my health continues to improve, it pains me to admit it, but Laitrech's role in all of this cannot possibly have been innocent. Someone capable of such treachery obviously has no place in my new administration. I have therefore revoked his status as Ordinal and ordered his immediate arrest to stand trial on charges of attempted murder. Since Armand tells me that Laitrech was in the vicinity this morning, I've asked both the Princess and the Crown to be on the lookout for his carriage. With any luck, he won't make it out of Trifienne. That, of course, raises the issue of his replacement."

Antoinette pulled at the cord around her neck. "I suppose you'll want this back then?"

"Ah yes, Laitrech's Relic. As a matter of fact, I will."

Antoinette placed it in her son's hand. Now that she'd given them what they wanted, perhaps they'd let an old woman get back to her plotting. Someone had to make sure these two didn't mess up the opportunity she'd given them. "We aren't going through the entire Ceremony of Ascendance, are we? I'm old, it's cold, and there's still a funeral to finish."

"That shouldn't be necessary. Armand assures me that the Canons allow for appointments by fiat when there are exigent circumstances. I think this qualifies."

"Excellent. Then why don't you appoint Armand and get this over with. I need to start planning my escape from whatever convent you're planning to banish me to next. At least while I'm here, I have the luxury of doing so with a nice glass of wine by a cozy fire."

"Not so fast," Darron said. "Against all odds, I've been granted a second chance, and I am not about to screw it up this time. That means, among a great many other things, that my Ordinal appointments will be determined solely on the basis of who is best-suited for the position."

"Seriously? Are you saying you've found a better candidate than Armand?"

"That's exactly what I'm saying."

It was a good thing they checked with her. Darron's track record on appointments left a little to be desired. "Are you sure you're feeling all right? Because, if you're not, you might want to recover a few more days before making any important decisions."

"I've consulted with Armand, and he agrees."

She shot Armand a sidelong glance. "Oh really? Did it occur to you that Armand's opinion might be a wee bit colored by a certain conflict of interest?"

"Armand? A conflict of interest? Are you kidding?"

"Good lord, you're right. What was I thinking? All right then—who is this super-candidate?"

"Why it's you, of course."

Antoinette's mouth fell open. It had been years since anything had rendered her speechless. "Me?"

"Frankly, this should come as no surprise. Although we both know Armand is eminently qualified, his interests and expertise are more aligned with crafting a rigorously humane and equitable institution than in securing the institution's stability in the first place. You, on the other hand, have spent a lifetime kingmaking within the context of the Church hierarchy, first on Father's behalf, and then, though I've been reluctant to admit it, on mine. Right now, those are the very skills I need most."

"But I'm not even ordained."

"That, too, can be remedied by fiat. It's not like you don't have all the appropriate training, and Armand assures me there's nothing in the Canons to prevent it. Once our position is a little more secure, we'll follow up with all the requisite pomp and circumstance."

Antoinette shook her head. They were sabotaging themselves—now was not the time. "I appreciate the offer, but I can't accept."

"I don't believe it—you're going to fight me on this too?"

"I know you're trying to do the right thing, but you can't do everything at once. At this stage of the game, it's vital to choose your battles wisely. Your situation is already precarious, and although necessary, your repeal of the Edict of Caprian will only make it more so. If you try to do this as well, you'll lose everything."

Darron pondered that for a moment, then sighed. "Ironically, it wasn't that long ago when winning itself meant so much to me that I was willing to compromise almost anything to achieve it. I told myself that even if I couldn't accomplish everything I originally intended, at least I had prevented selfish men from using my position to do worse things. Well, look where that got me. I'm under no delusions about the difficulties ahead. Make no mistake; this will be the toughest battle I've ever waged. To win, I'll need to give it everything I've got. For that to happen, I have to believe—*firmly* believe—that everything I'm fighting for is worth dying for. If, to regain the throne, I must continue to sacrifice the dignity of women, then what I will have won won't be worth the effort. Few among us are given a second chance. I intend to make mine count."

By now, she'd have thought they'd realize she didn't respond well to inspirational speeches. "Now you're starting to sound like Armand."

Darron smiled. "That's a compliment I don't yet deserve—but I hope to, one day. Mother, please, join my team. I promise I won't disappoint you. We may not win, but even in losing we'll be a shining example."

"And what about Armand?"

"He'll stay on as Inquisitor General to disband the Inquisition in an orderly fashion."

"And after that?"

"He's promised to take the next available Relic."

"Has he now?" Antoinette pulled out Jonas's medallion. "Well it just so happens I have it right here. As long as we are so determined to lose, we may as well all go out together in a blaze of nepotism."

Darron's eyes almost popped out of his head. "You stole another one?"

"No. This one I made."

"What are you talking about? You can't just make a Relic."

"Sure, you can. Where do you think the originals came from?"

"The original Martyrs—but the knowledge to make them has been lost."

Antoinette snorted. "Lost in plain sight. I found a scroll outlining the procedure some time ago in the Chapel. I figured the only way to get you to agree to retire the current Relics would be if we had a way to replace them. Well, now we do."

"Sure," Darron said. "All we have to do is round up nine more martyrs."

"Sarcasm is unbecoming in a Primal. Besides, it's not nearly as difficult as you make it sound. Just make it explicit that upon an Ordinal's death, the Relic is retired."

"I don't see how that solves the problem. By the end of a generation, we'd be completely out of Ordinals."

"Not if you had the current Ordinal take his Relic's place. That way there would be a constant supply of just the right number, and each participant would only be delaying his—or her—salvation for a relatively short time. The way it is currently done is unconscionable."

"You'd be willing to agree to that as a condition of becoming an Ordinal?"

"Actually, I would be willing to become an Ordinal only on that condition."

"And what about you, Armand?"

The Monsignor rubbed his chin. "Hmm. I'd want to know the details of the ritual, and I'd also want to know how the retirement of subsequent Relics will be assured, but in principle, it seems fair."

"I can't impose that requirement retroactively on a sitting Ordinal, but I'd be willing to impose it on anyone seeking to become an Ordinal."

Antoinette nodded. "I can live with that."

"So, you'll agree to be Laitrech's successor? Think of it—you'll be able to meddle along with me, instead of in spite of me."

Antoinette sighed. "Oh, if you insist. I never could seem to keep myself from spoiling you."

. . . . .

Thaddeus Nevinander opened his door to a roundhouse punch that sent him flying back into the tiny canvas-strewn hut he called his studio. Shaking out his hand, Damien stepped in after him.

"That's for killing our sister." He followed up with a kick to Thad's ribs. "And that's for turning me over to a Santine."

Thad spit blood from his damaged lip. He'd known Damien would come for him but hadn't expected him quite this soon. "Don't blame me if your assassin had the aim of a cross-eyed grandmother. You get what you pay for. I bet you thought I wouldn't remember him. Well, I've got news, when your big brother has his friends beat you up, you remember them for a very long time."

"I wouldn't have needed him at all if you hadn't been so unreasonable."

"You're just mad because you were forced to sacrifice your friend instead of me. I suppose you told him the promise stick held a Darkness and that his escape would be child's play, right?"

Damien sighed. "And now I'll need to find someone else to do the monthly dock collections."

"What's the matter? Running out of friends?"

Damien paused by a large landscape of the bridge to the island. "Pretty." With a *snick*, a knife appeared in his hand. "Too bad you never seem to learn how unproductive goading me can be." He slashed diagonally across the painting.

Thad winced. That one had taken him a week.

"Now—you were saying?"

"So what will Reg and Jed do to you when they find out what you've done?"

"Do to me? Congratulate me, probably. The whole thing was their idea."

Thad had been appalled to learn the depths to which Damien had stooped to safeguard his inheritance. That all three brothers had sunk so low was chilling. "Killing Verone was their idea?"

"Not exactly, but if Theratigan had died like we'd planned, Verone might still have married someone else. There's no chance of that now, is there?"

"And their hands stayed pristine. I should have guessed they were in on it. But unlike you, they had the sense to stay away from the wedding, no doubt to establish an airtight alibi. Don't you ever tire of doing their dirty work?"

Damien drew his blade across another canvas. "Well, what do you know? It's still sharp."

"Too bad it was all for naught. Not only are you out an inheritance, you're out of a job as well. Unless, of course, you expect Theratigan will continue employing his wife's murderer."

Damien ravaged another canvas. "Don't you worry. That imbecile won't inherit a thing."

"You murdered his wife. Correct me if I'm wrong, but doesn't that have exactly the opposite effect?"

Damien viciously stabbed another canvas. "I was wrong about you. All this time I thought you were an art lover."

"You know what I love even more? The artful way Verone made you bastards squirm when she disinherited you."

"I told you, it never happened."

"Come, now. I've seen the papers."

"There were only ever two copies of those papers—Dad will destroy his, and I already took care of the others."

Thad had been looking forward to this moment. He spoke the words with particular care for maximum impact. "You aren't referring to your botched attempt to incinerate them in Celeste's vestibule, are you? Because if you are, I've got news for you."

Damien's smile faded. "How do you know about that?"

"I was there."

"I didn't see you."

"Must have been right after you left—the bench cushions were still burning. Curiously, the relevant papers didn't seem to be affected. Don't worry, though, I'll be sure they make it into the hands of the appropriate authorities."

Damien's eyes burned like twin coals. "I see now that a warning isn't going to suffice this time."

"Want me to show you them?"

"Don't trouble yourself. I'll deal with them while you're napping. Such a pity all these pretty paintings are so flammable." Damien launched into mnemonics, completing them with a flourish.

Thad pulled himself to his feet.

"So you protected yourself against that, did you? And here I was being so nice by sparing you the pain. Tell me, smart boy, did you protect yourself against this?"

With deadly precision, he hurled the switchblade at Thad's still-heaving chest. As it neared him, the blade crumbled. The handle bounced harmlessly away.

Newcomb stepped across the threshold, his crossbow leveled. "Hands over your head."

Damien reluctantly complied.

"Did you hear enough?" Thad asked.

Michlos followed Newcomb in. "More than enough. You shouldn't need to worry about your brothers bothering you ever again."

Damien spat. "You gave me up…to a *Serrola?*"

Thad ignored him. "And the papers?"

"Safe and sound." Michlos dropped his Amulet just long enough to Sleep Damien. "I'll make sure they get where they need to go. I'm sorry about the physical attacks—we didn't see those coming. I barely caught the knife in time. You should come back to the Keep for treatment."

Thad rubbed his jaw. "I'll be all right. I've had far worse than this, but never for such a worthy cause. It was the least I could do for my sister."

# CHAPTER TWENTY-FOUR

---

# ЄPITΛPҺ

"Ma is going to kill me."

The carriage that had borne Dona and Alexi to Ranselard Keep was now carrying them back down the bumpy trail toward the bridge to Trifienne on its way to the Nevinander estate.

Alexi's brow furrowed. "Doesn't she like me?"

"It's not that. She's going to say I'm too young. She was having trouble letting go of Rayen, and he's old."

"Don't you think that's normal for moms?"

"Most moms get over it eventually—I'm not sure mine will. She'll want me to wait until I graduate."

"We'll just have to convince her it would be better not to wait."

"And how do you propose doing that?"

"Um, well—"

The carriage lurched to one side.

Dona peered out the window "Now what? We're already frightfully late."

"Looks like we're just passing someone on the road."

"Hmph. You'd think a horse could move faster than a carriage. I wonder what his problem is? Wait a second—isn't that Verone's horse?"

Alexi poked his head out the window as horse and rider receded into the gloom. "I don't know about the horse, but the rider sure looked like Professor Everson."

"Everson?" Are you sure?"

Alexi nodded. "He showed up for the funeral too"

"He did?"

"Is that really so surprising? They did know each other after all."

"Well, he certainly wasn't on the guest list."

"Maybe she invited him to the wedding in person?"

"If they were so close, why would he steal her horse?"

"Maybe he was afraid it would be overlooked in the commotion—he might be doing it as a favor."

Given their history, Dona was unconvinced Everson was capable of such a charitable act. "Maybe."

"Did you want to go back and ask?"

"And miss the interment entirely? If I never have to deal with him again, the horse is a small price to pay."

"You know what I think? I think someone needs to spend less time worrying about unpleasant things from her past and more time thinking about all the wonderful things in store for her future."

"Such as?"

"Such as how her fabulous fiancé is going to come up with an inspired pretext for putting his arm around her and holding her close for the rest of this trip."

She snuggled up against him. "You know—I think you might be onto something there."

She didn't bat an eye when, in the middle of Trifienne, their carriage was briefly stopped and redirected by the militia without explanation.

"I bet they're searching for that Ordinal," Alexi said.

Dona didn't lift her head from his shoulder. "Let them search."

By the time they arrived at the villa, the interment was well underway. The Nevinander Mausoleum was flanked by two ancient braziers—their oil-fed flames smoking and sputtering in the wind. The Monsignor stood between them on the steps pronouncing one last benediction. At the base of the steps lay the stretcher, its tragic occupant still decorated with the few stalwart blooms that survived the journey. To the left, Rayen looked on stoically, while on the right, Nathalie wept quietly beneath her veil, Olivia by her side. Nathan and Irina sat front and center, while Marguerite stood several steps back from the rest, seemingly lost in thought.

Dona took one last look at the lifeless form in the wedding dress with the tiny bloodstain. Verone had played so many contradictory roles in her life over the past few weeks, she really didn't know how to feel about her anymore. She settled for numb. She wanted badly to be more empathetic with her uncle, but try as she might, she couldn't make herself see Verone in the same saintly light.

When it was time to help Rayen move the stretcher into the crypt, Nathan stepped forward.

"Hey," Dona said suddenly. "What happened to her ring?"

"What ring?" Rayen asked.

"Her wedding ring. Don't you want her to wear it?"

Rayen set down the stretcher. "It's not on her finger?"

"No. She's not wearing any jewelry at all. Did you ever give it to her?"

Rayen felt his coat pockets. "I must have. I don't seem to have it on me."

Antoinette spoke up. "No doubt the Sisters removed her jewelry when she was taken to the infirmary. I believe that's standard practice."

Rayen's ears flushed. "Yes, that must be it."

"Do you want us to go back for it?" Dona asked.

Rayen shook his head. "It's all right. I don't want to make all these people wait."

Dona eyed Rayen dubiously. "Are you sure? I certainly wouldn't want to be buried without mine."

Dona's mother gasped. "What is that on your finger, young lady?"

Dona froze for an instant, turned to face her mother, and held up her hand. "Isn't it wonderful? Alexi proposed."

Amanda's eyes narrowed. "It's time we had a little heart-to-heart."

"Ma, don't blow this out of proportion."

"Tonight." Her tone brooked no further discussion.

A cry from the back of the assembly shattered the tension. "Mrs. Nevinander—come quick." Huffing and puffing, Eloise pushed through the guests. "It's Master Alistair—he's out of his mind."

Nathalie rushed to her side. "What happened?"

"I've never heard such howling and wailing and carrying on. He smashed most of the liquor cabinet before staggering upstairs, a bottle in each hand."

"Where is he now?"

"In his office. There've been some awful noises up there."

Nathalie sighed. "I'll come."

"Don't you do it," Olivia snapped. "You know how he gets."

"You want me to let him destroy the house?"

"I want you to call in the Constable. Stop risking yourself like that. It isn't right."

"I'll come with you," Nathan said.

Nathalie shook her head. "No, that would only make things worse."

The Monsignor clasped Alexi's shoulders. "Perhaps you should take Alexi, here. I doubt your husband would view him as a threat, and he could be helpful in a pinch."

"I appreciate your concern, Monsignor, but I've been doing this a long time now. I don't need help dealing with my husband, but I would be grateful if you could finish up here without me. I'm not sure how long I'll be, and it wouldn't be fair to make everyone wait."

The Monsignor bowed his head in acknowledgment, and Nathalie and Eloise started back toward the villa.

Olivia crossed her arms as she watched them go. "It's a wonder she's still alive."

At that, the Monsignor caught Alexi's eye and tilted his head subtly in Nathalie's direction. Alexi nodded in return, and the Monsignor returned to the crypt.

"What was that about?" Dona whispered.

"I think he wants me to keep an eye on her," Alexi said.

"Over my dead body. You have no idea what that man's capable of."

"Quit worrying. If things get ugly, I can always resort to my secret weapon."

"Or he can resort to his. Don't you get it? His family has been doing that sort of thing for generations. His arsenal probably makes your 'secret weapon' look like a pea shooter."

"Look, I've got to go. If he's half as drunk as the maid said, he'll probably pass out before I even get there."

"All right then, I'm coming with you."

"No, you're not.

"In case you haven't noticed, the world has recently become a very dangerous place. Or haven't you been keeping track of the body count?"

"He's just drunk. It's no big deal."

"Then I'm going too."

. . . . .

The Nevinander's courtyard was a gloomy conglomeration of sil-houettes and half-seen shapes. Other than the moon, the only light was a wan glow that filtered through the curtains behind the multipaned glass of a set of balcony doors far above.

Alexi hesitated, casting about for Nathalie and Eloise. "Where'd they go?"

"I imagine they went to Alistair's office."

"Uh, any idea where that is?"

Dona sighed and pointed out the balcony. "It's up there."

Shadows flickered across the curtains. Someone was moving about behind them.

A sharp knock froze the shadows in place. "Alistair, open this door," Nathalie said.

The shadows on the curtains shuddered. "Go away." The thick growl sounded only vaguely like Alistair.

The rapping resumed, more insistent. "Alistair, I said open this door. You need to sleep this off."

Something fragile shattered against the study door. "Leave me alone."

"How do I get up there?" Alexi asked.

"Don't stick your nose in this. She knows what she's doing."

"He's drunk and violent. There's no telling what he'll do. I can't risk letting the Monsignor down. How do I get up there?"

Although her better judgment howled in protest, Dona pointed across the courtyard. "Over there. Once you're inside, take the stairs to the right. It's down the hall from there."

He planted a hurried kiss on her cheek and headed off.

"Alistair," Nathalie said. "I'm worried about you. Please, let me in."

"No, you're not," Alistair slurred. "You hate me."

"Oh Alistair, that's not true. I love you too much to ever hate you."

The rage in Alistair's voice lessened. "Really?"

Even from where she stood, Dona could hear him fumble with the latch. "You really don't hate me?"

"Of course not. Now let's get you to bed."

"Our bed?"

"Yes," she said gently, "our bed."

"You're not going to leave me?"

There was a long pause. If Nathalie answered, Dona didn't hear it.

Alistair's voice suddenly took on a note of deep suspicion. "Who's that? Who's there?"

"What are you doing here?" Nathalie said.

"It's me—Alexi. The Monsignor asked me to check on you."

In the courtyard, Dona shook her head and clapped a hand to her face.

Alistair cried out, his rage redoubled. "I knew it—it was a trap. He never repealed the Edict. He'll never take me alive."

"Go away," Nathalie rasped. "I don't need your help."

In a clear voice, Alexi recited mnemonics from Reston's book, but before he finished, Dona heard the slow squeak of hinges and a metallic thud from inside the study. Then a door slammed, followed by frantic pounding.

"Alistair, come back," Nathalie cried. "It's not what you think."

"I'm so sorry," Alexi said. "How can I help?"

"Haven't you helped enough? Just go!"

The pounding resumed and Nathalie continued shouting Alistair's name.

In the courtyard, Dona watched in horror as the study was engulfed by a blinding flash of light. The balcony curtains burst instantly into flame. Heat radiated across her in waves. No sooner did the first flash wink out than the second hit, then a third. Within the inferno came a terrible heartrending wail, cut short by a fourth flash. The cry was echoed by Nathalie, who pounded all the more frantically.

Dona sprang across the courtyard. By the time she made it to the top of the stairs, the smoke was already making it difficult to breathe. Alexi limped toward her carrying Nathalie in his arms.

"Is she all right?"

He spoke through tears. "She wouldn't come away from the door. I had to do it to save her."

"Quickly, this way."

She led him back to the courtyard, but once there, Alexi could carry Nathalie no longer. He laid her gently on a bench. Eloise was already there, hovering with concern. Several panes in the balcony door shattered, peppering the courtyard with searing shards. Smoke billowed through the gaps.

Marguerite dashed into the courtyard. "Are any of you hurt?"

"We're all right," Dona said.

"Where's Alistair?"

Dona pointed. "He was in there."

Marguerite blanched. "Oh my lord. Stay here and keep a tight rein on Nathalie."

"What are you going to do?"

Marguerite pulled out her wrap and wound it around her face. She raced across the courtyard and into the villa.

Dona started after her, but Alexi held her back. "What's she doing? She'll die in there."

She pummeled his hands, but he held her fast. "Just let her go."

A moment later, the inferno winked out of existence. A few errant flames still danced for a bit longer until, one by one, they, too, simply ceased to be. The smoke was another matter, and it wasn't long before Marguerite leaned out a window and gasped for breath.

"I can't get to him," she wheezed. "Even if I could survive the smoke, it's still too hot in there. It wouldn't matter if I could, though. No one could possibly have survived that." She shook her head sadly. "Thus ends an era."

Alexi went stark white. "This was all my fault," he said softly.

# CHAPTER TWENTY-FIVE

---

# RESOLUTION

Arerio placed the steaming cup before Marguerite, who looked up from a stack of singed ledgers and smiled. "Why thank you. By the way, how are you feeling? Have there been any ill effects?"

"I've noticed one thing, but it's minor. It would be indelicate to mention."

Marguerite's eyes danced with amusement. "I'm a big girl. I think I can handle it."

"Then perhaps it would be easier to show you." He screwed up his mouth and spat. The ejected material sputtered, steamed, and evaporated before it made it even halfway to the floor.

Marguerite chuckled. "I do hope you won't let that get in the way of any of your duties."

"I shall do my best, Mistress. I should mention that Master Michlos is here to see you."

"Please, show him in."

"Ah, it seems he's found his way on his own."

Michlos strode into the dining room. "We haven't been able to find his body anywhere, and no one saw him leave Ranselard or the infirmary. I even tracked down Professor Everson to question him, since he was in the infirmary at the time."

"What did he say?" Marguerite asked.

"He said he doesn't remember anything at all after being chloro-formed until he woke up the next morning."

"And Vane's corpse was long-gone by then?"

Michlos nodded. "It's as if it vanished into thin air."

Arerio exchanged a discomfited glance with Marguerite. "If you'll excuse me."

"Thank you Arerio."

"Well, I'm at a loss," Michlos said.

"Are you saying you think Vane may still be alive?"

"I don't know. The Sisters say there was so much going on they never properly examined him. The pronouncement of death was made by some unnamed bystander at the scene."

"A co-conspirator, perhaps?"

"I have no way of knowing."

"Good morning, you two," Amanda said, breezing in. "How's the research going?"

"The research is fine," Marguerite said, "but you may not like the results."

"We're just so grateful you were willing to help."

"It's the least I can do. I'm arranging repairs, but it is going to be quite some time before my own house is habitable. It was gracious of you to offer me a place that's both comfortable and familiar in the meantime."

"Oh, it's my pleasure. So what did you find?"

Marguerite frowned. "It seems Alistair was so bent on repairing the damage from the division of the estate that he was willing to do almost anything to make up the difference."

"I don't understand."

"He became a thug. Many of these transactions would be consid-ered shady at best. At least a quarter are downright illegal."

"So Rayen is broke?"

"Oh, heavens no, but once this is all cleaned up, the revenues won't be anything like what they once were."

Amanda sighed in relief. "You had me worried there for a second."

Arerio appeared at the door. "Ordinal Goodkin and Monsignor Goodkin to see Mistress Nevinander."

"Nathalie's just finishing up," Amanda said. "Show them in, and I'll get her."

Marguerite stood to greet Antoinette and the Monsignor. "Please, have a seat. If I may say so, Your Ordinence, you wear the vestments well."

"Thank you," Antoinette said. "Darron gave me the option of designing a gender-specific set, but I declined. The last thing we need is any indication that a woman in this role is different in any way from a man."

"And how is the Primal?"

"He continues to improve. I expect he'll be back to his former self very soon."

"Did you ever apprehend Ordinal Laitrech?"

The Monsignor brushed a speck of lint from his vestments. "Not yet, but there's still a good chance of it. The Crown has all routes out of Trifienne under surveillance. If he wants to avoid capture, he won't be leaving by carriage."

"Have you established his guilt?"

"The evidence we've accumulated so far is pretty convincing, but he'll be given a chance to answer the charges. I certainly don't want to convict the wrong person. Speaking of which, I've been talking with Father Cartier, and I want to reiterate my apologies for his decision to attack your residence. The wrap and the documents Michlos provided, combined with the corroborating story of the Inquisitor who assisted Vane in his ambush on you, all make a convincing case that Verone was behind the incidents at Exidgeon. If she hadn't passed away, we would certainly bring charges."

"Even though she had those Indulgences?"

"They wouldn't protect her from charges of arson."

"And what about the deaths at the vicarage?" Michlos asked.

"I'm inclined to agree with your assessment. I can think of no reason for Marguerite to capture the four of them, release them, and then kill two of them—whereas Vane would have had every reason to want them out of the way."

"You believe he was a heretic, then?"

"I had a chat with Princess Celeste about that very issue. It was hard to argue the point with his name scribed in the rolls of that Academy of hers."

"She told you about that?"

"Indeed, and she coupled the revelation with a most intriguing

suggestion. She pointed out that if the Primal was serious about repeal-
ing the Edict of Caprian, then he should be prepared to deal with the
inevitable abuses likely to flow from that decision."

Michlos cleared his throat. "Abuses?"

"Given I'd just seen the Academy rolls, I had a pretty good idea
what she was referring to. Anyway, she pointed out that Father Albert won't be around forever and that the Church is unlikely to have
the requisite expertise to handle the many challenges the repeal will
likely cause. In short, she suggested we might want to partner with
the Academy to meet those challenges."

"So the Church will take over the Academy?"

"It's too soon for that. Even if everything works out perfectly, it
will take time for the stigma associated with what was once Phrendonic Heresy to fade. The Primal will need to tread carefully, or this
entire enterprise may backfire. Still, the suggestion has some merit.
Rest assured we'll be discussing it."

"So sorry to make you wait." Nathalie swept through the door in
full mourning—complete with black gown and veil. Eloise tagged
along behind her, lugging several enormous bags at once. Amanda
brought up the rear.

"You know you don't need to do this," Amanda said. "This is your
home—Rayen and I would never dream of turning you out."

Nathalie sat on one of her trunks. "You're a dear, but we've been
over this. Alistair and I were planning to leave once he passed the
estate to an heir anyway. Besides, there's nothing here for me now
but ghosts. So long as I keep looking mostly forward instead of back,
I'll be fine. I'm just widowed, not dead, right?"

"Will you have everything you need?"

"Of course not, but I'm only moving into town. It's not like I won't
be back. Did I tell you I've decided to take the quaint little apartment
near St. Sophia's? That way I'll be able to help Father Cartier over-
see the construction of the new vicarage. That will give me valuable
experience for my next project."

"And what project is that?" Marguerite asked.

Nathalie locked eyes with Antoinette. "What do you think? Should
we tell them?"

Antoinette shrugged. "Be my guest."

"Well, Nathalie said, "since I stand to inherit a bit of Verone's estate, I figured I might as well put it to good use. I trust you are all aware that the Sultan's Respite burned down recently? I got to thinking that, if we act fast, we could buy up that land for a song."

"Probably so," Marguerite said, "but what will you do with it?"

Her eyes gleamed with pride. "I plan to build a seminary."

"A seminary? Why that, of all things?"

"I know it seems odd, but just wait until you hear what we're going to call it. After much discussion, we've decided on 'The Antoinette Barget Theological Seminary…for Women.'"

Michlos raised an eyebrow. "Don't you mean Antoinette Good-kin?"

"No, she had it right," Antoinette said. "While I loved him dearly, there are certain things for which my late husband simply does not deserve credit."

Rayen's voice carried in from the next room. "Mandy, have you seen my cane?" The door opened, and he and Dona strolled in. "Oh, hello—it seems we have guests."

Amanda spied the cane in a wicker basket next to the coat rack. "It's right there. What do you need it for?"

"For a little walk. Since the sun has struggled so valiantly to appear on our behalf, we felt obliged."

Dona's face lit up. "Is Alexi here too?"

"He was seeing to the carriage," the Monsignor said. "He should be in any minute."

"Miss Merinne," Antoinette said. "As long as you're here, I've been told that you are acquainted with Mathilda Harcourt. Is that true?"

"I'm proud to call her my friend. Why do you ask?"

Antoinette produced a packet from her vestments. "I was wondering if I could impose upon you to deliver something for me. I would do it myself, but our past interactions have been a bit…tense."

"Of course. What is it?"

"It's the deed to the Harcourt estate in Caprian. I purchased it when Thurman was a babe, planning that someday he would inherit it. At the time I was more than a little concerned his father would fritter away everything he owned helping the poor and leave nothing to his son. Isn't that right Armand?"

The Monsignor was staring quizzically up at the dining-room ceiling.

"Armand?"

"Oh, sorry," he said, blushing. "That's quite a fresco you've got there."

"Anyway, please tell her that despite how things turned out, I truly appreciate all she did for us."

Dona grinned ear to ear. "I will." She turned to see Alexi in the doorway.

"By the way," Antoinette said. "Armand told me about your polemic on my behalf during Professor Hepplewhite's class the other day."

"I'm sorry if I offended."

"Don't be. Sometimes wrongheadedness becomes so firmly entrenched that its proponents seek to mask the weakness of their position by labeling as offensive the mere discussion of the issue. In this way, they can perpetuate an even patently indefensible viewpoint, not on the merits, but instead by vilifying any who dare to question them. Where they succeed, the only way to broach the subject is to be offensive. Sadly, it can take real grit to call them out on something like that, since it's a tactic for which the weak-minded are all too prone to fall. I just wanted you to know I admire that kind of grit."

Dona brightened at the compliment. "I'm glad that justice was served in the end."

"Justice doesn't serve itself, you know. You might want to ask yourself if Armand would still have thought to suggest my Ordination and Ascension had you not so recently raised the issue. I know I have."

"I don't know what to say."

"Well, I do. Thank you. That, and please don't ever stop arguing for what you believe in. You never know who might be listening."

"I won't, I promise you."

"Well, this old lady has taken up more than enough of your time. Go ahead. Go to him."

"Thank you, Your Ordinence." Dona curtseyed and turned to smile at Alexi.

. . . . .

Safely out of sight of the dining room, beneath the foyer's grand stair, she fell into his arms.

"Wow," Alexi said. "You sure seem to have impressed her."

"She exaggerated my role—she probably got the position in part because it was politically expedient and in part because she was far and away more brilliant than any other candidate. While I'm glad it happened, I'd hardly call it a triumph of equality."

Alexi nodded, "Maybe not, but it goes a long way toward knocking down the barrier for others, and you played a big part in that. I'm proud of you."

"Ahh, but do you love me? That's what I really want to know."

"Tons and tons. I even brought you a present."

She tore at the strings that bound the package. "What's this?"

"An early wedding gift."

"From whom?"

"Professor Reston. He's planning to take a leave of absence, and he's not sure if he'll be back in time for the wedding. Have you made any progress with your mother?"

"Not yet. She still says it can't happen until I graduate."

"On the brighter side, I might be around for a while after all. The Primal expects that reclaiming his throne may take some time, and he's keeping his base in Trifienne until things solidify. As long as that's true, the Monsignor says I should stay in school."

"Oh Alexi, that's wonderful."

"Go ahead, open it."

She peeled the paper away. "Wait a minute, this isn't—oh my word, it is. This is the copy of *Practical Phrendonics* that Damien stole from Miranda. How did Reston ever find it?"

"He didn't say, but he did mention that since he would be traveling, he couldn't give it the care it deserved, and that he couldn't think of a more appropriate place for it than here with you."

Dona opened the front cover. "Wait—this is inscribed to Julienne, from Marguerite."

"Yeah, Reston wondered about that too. The only thing we could figure was that Verone must have been intending to use it as additional evidence that Marguerite was a heretic."

Dona whistled. "Can you imagine the chaos Julienne could wreak with this?"

Alexi's ears flushed. "Nope. As I understand it, I am not permitted to imagine anything at all pertaining to said person."

She shot him a sly smile. "You're learning. Well as long as you're around for a while, we should all get together and celebrate."

"You might have trouble finding a time when Helena's available—Alphonse says the Princess has her working night and day on some huge project. She's loving it, but she has no time to spare."

"What project? We've been so busy around here I haven't had time to talk to her."

"It was Michlos's suggestion, something about designing new guard uniforms. It seems Newcomb has been driving her crazy with all sorts of helpful style suggestions."

"Funny, I would never have pegged Newcomb as the designer type."

"I suspect Helena would agree with you."

Alexi pulled away as Nathalie strode into the foyer. A parade of followers trailed behind in a colorful melange of luggage, gowns, and vestments.

"Did you see that ceiling?" the Monsignor said softly to Antoinette as they passed.

"I did indeed. I sort of liked it."

The Monsignor snorted. "You would."

"Oh, stop being such a prude—you're embarrassing me."

"I've got to go," Alexi said. Mindful of the audience, he leaned down to give Dona a chaste peck on the cheek. "I'll stop by later."

Dona winked. "I'm holding you to that, Mr. Reysa."

In moments, the guests cleared out, leaving Dona and Rayen staring at each other across the foyer.

"Ready?" he asked.

"Sure. Where are we going?"

"He gathered up a bouquet of dark red roses from the foyer table. I'd thought maybe we could take these to the crypt. Would that be all right?"

"Of course."

They strolled outside and around the villa without further conversation, each content in the sunshine, the beauty of the grounds, and the company of the other. It was some time before Dona broke the silence.

"You really do miss her, don't you?"

"I'll survive. After all, it's just a matter of time before I see her again."

"Do you really believe that?"

"With all my heart."

"Does it ever bother you? That you were so wrong, I mean?"

"Wrong? Was I wrong?"

"You told me you'd seen yourself and Verone living happily ever after."

He paused a moment, considering. "Oh, that."

"Doesn't it bother you that you didn't get it right?"

He shrugged. "Not really."

"I don't understand. How can you put so much faith in your ability and then not be crushed when it so completely betrays you?"

"Ah, now I see the problem. You're confusing ability with entitlement."

"What do you mean?"

"I see this all the time. The more ability people have, the more likely they are to use it in a misguided attempt to harness fate. Sadly, the more convinced they become that they are the masters of their own destinies, the more effort and resources they pour into those attempts. They naturally then expect a return on the investment—feeling entitled to the outcome they worked so diligently to achieve. If, by chance, things turn out the way they'd hoped, that only encourages them to invest even more effort. Eventually, though, they are bound to find that we can no more control our own destinies than we can control the weather. The inevitable result: crushing disappointment and a feeling of betrayal."

"I guess I've never really looked at it that way before. So you're telling me you weren't the slightest bit disappointed that your plans with Verone didn't work out the way you'd expected?"

"Actually, I'm simply trying to explain why you would have felt that way."

"Now you're being evasive. Are you hiding something from me?"

"Can you keep a secret?"

Dona made the secret sign. "Pirate's honor."

He took a seat on the crypt's bottom step. "All right, do you remember when Verone had the seizure?"

"You mean in the infirmary?"

Rayen nodded.

Dona sat beside him. "I sure do. For a moment, I thought Ordinal Goodkin was going to wet herself."

"What I haven't told you is—she had a vision."

"She did? What was it?"

"It was mostly about a specific card."

"As in a playing card?"

He nodded.

"Which one?"

"The Hanged Man."

"Oh—like in Trumps of Doom."

"Exactly."

"So what did that tell you?"

"It didn't tell me anything—it's what it told her that matters."

"Did she ever get the chance to share it with you?"

"She did. She said it meant that the only way she could still win was by first losing everything."

"Wow. That's profound for Verone. I know she was active in a Church group, but she never struck me as all that religious."

"She's not."

"Oh, I don't know—that's got some pretty serious religious over-tones."

"You see that tree over there? The one near the horses?"

"Sure, what about it?"

"Take a closer look."

"One second—I have just the thing." She retrieved her opera glasses from her satchel and held them to her eyes.

"Oh my word. Is that— No, it can't be— It is! But how? Isn't she supposed to be buried here in this very crypt?"

"Well, someone's buried here anyway"

Dona's eyes went wide. "Vane! That's why they can't find him. So that night, when we saw Professor Everson on Verone's horse, that wasn't really Professor Everson either, was it?"

Rayen just smiled.

"Well, that's starting to make sense, then. What I still don't under-stand is how she got Antoinette to go along with all this."

Rayen shrugged. "Someone had just tried to kill her. She made the case that her father was behind it and that he would likely try again.

From that standpoint, cooperating with us made perfect sense. After Alistair was gone, though, the case for keeping the secret got pretty weak."

"So, what did you do?"

Rayen scratched the back of his head. "I'm not at liberty to say, but next time you see her, you might want to ask the esteemed Ordinal how construction on her eponymous seminary is going."

Dona's jaw dropped. "It's been quite a week for Her Ordinence, hasn't it? What happens now?"

"Now we say our fond farewells. I've already arranged the transfer of the estate to your mother. You'll both be well taken care of."

"What do you mean? You're not leaving, are you?"

Rayen got to his feet. "Given everything that's happened, we really don't have a choice, do we? Now, come give your favorite uncle a goodbye hug."

Reluctantly, Dona embraced him. "But when will I see you again?"

"Whenever fate wills it, of course. Now I'd better be going. As you've probably surmised by now, my wife is not a patient woman."

She hugged him again, this time with conviction. "I love you, you know."

"I'm well aware. They don't call me 'the Magnificent' for nothing."

She stood near the crypt and watched as he strolled across the field with a spring in his step that was unusual even for him. When he reached Verone, he presented her with the roses, and they embraced for a long time. Then, he helped her up onto Venji, and he climbed atop the horse she'd brought for him. For a brief moment, they looked back toward the crypt. Then, with a final wave, they trotted off out of sight.

# CHAPTER TWENTY-SIX

# POSTSCRIPT

The front room of the Bursar's office lay in ruins, but Randolph Brent barely noticed. He picked a path across the debris-littered floor, careful not to misstep for fear of damaging the sacred artifact he carried. Once in the back room, he produced a collection of keys and inserted them into their slots in the massive vault door, adjusting them in the secret ways he was the last living man to know. When the final key clicked into place, a gentle tug was all it took for the door to swing silently open. After a glance over his shoulder, he slipped inside.

Pausing to wonder that the pit was still exposed, Brent took a moment to unwrap the Morgatuan—but its eyes were dark and its rings misaligned. He made a mental note to seek out a switch on his way back up and proceeded down the spiral stairway. He reached the landing before the second doorway and held up his lantern to double-check that he'd chosen the correct one. Satisfied, he ducked into the corridor, following it until he came to the arch. His lips moved as he read its Tep'Chuan inscription, and when he finished, he nodded. Counting each pace, he moved beyond the arch. When he'd reached the appointed number, he put down his lantern and adjusted the rings of the Morgatuan to recreate the Canticle of Obsequy. He held the scepter aloft, exultant as the dust gusted and swirled about him. Although the draft blew out his lamp, the gentle glow from the chamber beyond allowed him to strike a lucifer and relight it. He approached the altar with great care, fearful of triggering some trap he may have missed during their last visit. Despite the chill of the chamber, his brow glistened as he stepped on the dais—he was now close enough to touch the altar. But as he surveyed its surface, triumph turned to disbelief.

The three boxes that had once contained the skull, the ring, and the cloak were still where he'd left them. The skull was there, along with the rods from the cage that once contained it. But the wands—the precious irreplaceable wands so integral to the fulfillment of Chervil's Promise—were nowhere to be seen. In a panic, he scanned the dais, examining and tossing away several skull-cage rods. He upended each of the boxes, and, when they proved empty, threw them across the chamber. In desperation, he circled the dais, searching its edge in case a stray gust had blown them off the altar—but they weren't there.

"Where in consecrated damnation can they be? No one could have gotten in here. They must be here."

Frantically, he went back over the events in his mind: how they'd been trapped by the pit, his suggestion to follow the instructions on the altar, and how he'd convinced the rest of them to leave while he followed those instructions. The appearance of the Vismort had brought them all back into the chamber, but no one had approached the altar. They had all then left with the Vismort to find the switch, eliminate the pit, and seal the chamber.

Wait…there was one possibility.

Yes, he'd sent her back. It was only for a few minutes, but she had been alone in the chamber. No wonder she'd encouraged the Monsignor to yield the Morgatuan to him.

His eyes narrowed dangerously. "I don't know what game you're playing, little girl, but the stakes have just gone way up."

. . . . .

*Fin. 12:50 a.m. 11/21/2011.*

# ΛCKNOWLEÐGEMENTS

**Jean Jenkins**, whose breathtaking editorial expertise has once again helped me produce a product of which I am immensely proud.

**Mike Curdic**, whose enviable artistic gifts made Trifienne leap from the page and helped make my vision for the cover a reality.

**Adeela Syed**, whose incisive feedback helped not just with the story, but with my whole perspective.

**Brett Barbaro**, whose interest in the manuscript ranged beyond mere text. I hope one day to oblige him with a game of Trumps of Doom.

**Cindy Pury**, whose thoughtful and meticulous suggestions on motivation and plot were absolutely indispensable.

**Mary Vensel White**, wordsmith extraordinaire and Author of *The Qualities of Wood* and *Bellflower*. Her keen eye ferreted out the dull spots and helped make them gleam.

**Elspeth (Beth) Riley**, editor par excellence, whose seemingly effortless facility with language informs not just my fiction, but my life.

**Daniel Mendyke**, whose keen ability to think several steps ahead helped lay a solid magical foundation, and may even have won him a game or two of chess.

**James Czarnik**, who read despite all the other demands on his time—he taught me, once again, that "love is a verb."

**Yergalem Meharenna**, whose inexhaustible enthusiasm keeps me going even through the hard parts.

**Marianne Smith**, who believed enough in my writing and editing that she hired me to do it, and thereby changed everything.

**Lisa McLendon**, whose boundless editorial expertise guided the resolution of various pesky last-minute issues.

**Genelle Belmas**, my inspiration and my love. I strive to make her proud in ways she does not expect, as she continues to do for me.

**The Southern California Writers' Conference**, who opened my eyes to the existence of publishing conventions and practices and made me appreciate their value. Their tireless efforts help me "suck less."

**Nero**, who warmed my feet throughout those long first-draft years. I shall miss him always.

**Reshi**, who after Nero left, decided I needed him and moved in. He was right.

The Pocket Watch used for the paperback cover spine was designed and crafted by **Lady Pirotessa** (at Blue Rose Creations). I *still* marvel at it.

# GLOSSARY OF TERMS

**Attunement:** This property determines what constitutes a single object for purposes of vesting a spell—two or more objects attuned and in contact means a spell cast on one will spread to all of them. In general, items that remain in close contact for extended periods of time (about a year or so) become naturally attuned to each other. Thus, if a dagger blade is attached to a handle, and the two remain together for long enough, they become a single object for purposes of vesting spells (as long as they remain in contact as the spell vests) (see Vest). Certain Phrendonic spells from the Category of Enchantment can accelerate this process. In general, objects that are 95 percent attuned to each other behave as though they are 100 percent Attuned, while objects less than 95 percent Attuned behave as though they are not Attuned. Thus, once separated, Attuned items can lose their Attunement comparatively rapidly.

**Category:** Phrendonic spells can generally be grouped into one of seven categories based on how they function. Category dictates not only a spell's function, but also places limits on spells that affect it. For example, a Dispel spell cannot generally affect more than one category. Thus, if two spells on the same object hail from different Categories, to dispel both, two different Dispels are required—one tailored to each of the Categories represented by the affected spells. The seven Phrendonic Categories are: Alteration Divination, Enchantment, Encryption, Evocation, Kinesis, and Summoning.

**Charge:** Some spells, referred to as Numeni (plural of Numenus), require an energy supply to maintain their effects. Charge spells collect and provide that energy—termed a 'charge.' A Numenus can only accept a new charge when it is empty of charge or very nearly so. A Reservoir spell can hold a charge until a Numenus vested on the same item is ready to receive one. Numeni, Charge spells, and Reservoirs all possess a trait called Tolerance. A charge can flow from a Charge spell or Reservoir with a higher Tolerance to a Reservoir or Numenus with a lower Tolerance. If multiple receptive Numeni are available, the charge flows to the one with the lowest Tolerance. Once a Numenus receives a charge, it retains it until the charge is exhausted. Thus, if an Incinerate spell and a Light spell are both vested on the same item, casting a Charge spell on the item will have different results depending on the Tolerances of the three spells. If the Light spell has the lowest Tolerance of the three, the Light spell will receive the charge and the object will light up. If the Incinerate has the lowest Tolerance, the object will instead blow up. If the Charge spell has the lowest tolerance, the charge will have nowhere to go and will dissipate without effect. Only the Tolerances of empty or (nearly-empty Numeni capable of accepting a Charge) are considered for purposes of distributing charges.

**Chervillian:** Member of a heretical "death-worshipping" sect thought by some scholars to have arisen from an ancient schism within the Church. Chervillians believe that, unless preserved, souls of the dead are forever obliterated instead of passing to an afterlife. Chervil's Promise states that if the soul is preserved long enough, it will be accorded renewed life.

**Demon/Daemon:** A soul displaced from its native body. The Church uses the term "Demon." Phrendonic practitioners prefer "Daemon."

**Diffract:** A type of Suppression spell that works on radiant effects (effects that extend beyond the target object in a radius, such as Darkness). Typically, a Diffraction spell is limited to affecting spells within a single category, e.g., Summoning. Since it only suppresses the effect without disturbing the spell's pattern, a Diffraction will not prevent a spell of the Diffracted Category from vesting within its radius. For that, one would use a Hedge, which is the corresponding radiant Dispel. See Dispel.

**Dispel:** A spell of the category of Alteration that disrupts the pattern of another spell vested on the same object causing it to dissipate. It is distinguished from a Suppression, which disrupts the effect of another spell but leaves the pattern intact. If a Dispel is subsequently removed, the affected spell is still gone (provided it wasn't Patterned). By contrast, if a Suppression is removed, previously suppressed spells can often reassert themselves. A given Dispel is generally limited to Dispelling only spells within a single category. To be successful, the Dispel must be inherently stronger than the spell to be dispelled. Ordinals use the term Disrupt for essentially the same effect.

**Evoke:** To use a spell from the Phrendonic Category of Evocation. Evocation encompasses a Category of magic in which surrounding gasses are recruited into the pattern of a spell as it vests. Thus, solid objects may be created from air, although the spell itself must generally be cast upon an object to seed the effect. If the Evocation is dispelled or expires, the gas returns to its previous gaseous state. See also Category.

**Hanged Man's Gambit:** The Hanged Man is a card used in the poker variant *Trumps of Doom*, which is played using a Tarot deck. Playing trump cards modifies the game rules depending on the specific trump played. For example, if a round ends while the Hanged Man is in play, the lowest hand wins. The Hanged Man's Gambit tactic takes advantage of that card—players destroy their hands' value hoping the round ends with the Hanged Man still in play. The Gambit is considered risky, since, if the Hanged Man card is supplanted by another trump, those who attempted it are left with poor hands.

**Kinesis:** The Phrendonic category of magic associated with spells that attract or repel.

**Numenus:** See Charge.

**Ordinal:** The nine Ordinals are appointed by the Primal, customarily for life terms. They rank just beneath the Primal, and upon a Primal's death, the Ordinals vote to determine his successor. Beneath the Ordinals are Archbishops, Bishops, and Priests, in that order. The Inquisitor General is not technically part of that hierarchy—his role is to administer the Inquisition, and he serves at the pleasure of the Primal. Thus, in his official capacity, the Inquisitor General reports only to the Primal, and his authority is as extensive or as limited as the Primal allows.

**Passive Charge:** Passive Charges are a special form of Charge Spell that collect energy over time and, when full (usually after about an hour), dump the accumulated Charge into an available Reservoir or Numenus vested on the same item. Once emptied, they resume gathering energy, and the process repeats as long as the spell remains in effect. See also Charge.

**Patterning:** A Patterned spell is one that has undergone the process of Patterning to make the spell's pattern integral to that of the object on which it is vested. In essence, a Patterned spell becomes permanent, as long as the object it's vested on remains intact. Thus, a Color spell Patterned on a Promise Stick to turn it red would no longer have a duration—instead, the stick would remain red indefinitely. However, if the stick is broken in half, the spell dissipates like normal, except that if the stick is reassembled (provided the two halves remain attuned), the Patterned spell manifests once again and the red color returns. Patterned Numeni still require Charges to take effect. Like Attunement spells, Patterning spells reside in the Category of Enchantment.

**Phrendonic Heresy:** Practicing Phrendonic magic, as outlined in the work *Practical Phrendonics*, was officially declared heresy by the Edict of Caprian in the year 887. Some related practices, such as demonology, had been deemed heretical long before that. Prior to 887, a number of canon scholars viewed Phrendonic practices as already subject to those previous edicts. To them, the Edict of Caprian was little more than a clarification of existing canon.

**Profanity:** This term is used by the Church to denote an object upon which a Phrendonic spell is vested. Since Phrendonic spells generally don't last long unless they've been Patterned, it is usually presumed that a Profanity bears spells that have been Patterned.

**Promise Stick:** In its simplest form, a Promise Stick is a stick notched so that it may be easily snapped in two, usually to quickly break a spell without the bother of having to dispel it. In general, once a spell is vested on an object, at least 80 percent of the object must remain intact, or the spell is broken. Thus, if a Color spell is cast upon such a stick to turn it red, when the stick is broken, the spell is broken as well, and both pieces return to their normal color. However, if the stick is broken unevenly such that one piece retains at least 80 percent of its mass, the spell remains in effect on the larger piece and dissipates from the smaller.

**Reservoir:** See Charge.

**Ritergy:** A closely guarded magical tradition confined to the Church's upper echelons. In its current incarnation, a Relic is required for the Rite to create its intended effect.

**Sacrifice (Incinerate):** Incinerate is a Summoning spell that instantaneously converts a Charge into light and heat in a radius around the targeted object. During the Caprian Inquisition, a number of Phrendonic Heretic prisoners used this spell to immolate themselves rather than endure torture that might induce them to betray their compatriots. Inquisitors who got too close were often injured or killed as well. The Church's term for the practice, "Infernal Sacrifice," gained traction at that time. Such a Sacrifice was an avenue of last resort for a heretic, usually attempted after having been bound and masked or blinded. By casting the Sacrifice on themselves, they obviated the general requirement for the caster to see a spell's target to vest it. Since it's a Numenus, the Incinerate additionally requires a Charge to take effect.

**Slept:** Term of art used by Phrendonic practitioners to indicate that someone under the influence of a Sleep spell.

**Sorcel:** Phrendonic term for spell, specifically, one that has not been

Patterned and is therefore ephemeral.

**Spell Radius:** Radiant spells generally affect a 30-foot radius surrounding the targeted object. Skilled Phrendonic practitioners can modify radiant spells to have a smaller radius, but not a larger one. Spell Radius is to be distinguished from Casting Distance, which is generally line-of-sight up to a maximum of 150 feet.

**Spells vested on persons vs. Spells vested on objects:** Spells vested on people or animals behave differently in some particulars than they do when vested on inanimate objects. For example, the maximum duration of a spell on a person is approximately an hour, whereas on an object, a spell can last up to a day. The difference is thought to result from an interaction between the spell and the person's soul.

**Tag:** A Phrendonic spell that creates a standard (though invisible) magical pattern, generally useful for interacting with other spells, such as Attractions or Repulsions. The term is also used to refer to spells that create non-standard patterns that are able thereby to avoid interaction with the standard spells.

**Talis:** Phrendonic term for a Patterned spell effect.

**Vest/vesting:** The nearly instantaneous process whereby the pattern of a spell spreads across the target object. Once initiated by casting, a spell spreads to encompass all solid material that is both attuned to and touching the point at which the vesting initiated. Thus, if one were to cast a Color spell on the blade of a knife to turn it red, the spell would initiate at a point targeted by the caster and spread until it encompassed everything that was attuned to the blade. If the handle had been in association with the blade long enough, they would be Attuned, the spell would vest on the handle, and the handle would turn red as well. If the blade and handle were only recently assembled and therefore not Attuned, the Color spell would vest on the blade only, and the handle would not be affected.

**Vismort:** A title accorded to a highly ranked Chervillian, roughly equivalent to Archbishop.

# ABOUT THE AUTHOR

Doug Bornemann fondly recalls the dawn of civilization—a time when games were popular, but *gaming* was virtually unknown. The year was 1976. Doug had only recently discovered Tolkien's trilogy and was devouring *The Two Towers* on his bus ride home from school, when fellow busing victim Tamarack Czarnik observed Doug's choice of reading material and exclaimed, "I didn't know Douglas J. Bornemann liked *Lord of the Rings*." (While use of Doug's middle initial was not common at the time, Tam could be eerily prescient about such things.) Of course, Tam, being Tam, let the matter drop. After mulling for a few minutes, Doug concluded that Tam's declaration was unusual. In that time and place, Doug might have understood an exclamation upon learning one read at all, but Tam's fascination with that specific book struck him as peculiar, and Doug insisted on knowing what drove it.

Turns out, Tam had been playing a new game called Dungeons & Dragons, and in Tam's experience, readers of Tolkien were predisposed to develop an irrational fondness for it. Doug already had an irrational fondness for games like chess and was eager to expand his game horizons. Using a few six-sided dice (all he had at the time), Tam, who conveniently lived across the street, offered a small demonstration. Since single-player D&D games are not optimal, Tam recruited Doug's brother together with suitable candidates from among his own nine siblings, and an addiction was born.

At that time, D&D consisted of a small number of pamphlets, but the basic D&D boxed set followed soon thereafter. It contained fragile plastic polyhedral dice that dissolved on extended use and a thin soft-cover booklet that described basic character generation and rules of play, some "monster" characteristics, and a sample dungeon. Tam eschewed the sample dungeon in favor of developing an interconnected universe of wonders populated by nuanced villains and complex allies in which players struggled for survival, wealth, and personal glory as they strove to discover its secrets—Tam was a master of the unrequited hint. That group also quickly learned the value of teamwork. Unfettered by the proliferation of D&D rules in the years that followed, the game's focus never strayed from the story, which made the experience both immersive and compelling to an extent subsequent games rarely achieved. Even all these years later, were Tam to pick up where he left off, most of his players would magically appear, dice in hand.

Doug's sense of story was forged by Tam's early games and later refined by his own game-running efforts. Tam's insightful perspectives on how game universes, magic, and souls should work have informed both Doug's games and these pages. Truly, as did the Elves for the Ents, Tam gave Doug his voice.

www.ingramcontent.com/pod-product-compliance
Lightning Source LLC
Chambersburg PA
CBHW030919260626
47169CB00002B/327